Praise for *Shot Through the Heart*

'A deliciously sexy romp that blows open the
scandalous secrets of Hollywood'
Daily Express *****

'Scandal, glamour, love, sex: this novel has all of them in spades,
and the plot scurries along at a pleasing pace . . . Need a
companion for your beach holiday? Look no further
than this fun, glitzy tale'
Heat ****

'Rollicking good fun . . . sexy, funny, I couldn't put it down'
Attitude

'Brilliantly written and utterly engrossing, Matt Cain's
debut novel is a wonderful read'
Sun ****

'Jackie Collins, watch your leopard-print back!
Matt Cain is in town with a biting wit and some
good old-fashioned romance!'
Jonathan Harvey

'This debut is the shamelessly fabulous story of
Hollywood's biggest star falling for a Brit paparazzo,
from someone who knows LA inside out'
Elle

'A first-class ticket to Tinseltown. A novel full of glitz,
sex and secrets, it's over the top and fabulously good fun.
I raced through it'
Fanny Blake

Nothing But Trouble

Matt Cain was born in Bury and brought up in Bolton. He spent ten years making arts and entertainment programmes for ITV before stepping in front of the camera in 2010 to become Channel 4 News' first Culture Editor. Now a full-time writer, *Nothing But Trouble* is his second novel, following his debut, *Shot Through the Heart*. He lives in London.

You can follow Matt Cain on Twitter @MattCainWriter

www.mattcainwriter.com

Also by Matt Cain

Shot Through the Heart

MATT CAIN

Nothing But Trouble

PAN BOOKS

First published 2015 by Pan Books
an imprint of Pan Macmillan
20 New Wharf Road, London N1 9RR
Associated companies throughout the world
www.panmacmillan.com

ISBN 978-1-4472-3830-0

1 3 5 7 9 8 6 4 2

A CIP catalogue record for this book is available from the British Library.

Typeset by Ellipsis Digital Limited, Glasgow
Printed and bound by CPI Group (UK) Ltd, Croydon, CR0 4YY

Visit www.panmacmillan.com to read more about all our books
and to buy them. You will also find features, author interviews and
news of any author events, and you can sign up for e-newsletters
so that you're always first to hear about our new releases.

For my mum and dad,

who are cooler than any pop star.

1

'Ladies and gentlemen, please welcome tonight's guest of honour and a woman the whole country's talking about . . . Lola Grant!'

Lola blinked away her nerves and fixed her face into a bright grin. As she stepped onto the stage she couldn't help feeling overwhelmed by the sound of the applause. *Come on,* she told herself, *keep it together and don't start crying.*

'Oh my God,' she began in her strong south London accent. 'Thanks guys, thanks a lot. I hope this means you all like my new album!'

There was a howl of agreement from a prematurely drunk PR girl that grew into a widespread roar. The bright grin spread its way across Lola's face. *I can't believe this is happening to me!*

'You know what,' she went on, 'it's no secret it took me ages to get here. I couldn't get a record deal for years and the whole thing blatantly hammered my confidence. And then the first album was great and everything but after so many knock-backs I was convinced people would think I was shit – that I was just some rough bird with a good pair of lungs on her.'

'We love you, Lola!' shouted a group of excited fans from the back of the crowd.

'Thanks guys,' she smiled bashfully, 'but I didn't think *anyone* loved me a few years ago. So I was a bit scared to be myself on that first album. Actually, I was more than a bit scared – I was totally shitting it.'

The audience laughed then settled into an intent silence. Lola looked out and recognized a pair of fustily dressed music execs and the distinctive rust-coloured hair and beefy build of Freddy Jones, the entertainment correspondent from Channel 3 News.

'Anyway, you might be pleased to hear that I've stopped shitting myself now and haven't held back at all on *Trouble*. So when you listen to the album, for the first time you're listening to the real me – even if I am just some rough bird who can belt out a tune.'

As the crowd hollered and whooped their approval, Lola felt a rush of such intense joy she had to stop herself from staggering backwards from the impact. Here she was on a bright June evening in To Dive For, an exclusive rooftop bar with a full-length swimming pool and the most incredible views of London. And cheering her on were some of the most important people in the media and the music business – all of them here to celebrate the launch of her new album. It was everything she'd ever wished for and almost too much to take in. She paused for a moment to compose herself.

'But even though it's a very personal album I blatantly couldn't have made it on my own. I know speeches are boring and you all want to get pissed but I just want to say a quick thank you to everyone who worked with me on *Trouble*. And to one man in particular – my brilliant manager and best mate, Harvey Sparks.'

She looked around for Harvey but instinctively knew where she'd find him. He was standing at the front of the crowd just a couple of paces to her right — as he himself liked to say, always at and on her side. She grinned at the sight of his dirty blonde hair, gentle brown eyes and self-conscious smile.

'Harvey, you've always been there for me, and even when everyone thought I was shit you never stopped believing in me. So this album might have my name all over it but it's just as much yours as it is mine.'

As she held his gaze she felt a tremble of emotion. She turned back to address the crowd and gestured to Harvey with her thumb.

'You know what, I couldn't even *be* me if it weren't for this bloke. So please raise your glasses and drink to my rock and right-hand man . . . Harvey Sparks.'

*

Harvey tried not to blush as everyone turned towards him and raised their glasses.

'Harvey Sparks!' they boomed.

He took a sip of his fizzy water and did his best not to squirm. Drop him into a meeting with the biggest ball-breakers in the business and he always knew he could nail it, but stand him in front of any kind of audience and for some reason he went to pieces. He guessed that was one of the reasons he and Lola were so well suited professionally: she was happiest doing her thing on stage and he was at his best working away behind her. Except that right now she'd just yanked him out from behind her and thrust him into the spotlight. He straightened up and did his best to look authoritative and managerial.

Lola winked at him and then stepped back, handing the mic to a glassy-eyed record exec with shocking dandruff and horrendous buck teeth. As Harvey watched her swig from a glass of deep red sangria he listened to the exec explain to the crowd what he already knew: that Lola's first album had been a big success but now *Trouble* was going to take her to a whole new level. In fact, confidence in her career was so high that once she'd finished promoting the album in the UK and Europe and completed the first leg of her mammoth tour, she was going to fly out to the States to launch her career there. And with that he formally announced that Lola had just signed a major deal with the American arm of her record company – and predicted that this year she was going to conquer the world. There was another eruption of approval.

Flippin' 'eck! thought Harvey. *They really do love her.* It was all very encouraging – and came as something of a relief. Because yeah, hopes were high for Lola's career, but Harvey was all too aware that as they rose so did the stakes; the record company was investing millions in her future and needed to see a return on its investment. It was a big gamble but he reassured himself that there was nothing to worry about. In fact, the bosses at the record company were so bullish about Lola's career they were even thinking of dropping her surname to confidently position her alongside those music megastars known only by their first names – Madonna, Kylie, Rihanna . . . If everything went according to plan, Lola was heading for the international elite of pop's premier league. *I only hope we don't hit too many bumps along the way.*

Just then he was distracted by a pair of trashy-looking blondes with million-dollar bodies but one-dollar faces standing at the bar and talking at the tops of their voices. 'I swear to God his dick was so big it was like a beer can,' he heard one of them say. 'Honestly, I couldn't get it in my mouth never mind anywhere else!'

Harvey watched them cackle with laughter as they smoked fags, chewed gum and knocked back shots of vodka. They beckoned to the barman for more and Harvey smiled as he remembered his own days as a heavy drinker, always the life and soul of this kind of party – and the first to sacrifice his dignity to make sure everyone was having a good laugh. If he were ten years younger, by this stage of the evening he'd probably have ripped his clothes off and dived into the pool – either that or he'd be getting down and dirty with one of the waiters in the disabled loos. *Those were the days* . . . Three years ago, in his early thirties, he'd taken the decision to stop drinking when his life had begun to spiral out of control – but before things had reached that point he'd had a hell of a lot of fun getting there. And it looked like these two blondes were having plenty now.

As he watched them completely ignore the speeches and down another round of vodka, it dawned on him that this kind of industry party wasn't half as much fun when you weren't drinking. At least not now that he'd reached such a senior role and felt a real sense of responsibility for Lola's career – and well-being. But he was happy with his new focus in life and had become much more successful since he'd given up the booze. He felt a shiver of excitement as he thought of everything he'd lined up for Lola over the next few months.

Appearances on the biggest TV shows in Europe, a headline slot at a huge anti-drugs benefit, and that all-important multi-million-pound tour sponsored by the soft-drink brand Twinkle. With his help Lola really was on the cusp of taking on the world. *Hmm, not bad for a lad from a council estate in Wigan.*

His only concern right now was Lola's own drinking. Sure, fans couldn't get enough of stories of her wild partying, and pap shots of her falling over on her way home from clubs only seemed to make them love her more. Her appeal was very much that she was a real woman rather than just another bland, polished pop star. But there were times when Harvey looked at her drinking and recognized his younger self — and worried that she drank with an angry edge, out of some kind of urge to self-destruct.

Tonight she'd promised him not to get too hammered, at least not until she'd spoken to all the important industry people and recorded her interview with Freddy Jones. Freddy had been granted the TV exclusive of the launch party because he was known as a friendly, respectful interviewer who was never the slightest bit of trouble. Channel 3 News was the top-rated news programme on British TV and the interview would be broadcast live as the 'And finally' item at the end of tonight's nine o'clock bulletin. But Harvey was starting to worry that Lola would get carried away and say too much if she didn't stay sober. Because yes, she was a real woman – but there was only so much reality the public could handle.

*

As some buck-toothed bloke with dandruff droned on about the record company's latest financial results, Freddy Jones couldn't take his eyes off Lola. Of course there was no pretending she was a natural beauty in any conventional sense, but with her jet-black spiky hair, cute little face and dark, olive skin he found her seriously attractive. Tonight she was looking better than he'd ever seen her, in a fitted metallic minidress and thigh-high black leather boots with a pair of Marc Jacobs sunglasses perched on her head. And he loved the fact that she was much more rebellious and outspoken than other pop stars, who were usually so worried about offending potential album buyers that they failed ever to give away anything of the slightest interest. He gave a little chuckle. *No one could ever say that about Lola.*

On his way over here he'd read an interview in which she talked movingly about her difficult childhood growing up in the care of a hopelessly drug-addicted mother. He'd never come across a pop star speaking so openly before, and although some of the details of her story were pretty grim and difficult to swallow, it only made him like and respect her more. He was hoping she'd be similarly honest later that night when he interviewed her live on Channel 3 News.

The truth was, he didn't see how he could go wrong. Practically everything Lola did right now made the news, and her daily appearances in the tabloids had helped her latest hit *Lost in Love* reach number one and become the fastest-selling single of the year. Her surging profile had also helped build up a massive buzz around tonight's album launch — and attract some of the biggest stars in town. Freddy had already spotted footballer Slam Carter, TV presenter Ruby Marlow and celebrity sex therapist Bunny Love, all of them eager to soak up some of the overspill of Lola's glory. He made a note to make sure his cameraman filmed shots of each of them to give his report the maximum glamour.

Not that it would be lacking in glamour. In the two years Freddy had worked as an entertainment correspondent this was by far the glitziest showbiz event he'd been to. To Dive For was already the hottest venue in London and thousands of pounds must have been spent transforming it into the setting for tonight's themed beach party. The pool was surrounded by rows of retro deckchairs and real palm trees and the floor had been covered with inches of deep, soft sand. Waiters and waitresses dressed in ball-crushing Speedos and boob-busting bikinis padded around barefoot, serving little bowls of Spanish food like paella, chorizo and tortilla and topping up the guests' glasses with an endless stream of extra-strong sangria. Freddy assumed it had all been inspired by *Lost in Love*, Lola's upbeat summer anthem laced with hints of Spanish guitar which told the story of a whirlwind holiday romance. But whatever the inspiration, the party was a huge success — and he was thrilled to be the only TV journalist allowed inside to film it.

As the ugly bloke finally wound up his speech, Freddy signalled to his cameraman Big Phil to carry on filming. And he was pleased that he did; just when everyone thought the speeches were over, Lola surprised them all by stepping forward and grabbing hold of the mic.

'All right you lot,' she bellowed, waving her glass in the air, 'it's time to get this party started!'

To a roar of agreement she knocked back a huge swig of blood-red sangria.

'Come on guys, let's sip till we slip!'

Freddy smiled. It certainly looked like her guard was down and he'd be getting a good interview. *I only hope she doesn't get too drunk and embarrass herself in the process.*

*

Feeling the drink go to her head, Lola stumbled as she stepped down from the stage. She quickly checked herself and held out her glass to a passing waiter who filled it with sangria. Tonight she'd promised Harvey she'd only have one drink, but it was difficult to keep track when the waiters were constantly topping up her glass. *Mind you,* she reassured herself, *I haven't actually emptied it so technically I'm still on my first.*

As she entered the adoring throng she was instantly flanked by Harvey and her publicist Barbara Bullock, a bosomy lesbian who only ever wore men's suits and whose passion for promoting her artists was matched only by her passion for playing golf. Harvey and Barbara summoned security and guided Lola through the crowd as the opening notes to *Lost in Love* blasted out from the sound system. Once the chorus kicked in everyone around her began singing along.

> *That hot summer's night,*
> *It felt oh so right,*
> *And I was lost, lost,*
> *Lost in love.*

To have so many people singing her words back at her made Lola feel emboldened and uplifted. Her whole body fizzed with excitement at what she knew was going to be a great night.

Once they were clear of the crowd, Harvey steered her towards a reserved seating area.

'You all right, Trouble?' he asked.

'Yeah, fantastic thanks, darlin'. Was my speech all right?'

'Yeah, it was great — just the right balance between polish and personality. And thanks for embarrassing me in there.'

'My pleasure,' she teased. 'I'm sure there's plenty more where that came from.'

'Yeah, well don't forget you're being interviewed live on Channel 3 News later,' interrupted Barbara. 'And we also have photo opps with a load of celebs and competition winners.'

'That's not to mention all the industry people you have to charm,' added Harvey.

Lola pulled a mock pout. 'My God, I thought this was supposed to be a party!'

'Oh come on,' coaxed Harvey, 'you know the drill as well as we do. It's work for the first couple of hours and then play afterwards — once the cameras have gone.'

'All right, all right. Well, we'd better get the work bit out of the way then. And before we do I'm blatantly going to need a drink.'

Barbara clicked her fingers and from out of nowhere a waiter appeared and topped up her glass.

'Oh thanks, darlin',' Lola purred, almost draining it in one. 'And don't worry, Harvey — I'm still on my first!'

'Yeah, yeah,' he smirked, 'I've heard that line before — I used to use it myself once upon a time.'

There was a huge splash and the three of them looked over to see a pot-bellied A&R man bobbing up to the surface of the pool. Several guests wailed that he'd got them soaking wet but when this only made him splash them all more, they began to strip off their clothes and jump in after him. As *Lost in Love* reached its rousing conclusion, the party descended into a full-on water fight. *This is more like it!* thought Lola, shooting Harvey a mischievous look.

'Ah-ah,' he frowned. 'Don't even think about it.'

She folded her arms with a sulk. 'Well in that case let's get the boring stuff over with. Because sooner or later I'm going in that pool — and I can't hold myself back much longer.'

*

As soon as Harvey guided Lola back into the crowd, the commotion in the swimming pool calmed. Now there was a new focus of attention; within seconds a ripple of excitement tore around the party and Lola was besieged by guests baying for just one magical moment in her presence.

'Congratulations on the number one!' shouted a skinny man with enormous nipples.

'*Love* the new album!' shrieked a severe-looking brunette, stepping on Harvey's toe.

'Can't wait for the tour!' spewed a wasted bald guy, blowing chorizo breath into his face.

With the help of security he wrestled Lola through the crowd and began to pick out the important industry execs he wanted to treat to a blast of her high-voltage charisma. Despite the fact that she was continuing to knock back the booze, he was relieved to see that she didn't let him down, delighting a huddle of honchos with a mucky sense of humour most stars would keep well hidden.

'So there's these two rats in a sewer eating shit, right?' she began, a naughty twinkle in her eye. 'One says, "I'm sick of eating shit all day," and his mate says, "Cheer up, we're on the piss tonight!"'

Harvey reeled at the force of their laughter. *If she can keep this up then maybe she really IS going to conquer the world.*

'She's so normal!' gushed a tall guy with terrible nasal hair.

'I *love* her accent!' fawned a square-jawed, super-sized American.

'Where exactly *is* Tooting?' asked another, clueless.

As they left the execs and worked their way around the party, Harvey and Lola were trailed by the official event photographer, who occasionally stepped forward to take a snap. Whenever Lola met one of the celebrity guests, Barbara would make sure he had access to the best angle. He shot her feigning interest in Slam Carter's explanation of the offside rule, imitating the latest internet dance craze with Ruby Marlow, and being advised on how to give the perfect tit wank by Bunny Love.

Layla Lloyd was the only celebrity guest who didn't appear on camera. The glamour-model-turned-fashion-designer had recently seen her popularity plummet since splitting up with her fourth husband, a bricklayer and occasional stripper who'd won the hearts of the nation after coming second in a reality TV show set on a sewage plant in Barrow. With her fashion empire teetering on the brink of bankruptcy, she'd clearly come to the party to bask in any stray rays escaping from Lola's spotlight.

'What's *she* doing here?' Harvey asked Barbara.

'Sorry,' she grimaced. 'My call — bit of a guilty pleasure, I'm afraid.'

He rolled his eyes and smiled. He and Barbara had worked

together since Lola's debut single was released two years ago, and not only did he respect her professionalism but he was also very fond of her as a person. He could forgive her this one indiscretion, especially since her girlfriend of five years had just left her for a chubby cake baker from Cambridge. But that didn't mean he wanted any of Layla's tawdry reputation rubbing off on his artist. Before she had a chance to sidle up for a photo, he steered Lola away towards a group of fans who'd won a competition to meet her at the party.

From the moment she said hi they swooped.

'Oh my God, I can't believe it's you!' squeaked a girl who introduced herself as Pinkie.

'You're like my ultimate idol!' gasped another with horrendous hair frizz.

'I love you so *so* much!' breathed a gay guy reeking of Jean Paul Gaultier.

'Well, I love you all too,' said Lola, totally calm and comfortable in their presence. 'Come on, let's all have a little drink, shall we?'

The fans' faces beamed like a row of lights on a Christmas tree.

'Oh my God, it's like my ultimate ambition to get pissed with you,' said the one with the hair frizz.

'Well, come on then,' Lola smiled, summoning a waiter. 'You know my motto . . .'

'*Let's sip till we slip!*' they roared in unison.

As he watched them fill their glasses, Harvey started to seriously worry that Lola would be blind drunk by the time of the interview. 'Barb, do you really think we should be doing this news thing?' he asked.

'Yes! What's the problem?'

'Just look at her! She's going to be shit-faced soon – she's almost there already.'

'Oh relax, everyone loves her when she's pissed. It's part of the Lola Grant brand. And it'll be great publicity for the album.'

'Yeah, but what about her self-respect? I don't want her to say something she'll regret later – or look back on and cringe.'

'Well, I hate to tell you this, doll, but there's no ducking out now; the interview's live and they've reserved a slot in the programme for us. So unless you want to piss off the entire channel, we've got to go ahead.'

Harvey took a deep breath.

Is all the pressure making me worry too much?

Should I just try to relax and enjoy the moment?

Do I really have to keep thinking about the bigger picture?

'OK,' he conceded eventually. 'What time's it happening?'

'Ten to ten. Right at the end of their programme.'

He looked at his watch; it was nearly nine o'clock. He had just less than an hour to sober her up.

*

Lola looked at the phone thrust into her hand and tried to pull herself together.

'Come on, doll,' Barbara said, 'we need you to send a quick tweet. Something that makes your fans feel like they're at the party with you.'

She nodded and did her best to focus on the keypad. But the letters began to swirl in front of her eyes in a kaleidoscopic haze.

'Album party fierce,' she typed. 'Am very happy girl. But blatantly leathered and going on news in bit. Oops!'

She tried to hashtag the word *Trouble* but kept hitting the wrong key. In the end she gave up and hit Send. *Oh it'll have to do.*

A waiter offered her a bowl of paella but she declined; she didn't want food to slow her down. *Eating is cheating,* she reminded herself. Instead she held out her drink for a refill and felt another rush of joy.

The truth was, Lola still experienced a little thrill every time she was served a free drink. And she couldn't help feeling overawed by glamorous parties – especially when they were being thrown in her honour. Sure, she'd been in the music business for a few years now so she was getting used to it. But before that she'd spent more than twenty years struggling to get by, and as a child had grown up with so little money that most meals had consisted of bags of crisps, Pot Noodles or, if she was lucky, jam sandwiches. She still had clear memories of her mum dragging her down to the jobcentre every other Thursday to pick up her dole money, stopping off at her dealer's on the way home so she could spend the next few days utterly annihilated. Of course, when things became really bad Lola would be packed off to care homes or foster parents, while her mum was sent to understaffed treatment centres or put on half-hearted rehab programmes. But sooner or later, she'd always be sent back to a home which stank of unhappiness – and sooner or later her mum would go back to spending all their money on drugs.

Lola sighed and took another swig of her drink. Even though free booze still had the ability to make her feel special, at the same time being at this kind of party always felt a bit wrong. And that only made her want to drink more to obliterate the feeling.

She turned to Barbara but saw that she was transfixed by the spectacle of a now seriously dishevelled Layla Lloyd showing off her latest boob job to an obviously aroused Slam Carter. At least security were still concentrating on their job so she could have a quiet minute on her own to gather her thoughts. She gulped down more sangria and felt a shudder of fear.

There was no question that right now Lola's career was exactly the way she wanted it. But this only made her feel eerily uneasy. It wasn't the usual imposter syndrome that people talked about, when they felt like a fraud once they'd become the person they'd always wanted to be. No, this was something slightly different. It was almost as if she felt like she didn't deserve her success. And because happiness was still a relatively unusual experience for her, it made her feel awkward and anxious. More than anything, it made her worry that someone was going to come and snatch it away from her. Or that she'd snatch it away from herself by making some kind of huge mistake and messing it up.

Oh this is all a bit much, she thought. *I'm not sure I really know how to be this happy.*

She told herself to stop overanalysing things and have another drink. She looked around for a waiter and called one over.

'Top me up please, darlin'.'

As she watched the deep red liquid fill her glass, she realized that there was no more pretending to Harvey that she'd only had one. Come to think of it, where *was* Harvey? She hadn't seen him for ages. It wasn't like him to leave her side, especially not at a time like this.

Where the hell's he got to?

*

On the other side of the swimming pool Harvey was grappling his way through the crowd towards a young man who'd caught his eye. He wasn't his usual type but there was something about him that he found really attractive. Gym-toned, black and wearing a baseball cap teamed with the latest street fashions, he must have only been about twenty-five – a good ten years younger than Harvey. *Does that make it indecent?* he wondered. Right now he didn't care; he couldn't take his eyes off him.

He edged forwards but it was proving more and more difficult to negotiate the increasingly drunk and unruly crowd. The style and sparkle of earlier in the evening had been stripped away to reveal a bedraggled and undignified heap of humanity. A skinny waitress almost crashed into him, not realizing she had a cigarette butt attached to her cheek and one half of her bikini bottoms wedged up her bum. And he saw the rough blondes he'd spotted earlier looking like they were going to wet themselves with laughter as some slime-bucket of a man leered over them, unaware that the pool water had made his underpants totally see-through. Harvey couldn't help wondering if this was the kind of state he'd ended up in when he used to get drunk, and suddenly remembered why he'd given up the booze. *Thank God I'm over all that,* he told himself.

Just as he was finally approaching the guy in the baseball cap he spotted Freddy Jones emerge from the crowd and start talking to him. When the guy took out a pad and wrote something down, Harvey realized that he must be Freddy's work colleague. Straight away he spotted the chance to introduce himself.

'All right, lads?' he said, moving in. 'I'm Harvey Sparks, Lola's manager.'

'Oh right,' said Freddy, holding out his hand, 'good to meet you. Freddy Jones, Channel 3 News.'

'I know,' smiled Harvey, trying not to stare at the black guy. 'And you must be?'

'I'm Spike,' he said, 'Freddy's producer.'

'Well, good to meet you, Spike.'

'What up.'

They held each other's gaze and Harvey felt a tremor of nervous energy bounce between them. He couldn't help wondering if Spike felt it too.

'Well, we're all set, like,' interrupted Freddy, 'and we've just checked and everything's working fine.'

'I'm sorry?' asked Harvey.

'The interview? We've gone through all the details with Barbara and we're basically ready to go.'

'Oh right, sorry, the interview.' Harvey was entranced by Spike; he wasn't sure he'd ever met anyone quite so attractive. His heavily tattooed arms and gold tooth gave him an air of toughness but it was softened by a sweet, gentle smile which brought Harvey out in goose bumps.

'So are you still cool to bring her over about 9.40?' asked Spike.

'Yeah, yeah, all good. She's really looking forward to it.' He thought it best not to mention that she was completely off her face. Then he remembered that he was supposed to be sobering her up. 'Actually, I'll just go and check up on her. But let me give you my number in case there are any problems.'

He took out a card and before Freddy had the chance to take it handed it to Spike. *Was that too obvious?*

'Genuine,' said Spike, flashing him another of his spellbinding smiles.

Harvey suddenly came over all light-headed. *Maybe he does feel the same way as I do . . .*

'Well, I'd better go,' he managed. 'I'll, urm, I'll see you later.'

'For real,' nodded Spike.

Harvey turned around and felt slightly out of breath. He filled his lungs with air and told himself not to start acting like a lovesick teenager. *Come on, lad, you're a bit old for all that. And you've got a job to do, remember?*

He stood on his tiptoes and looked around for Lola. It was usually easy to find the artist at an album launch as they were always surrounded by an excited cluster of people trying to push their way to an introduction. But he couldn't spot her anywhere and he'd only slipped away ten minutes ago. He told himself not to worry; she was with Barbara and the security team so would be safe from any harm. *Except the harm she might inflict on herself . . .*

His phone beeped to say he had a Twitter alert and he took it out to see Lola's latest posting.

'Am very happy girl,' he read. 'But blatantly leathered and going on news in bit. Oops!'

His heart plummeted. That tweet had just gone out to over

half a million followers – and if they hadn't been planning to already, now they'd all be watching Channel 3 News.

*

Lola crashed out of the party and into a corridor leading to the toilets and her green room. She hurtled straight into a haughty-looking blonde who was shovelling an unfeasibly large spoon-ful of ice cream into her mouth while she thought no one was looking.

'You dizzy bitch!' screeched the girl, wiping the ice cream from her chin. 'You want to watch where you're fucking going!'

'Sorry darlin',' croaked Lola, 'I'm really sorry.'

The girl's scowl snapped into a smile as she realized who she was talking to. 'No, *I'm* sorry!' she gushed. 'I had no idea it was you, Lola. Honestly, I'm *such* a big fan!'

Lola did her best to smile before she staggered on, almost tripping over a tearful Bunny Love who was slumped against the wall confiding in a friend that she hadn't had sex since her boyfriend ran off with a Bulgarian masseuse three years ago – and she wasn't even sure she could remember how to do it.

'Sorry!' squeaked Lola again before Barbara appeared, linked her arm and guided her over to the green room.

How the hell did I get so pissed? She could remember having a laugh with the competition winners but as usual she hadn't known when to stop. She wasn't even sure she was enjoying being drunk anymore.

Inside the green room, her hairdresser, make-up artist and stylist were standing in a huddle waiting to begin work. Harvey always called them the Style Council but right now she was too drunk to remember why. Was it something to do with some band from the Eighties?

'Hiya girls,' she groaned, collapsing onto the sofa.

Before they had time to reply, Harvey burst through the door.

'Lola! Are you OK?'

'Yeah, course I am, darlin', I'm just pissed, that's all. And I couldn't half do with a lie-down.'

'Well you'll have to wait a bit longer for that, I'm afraid – you're live on Channel 3 in half an hour.'

She let out a moan and buried her head in a cushion. 'Half an hour? How did that happen?'

'Never mind that now, let's just concentrate on getting you ready – and sobering you up. Here.'

He held out a can of Twinkle.

'Come on, get it down you. I know it tastes like suntan lotion but you might as well get used to drinking it. And hopefully the sugar will sober you up.'

She nodded and reluctantly took the can.

'Now is there anything else I can get you?'

He waited while she glugged it down, trying not to grimace at its sickly sweetness.

'Actually,' she said, wiping her mouth, 'you know what I really fancy?'

He smiled, already guessing what she was going to say. 'Turkish Delight?'

'Oh Harvey, I'd love some!'

'Well it's a good job I brought a secret stash, isn't it?' He rolled his eyes at her fondly. 'I'll go and get it – just you concentrate on sobering up. And girls, work your magic!'

He left the room, closely followed by Barbara who announced that she was going to check on the film crew. As the door clicked shut Lola stumbled over to the dressing table and looked at herself in the mirror. She realized her eye make-up was smudged and she had a false eyelash stuck on the end of her nose. She let out another groan.

'Girls, I'm completely shit-faced.'

'Oh don't worry about it!' they all raced to reassure her.

'You'd never be able to tell!'

'Honestly, you look totes *amazing*!'

She could always rely on Belle, Scarlett and Trixie to pump her with affirmation – even when it was deplorably undeserved. The three of them had worked for her since she'd first signed to her record company and were hard core goodtime girls who'd often make her eyes water with stories of their wild partying. But they knew how to enhance her appearance in record time – and along the way massage her morale.

'You're going to be just fine,' soothed Belle, a statuesque black girl known as the best hairdresser in the business.

'You just need tidying up a bit, that's all,' reassured Scarlett, a beautiful blonde who used make-up like magic.

'You know, if you really want to perk up we could give you something stronger than a Twinkle,' breathed Trixie, a cute Chinese girl who could make even Mariah Carey look stylish.

'Oh yeah?' asked Lola. 'What's that?'

The three girls stepped back and looked at each other conspiratorially.

'A little bump of coke,' whispered Trixie. 'Ruby Marlow does it all the time.'

Straight away Lola's smile dropped. Didn't they realize her

entire childhood had been ruined by drugs? It wasn't as if she'd ever tried to hide it; she'd done enough interviews on the subject and was always making speeches for anti-drugs charities. But she didn't want to come across as a boring kill-joy so did her best to sound polite. 'Sorry, girls, but you know coke's not really my thing.'

'Yeah but you could always try a little bump . . .'

Lola sat up firmly. Suddenly she was six years old again, watching in horror as her mum maniacally bounced around the kitchen on a crack high, only to zonk out with depression for hours afterwards. The feeling of revulsion was just as strong now as it had been all those years ago. But she tried hard not to snap. 'No, sorry girls but you know I'm totally anti-drugs. Can you imagine what everyone would say if I went on live TV coked out of my mind?'

'Yeah, but we're not talking about you getting coked out of your mind,' breezed Belle. 'And coke's nowhere near as strong as crack.'

'Big time!' agreed Trixie. 'It's in a completely different league.'

'And a nice little bump might stop you looking so pissed,' suggested Scarlett.

'But I thought you said I didn't look pissed?'

The three of them were flummoxed.

'No . . . but we're just trying to make you look as good as possible, that's all,' ventured Scarlett. 'We only want what's best for you, Lola.'

Lola held up her hand as if she didn't want to discuss it anymore. 'Trust me, girls, what's best for me isn't to start cramming a load of coke up my conk – however pissed I am.'

There was a tense silence and the three girls looked down awkwardly.

'Now come on, sort me out, will you? I look like a total wreck.'

The girls resumed their work as Lola sat in silence. She wondered why she didn't seem to be able to make herself stop when it came to booze, yet she could always resist the temptation to take drugs, however drunk she was. She guessed she just had too many unhappy associations lodged deep in her memory – and whatever anyone said, nothing could dislodge them. She let out a long sigh.

'Could somebody please pass me another Twinkle?'

*

Freddy looked at his watch. It was 9.40 and there was still no sign of Lola.

'Ten minutes to air!' blasted a voice in his ear. He reached for the control pack fastened to the back of his belt and turned down the volume. They'd set up the camera and lights on the raised platform where earlier in the evening Lola had delivered her speech. But this time she'd be standing with her back to the crowd so as not to attract attention and to give the best possible view of the party raging on behind her. Of course there was always the worry that drunken guests might spot the bright lights and start waving at the camera or, even worse, try to interrupt the interview. In his two years as a news correspondent, Freddy had already had to cope with every embarrassing eventuality. But on this occasion the interview area had been cordoned off – and was already being fringed by security.

Just then he spotted Lola being escorted through the crowd by Harvey and Barbara. She was swigging from a can of Twinkle while a gaggle of girls fussed around her clothes, hair and make-up. She seemed a little bleary-eyed and was swaying slightly but, to Freddy at least, she still looked amazing.

'Man, she is proper wavey,' said Spike, standing next to him. 'This is going to be off the hook.'

Freddy felt a flicker of nerves take hold of him. He was always a bit agitated before a live broadcast: he couldn't help thinking about all the things that could go wrong in front of millions of viewers. And tonight there was the added pressure of dealing with a drunk interviewee – one he happened to find exceptionally attractive. He really hoped neither of them went to pieces.

Lola tottered onto the stage and gave him a bright smile. 'Hiya,' she beamed. 'Nice to meet you.'

'Urm, all right?' he managed, trying his best to look relaxed. 'I'm F-F-F-Freddy.' *Come on, champ, get it together!*

She didn't seem to notice his nerves and peered at him through a drunken haze. This was going to be a challenge . . .

'I'm Lola,' she slurred, 'and I'm shit-faced. Hic.' She gave a little giggle. 'Sorry darlin', I've been downing Twinkles to try and sober up and now I can't get rid of these hiccups.'

'Two minutes to air!' bellowed the voice in Freddy's ear.

'I hope I don't mess up your interview,' Lola went on. 'Hic.' *Is it my imagination or does she smell of Turkish Delight?*

'Oh don't worry about it,' he soothed. 'I'm sure you'll be cracking. I'll steer us through and look after you, I promise.'

She smiled at him and tilted her head to one side. 'Oh Freddy, you're so lovely!'

'Lovely'! There it was again – that awful word. He'd wondered how long it would take to make an appearance. Girls always seemed to describe Freddy as 'lovely', never 'sexy'. It usually meant they wanted to be friends rather than jump into bed with him. And it had already led to several romantic disappointments in his life – and lots of heartache. Of course he wasn't seriously thinking that a hugely successful pop star like Lola Grant would want to jump into bed with him. But he couldn't pretend that he found her anything other than out-of-this-world gorgeous.

Big Phil stepped forward to fit Lola's radio mic and once it was attached tested the sound levels.

'One minute to air!'

'OK we're nearly on,' said Freddy. 'Good luck!'

'Good luck!' echoed Harvey and Barbara from the sidelines. 'And don't get carried away and say something you'll regret later,' added Harvey.

'Carried away? Me?' teased Lola. 'Hic! By the way, Freddy, I love your accent. Where exactly in Wales are you from?'

'Port Talbot,' he shrugged. 'It's home and I love it but it's not very exciting, I'm afraid.'

She smirked at him. 'Darlin', have you ever been to Tooting?'

'Thirty seconds to air!'

Freddy readjusted his earpiece and smiled at her.

'You know you're blatantly much more handsome in real life than you are on the telly,' she said.

He felt his knees almost give way. 'Really? Oh right. Thanks, like.'

Is she flirting with me? Or is she just flashing me a bit of her pop-star charisma? He was confused. He'd interviewed plenty of pop stars in the past but none of them had told him he was handsome. But hadn't she also just said he was 'lovely'?

'Ten seconds!'

Freddy gave her a firm nod and then looked at the camera as he listened to the presenter Amanda Adams introduce him from the studio. He could feel his heart pounding in his chest and hoped Lola couldn't hear it. *Come on Freddy, you can do this.*

'And cue!'

'Yes, Amanda, I'm here in central London for the launch of *Trouble*, the new album by Lola Grant, who's with me now.' He turned from the camera to face his guest. 'Lola, you must be thrilled by the response to the album.'

'Hic. Yeah, sorry, I've got hiccups but it's all brilliant. I'm totally made up.'

'And we've just heard tonight that you've signed a record deal in America . . .'

'Yeah, I know, isn't it fierce? I'm going to promote the album over here, go on this massive tour and then hit the States. I'm really excited, hic. To be honest I think that's why I got so pissed tonight.'

From the corner of his eye Freddy could see Harvey visibly stiffen and shoot him a look of panic. He tried to steer them back onto safer ground.

'Yes, well, urm, the party, urm, the theme of tonight's party . . . Am I right in thinking it's inspired by your latest single?'

'Yeah, hic. Sorry, I'm so pissed. Yeah, it's inspired by *Lost in Love*.'

'Which is about a holiday romance, isn't it?'

'Yeah but to be honest it's a bit more personal than that. Hic. You know, I probably shouldn't tell you this but the song's about my mum's holiday to Spain when she was fifteen – when she came back up the duff with me.'

Freddy was momentarily disarmed by her bluntness. 'Oh, right. So it's about *her* holiday romance rather than yours?'

'Kind of. Hic. Although the truth is she's never told me much about it so I had to make up most of the story. You know, I've always imagined she fell madly in love with some gorgeous Spaniard, but knowing my mum, she probably just had a knee-trembler with some total stranger round the back of a nightclub. Hic.'

'This is sensational!' the editor's voice blasted into Freddy's ear. 'Keep it going – keep pounding her for more!'

*

Lola saw that Harvey had moved to stand behind Freddy and was waving at her to shut up, shaking his head furiously and miming the signal to 'cut'. *Oh what's the problem?* she thought. *I'm only telling the truth . . .*

'So urm, you, urm, you never knew your dad then?' Freddy asked.

'No. And my mum's never really told me much about him – except I'm pretty sure he must have been Spanish. Hic. The other thing I know is that, according to my grandma, when Mum came back from that holiday, that's when her life hit the skids.'

Freddy nodded sombrely. 'You've talked openly in the past about your mum's drug problem. Are you saying now that you think the two things could be linked?'

'Blatantly, yeah. Hic.'

'And how's your relationship with your mum at the moment?'

At this there was a thoughtful pause. Lola knew she shouldn't say too much but with Freddy she felt safe. She wondered whether she could ever fall in love with somebody like him. *This is the kind of man who'd be good for me. But do I actually fancy him?*

'It's difficult, to be honest, Freddy. I didn't have the best time growing up, as I'm sure you know, so I still find it hard to forgive her. Hic. But at the same time she's still my mum, you know?'

He nodded. 'So if she's watching now, is there anything you'd like to say to her?'

She bit her lip and took a second to reflect. 'Just give up the crack, Mum,' she said directly to the camera. 'It's a really nasty drug. And I hope we can be mates one day.'

Freddy fell silent to give her words maximum impact.

'Well, I'm afraid with that we're going to have to leave you,' he said, fiddling with his earpiece.

'That's all right, darlin'—' She suddenly stopped and slapped her hand to her chest. 'Ooh! My hiccups have gone! You've cured them, Freddy – you're a hero!'

Oh what am I doing flirting with him? He's lovely but there's no way it'd work – I'd only get bored and balls it up by having a fling with some bad boy. She consoled herself that she could always blame her flirting on the booze and told herself to cut it out before she went too far. But the funny thing was, she wasn't sure she wanted to.

Freddy smiled at her bashfully. 'That's my pleasure, Lola. And enjoy the rest of your evening.'

'Oh I will,' she sparkled. 'I've been dying to jump in that pool all night and there's nothing stopping me now!' As she took off her mic and picked her way down from the stage, she tossed her sunglasses over to him. 'Here, look after these for me, darlin'!'

Well I've got to find some way of seeing him again. At least when I'm sober . . .

Freddy caught the sunglasses just as he was turning to face the camera to hand back to the studio.

'Well, this is Freddy Jones with Lola Grant – a woman I'm sure we'll be hearing a lot more from over the next few months.' And then, right behind him, there was an almighty splash.

Lola gave a loud whoop as she bobbed to the surface of the water. All around her people began to giggle and gasp as they realized the biggest pop star in the country had just thrown herself fully clothed into a swimming pool on live TV. As she wiped the water from her eyes, she could just about make out Freddy gesturing behind him and winding up his chat to camera by saying something about her knowing how to make a splash.

Oh you'd better believe it, she thought as she leapt up into the air and shook the water from her hair. *And if you think that's making a splash, you ain't seen nothing yet . . .*

2

At the kitchen table of her flat in Camberwell, Gloria Montero was trying to persuade her daughter to eat a pot of yoghurt.

'Come on, honey. It's strawberry – your favourite.'

'But I'm not hungry, Mummy,' Chanelle sulked. 'I don't want it!'

Gloria let out a long sigh. This kind of performance was fast becoming routine and had already gone on for half an hour this morning.

'Please, Chanelle,' she tried again. 'One more spoonful for Mummy?'

Chanelle shook her head, turned away and began playing with her favourite princess doll. Gloria gave up. She had better things to do with her time than shovel food into the mouth of an unappreciative four-year-old. She finished the yoghurt herself, quickly checking that her own mum wasn't watching from her position at the sink, where she was powering through the washing-up.

'Good girl!' Gloria warbled, loud enough for her mum to hear. 'My Chanelle is such a good girl!'

'You know, I hope you're feeding that girl properly,' her mum called out over her shoulder, plonking the dishes down onto the draining rack. 'She's been looking a bit thin lately.'

God, what was it with her mum? She'd only arrived five minutes ago, already she'd complained about the kitchen looking like a pigsty and now she was telling her she didn't know how to feed her daughter. Gloria was just about to tell her to shut up when she remembered she needed her mum to look after Chanelle today – and would be relying on her a lot more for childcare now that she'd been hired to sing backing vocals for Lola Grant.

'Yeah, I suppose she has been a bit off her food lately,' she managed. 'But I wouldn't worry about it, she seems perfectly happy.'

Gloria looked at Chanelle dressing up her doll and smiled to herself. She was so innocent, so full of hope. Gloria had been like that once too. Although it seemed like a long time ago now.

'Well, I hope she's getting her five a day,' her mum clattered on. 'You know, I used to make sure you and your brother ate an apple and an orange every morning.'

Oh give me a break! I gave her a few Jaffa Cakes last night – and I always smother her chips in tomato ketchup. And all right, Gloria knew she wasn't the perfect mother but at least she was trying her best – and holding everything together really hadn't been easy for the last few years. Although hopefully it would be getting a bit easier now she was starting her new job. She might even be able to afford to finally get the washing machine fixed. She looked at the heap of laundry piling up next to it and realized she'd forgotten to go to the launderette yet again. Never mind. If she sucked up to her mum enough this morning she might go for her later.

'Oh yeah, I'm really strict about that, Mum,' she lied. 'Which reminds me, there's a box of strawberries in the fridge for lunch today.' *Yeah, and let's see how you get on forcing them down her!*

Her mum pulled the plug out of the sink and snapped off her washing-up gloves. She turned to face Gloria with her usual wintry smile. 'Well, at least this place is looking a bit cleaner.'

'Yeah, thanks, Mum.' *Now get off my back!*

Just then her mum spotted the overflowing bin and pulled a face as if she'd swallowed some out-of-date orange juice. 'My God, Gloria, look at the state of this!'

Gloria tried not to roll her eyes as her mum made a big show of emptying the rubbish into a black bin-liner, picking out takeaway cartons and tutting loudly. 'Posh Spice? Is that some kind of curry house?'

Yeah, all right, Mum, you know I can't cook! Now give it a rest!

As she listened to her mum launch into a long lecture about E-numbers and the dangers of eating too much salt, Gloria consoled herself with the thought that she'd lied to her about the start time for today's rehearsal. In fact, it wasn't really a rehearsal at all but more of a meeting, the first time Gloria and the rest of the band would be getting together with Lola. It wasn't happening till late afternoon but she'd told her mum she was needed in the morning so she could nip into her favourite beauty salon to have her hair and nails done. She knew she couldn't afford it but today was a day she'd been dreading – and she really needed to be feeling her best to get through it.

She switched on the TV, hoping to drown out the sound of

her mum's nagging. As a personality-free blonde she'd always found annoying ran through the latest showbiz news, she sat back down and gave Chanelle a kiss on the head.

'But the big news of the day,' announced the presenter, 'is last night's launch party for Lola Grant's new album . . .'

'Turn it up a bit, Gloria,' her mum chirped, tying up the bin bag and dumping it by the door. 'Look, Chanelle, that woman on the telly is your mummy's new boss.'

Oh, thanks Mum. Rub it in, why don't you?

'But I thought Mummy was a singer?' Chanelle asked, looking up from her doll.

'She is, sweetheart, she's a *backing* singer.'

Yeah and she'd been a damn good solo singer too – not that anyone remembered. In fact, the only person who listened to her music now was Chanelle when Gloria put it on at full blast and the two of them danced around the table having a kitchen disco.

'What's a backing singer, Mummy?' Chanelle asked.

Gloria stroked her hair and smiled. She couldn't bring herself to explain; she couldn't bear the thought of disappointing her daughter.

'Wait a minute and I'll tell you,' butted in her mum. 'Just let me watch this first.'

The three of them fell silent and listened to the report on Lola's album launch, which Gloria hadn't even known was taking place, let alone been invited to. Talk about putting her in her place. After two torturous minutes the report ended by repeating a clip of Lola jumping into a swimming pool live on Channel 3 News, which for some reason Gloria's mum and daughter found hilarious. Gloria couldn't bear to watch it and stood up to switch off the TV.

'What did you do that for?' asked her mum.

'I'm not in the mood.'

'No, well,' she sighed, 'I guess today can't be easy.'

You can say that again.

'Well, try not to be too miserable, Gloria. I'm sure it's not going to be as bad as you think. You never know, you might even *like* your new job.'

Yeah but I'm pretty sure I'd have liked my old one better.

'And, you know, it's a shame your solo career didn't work out but maybe you'll be better suited to being a backing singer. Not everyone's cut out to be a star, you know.'

Gloria couldn't listen to her anymore. 'Look, Mum, I don't want to talk about it.' She picked up the kettle and began filling it with water from the screechingly loud tap.

'And you've got to admit,' her mum wheedled on in the background, 'that Lola does look like a laugh. I bet you two will get on really well.'

Yeah, Mum, for your information we always did.

She turned off the tap and switched on the kettle.

What would it be like seeing Lola again after everything that had happened? She had no idea. But she guessed she'd be finding out later.

*

'How do you feel about chest hair?'

Lola looked at Barbara and rolled her eyes. It was going to be a long morning. It was only 9 a.m. and already she'd been interviewed live on Britain's most popular radio show, chatting brightly to the DJ as if she'd just dropped in for the fun of it. Now she was ensconced on a sofa in Barbara's office doing a round of print and online interviews with a succession of hungry-eyed journalists, each of them eager to make the most of their allotted ten minutes and come away with a different set of quotes from their rivals – which meant that their questions were becoming increasingly random.

'Urm, chest hair, urm, yeah it can be sexy, I suppose,' she answered. 'But only on the right man.' She found herself wondering if Freddy Jones had chest hair and then blushed as if the interviewer could read her mind.

'What's your favourite food?'

'Curry, blatantly.'

'Which member of the royal family would you most like to get drunk with?'

'Piece of piss – Prince Harry!'

Unlike some pop stars, Lola didn't mind the endless round of interviews and promotion. Harvey had explained from the start of her career that it was becoming increasingly difficult to sell albums – and pop stars were having to work harder and harder for their money. She'd always told herself that if she ever made it she wouldn't moan about having to speak to journalists and would do her best never to send them away disappointed.

Nevertheless, today she was finding it unusually difficult. Last night's launch party had gone on till late and she'd only had a few hours' sleep. After jumping into the pool she'd started on the shots, and the last thing she remembered was being carried down through the fire escape by security and dropped onto the back seat of a car waiting by the goods entrance. She'd woken up this morning wearing only one boot with her ripped minidress on back to front, a slice of lemon trapped down her cleavage and the taste of barbecued sewage in her mouth. Three hours later she was still suffering. In fact, she was so hung-over even her hair hurt.

In the brief breaks between interviews she held her head in her hands and let out low, whimpering moans. When she closed her eyes she could actually see stars, like some kind of cartoon character after a comedy fight. Barbara had subtly left a packet of Smints on the table next to her, presumably because she stank of booze. She popped another couple in her mouth and sucked on them as hard as she could. By now she'd gone through so many she was starting to get wind. She stifled a burp and dropped a hangover remedy into a glass of water. *Thank God I'm not on camera so I don't have to look good,* she told herself as she watched it fizz.

'Who would you rather sleep with, David Cameron or Nick Clegg?' asked a leather-skinned bald man who edited the showbiz section of one of the red tops.

'I'm sorry,' interjected Barbara from behind her desk, 'but Lola doesn't do politics. She'd much rather talk about the new album.'

'OK, well, tell me about the song *Tramp*,' the journalist went on. 'What inspired you to write it?'

Lola did her best to perk up. 'Well, I suppose it was the frustration I felt about the fact that a woman who sleeps around gets labelled a tramp while a slaggy man blatantly always gets away with it.'

'I see. And did you write it about anyone in particular?'

'Yeah I did actually – my ex-boyfriend who was a total dick

and cheated on me with some bird I was actually working with. Oh I'm sure you heard the story, it was all over the papers.'

The journalist smiled. Like everyone, he knew about Lola's fling with Fox Marshall, the neck-twistingly handsome guitarist in her last backing band. Fox was tall with wheat-coloured hair and bright blue eyes – and he was hugely talented, which Lola always found attractive. But he was one of those men who knew just how attractive he was and in her experience this always meant trouble. She should have stayed away from him from the start but had been lured into a steamy fling during a promotional trip to Denmark. And while she'd ended up falling in love with him, it had become more and more obvious that all he wanted from her was a bit of fun. When she discovered that he was also having fun with a dance coach he'd met on the set of one of her videos, she'd been devastated. And once the story had been splashed all over the tabloid press she'd felt like the whole world was laughing at her. At the time she'd been too upset to talk about it, but now it had inspired one of her best ever songs she felt differently – and was more than happy to open up.

'Anyway,' she breezed on, '*Tramp* is kind of my way of getting my own back on him – and telling the world what a wanker he was.'

The journalist nodded, clearly thrilled with the turn the interview was taking. 'And how would you like Fox to feel when he hears it?'

'Oh I couldn't care less, to be honest – I was over him ages ago. But I'm pleased I got a good song out of him. I'm only sorry I couldn't come up with any lyrics about his tiny dick.'

'OK, time's up!' Barbara butted in. She shot Lola a steely look and tightened her mouth.

'Sorry, darlin',' Lola frowned. 'I shouldn't have said that, should I?'

The truth was that Lola was glad she'd left the journalist with the bombshell about Fox's tiny dick – not that it was strictly true. In fact, far from it. But maybe reading about his inadequacies in the tabloid press would teach Fox a lesson. *And you never know, maybe this means he won't be able to hurt anyone else like he hurt me.* She wondered if Freddy Jones had ever hurt anyone. She doubted it. Which meant he could be just the right man for her . . .

'Tell me about the song *Miss Chief*,' asked the next journalist, an overweight brunette wearing a badly fitting bra that made her look like she had four boobs. 'What kind of message are you hoping it sends out to your fans?'

'Well, it's all about empowerment,' began Lola, trying her best not to sound pompous. 'I wanted an anthem to make my female fans feel strong and confident – and inspire them not to stand for any shit.'

'Sounds very admirable,' the journalist nodded. 'And is it about your break-up with Fox Marshall?'

Lola smiled. 'Not exactly. I wrote it when I found out my assistant had sold the story to the press.'

The woman nudged towards her. Lola knew she had to give each journalist something slightly different for their articles to have maximum impact – and it looked like this one was taking the bait. 'So what happened exactly?' she asked, her head cocked in interest.

'Well, some so-called "anonymous source" blabbed all the

gory details about Fox cheating on me,' Lola chirped. 'So first of all I was gutted about being dumped, but knowing that someone close to me had flogged the story made me feel even worse. So my manager came up with this idea: he planted three slightly different pieces of fake gossip with three different people he suspected of being the leak. And it turned out the story that ended up in the papers came from my assistant – so we sacked the silly cow.'

There was a nervous cough from the corner of the room and Lola spotted her new assistant Amina reaching for a glass of water. A quiet, shy girl, Amina had only started working for her earlier that month and until now had had no idea what had happened to her predecessor. Finding out was obviously coming as something of a shock.

Lola acted quickly to reassure her. 'But it all worked out fine in the end,' she beamed at her from across the room, 'because I've got someone much better working for me now. My new assistant Amina's way too fierce to do anything like that. And I'm sure she'll be sticking around for a long time yet.'

Amina gave her a grateful smile and went back to tapping on her iPad.

'And how about *Mess It Up*?' asked the next journalist, an intense-looking man who sounded like he was whispering and shouting at the same time. 'Don't you think it sends out the wrong message about binge-drinking to your young fans?'

'No,' Lola answered firmly. '*Mess It Up*'s about how *I* feel when I want to get drunk and messy. I'm not saying anyone else should.'

'But isn't it irresponsible to sing about drinking and make it sound cool?'

'Not at all. Everyone knows I'm anti-drugs but young people need *some* way of going out and letting their hair down. And don't tell me you don't like messing it up sometimes?'

The journalist tried his best not to smile.

'Oh come on,' she teased, 'I can blatantly see that naughty twinkle in your eye.'

She nudged him on the shoulder and he gave in to a big grin.

'Well, I've got to hand it to you, doll,' Barbara said once he'd left. 'You can play the press like a Steinway grand.'

'Even when I'm hung-over,' Lola shot back with a mischievous wink.

'Even when you're hung-over.'

As another journalist came in she reached for the Smints and popped three in her mouth. She sucked on them hard and braced herself for the next question.

'Where's the weirdest place you've ever had sex?'

It really was going to be a long morning.

*

Freddy hit Play and gazed at the screen as an obviously drunk Lola hiccuped and swayed her way through last night's interview.

'You know, I probably shouldn't tell you this,' he watched her say, 'but the song's about my mum's holiday to Spain when she was fifteen – when she came back up the duff with me.'

He pressed the Pause button and smiled. It was a great interview and he knew he'd nailed it. He breathed a sigh of relief. *That'll get the editor off my back – at least for the time being.*

That morning Freddy had come into the newsroom early to watch back last night's live broadcast before starting on the new working day. He felt great, having left the party shortly after the interview, as was expected of journalists in case they saw something they shouldn't. And he didn't mind the early start as at the moment work was his number-one priority. For weeks now all the correspondents at Channel 3 News had been under pressure to up their game: ratings had been falling and a new editor had been brought in to revamp the programme. As the show's entertainment correspondent, Freddy had repeatedly been told he had to nail bigger exclusives and be tougher on interviewees. Which was why at the moment he started every day watching back the previous night's report and seeing if there was any way he could improve.

He sat back and listened to the broad south London accent reverberating from his screen. 'She probably just had a knee-trembler with some total stranger round the back of a night-club.'

Even a day later Lola's candid confession raised a smile. And there was no denying her surprise pool jump made for terrific TV. Three of Freddy's colleagues had already congratulated him on it in the lift up to the newsroom. It looked like nailing a high-profile interview had been just what he needed. And now he could sit back and concentrate on what was really on his mind – working out whether Lola had been flirting with him because she actually fancied him.

'Freddy?' He heard a voice calling out behind him. 'Can I have a quick word?'

He swivelled around and came face-to-face with the programme's editor Hugh Badcock, an ex-army, dick-on-the-table alpha male with a beer belly he often stroked as if it were his proudest possession.

'Yeah,' Freddy replied. 'Sure.'

Lola's flirting would have to wait. Finally he was about to get some praise from the big boss!

Doing his best to suppress a grin, he followed Hugh into his office and sprung onto the sofa. The room was decorated with ethnic tat his boss had picked up on the road during his time as a foreign correspondent, photos of him proudly sporting a bulletproof vest in various war zones, and portraits of the three children he had with a minor aristocrat Freddy was pretty sure was some kind of Lady. The combined effect was to make Freddy feel like he was walking into one huge trophy cabinet.

'So,' Hugh began in his posh voice, lowering himself into the seat behind his desk, 'what did you think about last night's live?'

'Oh I thought it was cracking, like.'

'Hmmm.' He began fiddling with his signet ring. 'Hmmm.'

Uh-oh, thought Freddy, *he obviously doesn't agree*. He could feel his grin starting to wilt.

'Well, I loved it when she jumped into the pool,' Hugh acknowledged. 'And it was great when she asked her mum to give up crack.'

Freddy nodded expectantly. *But . . . ?*

'But that's exactly when you should have gone in for the kill. Rather than backing off, that's when you should have pushed her for more.'

'Oh, right,' he managed. 'You do know I only had three minutes for the interview?'

'Yeah but three minutes is plenty, Freddy. You know the rule – you warm them up off-camera first and then you go straight for the jugular once you're on air.'

By now Freddy could feel his whole body starting to sag. 'Yeah, I know, but it was pretty difficult, Hugh. We didn't have any time together beforehand – she was so pissed she only turned up at the last minute.'

'Which reminds me – you should have pushed her on the whole pissed thing. Every time she mentioned it you looked embarrassed and changed the subject.'

Yeah, well I'm hardly going to give her a hard time when I want to pull her, am I? He wondered how Hugh would react if he said it out loud – or if he confessed that as soon as he'd laid eyes on Lola he'd realized he hadn't fancied anyone as much in ages. Not that he was about to when Hugh was making it perfectly clear he thought he was a crap correspondent in the first place.

'But I didn't want to make her feel uncomfortable,' he attempted.

'But that's exactly what you're supposed to do, Freddy. You're a journalist – that's how you get the best material.'

Freddy couldn't believe what he was hearing. Regardless of how he felt about Lola, this was completely unfair: he'd delivered a great interview which everyone else loved and now for some reason his boss was having a go at him. Well, he wasn't going to stand for it.

'Actually, Hugh, I'm not sure I agree with you. I only got those lines out of Lola because she felt comfortable and relaxed around me. And I only got the interview in the first place because her publicist knows she can trust me.'

'But Freddy, you're not a chat-show host. There's no such thing as "relaxed" or "comfortable" on a news programme. For God's sake, when she handed you her sunglasses it looked like you were some kind of couple on a beach holiday.'

With a jolt, Freddy realized he'd forgotten all about the sunglasses. He'd put them in his bag for safe-keeping and then left without returning them. But maybe that was the point? Maybe Lola had given him the sunglasses precisely so he'd have to see her again?

'From now on,' Hugh continued, 'this programme needs to be much harder. I'm just not sure you're a good fit, to be honest, Freddy – at the moment you're way too much of a soft touch. No wonder all the magazines call you the "housewife's favourite".'

Freddy did his best not to wince; he hated that nickname even more than he hated the word 'lovely'. Neither label was going to get him a hot girlfriend, which was what he really wanted right now. And listening to Hugh Badcock throw both of them in his face only made him think he'd been stupid to have imagined Lola might fancy him.

Oh and what's the point of arguing with him anyway? There's no way I'm going to win so I might as well just grin and bear it.

'OK, message understood,' he conceded, gritting his teeth. 'I'll do my best to toughen up.'

'All right, boyo.'

Hugh always insisted on making fun of Freddy's Welsh accent and it really riled him. He wouldn't care but nobody in Wales called each other 'boyo' anymore – at least no one under the age of forty. But he didn't want to be accused of being oversensitive so he forced out a weak smile.

'Good man,' nodded Hugh, standing up to indicate the meeting was over.

For Freddy it wasn't over soon enough. He'd started the day on a high but the last five minutes had brought him crashing right down to earth.

*

Lola gave a little chuckle; she was really starting to enjoy the day. By now she'd finished her print interviews and was just beginning a round of phone chats with major local radio stations around the country.

'Who would play you in a film of your life?' came a Liverpudlian accent down the line.

'Oh, I'm not sure I'd want *anyone* to play me,' Lola replied with a wry smile. 'I'm having way too much fun playing myself!'

She didn't understand why so many pop stars had such a problem dealing with journalists: all you had to do was be yourself and they respected you, whatever you said. It was something she'd learned while making the new album – and opening up about her feelings for the first time. So far the reviews had been overwhelmingly positive so she'd decided to adopt the same policy in interviews.

Lola's problem was she could be way *too* honest – and left to her own devices would probably answer any question thrown at her. She'd already learned that journalists tended to leave their most direct personal questions till the end of their interviews, probably because by then they thought they'd warmed her up – and if Barbara pulled the plug they had enough quotes to work with anyway. But Harvey had always told her that there were some questions it was better not to answer, that there were some things it was best to keep to herself. And while she knew he was right, she sometimes struggled to put this into practice. Which was why he'd given her the nickname the Mouth from the South. And boy had she lived up to it last night.

'How does your mum feel about what you said about her on live TV?'

'Does she really not remember who your dad is?'

'How did it feel growing up knowing you were a mistake?'

As she did her best to deflect a barrage of questions about her relationship with her mum, Lola reasoned that family was probably one of the things she should have kept to herself. Sure, ex-boyfriends were fair game – especially when they'd dumped her. As were assistants looking to make some easy money on the side. But her mum should have stayed off-limits, however bad a job she'd made of bringing her up – and however pissed Lola had been when she'd done the interview. She wondered if she'd have behaved with a bit more self-control if she hadn't felt that twist of attraction towards Freddy. Well, there was no point regretting it now – even though every journalist she met wanted to pick up on the story and come away with their own revelations.

The worst thing was, her mum was bound to find out what she'd said – that was assuming she hadn't watched the interview on TV last night. The two of them hadn't spoken for months and Lola had no intention of calling her now that she felt so guilty. At least there was no chance of her mum speaking to the press, seeing as Lola's regular handouts were her only source of income. They'd originally been given on the understanding that her mum would seek treatment for her addiction, but Lola had given up on that hope long ago and by now was resolved to the fact that she used the money to buy more drugs. Oh it was all so sad and depressing – and Lola had only gone and made it even worse by making out her mum was some kind of slapper who'd got pregnant on a one-night stand.

There's a fine line between being honest and being undignified, she told herself. *And clearly I still haven't worked out exactly where it is.*

She took a deep breath and downed a swig of her hangover remedy.

'Next!'

*

'OK so the top story's the earthquake in China,' Hugh Badcock bellowed at the assembled Channel 3 News team. 'The death toll's ten thousand and we've got footage of cute kids being pulled out of the rubble. Bomber Bancroft's all over it – and it's great picture.'

His assessment was met with a chorus of approval from most of the staff. They were seated on sofas in the soft area of the newsroom, surrounded by clocks showing the time in various cities around the world and screens broadcasting the mute output of a selection of rolling news channels. Nestled somewhere in the middle of the team was a disgruntled Freddy, hoping he could escape being put on a story so he'd have time to recover from his early-morning disappointment.

'Next up is this newly discovered paedo ring in Dundee,' Hugh rattled on, his eyes widening. 'Suggsy's already on a plane up there. And it's a big, juicy story – ten kids raped and abused for years.'

Freddy watched as everyone's faces lit up around him. He couldn't help being repulsed by their enthusiasm.

'Fantastic,' he heard someone gush.

'What a brilliant story,' agreed the producer next to him.

'Can we blame the government?' broke in deputy editor Janine Jury, a haggard-looking thirty-something who, as far as Freddy could tell, seemed to spend every minute of the day manically chewing gum and knocking back Diet Coke. 'Surely we can find someone to say they're not doing enough to catch paedos?'

'Great idea!' barked Hugh. 'Someone call the Home Secretary's office and see if she'll come on to disco with the do-gooder. We could have a brilliant ding-dong.'

'And if she won't do it we can always empty-chair her,' added Janine.

Freddy bristled at her aggression. If Hugh Badcock was the alpha male of the office then there was no question that his deputy was the alpha female. Freddy looked at Spike sitting opposite and roofed his eyes in exasperation.

As Hugh carried on running through the day's stories, Freddy zoned out and glanced around the room. At times like this he always felt like the odd one out, like an alien who'd somehow landed in the middle of the newsroom. Everyone else looked gripped by the stories on offer – and chomping at the bit to start work. *Maybe Hugh's right. Maybe I just don't have the aggression it takes to be a great journalist after all.*

The problem was, he wasn't sure he wanted to force himself to feel that kind of aggression. All right, he loved his job, but what he really enjoyed about it was interviewing singers, actors and entertainers, asking them about their work and then sharing what he'd learned with the programme's viewers. Was that really such a bad thing? All the audience research showed that the viewers loved him – so why should he be treated like some kind of failure?

He suddenly realized that his disappointment at Hugh's criticism had ended up distracting him from what had been on his mind all night – Lola's comment about him being handsome. He still couldn't work out whether she was just pissed and flirtatious, turning on the charm to deliver a good interview, or actually flirting with him because she liked him. Come to think of it, he didn't even know if she was single. But then again, she had thrown him her sunglasses when she had a whole army of assistants standing by to hold them for her. All he had to do now was come up with a way of returning them personally – and then he'd be able to work out exactly how she felt.

And not only that, but if *Trouble* was doing well in the midweek charts, Freddy was sure there'd be an appetite for following up his interview with a second on-screen instalment. He could suggest filming an exclusive report from the set of Lola's next video or a rehearsal for that massive tour she'd mentioned – and tell Hugh that this time he'd push her much harder.

Yeah, that's the way to do it. He'd line up a professional meeting and a personal one too. And in the process he'd hopefully be pleasing both himself *and* his editor.

*

Sitting opposite Freddy, Spike Adebayo was trying to focus on what was being said in the meeting. Ever since the new editor had started a few months ago, the office had buzzed with anxiety and insecurity. Correspondents and producers had been fired, new faces had been brought in to try and boost ratings and everyone on the team had been left fearful for the safety of their job, including Spike.

But the truth was that today Spike was having trouble concentrating on work. He couldn't stop thinking about Lola Grant's manager, the good-looking older geezer who'd chatted him up then carded him at the launch party last night. *Harvey Sparks, Harvey Sparks, Harvey Sparks . . .*

Sure, Harvey was probably ten years older than Spike – and not his usual type. He tended to go for gym bunnies or go-go dancers he met out clubbing, usually while both parties were off their faces on mephedrone or crystal meth. But the truth was that this policy hadn't exactly worked out for him in the past – and had left Spike trapped in a soulless cycle of wild partying and pointless, fleeting flings. There was obviously more to this Harvey Sparks: he seemed sensitive and intelligent and work obviously played a big part in his life. And crucially they'd met when both of them were totally straight-headed, which had to be a good start. *You never know,* thought Spike, *maybe it's time for me to give it a go with someone completely different.*

'Now what about this hot weather?' Hugh Badcock interrupted his thoughts in his comically posh voice. 'Surely this has to be the hottest June on record?' He turned to face Dolly Dawson, the show's mild-mannered and perpetually pregnant weather presenter. She shook her head apologetically.

'*One* of the hottest Junes on record?'

She carried on shaking her head.

'*Probably* going to be one of the hottest Junes on record?'

She shrugged her shoulders in resignation.

'Well, come up with some kind of topline – there's got to be a news story in there somewhere.'

'Can we blame the government?' spat Janine Jury, her eyes blazing as she chomped furiously on her gum.

'Brilliant idea!' beamed Hugh. 'I'm thinking hosepipe bans, water shortages, global warming . . . Let's make some noise. Dolly, we'll have you in a live two-way next to a sandcastle on a beach somewhere. I'm sure by tonight you can come up with something to kick up a fuss about.'

'Oh right, OK,' she bleated. 'I'll do my best.'

Spike felt sorry for Dolly and shot her a look of solidarity. As he listened to Hugh drone on about hospital closures and benefit scroungers, he found his mind wandering back to last night – and the connection he'd felt when talking to Harvey. He was pretty sure he hadn't imagined it but why would a high-powered music manager be interested in a lowly young news producer like him? Unless he was one of those white geezers who got turned on by the idea of re-enacting a Benetton advert, or creating what Spike always jokingly referred to as a chocolate and vanilla swirl.

But no, he didn't get that impression about Harvey. He'd seemed sincere and genuine. And if he'd given Spike his card he obviously wanted him to get in touch. So why should he hold back just because Harvey wasn't his usual type? He took out the card and ran his finger along the edge.

Harvey Sparks, Artist Manager.

He thought about texting him and programmed his number into his mobile. Well, what did he have to lose? He could always start by saying something professional and see how things went from there: even though Barbara Bullock had arranged the interview it wouldn't be ridiculous for Spike to text Harvey a quick thank you.

'What up,' he began typing. 'Cool to meet you last night. Interview with Lola was sick. Hope you not feeling rough today. Spike'

As Hugh Badcock was busy whipping up outrage about some low-ranking politician no one had heard of until he'd been accused of a minor act of molestation by an intern, Spike read the text back to himself. All right, it wasn't the most professional thing he'd ever written but at least he'd mentioned the shoot. And he hadn't put a kiss at the end or anything. *Oh it'll do. At least it'll get the ball rolling.*

He pressed Send.

'Well, that's everything on the list,' Hugh boomed, rubbing his hands together in delight. 'What else is out there?'

As his colleagues fell over themselves to suggest potential stories, Spike did his best to refocus on the meeting. He was just about to open his mouth and make his own contribution when he felt his phone vibrate on his lap. As he unlocked the keypad the chatter around him faded into a low hum. He searched for the message and looked to see who'd sent it.

It was Harvey.

*

'So when are we going out then? What you up to this weekend?'

Harvey had been texting Spike for hours now but knew he didn't have long till he'd have to end the conversation to introduce Lola to her band. If he didn't strike soon then he might miss his moment. He reread the message and hit Send.

'Who are you texting?' Lola whimpered from behind a pair of face-swallowing sunglasses. The two of them were sitting in the back of a car on their way to Musicmaker rehearsal studios in Bermondsey. She'd somehow made it through a full morning of promo but by now the hangover was really starting to show – hence the sunglasses. Harvey wondered why she wasn't wearing her favourite pair and remembered that she'd thrown them to Freddy last night. 'And don't pretend it's business,' she croaked, 'I can tell from that grin on your face it's some bloke.'

Harvey knew there was no point lying. And he didn't want to anyway – he told Lola everything, including every last detail about his love life. But it had been a long time since he'd felt this excited about a potential date and he didn't want to jinx things.

'For your information,' he began slowly, 'I have met someone, yes. But we haven't even been on a date yet so I don't want to make a big thing out of it in case it doesn't work out.'

'Shit the bed!' Lola squealed. 'You really like him, don't you?'

'Lola, stop it! That's all you're getting for now!'

Just then his phone pinged and his fingers glided over the keypad to open the reply.

'Busy Friday but Saturday good,' he read. 'We keeping it chilled or getting wavey?'

Harvey looked at the message, perplexed. It was taking him

a while to decipher Spike's street speak but at the same time he found it quite charming: it transported him back to his own twenties, when he too had cared about being at the height of cool. And while he was happy to have left all that behind, he sometimes worried that as he'd matured he'd become jaded and weary, particularly when it came to mustering up enthusiasm about potential dates. Although hopefully Spike would be the one to end all that.

'So come on then,' broke in Lola. 'Have you got yourself a date or what?'

'I told you already, that's all you're getting for now.'

She pulled a sulky pout. 'Well, all I can say is, it's about time. You know you spend way too long looking after my life and nowhere near enough on your own. I think it'd be wicked if you got yourself a new fella.'

He smiled at her as he typed his reply. 'Saturday good. Let's keep it chilled. Fancy lunch in the sunshine?'

As he pressed Send he felt a flutter of nerves. Ever since he'd given up drinking, he'd found dating a big problem. If he told his date he was teetotal, they thought he was either a boring stiff or a complete alcoholic, which wasn't too far off the mark but not the kind of detail he wanted to divulge when he was trying to impress someone. It wasn't that he was ashamed of his wild, drink-fuelled past but it took some time to explain properly without putting men off – or scaring them into thinking he still had a problem with booze and was only going to be trouble. And besides, he'd learned from experience that most people needed to take the edge off their nerves on a first date by knocking back a few drinks – and instantly felt uncomfortable if he didn't do the same. In the past it had only led to tension and a series of dating disasters. And he wasn't going to risk that happening with Spike. *No,* he thought, *I'll arrange something low-key during the day, just to get the ball rolling.*

As he waited for the reply he remembered that Lola was scheduled to take part in a live Twitter chat. The journey across town would take about an hour, so Barbara had wanted to make the most of the dead time, especially after last night's live broadcast on Channel 3 News had earned Lola another hundred thousand followers, instantly expanding the market for her album and tour. He looked at his watch: they were five minutes late.

'Lola, I'm really sorry but we have to do this Twitter thing.'

'Oh no, you're not serious?'

He wrinkled his nose. 'I'm afraid so.'

'But can't you do it for me? Then I can have a little kip?'

'Don't be daft. Can you imagine what your fans would say if they thought your manager was tweeting for you?'

'Oh come on, what's the big deal? You know you can do me as well as I can. Didn't I say that in my speech last night?'

He knew she was trying to win him round and his eyes sparkled fondly. 'And what happened to me looking after my own life for once?'

'Well, get on with it then,' she joked, giving him a playful elbow in the ribs. 'How long does it take to arrange a date?'

Just then his phone pinged to tell him he had a reply. 'Genuine,' he read. 'See you Saturday. Stay cool. Spike.'

He couldn't stop himself from breaking into a wide grin. *Flippin' 'eck! I've met one of the fittest guys ever and we're actually going on a date!*

He looked at Lola but saw she'd already fallen asleep. Never mind, it was probably better if he tried to keep the news to himself anyway. But she was right – he should look after his own life more often. And that was exactly what he was planning on doing this weekend.

*

By the time she woke up, Lola was over the worst of her hangover – and was gradually starting to feel human again. When Harvey told her the midweek charts had come in, she removed her sunglasses so she could look him in the eye. 'Is it good, darlin'? Please tell me it's good.'

The news was even better than either of them had been expecting. Not only was the album predicted to hit number one but in just a single week it looked like it was going to become the UK's fastest-selling album of the year. The news instantly eradicated the remnants of Lola's hangover but also made her feel a little scared. From now on, she knew everything she did would be scrutinized that little bit more and the pressure on her was going to rise. She took a deep breath and stepped out of the car.

She told herself to focus on the task in hand. She was about to meet the various members of the band who'd be accompanying her on the *Trouble* tour of the UK and Europe in just a few months' time. If all went well, the same band would be following her out to the States in the spring, where the plan was to launch her career with a handful of exclusive live shows as well as performance slots on TV and radio – before hopefully announcing a full US tour later that year. Of course, as a solo artist Lola knew that she'd be the focus of attention on stage and many of the band wouldn't even be visible. But she also knew that they needed to gel as a group for the music to sound good – and impress both the critics and her growing army of fans.

She was painfully aware that the break-up of her last band had been entirely her own fault. Her affair and subsequent split with guitarist Fox Marshall had caused tensions to rise within the group until eventually things had become unworkable. She'd been so distraught about being dumped that she couldn't even think straight and once the musicians' contracts had expired, Harvey had been forced to step in and take the decision to start afresh with a new band for the second album.

Of course that particular disaster had been splashed all over the press. But what the press didn't know was that the same thing had happened with her previous backing band, when Lola had tumbled into a torrid affair with the knee-bucklingly handsome keyboardist Nicky Finn. Pale-skinned with jet-black hair and a soft Irish accent, she'd instantly fallen for his easy manner and laid-back sense of humour, despite the fact that he had a cocksure charm that should instantly have rung warning bells. By the time she'd discovered he had a girlfriend back home in Dublin it had been too late – she'd been so in love with him that her only option had been to pathetically reassure herself that eventually he was bound to leave the other girl for her. But it soon became obvious that he wasn't going to leave her. And when the girlfriend was told about what turned out to be his third major infidelity, she'd given him an ultimatum – and he'd promptly dumped Lola seconds before she was due to skip onto the set of some upbeat, jolly kids' TV show.

Even now, when she thought back to the break-up, she couldn't help feeling heavy-hearted. She'd been so over-whelmed by what had felt like a bottomless sorrow, it had cast a dark shadow over the launch of her debut single – and taken the shine off her happiness as her career finally took off. But then she'd only gone and made a total fool of herself by repeating the same mistake with Fox Marshall. Well, she was determined that it wasn't going to happen for a third time.

I've had enough of womanizers. And enough of falling for members of the band! From now on she was sticking to nice guys – nice guys like Freddy Jones . . .

As Harvey led her through to the rehearsal room she was greeted by ageing rocker Mike Henry, who'd served as her musical director since the start of her career – and had been personally responsible for putting together what would now be her third band. Although she'd never really bonded with Mike in the way she had with Harvey, she thought of him as a kindly uncle and knew that she could trust him without question.

'All right, darlin'?' She greeted Mike with a warm hug and he patted her on the back with real affection.

'All set?' he asked her.

'Yep, come on, I'm dying to meet everyone.'

Mike guided her into the room and introduced her to guitarist Danny, who looked about twelve years old, had the worst sloping shoulders she'd ever seen and hair that made him look like he'd had electric shock treatment; keyboardist Smudge, who had dark sweat patches under his arms and thick brown hair sprouting out of his nose, his ears and even the back of his neck; and bassist Chuck, who was definitely the runt of the litter, with one brown eye and one blue eye, a bulbous, penis-veined nose, and a face like a punched lasagna. *Hmmm, I'm beginning to see a running theme here.*

'Well, it's great to meet you all!' she gushed, a little too enthusiastically.

'Great to meet you too,' the band beamed back at her.

Although she'd entered the room vowing never again to fall for a member of the band, now that Mike had introduced her to the ugliest line-up ever assembled she couldn't help feeling disappointed.

'Happy?' whispered Harvey in her ear.

'Ecstatic!' she fizzed, hoping no one could see she was grinding her teeth.

The more she thought about it the more it became obvious there'd been some kind of plan to save her from temptation by avoiding hiring anyone on the right side of even average-looking. And although she appreciated that what mattered was how they played their instruments, the realization only made her feel rebellious and want to get off with one of them anyway. *Oh I know I said I wasn't going to fall for anyone else in the band but fancying someone always makes touring so much more fun!*

'Now you must be the BVs,' she said, addressing two beautiful black women who stepped forward and introduced themselves as backing vocalists Gloria and Sharonne. *Hmpf! It's all right for the blokes to have something to look at but what about us girls?*

She bit her tongue and carried on smiling.

*

Gloria bit her tongue and leaned in to give Lola a kiss on the cheek, just about managing to force out a little smile. This was the moment she'd been dreading – the moment she came face-to-face with the woman who'd ruined her life. But she couldn't think about that now. No, if she was going to make any kind of success of this job she absolutely couldn't think about that.

But God, it was hard. The second she'd set eyes on Lola she'd felt a bitterness so strong she could almost hear it ringing in her ears. She'd had to grit her teeth and join in as Lola received a round of applause just for walking into the room. How could that kind of adulation not corrupt a person? Well, it obviously had with Lola.

For a start she seemed so wrapped up in herself she couldn't even remember that she and Gloria had already met. Talk about insulting. They'd actually hung out together a few times in the early days of Gloria's solo career; they'd got drunk at a music industry party and the following week had bumped into each other in the recording studio. *But why should Lola remember? So many wonderful things have happened to her since then.* Unlike Gloria, whose entire life had fallen apart.

She did her best to suppress the memories and told herself not to give in to bitterness. No, there was only one way she was ever going to get through this. And unless she wanted to live the rest of her life in abject poverty, she absolutely had to get through this. She plastered a smile over her pain and took hold of Lola's hand.

'You know, I can't wait for the tour!' she managed, throwing in a giggle for good measure. 'Us girls are going to have so much fun!'

*

Before long Lola was chatting to the girls as if they were old friends. In fact, she was pretty sure she knew Gloria from somewhere but was too embarrassed to say. She'd thought it would come to her during the course of the conversation, but by the time she realized it wasn't going to, it would have been rude to ask. However, she was glad she and Sharonne were in the band – the three of them could have fun girl-time together to make up for the disappointment of the shocking lack of hotties.

Just as she and the girls were going to try out their harmonies, the door swung open and in waltzed a tall man with long, messy hair, a few days' stubble and thick, muscular arms.

'Hey guys!' he called out in an American accent. 'Sorry I'm late. I've had a bitch of a trip – my freakin' plane was delayed by three hours.'

Well, well, well, thought Lola. *This is more like it . . .*

He strode towards them, dragging a battered old suitcase behind him. As he drew nearer, Lola saw that his chestnut hair was complemented by piercing green eyes and a sloppy grin which was nothing short of mesmeric. In fact, he was so head-turningly good-looking he probably induced whiplash wherever he went. *Witness the fitness!*

'You must be Lola,' he said, stepping towards her and looking deep into her eyes. 'I'm Jake, Jake Hunter. Your new drummer.'

'Ah, nice to meet you, Jake.'

As she flashed him a blast of her pop-star sparkle, out of the corner of her eye she spotted Harvey take Mike to one side and whisper something urgently in his ear. *Aha, so I was right*

– he must have told Mike to hire the ugliest band ever. So how on earth did this Jake slip through the net?

*

Harvey watched Lola's face brighten as she spoke to Jake and his heart sank like a knackered lift. The band's new drummer was so good-looking he could probably have any woman he wanted. And in Harvey's experience, that kind of knowledge could only ever corrupt a man.

Coming to terms with that little life lesson had been a long and torturous learning process he still remembered well. And as he often recognized aspects of his younger self in Lola, he knew she'd find it impossible to resist a man like Jake. But somehow this Jake had slipped through the net he'd tried to construct to protect her from more heartache. Mike had said something about only communicating with him via email but had insisted that his contact had told him he 'wasn't much to look at'. When he asked who'd made the recommendation, it turned out it had come from a female drummer who'd been unable to accept the gig herself because she was expecting a baby with her lesbian life partner. Harvey let out a long sigh. He really hoped Lola didn't make the same mistake with Jake as she had with Nicky and Fox.

Then again, he thought, *maybe I'm just turning into an old cynic.* There were plenty of people who he was sure would say he was walking straight into the same trap with Spike, chasing after some kid who could have whoever he wanted and who was probably only interested in him because he was Lola Grant's manager. He was pretty sure that wasn't Spike's intention, that he'd picked up on a genuine and gentle soul hiding behind the hip, tough exterior. *But how can you ever know for sure?*

If finding out about men had been a long and torturous learning process, Harvey wasn't sure he'd reached the end of it yet. And judging from her reaction to Jake, Lola hadn't got anywhere near as far as he had.

*

Lola watched Jake introduce himself to the other members of the band and was entranced by his every movement. He really was one of the sexiest men she'd ever seen. But as she saw the effect he had on the backing vocalists, instantly reducing them from feisty women to giggling schoolgirls, she reminded herself that she'd vowed never again to get involved with anyone in her band. And if she should have spotted that Fox and Nicky were trouble, then this Jake was a disaster waiting to happen.

But oh, those eyes . . .

She suddenly felt a clutch of fear. Her imagination jumped ahead of her and conjured up all kinds of messy outcomes if she so much as spent a single night with him. *No, I absolutely can't go there.* And besides, she was looking forward to seeing Freddy Jones again. Surely he'd take the hint and return her sunglasses soon?

As she watched Jake unpacking and assembling the various parts of his kit, she consoled herself with the idea of some harmless flirtation. Yeah, if Mike and Harvey were so convinced she couldn't control herself then she'd just have to wind them up by drooling all over Jake. *You never know, I might teach them a lesson in the process.*

At that moment Jake glanced up and caught her staring at

him. He gave her a cheeky wink and she returned it with a cute little wave.

Well, I was looking for some fun – and I reckon I might just have found it.

3

The loud ring of his cell phone jolted Jake Hunter out of a deep sleep. He'd already slept through his alarm and the hotel wake-up call but knew he couldn't put off getting up any longer. The car to take him to today's rehearsal had just arrived – and he really needed to spring into action.

'Hey, man,' he rasped into his phone, 'I'll be down in ten minutes.'

Of course he knew it would take him way longer than ten minutes to get ready but the driver would just have to wait. *At least now I've spoken to him he'll quit hounding my ass.*

He dragged himself onto the edge of the bed and looked at his watch. He was due at rehearsals in half an hour and knew there was no way he'd make it in time. He rubbed his eyes and hauled himself up and onto his feet.

Last night he'd spent hours drinking in Shoreditch with an old American buddy who was in town on a business trip. Just before midnight the two of them had ended up staggering into a lap-dancing bar called Rack and Crack. Several strips and countless shots later Jake had risked breaking the no-touching rule with one of the girls, a leggy brunette who'd been all over him since he'd told her he was the drummer in Lola Grant's band. But far from having him thrown out she'd led him through to a back room where she'd jerked him off to the sound of *Lost in Love*. And he couldn't remember much else, except that it hadn't taken him long to whisk her back to his hotel room where they'd spent the rest of the night having sex – and it had been wild.

He looked at the girl now, her long hair fanning out on the pillow around her, a couple of the cheap extensions which had broken loose scattered on the crumpled sheets by her feet. Her make-up and fake tan were smeared all over the white pillow and her tacky perfume was still so strong it was filling his nostrils and turning his stomach. He suddenly realized he couldn't remember her name. Was it Caroline? Candy? Candice?

He lugged himself over to the bathroom to pour a glass of water, picking his way through a room which when he'd moved in had been the essence of immaculately ordered minimalism but now looked like a bombed-out rathole. He almost stood in an ashtray full of the discarded butts of smoked joints and had to stop himself tripping over the girl's lacy red thong and perspex hooker heels. A pair of fur-lined handcuffs was hanging off the bedpost next to a leather whip and something he assumed was a sex toy but could just as easily have been a cheese grater. *How the hell did we use that?*

At the bottom of the bed he saw that his video camera was set up on its tripod and remembered that halfway through the evening he'd had the idea of making a sex tape so he could revisit the smoking-hot session if he ever had a night alone. Not that he was alone very often – and so far he'd been pleased to discover that the girls in London were proving to be just as receptive to his charms as they were anywhere else in the world. But he never knew when his luck was going to run out. *Although it isn't showing any signs of running out just yet.*

He rewound the tape and pressed Play. As last night's action unfurled before him he couldn't help raising an eyebrow. *Aha, so that's how we used the cheese grater.* When the girl on screen began to howl like a demented animal he broke into a confident smirk. *You're the man, Jake! You're the man!* He heard a whimper behind him and realized the recording of the girl's own howls was about to wake her up. He hit Eject and tossed the tape into his suitcase.

Trying not to make any noise, he sloped into the bathroom, turned on the shower and slid under the hot deluge. As he soaped himself all over he couldn't help feeling a shudder of satisfaction: yet again he'd got laid and yet again he'd delivered a dynamite performance. The very thought of it made him feel special. It made him feel alive.

In order to keep the supply of sex steady, over the years he'd learned to adapt his raw lust into more socially acceptable forms of flirting. Someone had once told him the key to success with women was to tell the pretty ones they were clever and the clever ones they were pretty. Jake had wasted no time putting this theory into practice and had been thrilled to discover that it worked without fail. Although it did have its drawbacks: last night in the taxi home he'd had to feign interest while the dumb lap dancer wittered on about her hopeless ambition to be a Shakespearean actress. That part of the night he unfortunately *could* remember. But it had all been worth it in the end. Boy, had it been worth it.

As he padded back into the room he took another look at the girl in bed and ran his fingers through his wet hair. He wondered whether he could sneak away without bothering to say goodbye. Sure, he revelled in the pleasure of the pursuit, and of course he loved the sex that followed. But the post-coital aftermath could sometimes be a major pain in the ass.

One thing was for sure: he couldn't go anywhere without styling his hair – even if switching on the hairdryer was bound to wake her up. But creating that messy, just-got-out-of-bed look that gave the impression he hadn't spent any time on it was a complicated operation and one that easily took Jake half an hour every morning. As he began his expert blow-dry, he looked at his reflection in the mirror and couldn't help thinking how lucky he was. It was every straight man's fantasy to have sex with a different woman every night and here he was living that life. Sometimes girls he met put him under pressure to settle down – especially if he carried on seeing them for a few weeks. But why would he want to put restrictions on his pleasure when he'd only just turned thirty? *And anyway, who wants to settle? Isn't that what dust does?*

Reflected over his shoulder he saw the girl begin to stir in bed.

'Morning,' she called out.

He switched off the hairdryer and slid it into a drawer. 'Hey, I was just getting ready for work.'

The girl gave a big stretch and one of her boobs slipped out from under the sheet. *Well, it's obviously fake but it's still pretty awesome.*

'Oh but aren't you coming back to bed?' she purred.

'Jeez, I'd love to but I really can't.'

'Are you sure?' she cooed, sitting up to reveal both boobs.

Jake could feel an erection begin to tent his towel. *Man, she is one fine-looking piece of ass.*

He looked at his watch. He was already late and if he didn't set off now he really was going to get his ass whipped. But he'd seen the way Lola had looked at him the day they'd met and she might be a big star but he could tell that deep down she wasn't that different from all the other girls. Maybe one day he'd have some fun finding out. Right now, though, there was someone else demanding his attention. And however late he was, he was sure Lola would forgive him.

*

Across town, Harvey and Spike were strolling along the South Bank as the sun sparkled down at them from high in the sky.

'Isn't this amazing?' gushed Harvey, stretching his arms up in the air.

'Yeah, man,' agreed Spike. 'It's beast.'

It was the first time the two of them had met since Lola's album launch. It had been a busy week for Harvey, what with the album campaign moving into overdrive and most of his time taken up arranging her next video shoot, an appearance at a huge anti-drugs benefit gig and an extensive promotional tour of Europe. Not to mention dance auditions and creative meetings for the massive tour she'd be opening in the autumn. But this hadn't meant he'd stopped thinking about Spike – far from it. And this morning he'd worked himself up into such a fluster as he was getting ready for their date that he'd forgotten to walk his pet pug Pickle – and the dog had ended up relieving himself all over the outfit Harvey was planning to wear.

It wouldn't have been so bad if choosing what to wear for a date with a hip twenty-five-year-old hadn't already posed Harvey all kinds of problems. For a start, he was approaching the age when he had to start worrying about looking like mutton dressed as lamb, but at the same time he didn't want to put Spike off by drawing attention to the fact that he was so much older. Not that thirty-five was particularly old, but Harvey was painfully aware that when he was twenty-five it would have seemed *ancient*. In the end he'd settled for a pair of trendy blue jeans which Lola's stylist Trixie had given him after she'd worked on a fashion shoot for an upmarket men's magazine and a fitted white shirt which showed off his swimmer's physique. He'd rounded off the look with his latest retro Ray-Ban sunglasses and as he walked forward in the sunshine he was feeling confident and upbeat.

'Well, it's really good to see you,' he said.

'Yeah, you too, blud. You must be proper manic at the moment.'

'Yeah, it has been quite bonkers, to be honest. But bonkers is good. Everyone wants a piece of Lola right now.'

'And I suppose it's your job to make sure they all get it.'

'Yeah but I've also got to make sure she doesn't get eaten alive in the process.'

'Oh yeah,' he smirked, his gold tooth sparkling in the sun. 'I didn't think about that.'

'That's because you're a big bad journalist and it's your job to hope everything goes wrong. Then you can pounce and reveal all the gory details.'

Spike feigned indignation. 'You got me all wrong, blud. I'm a proper softie. And I don't pounce. Well, only sometimes.'

They looked at each other and grinned. Harvey felt a flicker of happiness that everything was going so well. And he'd really needed today to go well. Since giving up the booze, not only were first dates much more tough but even pulling men was becoming a rarer and rarer occurrence. It wasn't as if he thought of himself as particularly inhibited, but he'd discovered that he didn't tend to launch into a full-on snog, let alone jump into bed with a stranger, when he was stone-cold sober. He'd started to joke that these days he couldn't even pull washing off a line, but behind the gags he was starting to suffer – and for the first time in his life he knew what it meant to feel lonely.

He was sure that Spike had never been lonely. Spike was smart and sassy with a mischievous sense of humour but also a sensitivity and a vulnerability Harvey had been right to identify when they first met. And his smile was like the bright sun emerging from behind a dark cloud.

They strolled on, passing a couple of amateur painters engrossed in the view of the river, a trio of Asian Goths smoking cut-price cigarettes in the shade of Tate Modern, and an ageing drag queen singing away to herself as she applied too much make-up on the steps of Shakespeare's Globe. All around them milled people of every conceivable colour, shape and size. And Harvey couldn't help noticing that all of them were smiling.

'You know, this is why I came to London,' he beamed, waving his arms around to take in the scene. 'This is why I love it here!'

He explained to Spike that he'd been brought up in Wigan, where his parents worked for the Post Office, his dad as a postman and his mum behind the counter. But he'd never felt like he fitted in and his withering spirit had gradually gravitated towards a city where creative or quirky individuals had the freedom to become the people they really wanted to be. Of course he'd also moved to the capital to be closer to the country's highest concentration of gay men, and for his first ten years in the city had worked his way through a sizeable proportion of them. In fact, they were about to pass an alleyway that led to the Male Box, a gay sauna where Harvey had ended up after many a drunken night out, engaging in all kinds of sexual activities he wouldn't have even thought possible when he was a little boy hanging around the Post Office in Wigan. But he wouldn't be sharing that kind of information with Spike just yet. *That kind of thing I'll save for much later.*

'Fancy fish and chips?' he asked, worried that Spike could read the shame on his face. 'My favourite chippy's just there.'

'All right, man. Sounds cool.'

He led Spike over to the Cod Squad, where they sat down outside at a picnic table in the sun. From behind his shades he allowed himself to gaze at his date as he perused the menu. So far Spike was proving surprisingly easy and enjoyable company and already Harvey could feel his emotions racing ahead. But he stopped himself; he'd learned his lesson years ago about what he called fast-track intimacy, when you get carried away and go much too fast on a first date, only for both parties to panic and pull back shortly afterwards. *No, I can't fall in love with him just yet. I've got to find some way to stop myself . . .*

As he called for a waiter he heard the sound of a Spanish guitar and recognized the intro to *Lost in Love* come lilting out of the restaurant. As the music built he could feel his spirit being infused with the heady excitement of a sexy summer romance.

But stopping myself is going to be difficult – very difficult.

*

Over in Bermondsey, Lola was starting to get impatient. She'd been here an hour now and there was still no sign of her drummer.

'Where the hell is he, Mike?' she asked her musical director. 'This is really starting to take the piss.'

'I know, I'm sorry, Lola,' he said, twiddling with the ends of his handlebar moustache. 'Apparently there was some mix-up with the car.'

She tutted and rolled her eyes. She really didn't need this.

Tonight she and the band were due to perform on *Lucky Star*, the TV show which currently commanded the highest ratings on Saturday prime time by combining the traditional talent-show format with the added twist of a star-shaped roulette wheel which randomly ruled out a different contestant each week. Already this week she'd had costume fittings and dance rehearsals but she'd been so tied up with promotional commitments that the band had been forced to practise without her – until today. Three hours had been set aside and she really needed to make the most of them; this wasn't the kind of platform on which she could risk messing up. Unfortunately, though, apart from working on her vocals with the girls, without a drummer there wasn't much else she could do.

Just then the door swung open and in waltzed Jake.

'Hey guys,' he breezed, 'I'm really sorry I'm late.'

As he strode towards them, Lola remembered his entrance

into the same room just a few days ago. On that occasion she'd been thrilled to see him. But if she remembered rightly, on that occasion he'd also been late. *Hmm, I'm starting to see a pattern here.*

'Look, it's no excuse,' he shrugged, 'but my goddam car didn't show.'

He moved over to Lola and flashed her those penetrating green eyes and that sloppy grin she was sure had never failed to get him off the hook in the past. But she wasn't having any of it. His hair was a mess, he looked like he'd just got out of bed and, if she wasn't mistaken, he smelled of women's perfume – the kind of low-rent scent she associated with glamour models or lap dancers. *Wait a minute, has he just been shagging some bird?*

'I'm not interested, darlin',' she snapped. 'You're more than an hour late.'

'I know, man, and I'm really sorry.'

Mike stepped in and put a calming hand on her shoulder. 'Lola, don't you worry about this, it's my job to sort it.' He turned to look at Jake. 'Mate, just go and tune your kit. We'll talk later but we really need to crack on now.'

Lola huffed as loudly as she could. She couldn't believe she'd been standing around for an hour while her drummer was off having sex with some slapper. And it wasn't just her who was offended; the rest of the band looked riled and the atmosphere in the room had soured.

'Can you believe this guy?' she whispered to her backing vocalists. 'What a dick.'

'Yeah,' agreed Gloria, 'sometimes hot guns and a cute smile just ain't enough.'

She tried not to give off a naughty cackle. 'Ain't that the truth?'

As Jake tuned his drums, Lola made a big show of standing behind the mic and tapping her foot impatiently. To think she'd planned on flirting with him to wind up Harvey and Mike. To think she'd actually found him attractive.

Well, from now on she'd just have to forget about Jake and concentrate on having a laugh with the BVs. They both seemed like fun and Harvey had reminded her that she'd met Gloria when she'd been signed to her record label as a solo artist. Unfortunately her first album hadn't taken off and she'd been dropped shortly afterwards. But at least she'd been in the same position as Lola so would understand the pressures she was under and hopefully be an ally.

'Right, come on then,' smiled Mike, obviously trying to defuse the tension. '*Lost in Love*, take it away.'

As the music kicked in, Lola had to admit it was sounding good – and exceptionally polished after just a few days' rehearsal.

> *Like a vision,*
> *He waltzed into my world . . .*

She launched into her vocal and glanced over at Jake. He was actually quite revolting and thinking about him while singing a song about falling in love was something of a challenge. He looked up and caught her eye. She was surprised to see that he held her gaze.

> *The scent of danger,*
> *The swell of desire,*

> *And I was lost, lost,*
> *Lost in love.*

Lola broke off from his gaze and allowed the beat of the song to run through her and carry her away. As her vocal loosened up she could feel herself gradually starting to relax. *Oh what does it matter if Jake's a wanker? What does anything matter when me and the band are sounding this good?*

Right now Lola realized that she wasn't interested in losing herself in love. Losing herself in the music was much more important.

*

As Gloria swayed to the beat and mouthed the odd lyric, she couldn't help thinking how humiliating it was to have been demoted to the role of backing vocalist. All she had to do was sing the words 'lost in love' during the chorus and whisper the odd 'ooh' and 'aah' during the verses. And to think that once upon a time she'd recorded her own album and everyone had told her she was a major talent. Well, this was quite a comedown.

And the worst thing was, she was having to sing some stupid song about being in love – when it was that long since she'd been in love she could hardly remember what it felt like. *Lost in love? Some of us don't have that luxury. Some of us can't imagine ever being in love again.*

Not that Gloria would be sharing those kinds of thoughts with Lola, even though she'd been trying her best to be friendly all day. But no, Lola wouldn't have the slightest idea how it felt to be lonely. Lola could probably have any man she wanted. And from what Gloria had heard she'd had several, most of them in her last few bands – which probably explained why this one was some kind of freak show. With the exception of Jake, obviously. And Gloria wasn't stupid; however much Lola moaned and bitched about her new drummer, she could tell she fancied the arse off him. No, that whole playing-hard-to-get act didn't fool her – not for one minute.

But who could blame her? Certainly not Gloria; she fancied Jake so much she'd hardly been able to take her eyes off him ever since he'd arrived. He was just her type. In fact, he reminded her of her last boyfriend, Ned. He too had been a drummer and like Jake he'd been tall with long, chestnut hair, stubble and thick, muscular arms. Of course he didn't have Jake's irresistible lazy grin or his piercing green eyes. But that hadn't stopped Gloria falling head-over-heels in love with him – so in love that before long she couldn't understand how she'd ever existed without him. And then Chanelle had arrived and she'd been overwhelmed with happiness; she'd thought the three of them would be together forever. But she'd been wrong. Shortly after she'd been dumped by her record company, Ned had packed up his stuff and walked out on her. *Lost in love? What a load of crap!*

Now that she thought about it, in a roundabout way her disastrous love life was all Lola's fault. Because if it wasn't for Lola she'd still have a solo career – and she'd still be with Ned. But instead here she was singing a load of stupid backing vocals while Lola screeched away into the main mic about falling in love. The irony of it was breathtaking.

God, that woman had a lot to answer for. But Gloria reminded herself not to go there – not to even think about what had happened. *You're not going to let all that get to you, remember?*

No, Gloria needed to keep a lid on her resentment – or she had no idea where it would take her.

*

Once they'd placed their order, Spike stretched out and let the beat of the music pulse through him.

> *Like a vision,*
> *He waltzed into my world . . .*

He looked at Harvey and felt a little rush of excitement. Meeting him had taken Spike by surprise – and he was surprised by how much he liked him. Last night he'd stayed up late planning his outfit, trying on all the options for his flatmate Serenity, a fashion-conscious party girl he'd met at journalism school who now worked as the gossip columnist for a downmarket women's magazine. Spike didn't want to draw attention to his youth and make Harvey think he was some uncouth kid who wouldn't fit into his high-powered, highly sophisticated world. Which was something of a challenge considering most of his clothes had been bought to impress the kind of man who'd only be attracted to him if he were dressed like a dodgy gang member who might whip out a knife on him on their way home. In just a handful of years on the scene, Spike had already discovered just how sexy some people found dancing with danger.

> *The scent of danger,*
> *The swell of desire,*

> *And I was lost, lost,*
> *Lost in love.*

Unfortunately, while trying to resolve the dilemma, Spike and Serenity had got blind drunk and when Spike had woken up this morning he'd seen that his flatmate had spilled her vodka and coke all over his chosen outfit. In the end he'd had to settle for a pair of three-quarter-length trousers he'd bought after seeing them in a fashion feature in *Attitude* magazine and a tight-fitting polo shirt that showed off his gym-honed physique. He was relieved to see that so far things seemed to be going well and Harvey was proving to be easy and enjoyable company.

> *I was lost, lost,*
> *Lost in love.*

There'd only been one awkward moment when the two of them had passed the alleyway that led to the Male Box, a gay sauna Spike often ended up in after a mad night clubbing. Of course that wasn't the kind of information he was going to share with Harvey – at least not on their first date. But as they'd passed the entrance to the sauna he'd been convinced Harvey had spotted him shudder with shame. He was just about to suggest they sat down for fish and chips when Harvey had beaten him to it. *Oh I bet he's never been anywhere as nasty as the Male Box,* Spike thought. Harvey was possibly the most amazing man Spike had ever met, with an absolutely mesmerizing smile. When he turned away it was like the light went out, like when you were sunbathing and a cloud came along and cast a shadow.

The blaze of the sun,
The beat of the drum,
And I was lost, lost,
Lost in love.

As their drinks arrived, Spike began telling Harvey about growing up in Peckham, the son of parents who'd emigrated from Nigeria and worked as a tube driver and an office cleaner. He explained that his real name was Abayomrunkoje, but he'd grown so bored of repeating it for people or having to spell it out over the phone that he'd started to introduce himself as Spike – a nickname he'd earned at the age of ten when his mum had found him trying to spike up his Afro hair with a jar of cocoa butter and a steaming-hot iron.

He gestured towards the National Theatre and a group of pink- and blue-haired students sitting by the entrance dissecting some old play and explained that although he'd been born in London, this kind of scene had never felt like part of his world – and he'd been brought up to think he and his family lived in their own little outpost of Nigeria.

'So what would your mum and dad think about you eating fish and chips with a white bloke from Wigan?' Harvey asked.

Spike smiled. 'Oh the fish and chips they've got used to, man. The gay thing I'm still working on.'

For years Spike had avoided telling his parents about his sexuality as they came from a small village in northern Nigeria with no experience of openly gay people. When he'd eventually come out they'd reacted almost as badly as he'd feared, as had everyone else from the community he'd grown up in. At the same time, he'd found it difficult to fit into the gay scene and make real friends rather than just clubbing partners. And there were times recently when he'd begun to understand how it felt to be lonely, although he wouldn't be sharing that kind of intimate detail with Harvey just yet. *Harvey's so cool, I bet he's never been lonely in his life.*

'Well, I think you're an amazing man,' Harvey whistled. 'And I reckon your story's just about trumped mine.'

'Yeah, well, the story ain't over yet, man,' Spike smirked. 'I'm still working on my happy ending.'

> *My head turned,*
> *My heart burned,*
> *And I was lost, lost,*
> *Lost in love.*

As the music reached its climax, Spike was growing increasingly excited about the possibility of new love. And already he could tell that it would be all too easy for him to fall for Harvey. But he tried not to get too carried away, reminding himself that this was only their first date so he should do his best to hold back.

But holding back is going to be tough – proper tough.

*

In the car park of the studios where *Lucky Star* was filmed, Freddy's eyes alighted on a long white trailer. There was a sign stuck to the door with two words written on it – *Lola Grant*. He took a deep breath and gave a little jog up and down on the spot. *Come on, champ, you can do this!*

All week he'd been thinking about Lola, reliving the moment when she'd called him handsome and turning it over in his mind. Of course he'd had no contact with her since the album launch but she'd been a constant presence in his life, appearing on the radio and in the tabloids every day as sales of her album soared. Resigned to the fact that he wouldn't know how she felt about him till he met her again, he'd spent much of the week negotiating with Barbara Bullock to secure permission to film a behind-the-scenes report from her next video shoot. But he knew what video sets were like and didn't expect to get any personal time with Lola – which was why he was here now.

He took her sunglasses out of his breast pocket and knocked at the door of the Winnebago. He was so nervous he felt like he was at the top of a mountain breathing in thin air. And as he felt the hot sun burning the back of his neck, he knew he was breaking into a sweat.

'Just a minute!'

At the sound of Lola's voice his heart began beating so strongly he could almost see it pulsing through his shirt. Just as he was wiping the sweat off his brow the door was flung open. But it wasn't Lola – it was Barbara.

'Oh, hi, Freddy.'

'All right, Barbara?'

'What are you doing here, doll?'

'I, urm, I wanted to return these, like.' He held up the sunglasses. 'Lola left them with me the other night – at the album launch.'

'Oh, right, yeah. But you didn't have to trail all the way out here – you should have just sent them with a courier.'

'Yeah, I, urm, I was here anyway. I had to call in and see a mate.'

Well, that was only half a lie. The director of *Lucky Star* did play on the same rugby team as Freddy but the truth was he'd had to bribe him with a pair of tickets he'd been sent to a film premiere to wangle his way into the studio. Although by the looks of things he'd wasted his time.

'Who's that, Barb?'

At that moment Lola stepped into view over Barbara's shoulder. She was dressed in a grey tracksuit with an electric-pink baseball cap and wasn't wearing any make-up. Not that Freddy noticed. All he noticed was her bright smile – the kind of smile that was like sunlight dancing on the sea. And if he wasn't mistaken, it was a smile that grew at the sight of him.

'Freddy!'

'All right, Lola? How's it going?'

'Hiya, darlin'!' She threw her arms around him and gave him a kiss on the cheek.

Now that's more like it!

'Come in! Come in and join us for a drink!'

Us? Who's us?

As he stepped inside he was greeted by another four women Lola introduced as her assistant, hairdresser, make-up artist and stylist. That was all he needed – an audience! So much for spending personal time with Lola. He was so nervous even his hands were sweating.

'You know, I'm sorry my Winne's not very glamorous,' Lola piped, pulling a face as she gestured at the plastic walls, Formica furniture and snot-green sofas.

Freddy smiled. 'It reminds me of my grandparents' caravan in Tenby.' *Oh why did I just say that? Now she'll think I'm really uncool*. He tucked his hands under his armpits and shuffled around on the spot.

'But at least it has a fully stocked minibar,' Lola chirped, flinging open the door of a fridge. 'Now what can I get you? We've got Coke, Sprite, water, beer or champagne if you fancy it?'

'I'll just have a water, thanks.' He lifted his collar and breathed down the front of his neck to cool himself down. After much deliberation he'd opted to wear a short-sleeved shirt an ex-girlfriend had once told him showed off his rugby player's physique. He hoped a sweat patch wasn't forming on his back. 'It's really hot today.'

'Tell me about it. And I've got to go on stage later!'

'Well, I'm sure you'll be cracking, like.'

'Thanks, darlin', I'll do my best.'

She handed him the bottle of water and he opened it and took a swig. He was suddenly conscious of Lola's team mosquitoing around him. And they might all be busy with work but they could still hear everything he said. *Oh what am I doing here? Lola's so gorgeous she could probably have any man she wanted. She's hardly going to fancy a big, burly ginger like me.*

'And are you sticking around to watch the show?' she asked him.

'Afraid not. I already said I'd go out with the lads from uni tonight so I'll have to watch it at home.' Well, he had to at least play a little bit hard to get.

'Oh, that's a shame.'

Lola's smile wilted; she looked genuinely disappointed. It was a look that told Freddy maybe he wasn't being stupid.

Maybe she did fancy him after all. But what was he supposed to do now?

'I, urm, I wanted to give you these.' He held out the sunglasses and Lola took them. 'You left them with me at the album launch.'

'God, I'd forgotten all about that! Honestly, I can be such a dizzy bitch sometimes!'

Freddy smiled at her. 'Well, I was coming here anyway so . . .'

'Yeah, well that's very nice of you. And it's good to see you again.'

Was it his imagination or was she blushing slightly? 'Yeah, it's good to see you too.'

'Although I'm blatantly not wearing any make-up at the moment – you must think I'm a total dog.'

'No, not at all! You look really nice, honestly.' *Really nice?* Was that the best he could do?

'Well, I should be looking a bit better tonight. At least I hope you'll think so.'

That was it, she *did* fancy him! In an instant Freddy's nerves dissipated. Lola Grant fancied him! He felt a surge of excitement and realized he was standing that little bit taller. But before he could take advantage of his new-found confidence there was a knock at the door. Everyone turned to look and Lola's assistant got up to answer.

'Five minutes, Lola!' called out a voice from the other side.

Lola turned back to Freddy and scrunched up her face. 'Oh, I'm sorry, darlin' but I've got to go and sound-check.'

'That's OK, don't worry. I should probably be making a move anyway.'

'But I'll see you again soon, yeah?'

'Yep, I'll see you next week.'

'Next week?'

'I'm coming to film on the set of your new video.'

'Really?'

'He sure is, doll,' Barbara pitched in from her spot in the kitchen. So everyone *was* listening in to their conversation. 'We arranged it the other day.'

'Well, that's fierce. That's blatantly fierce.'

Freddy said goodbye to the girls and leaned in to kiss Lola on the cheek. 'All right, I'll see you next week then.'

'Yeah,' Lola gleamed, 'see you next week.'

As he stepped out of the Winnebago, Freddy felt like he was smiling with his whole body. He felt so much happier than he had when he'd arrived just ten minutes ago. In fact, he was so buoyant with happiness he felt like he could levitate.

But he told himself to rein in his feelings before he got too carried away. After all, this was only the second time he'd met Lola; it was still early days. But as he sprung across the tarmac he knew that reining himself in was going to be a major challenge.

*

As the music rose to its climax, Lola allowed herself to be overcome by a somewhat giddy excitement. She was on the set of *Lucky Star* looking out at an empty auditorium as she and the band sound-checked for tonight's show. Even though they were just walking through the song and she wasn't giving the vocal her full energy, she was starting to feel confident about delivering a dynamite performance.

I was lost, lost,
Lost in love.

And there was no question why she was feeling confident; it was because Freddy Jones had just visited her in her Winnebago. Freddy Jones, that great big mountain of manhood, whose biceps bulged out of his shirtsleeves and who turned up all bumbling and nervous without the slightest idea of just how gorgeous he was. Lola remembered how the sweat had glistened along his collarbone and on the short rust-coloured hairs on the nape of his neck. God, he was sexy. How could she have ever doubted that she fancied him? Well, she wouldn't doubt it anymore. And the best thing was, he was so nice – so much nicer than that bastard Jake. She couldn't wait for him to watch her performance tonight.

I was lost, lost,
Lost in love.

As the dancers gathered around her and together they struck their final pose, the music boomed to a stop and a huge explosion of ticker tape filled the studio. The show's producer Cassian Blunt, a whippet-thin man who'd done so many drugs he couldn't keep his face still, burst into a solo but maniacally enthusiastic round of applause. A few clipboard-clutching production staff and Lola's team soon joined in while Barbara let off a loud wolf whistle.

As Cassian collared the clipboard-clutchers and began twitching and mugging his way through what looked like crisis talks about a faulty jet of dry ice, Lola turned to face her band. 'Well done, guys,' she beamed. 'I reckon tonight's going to be fierce!'

And she needed tonight to be fierce as she had a major point to prove. Before landing her record deal, she'd auditioned to be a contestant on *Lucky Star* but hadn't even got through to the second round. Now here she was making her debut on the show as a guest performer and a hugely successful recording artist. If all went well she'd finally be laying to rest some painful memories.

As a squadron of sound engineers began fiddling with her microphone and earpiece she spotted Rex Watson picking his way through the auditorium towards the stage. A former member of a moderately successful and long-forgotten Eighties boy band, Rex was now world-famous as the head judge on *Lucky Star* in the UK, the US *and* Australia. In each continent he was equally famous for his contemptuous criticisms of contestants, his grease-covered forehead that seemed to glow through even the most heavy-duty studio make-up, and his penchant for wearing chinos so tight you could see exactly what he was thinking. He wasn't supposed to be on set until just before the show so Lola had told Harvey not to bother turning up to support her until much later. But now here he was. Without her manager and best friend, Lola felt alone and exposed. And as she gaped at Rex bounding onto the stage towards her, her heart froze with fear.

'Lola!' he trilled, blasting her with the smile of a man who was eternally pleased with himself. '*Great* to meet you!'

As she shook his hand she found herself squirming at the memory of him sitting in the audition room telling her she had a face 'like a carpenter's nailbag', a voice like 'a poodle being raped by a pony' and 'all the passion of an over-cooked cauliflower'. Thankfully none of the footage had been broadcast at the time and as yet hadn't been unearthed. But the memory was still sharp in her mind – and still had the power to strip away her self-belief.

'You know I *love* your new album!' Rex gushed, clearly oblivious to his earlier assessment of her talent. 'It's so fresh and ballsy and so *now*.'

'Thanks,' Lola gasped, a knot of bitterness tightening in her chest. 'Thanks a lot.'

'And I hear it's going to be number one tomorrow. Congratulations!'

'Yeah, thanks, I'm, urm, I'm really made up.'

Even though she'd rehearsed this scene in her mind over a thousand times, now it was finally happening Lola felt too overwhelmed by a mess of emotions to deliver the lines she'd so carefully worked out. She found herself regressing to the nervous girl who'd queued outside the audition venue, only to leave hours later crushed by Rex's criticism. He'd seemed so sure of her lack of talent she'd begun to believe he was right, even if Harvey had repeatedly reassured her she was good enough and told her to use Rex's negativity to spur her on, to 'turn that shit into fertilizer'. More than anything she wanted to forget about the pain of the past and start to enjoy her success – yet here was Rex, reminding her of the misery he'd inflicted on her all those years ago. If only she'd asked Freddy to stick around and watch her rehearsal; if he were here now she wouldn't be feeling half as insecure.

Just then Jake began tapping out a slow beat on his drums. As she glanced over at him he gave her a reassuring wink. She realized that he must have sensed how she was feeling and was doing his best to bolster her confidence. She listened to the rhythm of his stroke and could feel herself filling with a rush of warm energy.

'You know, I wish you'd auditioned for this show,' Rex joked. 'Eight years I've been doing it and still talent slips through the net!'

Lola could feel her heart start to race as she spotted her chance. 'Well maybe you put some people off,' she managed. 'Maybe you need to spend less time thinking about your own performance and more letting the kids shine. Because in my experience people only pick on kids when they're insecure about themselves.' She looked at his crotch and raised her eyebrow. 'And I wouldn't like to imagine what you've got to be insecure about.'

As she finished speaking, Jake played the rim-shot used to punctuate the punchline in classic comedy. Rex visibly winced. He'd been challenged before but only ever by disgruntled contestants – never a star of Lola's stature. And never on a stage in front of the show's entire production team. He was stupefied. There was a clatter from the auditorium and Lola realized a production assistant had dropped her clipboard.

'OK guys!' broke in the producer Cassian in a flurry of twitching. 'We need to crack on. One more time please!'

Rex gave her a nod and backed away, obviously frustrated at not being able to hit back at the show's star guest. Lola could feel her heart begin to slow and felt a shiver of satisfaction. As she walked towards the stairs at the rear of the set, she passed Jake and stopped to give him a smile.

'Thanks for that, darlin'. I really needed the back-up.'

He narrowed his eyes and tilted his head. 'My pleasure. The

dude's a total douchebag – it was cool to see you take a bite out of his ass.'

'Positions please!' barked Cassian.

Lola grinned at Jake and backed away. Once she'd climbed the stairs and settled into her opening position, she closed her eyes to gather her thoughts. She'd obviously underestimated Jake and he'd shown himself to be surprisingly sensitive. But more importantly she'd faced Rex Watson and given him a taste of his own medicine. *I did it! I really let him have it!*

As the lights went to black and the intro to the song started up, she breathed in as deeply as she could. She could feel the self-belief gradually returning and swelling inside her.

Now all I need is to prove him wrong . . .

*

At his home in Tufnell Park, Freddy felt a ripple of excitement as Lola blasted into vision on his TV screen. He'd only been half watching the show whilst getting ready to go out, but once Lola's performance was announced he sat down in his boxer shorts, opened a bottle of beer and stretched his legs onto the stack of rugby magazines that, in the mess of his cluttered bachelor pad, served as a surprisingly sturdy footstool.

His eyes were immediately transfixed by the image of Lola dressed in dark, tight-fitting matador trousers, a black and red striped top and a cute Spanish-style hat that added an impish touch. *Wow! She looks cracking!* And the best thing was she fancied him. She actually fancied him! He took a swig of his beer and felt himself swell with satisfaction.

Of course it was a high-risk strategy to pursue someone

both so desirable and so clearly in demand – particularly when he'd had such a long run of dating disappointments and wasn't sure he could handle yet another. It had been nearly two years now since he'd been in a serious relationship, and it was getting to the point where being single was starting to feel like part of who he was. He was finding it more and more difficult now that he and his friends were coming to the end of their twenties and so many of them were getting engaged. But he'd never been a quitter – and meeting Lola had given him new hope.

He watched spellbound as she slithered down the stairs to the intro of *Lost in Love*. He breathed in as deeply as he could and felt himself filling with positivity. Not only was *Lost in Love* a great song but its sexy summer vibe was infectious – enough to make even the toughest cynic want to fall in love. Freddy himself needed little persuading. And it might be a bit early to talk about love but he couldn't wait to see Lola again next week.

For the time being though he'd have to make do with her TV performance. He looked at the screen and broke into a huge smile as she stepped forward to begin her vocal.

*

As she stepped up to the mic, Lola felt the beat of the drum drive through her. Countless cameras circled and swooped around her, a reminder that there were millions of viewers watching her performance on TV. She wondered if Freddy was doing as he'd said and if he was one of them. At that moment, out of the corner of her eye, she spotted Jake nodding at her supportively.

Like a vision,
He waltzed into my world . . .

As she delivered her vocal, she felt as if her entire being was throbbing with happiness. This was what it was all about – singing. For as long as she could remember, singing had got her through the bad times and been with her for the good times. To Lola, singing came as naturally as breathing: it was an essential part of who she was and what she did – and doing it felt so right. When she sang she felt like nothing else mattered, that nothing could harm her. She felt beautiful and special, like a better version of herself.

The scent of danger,
The swell of desire,
And I was lost, lost,
Lost in love.

As she snapped the mic off its stand and began striding around the stage she felt the power of her band backing her not just musically but also emotionally. Gloria and Sharonne swayed to the beat as if immersed in a state of ecstasy, Danny, Smudge and Chuck played their instruments with expressions of such delight they almost looked attractive, and Jake was pounding his drums with so much passion Lola couldn't help but feel her body tremble. This was more thrilling than anything she'd ever experienced. She felt empowered. She felt free. She felt *sexy*.

The blaze of the sun,
The beat of the drum,
And I was lost, lost,
Lost in love.

Ranged over raked seating fanning out before her, the studio audience roared with such energy it almost knocked her back. Sitting in front of them, she spotted Rex Watson presiding over the judges' table, grinning through obviously gritted teeth, tapping out the beat of the song with enforced jollity. As she looked him in the eye she realized it didn't matter what she'd said to him earlier – *this* was the best revenge possible. He *was* wrong. She *was* good enough. And she was in the process of proving it to him – and to herself.

> *My head turned,*
> *My heart burned,*
> *And I was lost, lost,*
> *Lost in love.*

As Jake's rhythm drove the song to the middle eight, Lola was flanked by the show's troupe of dancers. She handed one the mic and launched into the short routine. Dancing wasn't her greatest strength but she'd worked with a really creative choreographer who'd come up with some moves that were less formal and much freer than a traditional routine and a better fit for her rebellious personality. As she flew through them now she could feel her spirit soar. She took back the mic and prepared to build the song to its rousing finale.

> *I was lost, lost,*
> *Lost in love.*

In the elation of the moment Lola knew that if she was lost in love then it had to be a love of music. Music made her feel strong. It made her feel brave. It made her feel ready for anything. Rex, Jake, Freddy, whoever she met and whatever happened in life, if she could just keep singing then she knew she'd be OK.

The music thundered to its finish and Lola broke into her final pose, the adrenaline soaring through her. Around her she could hear the dancers panting and catching their breath as the audience bellowed so loudly the cameras began shaking on their stands. The lights snapped on and she spotted Rex Watson standing on his feet cheering, a storm of ticker tape swirling around him.

Point proven!

*

'Here's to a brilliant performance!' proposed Harvey, holding up his glass of water.

'And loads more to come, blatantly!' added Lola with a whoop.

There was a growl of agreement and a swarm of plastic glasses were thrust into the air.

After the show Lola had invited the band and her entire team to squeeze into her Winnebago for an impromptu celebration. It always surprised Harvey how unglamorous stars' trailers were – this one reminded him of the mobile home where his family had stayed during many a wet weekend in Blackpool. Someone had gaffer-taped a heart-shaped cushion that a fan had sent to Lola over the smoke detector and cigarettes were being gaily waved around directly underneath it. As part of her rider Lola always insisted on a fully stocked minibar, but after just half an hour it had been decimated. A runner had been swiftly dispatched to the nearest off-licence and come back with what at the time had seemed like plentiful supplies of champagne, but these were already running low.

'Oh and here's to a number-one album!' Harvey boomed.

'A number-one album!' everyone yelled, grasping the opportunity to down more booze.

They were starting to become so raucous that the trailer was actually swaying. It reminded Harvey of the time he'd been working as personal assistant to Blake Striker, a long-haired rock god who sang guitar anthems about how tough it was to be a man but when it came to sex was secretly all woman. After one TV show the two of them had got carried away with such rowdy drunken sex that they'd actually tipped over Blake's trailer. Harvey chuckled at the memory. He wondered how many anecdotes like that would be in the making tonight.

'Let's all smoke cigars!' squeaked a paralytic Belle.

'Let's all take off our underwear!' screamed Scarlett, swigging straight from the bottle.

'Let's all get tattoos!' squealed Trixie as she slid off her seat.

The success of tonight's performance clearly had everyone fired up – and rightly so. Not only would it boost album sales and build excitement for the tour but it was a huge relief that the band were gelling musically.

'Tonight was immense!' gushed a thrilled Mike with what looked like a peanut but could just as easily have been half a champagne cork lodged in his moustache. Swaying arm in arm beside him, Danny, Smudge and Chuck were so drunk they'd lost all musicality and were droning their way through a tuneless dirge that Harvey could just about make out was supposed to be *Lost in Love*.

But it wasn't just the band who were feeling jubilant. The

usually shy Amina had lost all sense of personal space and was leaning right into Harvey to tell him how much she loved him, her breath smelling of cheese and onion crisps even though Harvey couldn't spot any around. And Barbara had drunk so much that for the first time Harvey could remember she'd actually removed the jacket from her men's suit and was twirling it around her head like a cowboy at a rodeo.

Not far behind them was Lola, who popped open another bottle of champagne and proceeded to glug her way through half of it. Harvey hoped she was all right – he felt terribly guilty that he hadn't been there to support her when she'd come face-to-face with Rex Watson. But from what he'd heard she'd coped admirably, slaying a stubborn and sizeable demon in the process.

'Oh and everyone,' he called out over the rising din, 'we need one final toast. To the best performance of the day – Lola pissing all over Rex Watson!'

As everyone raised their glasses and the trailer began to rattle from the racket, Harvey spotted Lola and Jake grin at each other with a frisson of what was obviously flirtation.

Flippin' 'eck, he thought, *here we go again . . .*

This was a situation he'd been dreading ever since he'd met Jake and he could see it was something he'd have to keep his eye on – especially as Lola was starting to look seriously shit-faced.

'Come on guys!' he watched her drool. 'Let's sip till we slip!'

As she held up the empty bottle in triumph, the naughty glint in her eye transported Harvey back to his own days as a heavy drinker. When everything was going well in his life he'd always found himself overwhelmed by the temptation to blow it all up in the air – and he worried that Lola suffered from the same compulsion. Unfortunately, he knew from experience that suggesting she stop drinking would prompt the same reaction as throwing water on a Gremlin. And he didn't want to spoil her fun but if she got any more pissed then he was going to have to step in – to protect her from herself.

*

Lola wasn't sure she'd ever been so pissed. As she reeled around the dance floor, shapes and colours began to whirl in front of her in a psychedelic blur.

Once she and her entourage had emptied the entire TV studios of alcohol they'd jumped into a fleet of cabs and raced over to Club Foot in the centre of Soho. As she'd recognized the introduction to *Lost in Love* blasting out of the sound system, Lola had led the girls onto the dance floor. But just a few minutes later she was feeling harassed by an excited huddle of members of the public who'd clustered around her, pushing through to introduce themselves and trying to take photos on their camera phones. She needed to get back to the safety of the VIP area – and fast.

As she staggered off the dance floor she felt Harvey appear from nowhere, take her arm and guide her through the crowd. 'Always at and on my side,' she smiled. And it was a good job – she felt as disorientated as a sailor back on land after years at sea. She careered through the velvet rope and slumped onto a sofa where the band were downing shots of sambuca. They welcomed her with a loud cheer.

'You know what,' she slurred, 'I've got the best band in the world!'

At that they cheered even louder. As they all put their arms around her for a group hug, Lola felt bad for having judged them on their looks. Sure, together they were rougher than a bag of spanners, but they were passionate about music – and damn good players. *And then there's always Jake . . .*

As a waiter brought over yet another round of drinks she had no idea who, if anyone, was paying for, Jake patted the space between him and Gloria. She slid into it with a mischievous smile.

'What have you been taking?' he asked. 'You look totally out of it.'

'Oh just booze,' she managed, biting her lip in what she hoped was an attractive way. 'I never touch drugs.'

'Shame, I was going to ask where I might score some weed.'

She felt her spirit sag but tried not to look disappointed. 'Trixie's your girl. Over there, the Chinese one.'

As they both looked towards Lola's stylist they saw she was itching her nose and erupting in a bout of aggression. 'What do you call this?' she spat at the bewildered waiter who'd just served her a drink. 'This tonic's as flat as my tits!' On either side of her, Belle and Scarlett cackled with laughter. The waiter picked up the offending drink and scurried away.

'Hmm, it looks like she's been overdoing it on the coke,' Jake mused, rubbing the stubble on his chin.

My God he's sexy, thought Lola, forgetting all about how she'd felt when he'd turned up late to rehearsal what now seemed like a lifetime ago. She leaned forward to breathe in the scent of his maleness and found herself fluttering her eyelashes. She couldn't pretend she was flirting with him now just to wind up Harvey or Mike. No, there was only one reason she was flirting with him and that was because she found him seriously attractive – so attractive in fact that she forgot all about how she'd felt when Freddy had visited her just a few hours ago. *But it's such a shame he's into weed – and such a turn-off.*

Gloria nudged her in the ribs. 'Hey,' she asked, 'is there anything going on between you and Jake?'

'Oh no,' Lola mouthed, pretending to be surprised. 'No. I'm just having a little flirt, that's all.'

'Well, if I were you, I'd stop at that. A friend of mine in New York warned me about him. Apparently he's the Pied Piper of trouble.'

'Oi, Lola!' interrupted Trixie, beckoning her over. 'Come and have a drink over here!'

As she extricated herself from the sofa, Lola narrowly avoided tripping over Amina, who'd fallen asleep in a huddle on the floor, and colliding into Barbara, who'd heard the sound of P!nk and was knocking over furniture in her rush to get to the dance floor.

'So are you going to get off with Jake or what?' Trixie asked when she finally reached the group.

'I don't think so – I reckon he might be bad news.'

'*No!*' chorused all three girls at once.

'He's a sweetheart,' said Scarlett. 'He's just a bit of a player, that's all. But he's perfectly harmless.'

'Do you really think so?' Lola wondered if she'd misjudged him after all. Maybe she was just being overcautious because of her experiences with Fox and Nicky. *And he was very gallant when he helped me face up to Rex Watson . . .*

'You need to loosen up, girl,' breathed Belle. 'Give yourself a little treat for doing so well today.'

'The only treat Lola needs right now is a glass of water,' broke in Harvey, wincing as he braced himself for her reaction.

She stood up to face him. 'Water?' she yowled. 'Water's for the shower! Why do I want *water*?'

He motioned her through to a quiet corner. 'I'm just worried that you've had enough to drink, that's all.'

'Oh please don't have a go at me, darlin'. I'm only just getting going.'

'Lola, you look shit-faced. And tonight was brilliant – I just don't want you to do anything to sabotage it.'

She leaned on the wall to steady herself but began sliding forwards. 'Oh chill out, darlin'. I'm fine, blatantly. I just need a little shot of tequila to perk me up.'

Just as she was about to slide to the floor she stopped herself and propped herself up again against the wall.

'Lola, I don't have the slightest problem with you drinking,' Harvey explained. 'It's the *way* you're drinking. It's like you're trying to punish yourself or something.'

She waved away his objection like a fly but part of her worried he was right. Meeting Rex Watson today had brought back that sense of not being good enough that had haunted her for as long as she could remember. It was a feeling that only seemed to go away when she was drunk. But she didn't want to think about that now. She just wanted to carry on drinking.

'Darlin', I think you've read too many self-help books. Honestly, there's nothing wrong with the way I'm drinking. I'm just not very good at finding my Off switch, that's all.'

'Well, you might have a better chance if you knock back a quick glass of water.'

She rolled her eyes affectionately. 'Oh all right – just as long as I can chase it up with a shot of tequila.'

'Deal.'

'Oh, and Harvey?'

'Yeah?'

'I promise I'm not trying to sabotage anything.'

But from the way he frowned at her she could tell he wasn't convinced. And as her eyes flickered onto Jake, she realized she wasn't either.

4

It was 6 a.m. and Lola crashed head first onto the sofa in her dressing room. She let out a low moan. 'Amina darlin', you couldn't get me a coffee, could you? I'd kill for a latte.'

'Course,' smiled Amina, stifling a yawn. 'Coming right up.'

'Oh and make sure you get yourself one too. I think we could both do with something to crank us up for the day.'

As Amina shuffled away, Lola stretched out and tried not to give in to sleep. She was still much too tired to be up so early. *But at least I'm not hung-over,* she consoled herself. And she'd had some stonking hangovers during the past week. The worst had been the day after she'd performed on *Lucky Star* and dragged her entire entourage on to Club Foot. She cringed as she remembered downing shots of tequila and then going back to flirt with Jake, only to beat a hasty retreat to the disabled loos where she'd spent the rest of the night throwing up, once so violently that some of it had splashed back all over her face. In the end she'd had to be smuggled out to her car through the back door, although someone had tipped off the paps and they'd been there waiting. The pictures of her being carried out of the club by Harvey had been plastered all over the Internet and the red tops over the next few days, but the funny thing was they'd only helped boost sales of the album.

And after today, sales would hopefully be boosted even further. Lola had been picked up at 5 a.m. and whisked to a film studio in Hertfordshire where she'd be shooting the video for her next single, *Tramp*. A rousing dance anthem, she'd already told the press she'd written the song after being dumped by Fox Marshall, but in reality it was addressed to all the slaggy men who'd ever mistreated her – or any woman for that matter. She'd wanted a video to really enhance this message and had insisted on a female director to create it. After much discussion the choice had been made to hire Hettie Spriggs, an endlessly enthusiastic twenty-something who always dressed in the full get-up of a 1950s rockabilly, with dyed-black hair in bangs and pigtails, a red polka-dot swing dress, matching open-toed heels and a gingham headscarf. She'd contemporized the look with a smattering of cheetah-print tattoos running up her arms and legs. Although it wasn't Lola's own particular style, she could see that Hettie really made it work. *Hopefully she'll be able to do the same thing with my video . . .*

'So,' Hettie began, pacing the room with her usual flurry of energy, 'just to remind you of the concept for the video. It's set in the future in a really cool world that looks like something out of a science fiction film. Spaceships, aliens, UFOs – they'll all be added later with CGI.'

'Sounds good,' nodded Lola, sitting up.

'What you need to know for today is that you're going to be playing a punky crusader whose job is to protect women from trampy men.'

'Now you're talking! And how exactly do I do that?'

'Well, you go on a rampage looking for men who are misbehaving – and you shoot them basically. With a stun gun that fires lasers.'

'I am *so* up for that!'

'But I also got the message that you wanted to focus on the music . . .'

'Well, yeah, I mean that's what I really care about. The music should always come first.'

'Well, don't worry – we're going to shoot a performance sequence with you and the band and mix this in with the other footage. Sound good to you?'

'Sounds *fierce!*'

At that moment the door opened and Amina re-emerged with the coffees.

'Just let me down this and I'm all yours,' Lola smiled, perking up already. 'And I can't wait to start shooting those tramps!'

*

In the Channel 3 newsroom, Freddy was packing his bag for today's shoot. He'd agreed with Barbara that they wouldn't turn up till late morning to give Lola and the crew plenty of time to settle into filming. Unfortunately, that also gave him plenty of time to get worked up about seeing her again.

The worst thing was, as it was a light news day there wasn't much going on in the office to distract him. Two business correspondents were half-heartedly trying to manufacture a scandal from a story they didn't actually believe had happened in a big City law firm. The flip-flop-wearing chubby girls on the admin desk were writing on each other's Facebook walls and sending each other links to YouTube clips of cats falling off tables. And the Home News team was organizing a sweepstake on the predicted death date of a nonagenarian senior royal.

'Why don't you have a go, champ?' Freddy asked Spike. 'Come on, you must have a good idea – isn't your new boyfriend about the same age?'

Spike gasped. 'That's well out of order, blud – he's only thirty-five!'

'Yeah and how old are you again?' Freddy teased.

Spike smiled and gave Freddy's chair a swivel with his foot. 'Twenty-five! And anyway, he's not my boyfriend, man.'

'Yeah, yeah, well I think we should have a sweepstake on how long till he will be.'

'Freddy!' interrupted Hugh Badcock's voice behind him.

He grabbed onto his desk to stop his chair from spinning. 'Yes, boss?'

'Come in here a minute – I want a little chat.'

He gave Spike a gloomy glare and followed Hugh through to his office. 'Is everything all right?'

'Yes, but I want to talk to you about this Lola Grant thing. It's going out tomorrow, isn't it?'

'Yep, sure is.'

'Well, we've got a problem – there's fuck all news around. Nobody's dying, all the politicians have pissed off on holiday and even the paedos have gone quiet. I never thought I'd say this but we could do with another right-wing president in America to start a few wars.'

Freddy clenched his teeth and forced himself to smile. *What a dick – and if he weren't my boss I wouldn't waste any time in telling him.*

'So anyway,' Hugh steamed on, 'you need to come back with something big. Ask Lola about that junkie mum again – there must be more dirt there. Actually, why can't we get *her* to speak?'

'I'm afraid she won't. Everyone's tried but she just won't talk. I think Lola gives her money.'

'Well, can't we give her more?'

'I don't think so. But don't worry, Lola knows how this whole thing works. I'm sure she'll give us something good in the interview.'

Freddy wriggled in his seat uncomfortably. He hated having to pander to Hugh. And the truth was, he was much more interested in flirting with Lola again – and maybe even asking her out – than he was in alienating her by asking awkward questions. He'd been looking forward to today all week and wasn't going to risk messing it up for anyone, even his boss.

'Yeah, well make sure you come up with *something*,' Hugh brayed. 'We've got a whole hour to fill tomorrow and nothing in the diary. And I'm sure I don't need to remind you I'm monitoring your work.'

Freddy tried not to clench his fist. 'No, no,' he managed. 'I haven't forgotten. And I'll do my best.'

'Good man,' Hugh nodded at him. 'Now off you go. I need to nip out for a Welsh breakfast.'

'Sorry, a what?'

'A Welsh breakfast – a leak. Get it?'

Freddy mustered a feeble chuckle while Hugh roared with laughter at his own joke.

'Come on boyo, keep up!'

I need to get out of here before I say something I'll regret, thought Freddy. 'All right, all right, I'd better make a move.'

'Yeah yeah, off you go. And don't forget – let's make some noise!'

*

In her dressing room, Lola almost jumped as a blast of noise came thumping through from the neighbouring sound studio. Once she'd collected herself, she recognized it as the opening notes to *Tramp*. She felt a flurry of excitement.

She did a last-minute check on her appearance in the mirror. She was dressed in a black PVC catsuit with matching high-heeled boots and a long hairpiece that had been tied to her head with a sparkling silver band. And she was fully made-up, with false eyelashes so long they almost touched her hairline and a futuristic look created with silver glitter eye-shadow and matching lip gloss.

Belle, Scarlett and Trixie stepped back to admire their work and Belle took a photo for Lola to tweet to her fans. 'Sweet,' she cooed, fiddling with the hairpiece, 'real sweet.'

'Are you sure?' asked Lola, pulling a face. The catsuit felt so tight she was worried that it gave her little rolls of flab on her back. Ordinarily, she didn't have to worry about her weight – and was lucky that she could more or less eat what she wanted without putting much on. And ordinarily, as so much of her appeal was built on the fact that she was a real woman, people didn't expect her to be stick-thin anyway; in fact, journalists seemed to love it when she spoke about her relatively normal diet and her love of everyday foods such as pizza and curry. But ordinarily she didn't go out wearing a PVC catsuit – or prance around a studio in front of Jake Hunter *and* Freddy Jones. 'You don't think it gives me bum back?' she asked the girls.

'No!' they chorused. 'You look totes *amazing*!'

'Really?'

'Yeah!' cheeped Trixie. 'And I'm sure Jake will think so too.'

'That's not why I asked,' pouted Lola with a little too much indignation, although she had to admit to herself that she'd thought about him a lot since abandoning him in Club Foot. And while she'd seen him at rehearsals for a big anti-drugs benefit gig they were headlining at the weekend, there hadn't really been the chance for her to follow up their flirtation – until now. The only problem was she was seeing him on the same day she was following up her flirtation with Freddy. There was no question that she fancied both men. But which did she fancy more? Perhaps today would be the day to work it out. Although it sounded like the girls wanted to work it out for her.

'You can say what you like about Jake,' quipped Scarlett as she stepped in to touch up her make-up, 'but he is fit as fuck.'

'You should totally do him,' agreed Belle. 'I bet he's a wicked shag.'

'Big time!' oozed Trixie, 'Can you imagine the cock?'

Lola tutted loudly. 'Yeah but according to Gloria, he's also the Pied Piper of trouble. Some friend in New York told her he was a total tramp.'

'Well, in that case,' grinned Scarlett, 'getting off with him today would be totes appropriate.'

Lola roofed her eyes and smiled. 'But the song's all about

being through with tramps. It's supposed to be about a strong woman saying she won't put up with any more shit.'

'Who says anything about putting up with any shit?' huffed Belle. 'We're only talking about shagging him!'

'Yeah but sometimes it's not as simple as that, is it?' sighed Lola. 'I've been here before, remember? And in case you didn't notice, the last few times I didn't handle it very well.'

The girls looked stumped as memories of Lola's devastation crept into the room, souring the atmosphere like a grief-stricken guest at a party. An awkward silence gradually imposed itself between them and they began busying themselves with last-minute adjustments to their work. After a while Lola couldn't help a mischievous grin lifting her face.

'Oh but I suppose he *is* hot . . .'

They all burst into laughter and Trixie whooped loudly.

'Now come on,' Lola broke in, 'I need to get on set. Will somebody hand me that gun? Something tells me I'm going to need it.'

*

As Gloria watched Lola bound onto the set like a Labrador out of a Volvo, she couldn't help feeling a twist of jealousy. She stood fixed to the spot as it tightened and tightened inside her until she felt it holding her in its grip like some kind of vice. It was as if she was being crushed, as if every last drop of goodness was being squeezed out of her. And that was when she knew she couldn't hold back her feelings any longer. No, it was all too much. Being here was just too much.

Lola's video shoot was taking place in exactly the same studio where Gloria had shot her first video just a few years ago. As she forced herself to greet Lola with a smile she hoped wasn't too strained, she couldn't help revisiting her own feelings of excitement as she'd embarked on the solo career she'd spent her entire life dreaming about. But it hadn't taken long for that dream to come to an abrupt end. As Lola's first single had become a hit, Gloria's had struggled to get playlisted at any of the major radio stations, and more and more of the label's resources had been diverted into packaging and promoting Lola's debut album while Gloria's campaign had been neglected. She'd eventually been told there wasn't enough money to film a video for her second single, which subsequently bombed. And when her album swiftly followed it to the bottom of the charts, dropping out of the top forty after just one week, that's when she'd been dumped from her deal. As she watched Lola skip around firing her laser gun like an excited child, the memory burned so furiously inside her she felt as if it were poisoning her from within. *That could have been me. That should have been me . . .*

'Morning, Lola,' she murmured, struggling to swallow as she almost choked on her jealousy.

'Hiya darlin',' chirped Lola. 'Check out my stun gun. Isn't it *fierce?*'

Gloria responded with the prerequisite gasp of approval as her mind transported her back to a particularly painful meeting she'd had with a hideous record exec with dandruff and buck teeth. She'd sat cowering in his office entirely on her own, deserted by all the arse-lickers who only a few months earlier had whipped her up into such a frenzy of excitement about her career that she'd thought she'd been invincible. When the exec had told her she lacked charisma and was 'just like any other black girl who can sing', something inside her had broken. 'You're not a star, not like Lola Grant,' she remembered him saying as she'd blinked back the tears. And that was when he'd explained that the record company had only ever taken on the two artists with the intention of sticking with one – and they'd chosen to back Lola. The exec suggested Gloria concentrate on finding work as a backing vocalist and at the time she'd dismissed his suggestion outright. But after nearly two years without working had decimated her savings, sheer desperation had forced her to go begging to the same exec who'd fired her – and he'd put her in touch with Lola's MD Mike Henry. And here she was now, reduced to watching with a smile as Lola flounced around the set flaunting her success as if determined to rub salt into Gloria's still festering wound.

She wished more than anything else she didn't have to be here. It had been torture having to get ready with the rest of the band in a communal dressing room that stank of unwashed sweaty balls and a shared bathroom that had a toilet seat covered in streaks of dried yellow piss while Lola had giggled at full volume in her plush suite next door. And now she had to carry on suffering while Lola swanned around a set that must have cost hundreds of thousands of pounds, simpering like some smug superstar. It was sickening to think that financing Gloria's second album would probably have cost the record label a small fraction of what they must be spending on this stupid video.

Oh and Gloria didn't buy all this crap about Lola being a real woman because she'd been through pain. *Pain? What does Lola Grant know about pain?* Gloria had experienced a pain stronger than anything she'd even thought possible – a pain so strong that for a while she'd actually thought it might kill her. *Not like Lola Grant, who makes such a song and dance about being dumped by the odd bad boy. Big deal! She wants to try being a single mother with no man, no money and no career.* Not to forget a nagging bitch of a mum who never ceased to remind her she was a failure.

'OK, positions please everyone!' called the voice of the director, some silly cow who was caked in make-up and looked like she'd turned up in fancy dress as a permanently grinning version of one of the Pink Ladies from *Grease*. Gloria watched in disgust as she fawned all over Lola, repeatedly telling her how amazing she was. Lola Grant, the woman who'd destroyed her own career – the woman who was the source of all her pain.

What Gloria would give to see her fall off that pedestal – and flat on her face. And if there was any justice in the world she had no doubt that one day she would. She had to believe that; it was the only thing that would keep her going.

And the higher she soars, the harder she'll fall.

*

'Roll cameras!' called Hettie with a burst of such enthusiasm Lola could almost feel it blowing through the studio.

'And roll playback!'

Stepping in front of her to hold up the timecode slate was a hairy clapper loader with a terribly distracting case of brickie's wink. Lola tried not to giggle but she caught Gloria's eye and the two of them couldn't help themselves. She was so pleased they were becoming mates; it couldn't be easy for Gloria to sing backing vocals for an artist who'd been on the same label as her. In fact, she couldn't believe how well she was taking it.

'And action!'

As the clapper loader stepped out of shot, Lola quickly re-focused and assumed her opening pose. The set looked like something out of a blockbusting superhero film and she shuddered to think what it must have cost. She still couldn't quite believe the record company had such confidence in her career that it was investing so much money. Determined not to disappoint anyone, she glared into the camera lens and delivered the words that opened the song.

> *This song's for all you tramps out there.*
> *So shut up and listen!*

As the music began to pound through her, she launched into the dance routine she'd been rehearsing all week and blasted her way through the lyrics with such a burst of energy that she surprised even herself.

> *All that talk and all those lines,*
> *I listened to you too many times.*
> *No apologies and no excuses,*
> *I think you've exhausted your uses.*

They were beginning the shoot by recording a wide master shot of the performance of the whole song, after which they'd pick out individual shots to record separately. This was only the fifth video Lola had made but she already felt familiar with the process.

> *Yeah you're hot but that's about it,*
> *And guys like you don't count for shit.*

She strutted her way through the moves, concentrating every muscle in her body on radiating a look of strength and defiance. She wasn't an actress so didn't really know how to play a part – but reassured herself that in this song she didn't have to. All she had to do was think back to how she'd felt when Fox and Nicky had torn through her life and torn up her heart – and how determined she'd been never to let any man make her feel that way again.

> *You're a tramp,*
> *Nothing but a tramp,*
> *A low-down dirty tramp,*
> *But I don't need no tramp.*
> *And I don't want you!*

As she scorched through the song, all around her the band mimed playing their instruments. They were dressed in black PVC outfits that matched hers and she couldn't help thinking Danny, Smudge and Chuck looked slightly ludicrous, like Matt Lucas playing the only gay in the village in *Little Britain*. But she knew they'd only be appearing on screen in the odd flash – and even then they'd be in the background. Perhaps unsurprisingly, Jake had been positioned further forward than the others and she saw that he was looking seriously hot, with his outfit slashed down to his waist to reveal an impressively muscular torso covered by a light smattering of chestnut hair. She remembered being asked by a journalist a few weeks ago how she felt about chest hair. At the time the question had seemed completely random and she'd mumbled something about it being hot on the right man. But now she knew the answer – it

was a massive turn-on. At least it was on Jake, even if he wasn't
the right man.

Right now though it was a distraction. And unfortunately,
Jake kept straying into her eyeline. As she mimed her way
through the lyrics she tried her best not to direct them at him.

> *What you did was just plain wrong,*
> *It's only gone and made me strong.*
> *No more pain and no more tears,*
> *I'm now the bitch of your wildest fears.*

Swaggering her way across the set, Lola couldn't help her
eyes being drawn to Jake's chest – and found herself imagining
how it would feel to be lying next to it, running her fingers
along that gorgeous ridge between his reassuringly manly pecs.

> *Yeah you're hot but you've no range,*
> *And guys like you don't ever change.*

As her imagination ran away with itself, her head rang with
the sound of Belle, Scarlett and Trixie urging her on.

'He's a sweetheart.'

'You should totally do him.'

'Can you imagine the cock?'

Lola stamped the thoughts out of her head by concentrating
on her angry dance moves. This was a song she'd written
about not going anywhere near men like Jake. But why was it
that, however passionately she believed in it, it still didn't stop
her fancying him?

> *You made me want you,*
> *But you never loved me,*

> *You think I need you,*
> *You don't deserve me!*

As she felt her conviction begin to waver, she threw herself into the song's middle eight with a vigour she hoped would be strong enough to protect her from the magnetic pull of Jake's attraction.

> *You're a tramp,*
> *Nothing but a tramp,*
> *A low-down dirty tramp,*
> *But I don't need no tramp.*
> *And I don't want you!*

She delivered the song's final lines and dropped down into the crouching pose that ended her routine. She looked directly at the camera with a snarl so furious she could hear Hettie gasping with delight from behind the monitor. The song thumped out into silence and Lola was left with nothing but the sound of her own breathing. She knew she'd stormed it when the applause erupted around her.

'And cut!'

*

As the applause faded, Jake couldn't help himself from breaking into an amused chuckle. Sure, it was a great performance and Lola had really thrown herself into the sentiment of the song. But she obviously didn't realize 'tramp' was a word most people used when talking about women. That was, unless she was trying to make some kind of feminist point. Well, whatever it was, she didn't fool him. *No, I'm not convinced she's through with tramps just yet . . .*

Not that he was particularly attracted to her or anything. But it kind of bothered him that so far she was proving immune to his charms. On top of that, he was well aware that his buddies back home would be *expecting* him to screw her – and he couldn't bear for them to think he was losing his touch. But why was it taking him so long?

He'd thought backing her up when she'd bumped into Rex Watson might at least have been worth a blow job – a bit of chivalry usually went down well with those girls who bothered to try and resist him. And when they'd all started drinking later that night he'd thought he'd been on course to get laid, especially when Lola had gone off to down a shot of tequila and then come back to flirt with him. But a few minutes later she'd said she didn't feel well and had disappeared, leaving him all fired up like a bull at a gate. He wasn't sure if she really was sick or just being a prick-tease – and it didn't help that her fag manager was looking out for her the whole time. Well, Jake didn't care because sooner or later he'd get what he wanted.

He watched Lola now, engrossed in a conversation about her performance with the director, some ugly chick who looked like she was going to a 1950s costume party and had taken so much Ecstasy she couldn't stop smiling. *Well, I can think of one way to wipe the smile off her face* . . . Just as he was drifting off into a fantasy about Hettie giving him head in the dressing room, he noticed that Lola's gaze had drifted onto him. He quickly pulled himself together and flashed her a twinkle of his sparkling green eyes. Oh no, he wasn't giving up on this one just yet. He'd just have to up the ante to make sure he got her.

But the truth was, he wasn't in any rush. Just last night he'd hooked up with a waitress with an indecipherable accent he'd met on her way home from work while he was strolling back to his hotel after a few drinks in Soho. He seemed to remember she was from somewhere in Eastern Europe but couldn't speak proper English – not that it had remotely bothered him. In fact, it had been quite handy, seeing as the last thing he'd wanted to do was talk to her. He was much more interested in her long blonde hair and smoking-hot legs – although once he'd got her under the harsh lighting of her roach-pit of an apartment, he'd seen that her hair had been dyed such a cheap shade of blonde it actually looked green and she hadn't bothered shaving her legs or waxing her bush for weeks. It had really grossed him out but of course he'd banged her anyway. He usually found that when a girl was grateful for his attention she went out of her way to please him. *The ugly chick always tries harder*. And last night had been no exception.

Once the girl had fallen asleep, Jake had sneaked out of her apartment to get back to his hotel bed for a few hours. But she lived in Lewisham and he hadn't been able to find a cab anywhere and eventually had to catch a night bus into the centre of town. It had been a major pain in the ass but he smirked at the memory; he'd been here for less than two weeks and already he'd slept with girls in practically every neighbourhood in London. *Well, it sure is a novel way to get to know a city*.

This morning he'd had to be awake at five o'clock to be picked up for this shoot and knew he couldn't risk being late after the way everyone had overreacted last time. He'd slept in the back of the car during the journey but hadn't had time to take a shower and worried that he smelled of sex. He'd had to nip into the shared bathroom to stand over the sink and quickly clean his dick and balls – what he always called a gentleman's wash. A little flirt with Lola's hairdresser and make-up artist had been enough to ensure his appearance benefitted from some professional attention before he'd made it onto the set looking so good Lola hadn't been able to take her eyes off him for the whole of the first take. He had to hand it to himself – he really was good at being him. In fact, nobody did it better.

All right, he might be a tramp. But right now the girls couldn't get enough of him. And he was going to make damn sure Lola was next. However much she protested in her stupid song.

*

'You know I really love your new song,' Freddy told Lola in his delightfully soft Welsh accent. They were sitting in a corner of the studio facing each other on a pair of canvas chairs that had been arranged with a view of the set behind them. A camera-man everyone called Big Phil tweaked the lighting, a young producer Lola assumed to be Harvey's new man Spike held up a sheet of paper to set the white balance, and her publicist Barbara assessed the shot through the viewfinder.

As Belle, Scarlett and Trixie stepped in to make the final checks on her appearance, Lola reasoned that seeing Freddy now could be just what she needed. It was a reminder of the kind of man she'd vowed to date from now on, the kind of man who could save her from Jake – and herself. She kept her eyes firmly fixed on him like the beam of a lighthouse in a storm. 'Thanks,' she smiled, 'it's one of my favourites too.'

'And you really don't hold back in some of the lyrics.'

'No, well, I was pretty pissed off when I wrote them. And I guess that comes through. But you know what, I couldn't actually give a shit – some blokes need to hear it.'

Freddy held up his hand and smiled. 'I tell you what, this is all cracking stuff but don't say anything else – save it for the interview or else we'll be repeating ourselves and it won't be as fresh.'

'All right, but I have to watch myself this time. Last time you interviewed me I couldn't keep my gob shut and said way more than I should. You know my manager's from up north and he calls me the Mouth from the South?'

Freddy laughed and she could feel his sparkle radiate onto her, prompting a smile to spread its way across her face. Her eyes drifted onto his wrists poking out of his shirtsleeves and she wondered if they could actually be thicker than her neck. *He wouldn't struggle to carry me home after a night out,* she thought, imagining how comforting it must feel to be swept up in his sturdy embrace. And maybe it was because she'd been singing about tramps all morning, but today she was enjoying being in his company more than ever – and that made her feel good about herself. It was a new feeling and one she wasn't sure what to make of. But one she wanted to get to know better.

What am I doing fantasizing about Jake? This is the kind of man who could make me happy. The only reason she'd ever doubted this in the first place was because she wasn't sure she could trust herself around a nice guy. She'd always thought that if she started seeing someone like Freddy, she'd go and destroy the relationship by having a fling with some tramp.

But maybe I'm over that now. Maybe writing the song has helped me through it.

'How we doing, fellas?' interrupted Barbara. 'Nearly ready?'

Big Phil stepped out from behind his camera and gave her a nod. 'Yep, all set. If you could just give us some levels for sound, please.'

'OK,' began Freddy, 'I'm Freddy Jones and I'm going to be speaking to Lola Grant about her new video.'

Big Phil nodded. 'That's great. And Lola, would you mind telling us what you had for breakfast?'

She let out a plaintive sigh. 'My God, I was so knackered this morning all I managed was a coffee. To be honest, I've been shit-scared about eating anything with this thing on – I'm too worried about looking fat.'

Freddy jumped straight in. 'But you're not fat at all! Honestly, you look well fit.' He stopped himself and frowned. 'Sorry, you look really pretty, like.'

She smiled and could feel a twinkle gleaming in her eye. *I could get used to this.* 'Well, thanks, Freddy. You don't look too bad yourself. But I've already told you you're handsome. And you're not getting any more compliments today.'

'OK guys,' broke in Barbara, looking at her watch. 'We really need to get going or else the crew will be back from their lunch.'

'No problem,' breathed Freddy, totally unruffled.

Lola couldn't help thinking he seemed so much calmer and in control than the last few times they'd met. And she was completely enchanted.

'Turn over, Phil,' Freddy commanded. 'And if we just give it five seconds . . .'

'OK,' said the cameraman, having one last check in the viewfinder, 'ready when you are.'

*

'Lola, it's great to see you and thanks for letting us on set today,' Freddy began, switching to a slightly more formal tone. 'Could you start by talking us through what you've been filming?'

'Yep, course. Today I'm filming the video for my next single, *Tramp*, which is on my new album. And it's about getting my revenge on all the trampy men out there on behalf of all the women they've messed around.'

Freddy allowed himself a smile. 'And how exactly do you do this?'

'Oh, I shoot them. I basically go around shooting them all with this really cool laser gun.'

As she held the gun up to the camera, alarm bells sounded in Freddy's head. Just last month a man had walked into a school in Texas and opened fire on hundreds of children. Ever since, the American media had been gripped by a furious debate about gun control and this was just the kind of thing Hugh would like him to ask Lola about – with the express intention of getting her to put her foot in it, a practice known in the business as 'delivering a newsline'. 'Lola Grant condones the use of guns,' he could hear presenter Amanda Adams saying now as images of injured children flashed up on the screen. Well, he didn't care what Hugh said – he wasn't going to do that to her. Especially not now the attraction was sizzling between them. No, some things were more important.

'So you aren't worried about glamorizing violence?' he asked diplomatically.

'No, I'd never do that, darlin'. The video isn't set in the real world and this is only a stun gun – it's just a bit of fun, really. And anyway, we've all wanted to shoot someone with a little laser from time to time. Don't tell me you haven't?'

Freddy smiled knowingly. *Too right I have – one person in particular.*

'And it's, urm, it's set in the future, isn't it?' he asked.

'It is, yeah. Which is why I'm dressed up in this catsuit – blatantly looking like the fat bird no one wants to get off with at Halloween.'

Freddy rolled his eyes. 'You can't seriously think that? You must be one of the most fancied women in the country right now.'

She smiled. 'Oh, I don't know. I'm not really sure that kind of thing's what I'm about, to be honest. I mean, it's girls who listen to my music – girls and gay men. I think a lot of straight men find me a bit threatening. But that's fine by me, I suppose – I'm not really doing this to make men fancy me. Although obviously it's nice if they do.'

She looked deep into his eyes and gave her long lashes a bit of a flutter. Not only was she flirting with him but she was flirting with him on camera – and not for the first time. It made him feel so strong. It made him feel indestructible.

But before he went any further, he reminded himself there was one question he really needed to ask.

*

Freddy cleared his throat. 'And is there a man in your life at the moment?'

'There isn't, no.' Lola was sure she spotted a look of relief flash across his face. 'To tell you the truth, darlin', there hasn't been anyone since I split up with the sleazebag I wrote this song about.'

'That's Fox Marshall, your last guitarist?'

'Yep. Although I haven't told anyone else this but there was another sleazebag before him – my keyboardist Nicky Finn, who was even more of a wanker than Fox. The whole time he was seeing me he had a girlfriend.'

From behind the camera Barbara shot her a glare and mouthed the word 'No'. But Lola didn't care: Nicky had treated her like shit and so far he'd got away scot-free. Why shouldn't he pay with a little public humiliation? *And anyway, I feel safe opening up to Freddy. And I want to give him a good interview.*

'Really?' he asked. 'So what happened?'

'Well, it was a disaster, obviously. By the time I found out about his bird, it was too late and I ended up getting hurt. And I suppose she must have done too, which I'm not very proud about.' She paused and shook her head. 'But to tell you the truth, darlin', for some reason I've always been attracted to trampy men who treat me like shit. It's like I can't help myself. And I can tell *you're* not one of them but unfortunately there's a lot of tramps around.'

'But according to the song you've moved on from all that now?'

'Blatantly. Enough is enough – I'm done with trampy men! What I'm looking for now is someone who respects me and treats me well. Oh, and he's got to be fit too, obviously. But from now on I'm absolutely not putting up with any more crap from anyone. However fit they are!'

As she chatted away she remembered that just a few hours ago when she'd been miming the words to *Tramp* she'd found herself magnetically tugged towards Jake. When she thought about it now she felt embarrassed and slightly ashamed of herself.

'So if you know anyone who fits that description,' she fizzed at Freddy, 'let me know. Because I'd love to meet him. That is if I haven't already.'

Freddy grinned at her and put down his pad.

'I'll make sure I do. Lola Grant, thank you very much.'

*

Spike watched as Lola withdrew into the distance, led by her publicist and trailed by her assistant, hairdresser, make-up artist and stylist. Just before she left the studio she stopped at the door and turned around to wave them all goodbye. Spike's spirit slumped to see her go. Lola could change the energy of a room just by walking into it – and when she left it was almost as if you could feel the atmosphere deflate.

He turned to Freddy. 'Well done, blud – that was off the hook.'

'Really?' asked Freddy. 'Do you think it'll be enough to keep Hugh happy?'

'Well, she was proper open and told you that whole story about the ex-boyfriend. And you did ask her about the gun thing – it's not your fault if she didn't bite.'

The two of them stepped to one side to make room for Big Phil and his assistant, who were de-rigging the cameras and dismantling the lights.

'No,' frowned Freddy, 'but I expect Hugh's going to tell me

127

I should have pushed her till she shot her mouth off and gave us a newsline.'

Spike shrugged his shoulders. 'Yeah but that's not your style, man. And anyway,' he smiled, flashing his gold tooth, 'never mind the interview – she was proper flirting with you.'

'Do you think so?'

'For sure! She practically asked you out on camera, man!' He raised his eyes with a look of impatience. He never understood why Freddy couldn't see how good-looking he was and had so little confidence when it came to women. 'Blud, you're the only geezer I know who can sit there while a girl flirts with you and just not see it.'

Freddy looked down bashfully. 'No, I saw it, Spike. And you know, I really fancy her too – I haven't fancied anybody as much in years.'

'Well, that's cool, man. That's proper cool.'

'Yeah, but how am I supposed to see her again? In case you haven't noticed, she's a massive star so I can hardly ask for her number. And every time I see her we're either filming or she's surrounded by her team. I just need to get her on her own.'

'I know!' said Spike, as if suddenly struck by a brilliant idea, 'why don't I have a chat about it with Harvey?' Over the past week he and Harvey had been on a few more dates and even though they were very different, Spike was starting to imagine they might have a future together. And after nearly two weeks of trying to hold back his feelings, he was finally allowing himself to give in to unrestrained excitement. 'Look, Harvey's going to be on set a bit later. Why don't I see if he'll have a quiet word with her? And ask if she fancies going out on a date?'

'All right, just so long as it is a quiet word.'

'For sure. I know Harvey – and he'll be as quiet as a mouse.'

*

'Lola, I think you should go out with Freddy Jones!' Harvey blurted out at full volume.

Lola looked around to check no one had heard him. They were standing in the middle of the studio while Hettie checked back a shot on the monitor. 'Harvey! You've only been here five minutes. Where did that come from?'

'Oh, nowhere. I was just thinking how gorgeous he is – and how he seems like a really nice guy.'

'Oh yeah? And presumably you've been talking to your new boyfriend about it too?'

'I keep telling you he's not my boyfriend! But since you ask, we might have had a little chat, yeah. And apparently you got on brilliantly in your interview. So I just thought it might be a good idea if you went out on a date.'

'Well, for your information, I do fancy Freddy so maybe I will go on a date with him, yeah. But in case you haven't noticed, I've already got a lot to think about today.' She aimed her gun at him and fired. All afternoon she'd been romping around in her catsuit filming endless shots of her walking in on men who were cheating on their wives, leering at lap dancers or having sex with their secretaries. In each scenario she'd had to mime outrage and shoot them before looking to camera naughtily and strutting off in search of her next tramp. It was all great fun, but with no training as an actress, she was starting to exhaust her repertoire of appropriate expressions – and there were still three hours to go.

To make matters worse, she'd been so starving at lunchtime that she'd stuffed her face on bangers and mash in the catering van – and was now worried that she had a gunt as well as a bum back. It didn't help that Jake had been hanging around the set for hours unleashing his lazy grin from the sidelines, despite the fact that he'd finished shooting his scenes halfway through the morning. Or that Freddy and his crew were following her every move, shooting footage of the video being made but often standing directly in her line of view so she couldn't help catching Freddy's eye. She'd felt pulled in both directions and wasn't sure what she felt about either of them anymore. That morning she'd told herself today could be the day to work out which of the two she fancied more. But now she felt more confused than ever.

Harvey obviously wasn't confused in the slightest. 'And what's going on with Jake?' he asked. 'Don't think I haven't seen the way you've been gawping at him all afternoon.'

She tried to stop herself from grinning. 'I don't know what you're talking about, darlin'.'

'No, of course you don't. But don't you think it's ironic that he's standing around giving you the eye while you're singing about being through with tramps?'

'I *am* through with tramps! I'm just not sure Jake's one of them, that's all.'

Harvey frowned at her affectionately. 'Well *I'm* sure. Trust me, Lola – I've forgotten more than you'll ever know about men. And I can tell you without any doubt that Jake Hunter's the biggest tramp of the lot.'

She folded her arms with a sulk. 'But Harvey, I've learnt my lesson the hard way too. And I just don't see how you can be so sure.'

'Look, Lola, you're talented, you're successful, you're beautiful—'

She snorted. 'Yeah, right.'

'Well, *I* think you're beautiful. And I think it's about time you realized how much you've got to offer. Because until you start loving yourself, you're still going to be attracted to men who treat you like shit. It's like an exercise in self-harm.'

'Hmpf! Now you're sounding like Jeremy Kyle – either that or you've had too much therapy.'

'I have had a lot of therapy, yeah. But I'm only telling you all this because I've been in exactly the same position. You don't think you're worthy of a loving relationship so you're attracted to men who won't give you one.'

'Oh yeah, and what about you with that Spike? He's blatantly got trouble written all over him. He's only a kid – how can he be ready to settle down?'

'He's twenty-five, actually, exactly the same age as you.'

She wafted away his objection like a bad smell. 'Yeah, yeah, and what do they call a gay guy who goes out with a much younger man? Is there a word for it? Like "bear" or "otter"? Or do you just say "dirty old man" like we do?'

'Flippin' 'eck, Lola! I'm not a dirty old man. But yeah, I do like Spike, actually. And since you mention it, we're going out for something to eat tonight.'

She raised an eyebrow. 'Just as long as you know what you're doing. I mean, how can you be sure he isn't still slapping his way around town? You were at his age – all those millions of years ago.'

Harvey sighed and raked his fingers through his hair. 'Oh I know what you mean but I just have a good feeling about this one. And obviously I've been wrong before, but I've grown up so much since then. And something tells me that Spike's worth getting to know better.'

Lola spotted her chance. 'And what if I've got a good feeling about Jake?' Not that she had, exactly, but she was too embarrassed to tell Harvey she just found him really sexy. 'What if I told you I wanted to get to know him better?'

Harvey's mouth twisted into a squirm. 'I'd tell you to be careful, Lola. But if anything went wrong I'd be at and on your side.'

She put her arms around him and pulled him to her tightly. 'I do love you, Harvey. And I promise I'm not going to do anything stupid. I've learnt from my mistakes and I'm not taking us back there again, darlin' – no way.'

'Good to hear it. And I love you too, Lola.'

'OK, that's all looking good!' interrupted Hettie with an animated squeak. 'Let's get on with the next set-up everyone!'

Lola kissed Harvey on the cheek and slipped away from the studio to catch five minutes in her dressing room. She could hear Amina, Belle, Scarlett and Trixie scurrying behind her into the corridor. And there was someone else following them. She looked over her shoulder and saw it was Jake.

She stopped in her tracks and looked at her team. 'You go on, girls. I'll catch you up in a minute.'

They looked over at Jake and hurried off to the dressing room, whispering to each other excitedly. Lola was pretty sure she caught the words 'big dick' drifting down the corridor towards them. She grimaced and hoped Jake hadn't heard.

'Hiya,' she chirped, beckoning him over. He came and stood next to her under a flickering old strip light. 'How's it going?'

'Yeah, cool thanks. The video's looking awesome. You're really knocking it out of the park, Lola.'

'Thanks, Jake, I'll be glad when it's finished, to be honest – I can't wait to get this catsuit off.'

'Well, I think it really suits you. And I've got to say, it's sexy as hell.'

He glared at her, his green eyes feral with longing. She wondered why people always used the word 'feral' as if it were a bad thing – because right now it struck her as being really good.

Over his shoulder she was distracted by the sight of Freddy leading his crew across the corridor and towards the exit. He was deep in conversation with his producer and didn't spot her. She was just about to open her mouth to shout out to him when something stopped her. She swallowed and looked back at Jake.

'Yeah, thanks, Jake. You don't look too bad yourself.'

'Oh you know, I just throw myself together in the morning. I'm not really into all this male-grooming bullshit.' As he fingered the edge of his shirt, once again Lola's eyes were drawn to his muscular torso with its light covering of mahogany hair. Jake caught her looking and for a few seconds they stood holding each other's gaze under the flickering light bulb. Lola couldn't help thinking of the energy shooting between them; it was so strong it made her feel slightly giddy. It was very different from the way she'd felt when she'd looked into Freddy's eyes. Freddy made her feel good about herself; he made her feel like a better person, which was delightful and totally intoxicating. Jake didn't. He kind of made her feel bad. *But why does it feel so good?*

'So I was thinking it might be cool if me and you went out for a drink some time,' he said, without breaking her gaze.

'Yeah, urm, that'd be nice, yeah.'

'Great.'

He reached out and touched her cheek. She felt it burn so intensely she wondered if he'd left a singed handprint. Her need for him was so overpowering she just wanted her body to melt into his.

If only I'd called out to Freddy . . .

But he was gone now.

'How about after the gig this weekend?' she managed, her voice cracking slightly. 'I guess I need to focus on work till then.'

'Yeah, sounds good.'

'OK, fierce.'

With all the confidence of a man who knew he wouldn't be refused, Jake leaned in to kiss her. As he approached, she felt her body go limp and her mouth fall open almost instinctively. His lips touched hers only lightly and ever so slowly, but it was enough to feel their hot breath intermingling – and to feel the energy between them intensify until it sent a flush of excitement racing through her. He pulled back and gazed so deeply into her eyes she felt almost naked.

Oh what am I doing?

She hadn't been lying when she'd told Harvey she had no intention of doing anything stupid with Jake; when she'd said the words she'd really meant them. But right now she wasn't sure she had any control over the matter. It was like she knew it was going to happen – whether she intended it to or not.

There was another silence filled only by the sound of the strip light flickering. Lola couldn't help thinking about the last week and her own feelings for Jake flickering on and off. It would be a relief to just turn them on now and let the light come flooding in. *My God it would be such a relief.*

'OK, well I'd better go and get ready for this next scene,' she said softly. 'I'll see you at rehearsal tomorrow?'

'Yeah,' he breathed, a grin lazily creeping its way up his cheeks. 'See you at rehearsal.'

She moved away in the direction of her dressing room but turned to stop and watch him walk away. Once he'd disappeared around the corner she held the gun up to her lips and nibbled on it. For better or worse, it looked like she'd chosen between Jake and Freddy. Or rather, the choice had been made for her – by a force far stronger than her own willpower.

This is it – now I know it's going to happen.

She couldn't see how she'd ever be strong enough to stop it. Unless Freddy could somehow step in and stop her. But how was he going to do that?

5

'And how's my new boyfriend this morning?'

Harvey stretched out his arm so that Spike could snuggle into his chest.

'He's pretty cool, man. And how's mine?'

'Oh he's brilliant, just brilliant.'

It was Saturday morning and for once Harvey didn't have to bounce out of bed and dive straight into work. Later that day Lola was due to perform at an anti-drugs benefit concert organized by charismatic stand-up comedian and former-junkie-turned-sex-addict Ace Bounder. It was a huge deal as Lola's recent success meant she had a headline slot and her performance would be live-streamed all over the world – and in particular in the US, where the exposure would help build up interest in her career before it launched there early next year. But however important it was, Lola wasn't due on stage till nine o'clock in the evening and wouldn't even be sound-checking till four, so there was no rush for Harvey to leave the comfort of his bed.

'I really enjoyed last night,' he said, running the back of his thumb along the groove of hard muscle in Spike's back.

'Mmm, me too, man. That place you took me to was sick.'

Early in the evening they'd been for dinner at Harvey's private members' club in Soho, an elegant yet homely Georgian townhouse that had been painted and papered by Farrow and Ball, stuffed with old bookcases and antique chaises longues, and then sexed up with a smattering of controversial contemporary art by feather-rufflers such as Tracey Emin and Jake and Dinos Chapman. They'd enjoyed a delightfully flirtatious meal before deciding to slope off to Harvey's flat in Islington, where they'd had a frank conversation in which they'd both admitted to developing strong feelings for each other and decided from now on to commit to an exclusive relationship. Harvey was relieved to wake up now and find there was no awkwardness between them. Of course that didn't mean he was going to start letting himself go, and he'd already nipped into the bathroom to let loose a sneaky fart and combat a particularly nasty case of morning breath before Spike woke up. Now that he had, they were curled up on a pile of pillows and immersed in a calm contentment Harvey was eager to savour.

'Man, I love your flat,' Spike breathed. 'It's beast.'

Harvey explained that he'd bought it six years ago with money he'd earned from the first act he'd managed – a bubble-gum boy band called Cleen Teenz, who'd been briefly successful until two of them had filmed themselves alternately spit-roasting an underage groupie and her over-the-hill mum and the footage had somehow found its way onto YouPorn just before they were due to launch their careers in the States. The scene totally jarred with what the band stood for as a supposedly wholesome quartet of friends who'd met in a Christian youth club, and they'd instantly been dropped by their US record company. It had been a difficult time and one that had left Harvey wary of mounting a fake front for any of his acts – including Lola.

But at least he'd come out of the experience with his first property – the top two floors of a spacious Victorian conversion on a pretty little square in Canonbury Village. It housed a large office as well as a roof garden and a dramatic attic lounge that light streamed into from spring through to autumn. It had been decorated throughout with bare floorboards and whitewashed walls that Harvey had warmed up by adding shelves of trinkets he'd picked up around the world, as well as photos of him and friends having fun. Although the pièce de résistance wasn't the decor but his pet pug Pickle, who very much embodied the spirit of his home and proved a hit with all visitors – including Spike.

'Come on, blud,' he called to him, patting the bed. 'Come up here and have a cuddle.'

Pickle shuffled over and waddled up onto the bed, where he burrowed under the covers, wriggling his head out of the other end.

'All right, lad?' soothed Harvey. As he patted him on the head he realized he felt happier than he'd been in a long time. But there was something he'd been meaning to do for a while now – something he couldn't put off any longer.

'Spike? There's something I need to tell you . . .'

'Oh yeah? What's that, man?'

'You know how I've never had anything to drink when we've been out?'

'Yeah.'

'Well, I know I said it was because I was working early and

I was on antibiotics and stuff. But actually I wasn't being completely honest . . .'

Spike turned onto his elbows. 'What? What's up, man?'

Harvey knew that he had to tell the truth now because if he waited any longer he'd be misleading Spike. *And besides, now that we're boyfriends, surely it's safe to tell him?*

He contorted his face into a grimace. 'It's just that I don't drink at all.'

There was a long pause and Spike creased his eyebrows. 'What, you mean you're like, teetotal?'

'Yep – I don't go near the stuff.'

There was another pause and Harvey began picking at a stray thread on the duvet. *Flippin' 'eck, maybe he's thinking of an excuse to back out now.*

'Is that all, man?' came Spike's eventual reply. 'Why didn't you tell me before?'

'Oh I don't know. I guess I was worried you'd think I was boring and not wild enough for you. To be honest, the wildest I get these days is sneaking the odd packet of chewing gum through the self-checkout at the supermarket.'

'You're proper daft, blud.' Spike smiled and slumped back down onto his chest.

As Harvey felt the calm rhythm of his breathing on his skin, his own tension began to seep away. *Maybe this is going to be all right after all. Maybe I can be happy like this every day . . .*

'And when did you give up the booze?' Spike asked

'Three years ago now. I was just drinking too much. It was making me do stupid things and I was unhappy, basically. I wanted to take control of my life and sort myself out – which I did.'

Spike reached up and kissed his cheek.

'What was that for?'

'Oh, you know, just for being brave. That's a cool thing you did, you know. Not everybody could do it, man.'

'Aw thanks, Spike.'

Harvey felt him wriggle awkwardly.

'While we're on the subject of confessions, I need to tell you something.'

Harvey sat up and Spike slid to the side. 'What?'

'It's just that I've made plenty of mistakes too, man. And a lot more recently than three years ago.'

'Spike, you really don't have to tell me about stuff like that.'

'No, but I don't want you thinking I'm someone I'm not. And if you knew some of the things I've got up to I'm not sure you'd be that into me.'

'Oh come on, don't be silly. We've all been around the block a few times. I can't even remember who I lost my virginity to; I shagged three blokes on a boys' holiday in Gran Canaria when I was nineteen and I was that pissed the whole time I can't even remember which one came first.'

Spike's throat clogged with laughter. 'Well, last month I got so wavey I lost all my mates and all my dough and had to shag some taxi driver so he'd take me home. Except the tight bastard only reduced the fare by a tenner and drove me to a cash machine to pick up the rest.'

The two of them burst into laughter so loud Pickle reared onto his hind legs and started yapping.

'But do you think you're over all that now?' Harvey asked.

'Yeah, man. At least I hope I am.'

Harvey couldn't help feeling a flicker of worry. He knew that

Spike *hoping* he was over all that wasn't the same as *actually* being over it. He remembered Lola saying something about him having trouble written all over him and wondered if that had been what she meant. But he was already in way too deep to pull back now. He gave Spike's shoulders another squeeze. With everything going so well he really hoped he didn't do anything stupid. Come to think of it, he hoped Lola didn't either.

*

I'm going to shag Jake tonight.

Lola looked at herself in the mirror and felt a quiver of excitement laced with dread.

I'm blatantly going to shag Jake tonight.

She dug out some lingerie she'd been sent by Agent Provocateur and tried it on. *Hmm*, she thought, *not bad.* She'd been fully plucked and waxed and her figure wasn't looking bad either; she'd stayed off the booze for the last few days and hadn't eaten much so she looked good for today's gig. *Oh yeah, the gig! I almost forgot about that . . .*

At the final rehearsal yesterday she'd been so overwhelmed by a desperate need to shag Jake she'd hardly been able to concentrate on her performance. At one point she'd been so distracted she'd mistimed a dance move and had whacked one of the dancers in the face. And on several occasions she'd even forgotten the words to her own songs – despite the fact she'd only written them six months ago. But it was as if she was possessed by some kind of savage desire for him, a visceral, animalistic need to feel her body fuse with his, that overrode everything else – even that voice in her head telling her to steer well clear.

And of course she knew that everything Harvey had said to her the other night was true. *That I'm only attracted to tramps because I've got a low sense of self-worth – blah blah blah.* But what was she supposed to do about it? It didn't stop her fancying Jake. Self-knowledge was all well and good but sometimes it just didn't help. She still hadn't worked out how to use it to control her emotions – or understood why it took so long for her feelings to catch up with her brain.

To top it all, now that she'd blabbed to the world about her fling with Nicky Finn, the last thing she wanted was to get mixed up with another tramp and the news to somehow leak out to the press. That would only make her look like some desperate basket case, not to mention a fake. But she decided not to think about that now – she'd made the decision to sleep with Jake and she'd just have to go through with it. Although part of her couldn't help wondering what Freddy was doing today. Was he going to be at the concert too? And if so, would he find some way of coming over and saying hello?

She picked her way across the bedroom and between the boxes and storage containers that lay strewn all over her flat. She'd first seen the place six months ago when she'd been recording *Trouble* and straight away had put in an offer with the money she'd earned from her first album and from the advance on her US deal. She hadn't really been able to afford it but everyone else seemed to be so confident about her future earnings she'd told herself that she should relax and go for it. It was a huge risk and she did sometimes worry what would happen if her career suddenly tanked. But she did have the most amazing home: it was a huge open-plan space that occupied the top floor of a former brewery in Shoreditch and when she'd viewed it she'd instantly felt an emotional connection, enough to convince her that it was her dream home. Or *would be* her dream home, once it had been gutted, refurbished and redecorated. The plan had been for her to be safely installed by the time *Trouble* was released so she'd have a sanctuary during the mad whirlwind of promotion. But unfortunately the sale had taken so long to go through she'd only moved in a few weeks ago. Harvey had wanted to put her up in a hotel or rent her an apartment while it was done up but she'd decided against it. She'd grown up living in squalor, so bare walls, a bit of dust and a few boxes really didn't bother her. They'd have plenty of time to do the building work once she was on tour.

She tottered into the kitchen and filled the kettle to make herself a cup of tea. Out of the corner of her eye she spotted a letter Harvey had given her the day before propped up on the worktop. She remembered him suggesting she read it before the concert, saying something about it putting her in the right frame of mind for her performance. She opened it and began reading.

It was from a fan who, like her, had seen her life blighted by the drug abuse of a single parent. She told Lola that she'd been an inspiration to her through some desperate times and explained that seeing Lola go on to enjoy such success had encouraged her to keep fighting. As she read, Lola could feel tears welling in her eyes. It was a moving story and evidence of just the kind of impact she'd wanted to make when she'd decided to share her own story with her fans. But as well as validating and emboldening her it also made her feel under pressure. The writer had called her a 'strong, emotionally balanced woman'. Lola remembered how badly she wanted to be one but couldn't help thinking about her attraction to Jake – and wondering if she was failing dismally.

She decided to shelve all thoughts about Jake and concentrate instead on the reasons why she'd agreed to perform at today's gig. It was being held to raise money for rehab centres and support groups for people whose lives had been devastated by drugs. It was a cause obviously close to Lola's heart and one about which she cared passionately. And from a selfish point of view, she'd always found that doing good for others helped take her mind off her own dramas and worries.

She took a sip of her tea and remembered that there was one worry she couldn't put off tackling any longer. It was something she'd been meaning to deal with since the night of her album launch, when she'd shot her mouth off about her mum's murky past and told Freddy and the whole country how it had sent her careering into a life of drug abuse. She knew that she owed her mum an apology – even if the booze had loosened her tongue. But the two of them hadn't spoken for months and their relationship had been strained since Lola had hit her teens. This was going to be a difficult call to make.

She reached for the phone and dialled the number.

*

'Lola?' asked Karen Grant. 'Is that you?'

She was somewhere in rural Berkshire, lying on her bed in the Abbey rehab centre, more commonly known by its nickname the Abyss. Her room reminded her of the chintzy hotel in Brighton where she'd often stayed with her parents as a child, with its tasselled pelmets, pretty prints of English country scenes, a horrific ceramic Pierrot she'd had to hide because it gave her nightmares, and so many scatter cushions in contrasting floral patterns that if she looked at them for too long they induced chronic nausea. But she wasn't complaining; it was much nicer than some of the dumps she'd stayed in when Lola was little – and a world apart from the shambolically run treatment centres she'd had to visit as an outpatient, where she'd often met other addicts or even dealers who'd entice her away to get high. Of course the money to pay for this new residential treatment was being deducted from the rather generous allowance Lola gave her, although it had been her manager Harvey who she'd called to arrange it. And she was glad she had; she'd been here for ten days now and it was the longest she'd been clean for years. Although evidently her daughter knew nothing about it.

'Yeah, course it's me,' piped Lola. Karen was sure she could detect a note of annoyance in her voice even though it was only the beginning of the conversation. 'Who else do you think it is?'

Well, that's a good start. Why's she bothered calling if she's not in the mood to speak to me? Mind you, Karen could hardly blame her. No doubt every time Lola spoke to her she thought back to what a lousy, neglectful mother she'd been and how she'd ruined her childhood. She wondered if this would ever change.

'Oh, I don't know,' she managed with a little sigh. 'How's it going? You seem to be in the papers a lot at the moment.'

'Yeah, it's all great, thanks. The album's doing really well and I just shot a video for my new single.'

As Lola spoke, Karen could feel her insides twisting into a

familiar knot of resentment and anger. Whenever she listened to her daughter or looked into her eyes, she couldn't help being transported back to that night in Spain – and being confronted by the image of the man who'd got her pregnant. And not just his image but his touch, his smell . . . It was a memory she never wanted to revisit, one she just wanted to annihilate forever. But that wasn't particularly easy when she'd been saddled with a constant physical reminder for the last twenty-five years. And just when she thought she was breaking free, just when she thought her daughter was stepping away from her life, she'd only gone and resurfaced in every paper and on every TV screen Karen happened to stumble across. It was as if she was deliberately taunting her.

And why should she be so happy when my life's been wrecked?

If Karen hadn't fallen pregnant with Lola, her first love back home in London wouldn't have dumped her, her parents wouldn't have turned against her and she wouldn't have had to drop out of school, where she'd always been one of the brightest girls and had been predicted to go on to A Levels and university. And it wasn't as if she hadn't tried *not* to fall pregnant; she'd taken a morning-after pill so had assumed she wasn't, even though she'd been so hung-over when she'd taken it that she'd spent most of that morning throwing up. But how was she supposed to know it wasn't 100 per cent effective? And how was she supposed to spot the signs of pregnancy when she went to a Catholic school where no one talked about sex and lived with parents who were so uptight they wouldn't even let her watch *Grange Hill*? By the time she'd found out it had been way too late to do anything about it – and a few months later she'd been lumbered with an ugly dead weight of a baby who didn't stop screaming, and so much anger at the injustice of the world that it had worked its way into her bones and gnawed away at her insides ever since. She tried shaking such negative thoughts out of her head but however hard she tried, she couldn't see how her relationship with her daughter would ever be anything other than tense, resentful and a huge effort for both parties.

'Brilliant,' she forced herself to say. 'You must be really pleased.'

'Where are you anyway?' Lola asked suspiciously. 'It sounds very quiet.'

'Well, since you ask, I'm actually in rehab.'

'*Rehab?*' She sounded astonished. 'What are you doing there? I thought you'd given up on all that.'

'Well, I had. But I thought I'd give it another go, you know. And this time I really think it's going to be different.'

She was pretty sure she heard Lola scoff but decided not to respond. A cupboard door opened and there was a rattle of cutlery; it sounded like she was in a kitchen making herself something to eat. She obviously wasn't remotely interested in what was going on in Karen's life.

'Really?' Lola asked, stifling a yawn. 'Well, I might believe you if I hadn't heard you say that a thousand times before. I mean, you've been saying it since I was about three.'

Karen felt a prickle of anger. *Oh, what's the point in even trying?* 'Yeah, well this time I mean it, Lola. And it might help if you showed a little support.'

She could hear her start to munch her way through a bowl of cereal. 'Course I support you, Mum. I'm just a bit surprised, that's all. And where did all this come from, anyway?'

'Well, since you mention it, it was seeing you ask me to give up crack on Channel 3 News. I don't know, when I watched it something just clicked and a little part of me buried somewhere deep down started to fight back.'

For the first time in the conversation Lola sounded pleased. 'Oh well, that's brilliant because I was actually phoning to apologize for that but I guess I don't need to now.'

Karen could feel her jaw stiffen. 'Well, it might still be a good idea, to be honest. I mean, some of your comments were a bit raw.'

Lola didn't appreciate the criticism. 'All right, all right! I'm sorry, Mum.'

'Thanks. Apology accepted.' Oh *why's it so hard for me to be nice to her?* She opened her mouth to say something else but nothing came.

She stood up and moved over to the window. In the clinic's lovingly tended gardens she spotted a young mother she knew from group therapy out walking with her teenage sons. There seemed to be genuine affection between them, even though she knew the mother's actions must have put a severe strain on the relationship. She wondered why she always felt such a stiff, unmovable barrier when it came to connecting with her daughter. If only she could jump over it.

Her new therapist had repeatedly stressed that she needed to let go of the bitterness that had ruled her life for the last twenty-five years if she was ever going to move on. But first she had to stop blaming Lola for everything that had gone wrong in her life and try to start seeing her as an innocent party. It was quite simple and, despite everything, she was sure that she had just enough love to do this – even if it was buried under a heap of rotting resentment. But she was sure it was there somewhere. After all, it was why she hadn't given up Lola for adoption in the first place, defying the advice of her parents, friends and teachers. It was why, no matter how far she'd sunk during her childhood, she'd always fought to keep her. And it was why, sitting in front of the TV less than two weeks ago, she'd still felt enough of a spark inside her soul to stir her into action – and have one last go at resurrecting her life and building a new relationship with her daughter.

'Anyway,' Lola breezed, interrupting her thoughts, 'in case you're interested, I'm performing at that big anti-drugs gig tonight. You know, the thing in Hyde Park?'

'Oh right, great. Well, good luck – it sounds fantastic.' There was a pause. 'Oh, and Lola?'

'What?'

'You know . . . you know I'm very . . . proud of you.'

'You what?' Lola spluttered. 'What do you mean?'

'Just that. I've never said it before but I'm very proud of you and your career – and you speaking out about all the shit that goes with taking drugs. It's really important you say it, that's all.'

She was surprised to feel her tension ebbing away as she said the words. She'd always thought that if she said anything like this it would feel wrong, but somehow it felt right. She could hear Lola lower her bowl onto a table. 'Urm . . . Yeah . . . Urm . . . Thanks . . . Urm, I've got to go now.' She sounded bewildered. 'But I hope you enjoy the show, Mum.'

'Oh I will,' she answered. 'I'm sure I will.'

She put the phone down.

Well, it wasn't brilliant but at least it's a start.

There was a time when this kind of conversation would have sent Karen racing to her dealer in a self-destructive rage. But instead she felt a sense of calm and a warm glow she recognized from the outer limits of her memory as satisfaction. Somehow she'd managed to be nice to Lola and for the first time in years express genuine affection. She couldn't wait to tell her therapist and talk about what to do next. Because this time she was determined to follow it through.

*

Eight hours later Lola was still feeling guilty about the way she'd spoken to her mum. *She told me she was in rehab and all I could do was scoff and take the piss.*

She tried to relieve her guilt by reassuring herself her reaction was perfectly natural when her mum had promised she was going to sort out her life on countless occasions in the past. But she couldn't help thinking that this time something seemed different. For a start her mum had said she was proud of her, expressing affection for the first time in as long as Lola could remember. It had hit her like a body blow and she hadn't known how to respond. However hard she'd tried, she just hadn't been able to bring herself to return the affection. And now she felt so unsettled by the experience that all she wanted to do was go out and get completely obliterated on booze. *Oh, and fuck the brains out of Jake.*

But for the time being she had to focus on her performance and prepare herself for what was being seen not only as the most important gig of her career so far but also as a taster of what people could expect from her all-important autumn tour. She was standing with her entourage backstage in the artists' holding area at Hyde Park. All around them there were flight cases, Portakabins pinned with laminates giving directions to the toilets, and monitors showing the live TV broadcast so that people could watch the action on stage. Rising from the grass beneath her and reverberating through her boots, she could feel the pounding bass line of the music currently being performed by American pop sensation and occasional actress Shereen Spicer, who'd chosen the event to premiere her newly dyed red hair. Judging from the roar of applause, the new look was going down well. Lola knew Shereen would be a tough act to follow and she couldn't believe she was appearing higher up the bill. She felt the boom of the bass mix with a rumble of nerves in her stomach. *Just a few more minutes and I'll be on . . .*

She was finding it particularly hard to relax when everywhere she looked she was confronted by the highest concentration of A-list celebs she'd ever seen. Just a few metres away, rock god Blake Striker was wearing cowboy boots and a leather waistcoat that showed off arms he was pumping up with a set of last-minute press-ups. Premier League footballer Slam Carter was teaching American baseball-player-turned-movie-action-hero Buck Andrews how to play keepy-uppy. Oscar-winning actress Lucy Cantrell was swapping make-up tips with achingly fashionable transgender DJ and remixer Candy Lunt. And even the sour-faced Home Secretary Lavinia Trout had turned up in her trademark maxi dress and Pixie boots and was rehearsing a speech about the government's commitment to drug rehabilitation to a crowd of nodding advisors. Flitting between them all was the event host and organizer Ace Bounder, who seemed so pleased with himself he looked in need of urgent medical attention. Lola watched as he shamelessly stroked the backside of *Lucky Star* presenter Ruby Marlow, who she was sure somebody had once told her was a cokehead. She watched as Ruby giggled at Ace in flirtatious annoyance.

Circling around them were journalists from the BBC and reporters from Radio 1 snaffling as many interviews as they could, although thankfully Barbara was keeping them away from Lola until after her performance. She looked around for Freddy, the only journalist she actually wanted to see, but she couldn't find him anywhere. Instead her eyes alighted on Jake, leaning on a Portakabin chatting to Sharonne. She felt a sudden prick of jealousy. *Is he flirting with her? Is he actually flirting with her?*

She told herself she was so nervous she was probably imagining things. After all, during their chat on the set of the video just a few days ago Jake had made it quite clear it was Lola he was interested in. But she couldn't stop her mind flashing forward to the future and she pictured herself descending into a deep, gloomy abyss of jealousy and paranoia. A man like Jake would always get attention from women, and previous experience had taught her she wasn't well-equipped to handle it. *Do I really want to go there?* She stamped her feet and reminded herself there was no turning back now. *At least not unless Freddy shows his face.*

Just then she felt a hand rest on her shoulder. 'How you feeling, Lola?' She turned and saw it was Gloria.

'Oh I'm shitting it, to be honest, darlin'. Have you seen how many people are out there?' From the other side of the stage they could feel the low growl of the one-hundred-thousand-strong live audience, occasionally erupting into colossal applause. Lola was gripped by an icy fear. She daren't imagine how many millions more would be watching live on TV. 'What if I fuck it up?'

Gloria put both hands on her shoulders. 'You *won't* fuck it up, Lola. You're a brilliant singer and a brilliant performer. All you have to do is go out there and be half as good as you've been in rehearsals and you'll blow everyone away.'

Lola took a deep breath and could feel herself calming down. *Thank God for Gloria!* 'Oh thanks, darlin'. Thanks a lot.'

Gloria nodded forcefully and released her. She suggested they perform some vocal exercises to try and focus their energies. Lola jumped at the chance.

'Scrumpity scrumpity scrump.'

'Scrumpity scrumpity scrump.'

'Scrumpity scrumpity scrump.'

They were silenced by another wave of applause and stepped back to watch Shereen Spicer and her band tear down the rickety stairs beside them in a flurry of hollering and high fives. Lola felt a stab of fear; she knew the pressure was on. The press always wanted to stir up rivalries between female singers, so if Shereen had been good, she had to be even better.

'Good luck, honey!' called out Shereen, a tattooed tit peaking out from behind her bra strap.

'Yeah, thanks darlin',' squeaked Lola.

As Shereen skipped away, Lola clenched and released her fists to try and relieve some of her tension. She turned back to Gloria but saw that she'd disappeared. She looked around for Harvey and instantly spotted him. *Always at and on my side . . .*

Just as she was beckoning him over she spotted something behind him that made her blink in disbelief. Stepping out of a Portakabin was Hollywood megastar Billy Spencer, who strode through the parting sea of celebs and started scaling the stairs to the stage. Lola had never been so close to such a huge international celebrity before and she gave an involuntary shudder. It seemed like only a few months ago that she'd picked herself up from yet another record company rejection by gorging on a weekend of Billy Spencer films on DVD. Of course it must have been years ago really, and at the time she'd had no idea Billy would one day come out as gay, not that it would have made any difference to her youthful fantasies. But here he was now standing just a few metres away from her, presumably taking to the stage to introduce her to millions of people. It suddenly dawned on her just how successful she'd become. She turned to a monitor and was transfixed by a shot of Billy looking out onto an ocean-like audience. It was as if she could suddenly feel the whole world opening up before her.

Harvey stepped forward and put his arm around her.

'You did it, Lola,' he said, pulling her towards him. 'You really did it.'

'No, *we* did it, Harvey,' she corrected him. 'We did this together.'

They watched Billy as he fought through the applause to explain that he was in London to shoot a movie but had wanted to come here today to introduce an artist whose music he'd fallen in love with during his time in the UK – and one he was really excited about breaking through in America. *Oh my God,* thought Lola, *can this actually be happening?*

As the crowd roared at the first mention of her name, she felt Harvey squeezing her hand.

'Off you go, Trouble. We might have done this together but it's you they're cheering for.'

She nodded solemnly and took to the stage.

*

From his position near the front of the golden circle, Freddy was so taken aback by the thunderous applause he instinctively ducked for cover. *Wow! Lola hasn't opened her mouth yet and already they're going mad for her.*

'Hiya everyone!' she cheeped in her south London accent. 'Are you all having a good time?' The response was almost deafening and the audience surged towards her. 'Good to hear it. But don't go anywhere just yet – because the fun's only just starting . . .'

As the band began playing the opening notes to *Lost in Love*, Freddy drank in Lola's every detail. She was dressed all in white, wearing a fitted waistcoat, a bandana tied in a bow and trousers held up with a patent leather belt onto which was attached the battery pack for her earpiece. Glinting in the low evening sun, a diamanté belt buckle, hoop earrings and bracelet complemented a sparkling letter L that hung around her neck. She looked incredible.

'Fuck me!' whistled his friend Rhodri, standing next to him wearing a T-shirt emblazoned with the slogan *Beaver Patrol*. 'She. Is. FIT. AS.' The two of them had been drinking lager in the sun all afternoon and it had clearly gone to Rhodri's head. 'I mean, she ain't a beauty or anything but I bet she's a cracking ride.'

Freddy tried not to baulk. 'All right, champ, take it easy.'

Rhodri didn't take his eyes off the stage. 'No but seriously mate, I'd love a go on that.'

'All right, all right! I get the picture.'

Rhodri turned to look at him and raised an eyebrow. 'Well, somebody's a bit touchy. Got a thing for her, have you?'

'Don't be daft. She's a massive star – she wouldn't look twice at me.'

'Well, she was flirting with you on telly last night – and it wasn't the first time.'

Freddy thought back to the interview he'd recorded on the set of Lola's video shoot. The chemistry between them had made such an impact on him that he hadn't been able to think about anything else since. Spike was supposedly asking Harvey to find out if she wanted to go out on a date, but he'd told him to be subtle and he hadn't heard anything since. But once the interview had broadcast last night he'd been inundated with people commenting on the flirtation between them and asking what he was going to do about it. Rhodri was only the latest in the long line.

'Seriously, mate,' his friend slurred, 'you want to get in there. I mean, get a load of those blow job lips – I bet she could suck a rugby ball through a hosepipe.'

'Oh give it a rest, Rhodri. I'm on it, all right? But right now I wouldn't mind watching her show.'

'Whatever you say, mate. Whatever you say.'

The two of them turned back to the stage and watched in wonderment as Lola scorched her way through her first number. Freddy tried to catch her eye but knew it was a long shot. And besides, she clearly had much more important things to think about than him. In fact, she was so immersed in her performance it was as if she wasn't really present – or that her energy was so intense it was somehow lifting her above the audience so the only way they could respond was by looking on in adulation.

Freddy had arrived at Hyde Park just before the show opened, assured of access to the golden circle for him and a guest. He'd been released from all work commitments for the day as broadcast rights to the show had been given exclusively to the BBC. At first he'd been disappointed to miss out on the chance of another meeting with Lola. But so far it had been an incredible day. The line-up of talent was outstanding and between performances the anti-drugs charity had used the screens at either side of the stage to play films about their work helping young people whose lives had been destroyed by addiction. It had all combined to create a very special atmosphere, helped in no small part by the blazing hot sunshine, which had people taking their tops off and spraying themselves with water to cool down. Earlier in the day Freddy had been plagued by hassle from people who recognized him but it was all good-natured and seemed to have calmed down now. Everyone was much too interested in the action unfolding on stage. And so far there was no question that Lola was proving the highlight.

'Do you want to hear some more?' she growled as *Lost in Love* boomed to its finish. She cupped her ear playfully, pretending not to hear the loud cheer crash through the crowd. 'I said, do you want to hear some more?'

The intro to *Tramp* began blistering its way through the applause and two male dancers marched onto the stage at either side of Lola. She looked at them impishly. 'This song's for all those trampy men out there. And all the girls who won't put up with them anymore!'

Leaning onto him to steady himself, Rhodri gave a loud wolf whistle and Freddy recoiled with his finger in his ear.

'Now I want to see everyone dancing!' Lola yelled. 'And that includes you, Freddy Jones!'

Freddy reeled as a hundred thousand people turned to face him. Rhodri's mouth fell open and he dropped his can of lager on Freddy's foot.

'Come on, darlin',' Lola yowled, her eyes sparkling at him from the stage. 'I know you're not a tramp but I still want to see you dancing!'

A grin lifted his face as two cameras swept in to shoot his reaction. But all he could hear was Rhodri gasping for breath next to him.

'Fuck me, mate. You are *well* in there!'

*

Lola took a few seconds to catch her breath and waited for the applause to die down. She couldn't believe how well the show was going; the energy of the audience was spurring her on to give what she'd known she needed to deliver – her best performance ever. Feeling the impact of a hundred thousand people clapping to the beat of her music instilled in her a happiness more intense than she'd ever imagined possible. And to top it all, she'd spotted Freddy in the audience. He *was* here after all! She stopped to collect herself and wiped her brow with the back of her hand. Gloria stepped forward and handed her a bottle of water. She nodded her thanks and took a long swig.

'My God it's so hot up here,' she puffed to the audience, 'I'm sweating like a whore in confession.' There was an eruption of laughter. 'Sorry, but you know me – about as subtle as a fart in the bath.' The laughter doubled.

'Anyway, I just want to be serious for a minute and tell you how made up I am to be taking part in this event today. I'm sure everyone knows that drug abuse has had a major impact on my life – and particularly my childhood. And I know from the experience of my own family just how much damage it can cause.'

The crowd settled into a respectful silence.

'But what I think's so important about this concert today is that it really sends out a message that, however low you think you might've sunk, there's still a way out. And the more money we raise, the more people we can help find that way out.'

Someone yelled their support from way back in the distance and Lola could feel her poise crumbling. She thought about her mum sitting watching her on TV in the rehab centre and felt compelled by a need to speak directly to her – to say something affectionate or even loving that she'd be able to use as encouragement to fight her addiction. But she just couldn't do it.

She thought of the lonely little girl she'd once been, trailing around after a mum she loved so much, a mum for years she hadn't even realized had been so broken. She was the only mum she'd known, which was why she'd cuddled up to the dead weight of her body as she lay racked by depression, rolling around on the filthy floor during yet another crack comedown. As she pictured the scene now, a tear sprang from her eye and ran down her cheek. She wiped it with the corner of her hand and tried to compose herself. There was just one more song to go and the last thing she needed now was to give in to an emotional meltdown. She forced her lips into a tight smile.

'Anyway, please give as much money as you can. Because I promise every penny of it will make a difference. And help people like me come out fighting.'

A low rumble of encouragement issued from the audience and began to build steadily. Lola jumped up and down on the spot and snapped her mic off its stand.

'OK, let's get back to business. I hope you all enjoy this next song. Come on boys, hit it!'

*

As she stood at the back of the stage watching Lola turn on the tears, Gloria tried not to curl up her lip in distaste. *Here she goes again, milking the whole junkie mum thing.* It was quite pathetic really and Gloria didn't understand why anyone bothered listening. Every artist had a sob story but some of them weren't so tacky as to wheel it out at every available opportunity. And anyway, she didn't see what the big deal was. *Are we all supposed to feel sorry for Lola just because her mum can't take her drugs?*

The band launched into the intro to their final number and Gloria began her usual moronic swaying from side to side. As she delivered her vocals with a pained expression on her face, all she could think was that *she* should be the one headlining this show – not Lola. For what it was worth, she had a much better voice and she'd trained as a professional dancer so could dance Lola off the stage. She was much better looking too and had spent thousands having her teeth and boobs done before Lola had come along and snatched her career away from her. But here she was now, confined to a dark corner where hardly anyone could see her. This morning she'd left Chanelle sitting in front of the TV with her mum, the two of them waiting to catch a glimpse of Gloria on screen. Her mum hadn't been able to resist asking if they bothered shooting close-ups of the backing singers. Gloria had refrained from giving her a mouthful, only to find herself positioned so far upstage she had a cat in hell's chance of featuring in a single shot, never mind a close-up. She could hear her mum crowing about it now.

She looked out onto the crowd and couldn't believe none of them could see Lola for the talentless charlatan she was. And what Gloria found most galling was she was so two-faced. Just today she'd been chatting away to her backstage, doing her best to calm her nerves, until Shereen Spicer had appeared and Lola had turned around and blanked her. The whole experience had been utterly crushing and had destroyed Gloria's confidence just before she went on stage. Not that Lola cared. The only thing Lola cared about was herself.

It was just so frustrating that the hundred thousand fans crammed into Hyde Park were oblivious to what she was really like. As Lola reached the end of her set and took a bow, they gave her the loudest applause of the day. After what seemed like an eternity of wallowing in the adulation, she finally led the band offstage. They all clattered down the rickety stairs and back into the artists' holding area, where Gloria forced herself to join in the self-congratulatory whooping and cheering.

'Well done, Gloria!' Lola frothed. 'That was blatantly fierce!'

'Yeah, thanks, Lola,' she forced herself to reply. 'You really smashed it!'

As Lola leant in for a hug, Gloria couldn't help feeling a stab of guilt. She hated it when Lola was nice to her – it only made things worse.

But then Lola suddenly broke away and ran over to her assistant, a few minutes later bounding back to Gloria with an envelope.

'Gloria, darlin', could you do me a favour?'

'Yeah, course, what is it?'

'Could you nip and find Freddy Jones and give him these? They're tickets to the after-show party.'

Gloria's mouth fell open. Had she just heard her right? *The cheek of it! What was she, Lola's errand girl?*

'I mean, I'd ask Amina to do it normally,' Lola went on, 'but she's got to come with me to do all the press.'

She gestured towards a scrum of journalists, cameramen and radio reporters all vying for prime position behind a long velvet rope. Not a single one of them recognized Gloria.

'No, it's fine, Lola,' she found herself saying, 'don't worry about it.'

'Did you see where he was standing? At the front of the golden circle?'

Oh, I saw him all right, I saw you throw yourself at him like some total slapper. And while they were on the subject, wasn't Lola supposed to be after Jake? Or would she drop her knickers for anyone?

'Yeah, I know where he is,' she managed to breathe reassuringly. 'Don't worry, I'll find him.'

'Come on, doll!' called out Lola's publicist. 'Everyone's waiting!'

'Thanks, Gloria,' Lola said, touching her arm. 'You're a real mate.'

As she watched her trot off towards the press area, Gloria fanned herself with the party passes. She couldn't believe it. Lola actually expected her to wade through the crowd of piss-heads and hand them over to some bloke she wanted to get off with. She wondered if she was deliberately trying to insult her.

And then it suddenly occurred to her that she didn't actu-ally have to do it. She could pretend she'd looked for Freddy but he'd moved on and she couldn't find him. Surely that kind of thing happened all the time in a crowd this size? That would certainly teach Lola not to treat her like some kind of gopher she could boss about whenever she wanted a quick shag.

But she couldn't really do something as underhand as that. Could she?

*

By midnight the after-show party was in full swing. Jake stood leaning against the ornate wrought-iron balcony of the elegant Café du Palais and looked down to survey the scene.

In the DJ booth, Candy Lunt was playing a dance remix of the latest single by Rihanna. On the dance floor, Shereen Spicer and Lucy Cantrell were so off their faces they were stag-gering their way through some kind of lesbian act as Ace Bounder looked on, leering. Blake Striker was becoming less and less masculine the more whisky he drank and was cur-rently puckering his lips, twiddling his hair and launching himself at Buck Andrews and Slam Carter, neither of whom was remotely responding but both of whom couldn't help being fascinated by his transformation. And some tart-looking politician called Lavinia Trout was drinking herself red-nosed on neat gin, wailing like a Spanish widow about everyone hating her to a group of sallow-faced, out-of-shape brown-nosers with cheap suits and coffee-stained teeth. And through it all clicked a high-heeled flat-chested waitress who seemed to think miming a look of extreme boredom in the face of major celebs letting their hair down made her look the height of cool. *Hmpf,* thought Jake, *I could think of a way of making her look a little less cool . . .*

But he reminded himself that tonight he had a prior assignation. Thanks to his little routine on the set of the video for *Tramp*, Jake knew that tonight Lola was all his. And once he'd upped the ante, he couldn't get over how easy it had been. *All I had to do was flash my eyes, touch her cheek and then move in for a little kiss and she was practically frothing at the snatch.* He thought back to the way she'd been looking at him in rehearsals since. He wondered how she'd be looking later – when he was inside her.

He quickly glanced at himself in what was obviously a fake antique mirror. He scraped his fingers through his hair and stroked the bristles on his chin. *Man, you are one smoking-hot sonofabitch.* He treated himself to a quick flash of his sloppy grin and then turned to walk down the sweeping staircase and join the party.

As he entered the unsteady throng he was overwhelmed by the smell of champagne farts and beer burps. He wrinkled his nose in disgust. Sure, everyone here had leapt to the stage to denounce the dangers of taking drugs, but Jake wasn't sure their consumption of booze was any more laudable. He tutted as he thought of how smug Ruby Marlow looked to have substituted her usual penchant for cocaine with enough champagne to drown a cartel of drug barons. He shook his head and stepped out of the way to avoid colliding with Slam Carter, who fell over a chair in his rush to escape Blake Striker.

Now where's Lola? As he leant on the bar to get a better view, his hand slipped into a puddle of spilled beer. He shook it off with a scowl. All right, this might be a classy venue with an all-star guest list, but right now it didn't strike him as being much different to any of the dives he'd been dipping into late at night to pick up an easy lay.

And speaking of easy lays . . .

He scanned the room and spotted Lola breaking away from a huddle of honchos who were clambering over each other to praise her performance. He watched as she gestured to Gloria and took her to one side. He stood on his tiptoes to peer over the mob and catch her eye. It took a while but after a few minutes his gaze finally locked onto hers. He gave just a flicker of a smile and saw her cheek tremble. *This is it,* he thought.

As he made his way through the melee towards them, he could just about catch a few snippets of their conversation. 'I'm sorry,' he heard Gloria saying, 'but I couldn't find him anywhere, honestly.'

'Oh it's all right, darlin',' Lola replied, clearly shit-faced. 'Thanks for trying.'

He hovered just a few feet away until Lola excused herself and made her way over.

'Hiya,' she slurred.

'Hey,' he breathed.

Just then Candy Lunt changed the song and began playing the latest single by Nicki Minaj.

'Oh I love this song!' Lola shouted over the music.

He pretended he couldn't hear so she'd have to lean in. 'Excuse me?'

'I said I love this song!'

He pulled a face. 'I'm sorry?' He moved in closer and allowed his stubble to gently catch her cheek. 'What was that again?' he said straight into her ear, his lips lightly tickling the lobe and his hand resting on her waist.

'I said I LOVE THIS SONG!'

'Good,' he nodded, stepping back to look at her intently. 'Remind me to play it later while I'm fucking you.'

She stopped dead and for a second he wasn't sure whether he'd overstepped the mark. She seemed to shiver ever so slightly. But then she glared at him and her eyes flared with yearning.

It was time for Jake to begin his performance. A performance he was sure would completely overshadow Lola's.

*

Across town, Freddy was still basking in the brilliance of Lola's performance.

'Yeah but did you see how much everyone loved her?' he asked Rhodri. 'I mean, did you hear how loud they were all cheering?'

Unfortunately Rhodri's attention was focused elsewhere. 'What do you think of that one?' He gestured towards a generously thighed whopper of a woman whose rolled up

G-string was poking out of the top of her low-rise jeans. 'I mean, she's not perfect, but I could always D.I.D.'

'D.I.D.?'

Rhodri looked at him as if he'd said something stupid. 'Do It Doggie.'

'Oh yeah, sorry.' Freddy plugged his frown with a bottle of beer.

The two of them had come to the Roaring Donkey pub in Bayswater, where Rhodri had carried on drinking like a pirate – and Freddy had lost all chance of catching up with him. Not that he was remotely interested in getting drunk – all that interested him tonight was Lola. He couldn't stop thinking about the moment she'd flirted with him on stage, the moment his heart had taken flight. He wondered where she was now. She was probably at some glamorous after-show party being showered with praise. But as he wasn't working the gig, he hadn't arranged to get hold of any invites – and had no idea how he'd go about it now.

'Or what about that one?' his friend asked. He pointed out a woman with a dramatic streak of red in her black hair and a faraway expression that showed she too had been drinking for hours. She gave a loud laugh like a drain, revealing a huge gap between her front teeth. 'Hey, do you reckon I could fit my cock in that gap?'

'I've no idea, mate,' Freddy answered. 'But why don't you go and chat to her? She looks like a nice girl.'

'Shit!' Rhodri gripped onto Freddy's arm and pulled him behind a pillar. 'Have you seen who's just walked in?'

Freddy peered around and spotted a trashy blonde with the

worst muffin top he'd ever seen stuffing her face on a bag of Quavers. 'What's the matter, mate? Who's that?'

'Ingrid Grimmer. You must remember her? I shagged her after the rugby ball last year.'

Freddy didn't have the faintest recollection but played along anyway. 'Oh yeah. She was all right, wasn't she?'

Rhodri pulled a face as if he could smell shit. 'Mate, shagging that was like putting my dick in a messy kebab. I ain't going back there again – no way.'

'Well, that's all right, like. We can just hide here for a while.'

'Do you mind?'

'No, it's fine, honestly.'

As Rhodri emptied his bottle and burped hotly, Freddy couldn't help wondering how he'd ended up in this position. What he'd give to be with Lola right now. Oh it was all so frustrating. He knew that if he could just wangle one date with her everything would be fine. But here he was stuck in some dump of a pub looking after his shit-faced mate as he hid from a dodgy pull while Lola was somewhere much more glamorous celebrating her success. Not to mention fending off the advances of every man who'd seen her sizzle on stage.

He took a swig of his drink and told himself not to worry about it. After what she'd said today there was no question there was a connection between them. He'd just have to be patient until he could act on it – until, to use a rugby expression, he could convert the try. But an awful thought suddenly occurred to him and started beating at the walls of his skull. *What if some other bloke gets in there before me?*

*

'What was the name of that song again?' Jake asked as he crashed into Lola's flat a few hours later. 'The one I said I'd play while I was fucking you?'

'Oh, who gives a shit?' Lola practically shrieked. 'Just shut up and snog me!'

She ripped at his jacket and tugged it onto the floor, giving in to an urge she'd been fighting ever since she'd set eyes on him at the after-show party. Actually, if she were being honest, it was an urge she'd been fighting ever since she'd first set eyes on him in rehearsals. She'd thought she'd come up with a way of resisting it when she'd flirted with Freddy on stage and then asked Gloria to give him tickets to the party. But her plan had failed – and now she saw no other option but to surrender.

Falling back onto a cardboard box, she felt Jake lowering himself onto her. As he pressed down, her legs gently fell apart, while her lips hungrily snatched at his. Now that she was giving in to her desire she couldn't for the life of her think why she'd spent so long resisting. This felt good. It felt right. And today had been such an unreal experience, Lola clutched at it as something that could once again root her in reality. Or at least a reality she recognized as hers. She kicked the door shut and heard it slam.

She could feel the proof of Jake's desire pressing against her from beneath his trousers. And the evidence that he wanted her made her flush with a feeling she could only identify as euphoria. Right now she was convinced she wanted him more than she'd ever wanted anything else in her life.

'Wait a second,' he said, detaching himself so that he was

just out of reach. Her lips carried on snatching at the space between them. 'I need to quickly use the bathroom.'

Lola let off a groan. He staggered back and she pointed the way. As he turned and receded into the distance, she clattered down off the box and onto the floor. She was so drunk she felt stunned. She came to a stop in front of a full-length mirror and settled into a glassy-eyed gaze at her reflection. Her vision began to dot like in one of those optical illusions she'd had to stare at when she'd had her eyes tested. For a brief moment the dots rearranged themselves into an image of her mum staring back at her after one of her heavy binges. She watched herself blanch with fear.

Come on, Lola, it's not too late to back out of this now.

She shook the thought out of her head and padded over to the kitchen to see what there was to drink. She flung open door after door but all she could find was a half-empty bottle of whisky she couldn't remember ever having opened. She held onto the worktop to steady herself and emptied the contents into two glasses. As she did so she heard the tap turn on in the bathroom. Jake was probably freshening up before coming back in to get naked. She let loose a little yelp and gripped her glass of whisky.

Come on, Lola, this is your last chance to back out.

Just as she was raising the glass to her lips, a pair of strong arms snaked around her waist and she felt Jake's hot breath on the nape of her neck. He nuzzled into her and whispered something in her ear. She was so turned on she couldn't make out a word he was saying; all she could hear was the sound of the blood pumping in her head. And she knew there was no way she could back out now.

She lowered her glass onto the worktop and turned to face him. Her fingers threaded into his hair and she drew herself into his kiss. The energy between them was so intense the only thing she could compare it to was the way she'd felt earlier that evening performing to an audience of a hundred thousand fans. Except this felt even better.

And then one last thought flashed through her mind.

I'm sorry, Freddy. I'm sorry.

6

Lola looked out over the Place de la Concorde. It was only 8 a.m. but already the August sun was burning dazzlingly bright in a clear blue sky. On her left she could see the Tuileries Garden, the water of the little boating pond glinting with sunlight as the trees fluttered in the light breeze. On her right, traffic slithered over the cobblestones and funnelled into the Champs Élysées. And straight ahead, the River Seine wound its way through a city that struck her as being so beautiful she had to clutch her chin to stop it trembling.

She'd arrived in Paris the previous morning for the start of a month-long promotional tour of Europe, kicking things off with a press conference to announce details of the *Trouble* tour and the release of tickets later that week. Obviously, most of the journalists had been much more keen on talking about her views on France, French men and French music. She'd had to confess that she had no time in her schedule for sightseeing and so far most of the France she'd experienced had been through a car window. But she didn't want to let them down so had regaled them with a story about her teenage fling with the school French assistant, who'd shown her how to French kiss, got her drunk on Pernod and taught her zero French apart from *Je veux te sucer la bite*, which she was pretty sure meant something rude and gaily trotted out for the assembled press, only to be told by one boggle-eyed journalist that it meant, 'I want to suck your dick'. *Oh, never mind, at least I gave them something to write about.*

She tightened the belt on her white towelling robe and leant on the stone balcony of the Hotel Pierrot. Down below, people were streaming out of the crowded metro station and rushing to work, fanning themselves with newspapers and nervously checking their watches. Lola couldn't help wondering about the variety of dramas that must be powering them through the start of their days. *Have any of them spent all night having hot, sweaty, riotous sex? Have any of them experienced the same kind of passion as I feel buzzing through me right now?* Her eyes settled on the tall, thrusting obelisk standing proud in the centre of the square and she thought about Jake with a wicked smile. *Je veux te sucer la bite* – maybe she'd reuse that line later.

But right now Jake was asleep in the enormous four-poster bed behind her; she could hear his low snores sailing through the suite of rooms and out onto the balcony. She knew he could afford to keep sleeping as he wouldn't be needed for hours, whereas she had to be up early to appear on some radio show. Stretching out ahead of her was a full day of interviews, performances and personal appearances, not to mention having to charm record company execs and wow competition-winning fans. The full schedule was documented on the call sheet she'd been given by Barbara the night before, which she'd left by the side of her bed having glanced over the details and registered the most important piece of information – her call time. Today it was 8.30, which gave her just a few minutes until the long sequence of wake-up calls would begin, ending with Amina nervously knocking at her door to whisk her away.

It was a strange existence but she knew that for this kind of trip to work she had to surrender control of her life. For the next month everything would be arranged for her – hotels, travel, meals, even her choice of clothes. Today's outfit was hanging on the door of her wardrobe next to a bottle of sparkling water, an empty glass and a pile of vitamin tablets and health supplements. She prickled at the idea of giving herself over to a state of unquestioning obedience, which she always found a real struggle, however temporary. But she knew that everyone working for her was on her side – and that Harvey would have liaised with record-company staff in each country to OK every last detail.

What Harvey didn't know was that Jake Hunter was lying in the bed behind her. In fact, nobody knew that little detail. Lola hated having to keep quiet about what was going on but she couldn't risk the press finding out and making a big thing out of it. Not that there *was* much going on, other than lots of sex. In fact, the week before they'd left London, Jake had spent every single night at hers – and the sex had been fierce. But that was all it was, sex. And she told herself not to forget it.

Then again, she couldn't help thinking how lovely it would be for the two of them to slip out into the street and stroll arm in arm along the banks of the Seine. It wasn't as if she was particularly romantic, but gazing out over Paris she couldn't help feeling infused with excitement at the possibility of falling in love. She stopped herself. *Don't develop feelings for him – that's when everything starts going wrong.* She distracted herself with the memory of last night and the powerful jolt of pleasure that had made her shriek out loud as their bodies had urgently come together on a satin chaise longue.

She heard the first wake-up call and rushed into the bedroom to pick up the phone. She watched Jake stirring under the sheets and realized she only had a few minutes to smuggle him out before Amina arrived. Because, just like all those thousands of people rushing across the Place de la Concorde, Lola had work to do. And her working day was about to begin.

*

Jake stretched out his legs onto the chair opposite and sipped at his surprisingly good machine-spluttered coffee. He was in the green room of a radio station somewhere in Berlin. It had been decorated with retro furniture he could only assume had been chosen in deliberately clashing colours and a huge central light fitting made out of old seven-inch singles melted into a variety of head-scrambling shapes. One corner of the room was piled high with cushions and beanbags while another held rows of plastic containers dispensing pick-and-mix sweets in the shape of strawberries, cola bottles and wiggly worms. It was like being in a children's playpen, although Jake assumed the intention was to crank up the artists' energy levels before they went through to the studio.

In just under half an hour's time Lola and the band would be performing a live session for the biggest and most important radio station in Germany. As this was the third they'd done in as many countries in as many days, no one seemed particularly nervous. Lola and Gloria were flicking through magazines and gurgling with laughter at a story about some woman who'd apparently had sex with a donkey *and* a Great Dane. Barbara was stuffing her face on sweets and chatting up a power-dressing brunette from the radio station who was just the kind of lesbian Jake might go for if she didn't blow it all by having an annoying laugh that sounded like a hiccup. And thankfully Harvey was just out of sight, talking business with some record exec in the corridor. Harvey was the only member of Lola's entourage who made Jake feel uncomfortable. He was the only one who was immune to his charms, which was funny as fags usually loved him. But not this one. There were times when he seemed to look at Jake and know exactly what he was thinking.

And right now he was thinking about sex. Not that that was particularly unusual as it was what he thought about most of the time. Once again he'd stayed up until the early hours of the morning banging Lola on the balcony of her suite in the smartest hotel in Berlin as he gazed out at the sleekly modern Potsdamer Platz, still bisected by tranches of the graffiti-covered wall that for so long had divided the city. He wondered what the rest of the band would think if they knew about his little late-night sightseeing activity, but it didn't look like any of them had the slightest suspicion. He scanned the room and saw Mike lying flat-out on a sofa running his tongue along the edge of his moustache, his hair now lightened by the sun so he looked like the Cowardly Lion from *The Wizard of Oz*. Danny, Smudge and Chuck were engrossed in a game of table football, although Jake spotted Danny occasionally glancing up at Amina. In his eyes Jake recognized the look of a musician who'd been on the road with the same team for a few days and was starting to find anyone attractive. It was a feeling he knew well, not that he'd ever been so desperate as to have to consider anyone as plain-looking as Amina, who had all the sex appeal of a slug crawling over a rotten cabbage. He looked at her tapping away on her iPad, her eyes intermittently alighting on Danny. *Then again, maybe she could have that whole shy-wild thing going on . . .*

'Hi Jake,' smiled Sharonne, sliding into the seat next to him. 'How's it going?'

Now Sharonne was more Jake's kind of girl. Tall and slender, she had dick-liftingly good legs and a sassy vibe that he knew from experience usually translated into great sex. *And I've always had a thing about black chicks . . .*

'Hey,' he said, switching on his lazy grin. 'What's up?'

'Oh, you know, just kicking my heels until we're on. But this schedule is kind of insane. It's all work, work, work – and I'm starting to feel like a caged animal.' She licked her lips in a not particularly subtle way but Jake didn't care; he'd never been a big one for subtlety.

'Well, I think we're off tonight – and this is meant to be a kick-ass city . . . Maybe me and you should go out for a drink or something?'

As he said the words, he knew there was no chance he'd be able to break free of Lola for an entire evening. They'd been sleeping together for less than two weeks and already she expected him to come to her room every night – and was showing the first signs of getting clingy. Sure, she was great fun and their sex life was off-the-scale, but she always tried snuggling up to him afterwards, even though he'd made it quite clear he didn't do cuddles as they annoyed the hell out of him. And she'd started nagging him about smoking weed, panicking that if anyone searched her room and found his stash, the story would leak to the press and her reputation would suffer. Jake couldn't help thinking it was selfish of her to hang all her anti-drugs shit on him. *Like it's my problem if her ass gets busted. What am I, her boyfriend?*

He remembered that she'd called him just that when they'd been having sex on their last night in Paris. He'd had to break his stroke mid-flow to tell her he didn't do relationships, but after the conversation he'd felt relieved he'd spelled it out so forcefully. It wouldn't be his fault now if she wanted to fantasize about him changing – or her somehow changing him. *And anyway,* he thought, eyeing up Sharonne, *the erect cock has no conscience . . .*

'OK,' she drawled, her eyes flashing as if she understood him completely, 'let's go for a drink. That'd be cool.'

This was the kind of connection Jake loved – one in which both parties knew exactly where they stood. Some psychology student he'd dated back in the States had tried to analyse him once, coming out with a load of crap about him using casual sex to 'narcotize deep-seated anxieties about being hurt by a woman'. He'd been so desperate for a blow job he'd had to play along and listen to her spout shit, bombarding him with questions about his childhood in Buffalo. He'd ended up confessing that his dad routinely cheated on his mom while he was away working as a sales rep, leaving her needy and desperate, smothering the children with an affection he found repulsive and had found repulsive in women ever since. The girl had concluded some bullshit about him 'internalizing the models of male and female behaviour' he was brought up with and going on to repeat them himself. He thought about it now and had to admit that maybe she had a point. But the truth was, Jake wasn't remotely interested in finding out why he was the way he was. And he wasn't remotely interested in changing. The truth was, he quite *liked* the way he was. And there were plenty of girls out there who did too – Sharonne being one of them.

'Well, let's keep it on the down-low,' he breathed, leaning into her ear. 'You know what these things can be like – and we don't want people talking.'

Sharonne nodded with a knowing grin.

'Don't want people talking about what?' snapped Lola, standing over them with her hands on her hips.

Uh-oh, thought Jake. *Here we go . . .*

'Oh, hi Lola,' he chirped, without losing his calm for a second. 'We were just talking about Amina and Danny. They've been making eyes at each other all day.'

'Oh, right,' Lola stammered, sitting on the chair on the other side of him. 'I hadn't noticed.'

'Yeah but they're both quite shy,' Sharonne cooed, 'which is why we were just saying we're going to pretend we haven't seen anything.'

Lola looked up and saw Amina catch Danny's gaze, distracting him from the game and causing him to let through a goal.

'Get in!' roared Smudge, pounding his fist into the air. 'Good old Smudge takes the lead!'

'Anyway,' Sharonne went on, 'if you don't mind I need to make a quick phone call. I'll see you guys later.'

They both smiled as she slipped away.

'So what you up to tonight, darlin'?' Lola asked once they

were on their own. 'It looks like we've got a night off. Fancy room service at mine?'

'Actually, I'm not sure I can tonight.'

The look of disappointment on Lola's face registered like a warning signal – as if her little outburst of jealousy towards Sharonne hadn't set sirens blaring already. 'You what?' she huffed. 'Why not?'

'Well, it's just that—'

'Lola,' Harvey interrupted, stepping towards them. He was accompanied by a dull-looking exec who was wearing glasses with those transitional lenses, which had gone into total blackout even though he was only standing under a sixty-watt light bulb. 'Can I introduce you to Mathias Muckenfuss? He's Head of Distribution at the record company here in Berlin.'

'Hiya,' Lola beamed, standing up to shake his hand. 'Great to meet you, darlin'.'

'Good to meet you too, Lola. We're very excited to have you with us in Germany.'

Lola slid back into her seat as Mathias began trotting out sales figures and distribution plans for the next quarter. 'Oh my God,' she cooed, eyeing him with an expression of the utmost fascination, 'that's blatantly amazing.'

As he droned on, Jake became aware of her hand sliding under the table and feeling its way over to his crotch. His mouth twitched slightly as she undid his fly and wriggled her fingers through the gap to start stroking his rapidly swelling cock. *Man, this is horny. This is so freakin' horny!*

'Germany has now overtaken the UK to become the biggest market for recorded music in Europe,' Mathias rattled on in his formal, heavily accented English.

'Which is why we're so pleased to be here,' Harvey quipped, 'and why we've given Germany such priority in the campaign.'

'Absolutely!' echoed Lola, her hand now expertly working its way up and down Jake's fully erect dick. His eyes focused on the exec's thin lips, which began to form abstract shapes as Jake zoned out of his words. He had to concentrate all his energies on stopping himself from whimpering with pleasure.

Damn, Lola's good at this, he thought, his legs splaying on the seat and his mouth twisting into a smile. Maybe he'd been a little hasty when he'd thought about telling her to back off earlier. Maybe he'd have a quick word with Sharonne and make up some excuse about tonight so he could be with Lola instead.

Because he had no doubt Sharonne would keep. And he wasn't through with Lola just yet.

*

'Kerfuffle,' said Belle.

'Codswallop,' said Scarlett.

'Canoodle,' said Trixie.

Lola and her Style Council were in the dressing room of a TV chat show in Stockholm. Already tiring of a seemingly end-less round of interviews, they were coming up with suggestions for a code word she had to somehow smuggle into today's live chat. And each time she mentioned it the girls would down a shot of vodka backstage.

'Oh I know!' yelped Trixie. 'How about "rambunctious"?'

'Yeah!' they all agreed. 'See if you can get *that* one in!'

'Wait a minute,' said Lola. 'What does that actually mean?'

They looked at her blankly.

'Maybe it's best if I stick with "kerfuffle".'

The girls began flitting around her, putting the finishing touches to her clothes, hair and make-up. Lola looked at herself in the mirror and could see that the cumulative lack of sleep was starting to show. Jake had come to her hotel room again last night and once again they'd stayed up until the early hours having sex, this time in an antique four-poster bed that for some reason had driven him wild. The problem was, even though she was trying her hardest not to, she knew she was starting to fall for him. On their last night in Paris she'd made the mistake of calling him her boyfriend and he'd instantly lost his hard-on. A full-on heavy had ensued — he'd accused her of pressurizing him into something he wasn't ready for and she'd spent most of the next day feeling guilty. At the time she'd plunged deep into a ditch of disappointment, but she'd since reassured herself that some men just weren't ready to get serious straight away and needed easing into a relationship. Which was why she'd resolved to be just the kind of low-maintenance, up-for-it girlfriend Jake wanted until she'd *made* him fall for her.

That had certainly been her strategy when she'd given in to his demands for increasingly athletic sex last night. But now she'd spent the day feeling like the old hag from a Disney cartoon. And her concentration was so low she was seriously worried about being able to hold a straight conversation with the chat-show host, never mind sneaking in secret words. She stifled a yawn.

'Hello, hello,' crowed Scarlett. 'What were we up to last night then?'

'Nothing. I just stayed up late watching a film, that's all.'

'Bollocks!' said Trixie. 'Lola Grant, you can't lie to save your life.'

Lola tried keeping a straight face but couldn't help herself breaking into a smirk.

'Come on, girl,' cooed Belle, putting down her can of hairspray and folding her arms. 'Spill!'

Lola wasn't sure she could keep her secret much longer; hiding her relationship with Jake was proving a real struggle. *If I just tell the girls, it'll make things so much easier . . .*

After making them all promise not to tell anyone, she admitted she and Jake had spent pretty much every night together for two weeks – and she was totally hooked. The girls were rapt.

'Oh my God, when did you first shag him?'

'Has it been good sex?'

'Does he have a big dick? *Tell* me he has a big dick!'

She answered pretty much all of their questions, her face blazing with a mixture of joy and excitement. And as she did so, she realized she didn't feel tired anymore.

Of course what she didn't tell them was that Jake had repeatedly stressed he didn't do relationships. Or that he'd been totally disrespectful when she'd asked him not to smoke weed and leave it lying around her room. Or that she was starting to be racked by a paralysing fear that one day he'd dump her. She felt a shiver of shame as she remembered how just the other day she'd been reduced to wanking him off under a table to keep him interested.

'Well, I think it's totes amazing,' crooned Scarlett.

'Absolutely,' agreed Belle. 'I'm sure you two will be really happy.'

'Big time!' chirped Trixie. 'And I'm so jealous that you've seen his dick!'

They erupted into a fit of filthy giggling and picked up their tools to get back to work.

'How come you all know him so well anyway?' asked Lola.

'Oh, you know, he comes in to see us quite a bit and we do his hair and make-up sometimes.'

Lola furrowed her brow. '*Jake?* You do *Jake's* hair and make-up? But I thought he wasn't bothered about that kind of thing.'

'Maybe he wasn't – until he met you.'

'Maybe he's just trying to impress you.'

'Maybe he's not quite as cool as he likes to make out.'

Lola nodded as she thought about what they said. For the last few days she'd been winding herself up into a nervous wreck thinking Jake was losing interest in her – or that all he was interested in was sex. But from what the girls were saying now it seemed he really did like her. *I'll just have to be a bit more patient with him,* she thought, her resolve strengthening. She cast her mind back to last night and the look on Jake's face as he'd entered her again and again. Surely he felt the same way she did? And how could a feeling so strong not eventually blast through his resistance?

She noticed Trixie yawn and the other two quickly followed suit.

'Eh-eh,' she piped, 'it looks like I wasn't the only one who stayed up late last night.'

For the next ten minutes, Belle, Scarlett and Trixie entertained her with stories of yet another raucous night out, including a long anecdote that ended with Trixie being fingered over a barrel by a colour-blind florist. Once their laughter had died down, the girls tried persuading Lola to go out with them that evening.

'Oh come on,' cooed Scarlett, 'we'll have such a laugh.'

Lola wasn't convinced; she really needed to catch up on her sleep and she wasn't sure how she felt about leaving Jake on his own.

'Chill out!' trilled Belle. 'I'm sure he can look after himself for one night.'

Lola didn't give in; she reminded them that they all had to catch a flight to Amsterdam first thing in the morning.

'Exactly!' fizzed Trixie. 'Which means we'll have plenty of time to sleep on the plane.'

'And Tiny's coming too,' said Scarlett, 'so he'll make sure we all get home OK.' Tiny was Lola's head of security – so-called because he was nearly seven foot tall and about the same size as a Ford Transit.

There was a pause as Lola thought it over.

Trixie raised an eyebrow. 'And you know Swedish men are supposed to have the biggest dicks in Europe?'

'Oh all right, all right!' Lola said, feigning a look of ex-asperation.

They all cheered.

'But I can't stay out late,' she added, raising her hands in defeat.

'Course not,' Belle reassured her. 'We'll be in bed by mid-night.'

'Yeah, yeah, yeah,' smiled Lola. 'Course we will. Now what was that word again?'

'Kerfuffle.'

'How appropriate,' quipped Lola. Although, if she knew the girls as well as she thought she did, something told her she'd need a much stronger word to describe what they were going to get up to.

*

Freddy gazed in horror at the YouTube clip of Lola Grant staggering out of a Swedish nightclub surrounded by a group of bedraggled girls. It was broad daylight, so the clip must have been filmed during the early hours of the morning. He couldn't help flinching as he watched Lola miss her footing and then tumble down the flight of stone steps, at one point almost flipping over a central handrail, only to land in a crumpled heap at the bottom, her legs bent open to reveal her underwear. As an enormous black guy in a dark suit stepped in to scoop her up, the camera started shaking and the clip came to an abrupt end. Freddy saw that it had already been viewed by nearly half a million people, even though it had only been posted earlier that morning. He hoped Lola hadn't seriously hurt herself. He shook his head and put down his smartphone. *Oh Lola, what are you playing at?*

He was sitting in the afternoon meeting in the Channel 3 newsroom, trying not to get involved as his colleagues discussed a bomb that had exploded in Baghdad, killing fifty Iraqis. At around the same time another bomb had gone off in the US, although it had only injured a few people. While the Washington correspondent had already been dispatched to cover that story and the plan was to sub-anchor the entire programme from the crime scene, for some reason there weren't any plans to even mention the more serious explosion in Iraq.

'I just don't think it's very interesting,' dismissed Hugh Badcock.

Freddy shifted forward in his seat. 'So how many people have to die before we cover a bomb in Iraq?'

Hugh looked at the head of foreign news, Colin Duffer, a balding fifty-something who panted like a carthorse with emphysema and had such strong fag breath you could smell it across the newsroom. 'How many did you say had died again, Col?'

'Fifty,' came the gravelly voiced reply.

'Then fifty-five,' Hugh answered calmly.

Freddy did his best not to look exasperated.

'Anyway,' Hugh went on, 'don't you worry about Iraq, boyo. What's the story with this footage of Lola Grant falling down stairs?'

'Oh nothing,' he shrugged, desperate to play it down. 'She just had an accident after a heavy night, like.'

'But didn't she miss a flight to Amsterdam?' asked a producer.

'And hasn't she had to pull out of some big show?' added another.

'And what about that tweet she sent a few hours ago?' came a voice behind him.

Freddy had read the tweet as soon as it had appeared. 'Blatantly feel like shit,' Lola had written. 'Do you think you can actually die of a hangover?'

'Well, she's obviously suicidal,' said Hugh. 'And I think it's a great story.'

'She's doing a Justin Bieber!'

'More like a Britney Spears!'

'Make that a Lindsay Lohan!'

As Freddy watched his colleagues whip themselves up into a frenzy of excitement, his stomach lurched in disgust. How could they all be so keen to exploit Lola's misfortune? Well, he wouldn't let them do it to her – especially not when he'd have to appear on national television fronting the attack.

'I think we should blame the government,' hissed Janine Jury, taking a sharp swig from her can of Diet Coke. 'Surely we can broaden out the story to do a disco about binge-drinking and feral girls roaming the streets? I mean, what's the government doing about it? That's what I want to know.'

'I'm sorry,' Freddy managed firmly, 'but I just don't think Lola Grant getting pissed is a big story.'

'Aha!' said Hugh. 'So the rumours are true then . . .'

'What rumours?'

'That you're shagging her.'

Freddy rolled his eyes. He hadn't seen Lola since she'd shouted out to him from the stage in Hyde Park two weeks ago. As she wasn't due back in the UK for another couple of weeks, he was already starting to worry about things fizzling out. The idea that he was somehow shagging her was nothing short of preposterous. Not that it hadn't crossed his mind – on many an occasion. Although unfortunately there was zero chance of it happening just yet. And there'd be even less chance if he made fun of her drunken accident on tonight's programme. 'No, Hugh, I'm not shagging Lola Grant.'

'Well then what's the problem? Surely you can give us a fat minute?'

'The problem is, on my desk it's all about relationships. And I do get on well with Lola, yeah. So I don't want to balls things up now and miss out on potential stories in the future. I mean, it's not as if this is an exclusive or anything – everyone's seen that footage already.'

Just as Hugh was opening his mouth to reply, Spike stepped in to stop him. 'Just a minute,' he began, looking at his mobile. 'Something's coming in from the wires.'

'Let's hear it, bro.'

Freddy cringed. He knew that Spike hated Hugh calling him 'bro' almost as much as he hated being called 'boyo'.

'Cooper Kelly's just died in LA,' Spike read. 'The family's releasing a statement.'

Cooper Kelly was an octogenarian Hollywood legend who'd been starring in hit films since the 1950s, as well as frequently recasting the role of his wife and in the process siring an entire acting dynasty.

'That's great news!' chorused the full complement of Freddy's colleagues.

'It looks like your girlfriend's off the hook,' added Hugh Badcock.

'Didn't Cooper Kelly shag Marilyn Monroe?' asked Janine Jury.

'No, it was Jayne Mansfield,' gasped Colin Duffer with a blast of fag breath.

'But I always thought it was Lana Turner,' chimed in the now unfeasibly pregnant weather girl Dolly Dawson.

'Actually,' sighed Freddy, 'I think you'll find he shagged all of them.'

'Great,' said Hugh, clapping his hands together. 'In that case, forget the films – let's hear about the shags. I want three minutes, Freddy. Let's make some noise!'

Freddy nodded, too worn down to protest that it might be worth mentioning Cooper's three Oscars rather than just the famous women he'd shagged. Ordinarily he hated doing obituaries but on this occasion he was relieved to have escaped appearing on screen predicting Lola's downfall – especially as tomorrow was the weekend and by Monday the story would have blown over.

He only hoped she didn't do anything else stupid in the meantime.

*

Gloria hit Play and felt a smile tickle her cheeks as she watched Lola tumble down the stairs. She just about managed to hold in her giggles when she saw her flip over the handrail and then carry on falling. But when she watched her land in a heap, exposing her underwear to the world, she couldn't stop herself from laughing out loud. On the next table a pair of badly dressed American tourists looked up and tutted.

She was sitting by the canal outside a café in Amsterdam watching the clip on her laptop. She saw that it had already been viewed by nearly a million people and laughed again as she read some of their comments below.

'I'll have what she's having!' joked one.

'That's more coordinated than some of her dance moves!' said another.

'Shame she didn't break her neck!' read Gloria's favourite.

The funny thing was, she'd only decided to slip her foot under Lola's ankle on the spur of the moment. She'd actually been hoping to inflict more physical damage; from what she'd heard today, Lola had got away with nothing more than heavy bruising. But Gloria hadn't spotted the fan waiting outside the club with his camera phone. And she was pretty sure that the damage done by his little film had exceeded anything she'd imagined possible. She took a sip of her coffee. She had no idea tagging along on a girls' night out could be so much fun.

Now that she thought about it, she had no idea being a bitch could be such fun either. It was a realization that had first hit her when Lola had asked her to deliver the pair of party passes to Freddy Jones after the gig at Hyde Park and she'd pretended she couldn't find him. She'd been surprised at how easily lying had come to her – and how good she was at it.

She pressed the Play button and watched the clip through again to make sure you couldn't tell it had been her tripping up Lola – and to check that she hadn't laughed as she'd tumbled down the stairs. But no, she'd kept a straight face and Lola was so unsteady as she emerged from the club she was dragging her feet and stepping on everyone's toes. Her eyes sparkled as she realized she was in the clear.

She gave a little start as a pair of teenage girls raced past on their bikes, clattering over the cobbles and ringing their bells at each other. She closed her laptop with a gratifying click.

Gloria had never thought of herself as a bitch before, but it looked like she was falling head-first into the role – and playing it to perfection.

*

The car sped past St Peter's Square, skimmed the side of the Castel Sant'Angelo and then crossed the river to begin rolling its way through the streets of Rome. Harvey wound down his blacked-out window and tried to breathe in the city. He was hit by a blast of scorching hot air and immediately wound it up again, keen to retreat to the comfort of the efficiently cooled car.

He was ensconced in a plush leather seat next to Lola and across from Barbara and Amina, while Tiny was squeezed into the ordinarily ample passenger seat up front and the others were following in a convoy of vehicles. Lola and the band were due to perform a short set at a music festival in the Villa Borghese. It was a big deal as the show would be broadcast live on Italian television and Lola was the headline act. But after seeing the state she'd been in on the YouTube clip and having to pull her out of a TV show in Amsterdam because she was too hung-over, Harvey only hoped she was up to it.

Come to think of it, he hoped everyone was up to it. A yawn spread its way around the car and he noticed that Barbara was doing her best not to nod off, her cheek sliding off her fist with a rhythm he couldn't help finding amusing. Clearly by this stage of the promo tour everyone in the team was starting to feel the strain of a schedule he was beginning to think might have been a little too packed from the start. He too gave into a yawn and squeezed his eyes tight to try and clear his foggy head. He'd just flown in from a difficult meeting in LA with the management team behind soft drink Twinkle to finalize their deal to sponsor Lola's tour – and was feeling flattened by jet lag.

He looked out of the blacked-out window and caught a glimpse of something that may or may not have been the Piazza Navona. He couldn't remember much of city as he hadn't visited since Cleen Teenz had crashed in and out to play a couple of gigs, and he'd had to spend most of that trip bribing doctors to prescribe the morning-after pill to fans their security had plucked out of the audience and invited back to the band's hotel. Either that or drunkenly chasing around after a handsome TV producer called Alessandro he'd met back-stage at a gig, who never seemed to take off his sunglasses and always had a jumper draped over his shoulders even though it was the height of summer.

But Harvey did also remember that the city he'd experi-enced back then had been achingly beautiful. The Colosseum, the Spanish Steps, the Trevi Fountain . . . He looked out of the car window now and caught the occasional flash but was so disorientated by a combination of jet lag and drunken mem-ories that he wasn't sure what he was seeing. Hopefully he'd get the chance to do a bit of exploring later when Spike arrived to watch the gig then take a short break. Harvey hadn't seen him for nearly a fortnight and the next few days would give him a chance to make up for it. He planned to make every-thing wonderfully romantic, in so far as he could whilst also fulfilling his various work commitments. For the moment, though, his main priority was looking after Lola – and making sure she didn't descend into freefall.

He looked across and gave her a warm smile. 'How you feel-ing, Trouble?'

'Oh, you know – like shit. I'm blatantly knackered, darlin'.'

'Well, hang on in there. We're nearly done now – only Spain to go.'

She nodded dolefully.

'Lola,' he asked gently, 'is everything all right?'

Her eyes flickered nervously onto Barbara and Amina, who

by now were both fast asleep. Amina's cheek was squashed against the window, a trail of dribble sliding down and pooling on the leather upholstery. 'Yeah, why?'

'I don't know. I just wondered if you wanted to tell me anything.'

Like whether I'm right to suspect you've been sleeping with Jake.

'About what?' snapped Lola. 'What are you on about, Harvey? Have people been talking?'

Uh-oh. Looks like I'm right.

'No, of course people haven't been talking,' he replied calmly. 'Well, no more than they always do on this kind of trip. But I've obviously seen the YouTube clip from Stockholm.'

She flashed him what he could tell was a forced smile. 'Oh yeah, isn't it hilarious? Me and the girls couldn't stop pissing ourselves.'

'Unfortunately the marketing guys at Twinkle didn't see the funny side.' Harvey didn't have the heart to tell her that he'd had to spend most of the last twenty-four hours trying to persuade them not to pull out of the deal, listening to them rant about Lola 'polluting the brand' and causing 'reputational damage'. He'd eventually managed to smooth things over but only on the strictest promise that Lola wouldn't be making a spectacle of herself again – and it was his job now to make sure that she didn't. 'Don't worry,' he smiled, 'everything's fine but I think they'd prefer it if we toned down the partying for a bit and concentrated on the music.'

He tried not to wince in anticipation of Lola's reaction. He already knew his words would go down like a soprano on a stag night.

'What do you mean?' she practically spat. 'I was only having a laugh! That's what I'm like – and I thought they were into the real me. I thought they liked me being all wild and rebellious?'

Harvey thought back to all the trouble he'd got into with Cleen Teenz and his vow never again to mount a fake front for any of his acts. Obviously he was way past that point with Lola, whose true self had been riotously romping its way through the tabloids for months. But it was already way too late to find another sponsor for the tour – especially one with as much clout in the US. He needed to make this deal work. And besides, they were booked to shoot both the ad campaign and the TV commercial shortly after arriving back in the UK. *Assuming Lola doesn't do anything to sabotage the deal first . . .*

'Lola! Don't get wound up about this. Honestly, it's not that big a deal. All we need to do is keep them sweet – everything else is going brilliantly.' He reminded her that the finished video for *Tramp* was looking amazing and about to premiere online at the same time as the single went to radio. As if that weren't enough, *Lost in Love* was still top five in most territories, *Trouble* was the biggest-selling album in Europe and tickets for the tour had sold out in minutes. 'Let's just enjoy all the success and not do anything to rock the boat.'

Lola smiled thinly but didn't respond.

The car slowed down as they approached the venue, hitting a speed bump which jerked Barbara and Amina awake. 'Ooops, sorry,' frowned Barbara as Amina wiped the drool from her face. 'I must have nodded off.'

Harvey smiled fondly. He didn't like to say that certain people in the entourage *had* been talking – and he'd heard all about Barbara's fling with the German radio producer who'd then followed her to Amsterdam, and Amina's ongoing involvement with Lola's guitarist Danny. It was great news that both of them had found someone and he knew it wouldn't affect either of their work. 'Oh don't worry about it, Barb. Me and Lola were just saying how pleased we are that everything's going so well.'

Lola raised an eyebrow and wound down her blacked-out window. Straight away a crowd of fans spotted her and began calling her name.

'*Lola!*'

'*Ti amo Lola!*'

'*Sei stupenda Lola!*'

She waved at them and wound the window back up again but it was too late. The fans stormed over the barriers holding them on the pavement and rushed towards the car, banging on the windows so it began to rock gently. In an instant, Tiny locked all the doors and windows.

'OK everyone, keep calm,' he boomed from the front seat. He said something to the driver in Italian and stepped out to take charge of the situation.

'Oh my God,' screeched Lola as his door clunk shut. 'What's going on?'

'It's all right,' breathed Harvey. 'We just have to go slowly, then we don't run anyone over. Tiny's probably guiding the car through, that's all.'

He tried to look out of the window but so many fans were squeezed up against the car that he couldn't make out what was happening. They inched forwards but the rocking motion was growing more and more violent.

'OK, so I really don't like this now,' stammered Lola, her face draining of colour. 'I'm actually starting to shit myself.'

'Don't worry, doll,' managed Barbara, although her hands were shaking so much it was obvious she was worrying herself. 'We'll be through it in a minute.'

Lola scraped her fingers through her hair. 'But it's getting worse, Barb, it's getting worse!'

'All right, let's all just try and stay calm,' Harvey said, having to raise his voice over the sound of shouting outside. Amina had put her head between her legs and was starting to hyperventilate. The car came to a stop.

Harvey could feel his heart rate quicken as the rocking continued.

Lola snatched hold of his hand. 'Oh make it stop, Harvey. Please make it stop!'

What can I do? What can I do?

'It'll stop soon, Lola,' he promised lamely. 'We're nearly inside now. Just everybody try not to freak out.'

He could feel the adrenaline surge inside him. The four of them fell silent and panic bounced between them. The car was now rocking so violently Harvey was sure it was being lifted off the floor.

'Lola, Lola, Lola!'

Lola scrunched up her face and opened her mouth to scream.

At that second a police siren sounded and the rocking came to a sudden halt. Harvey looked through the window and could see most of the fans stepping back as the police moved in.

'Oh my God,' exhaled Lola. 'Oh my God.'

Once again the car began to crawl forward. Through the windscreen he saw two huge iron gates swing open and the car zipped through, swept across a gravel path and crunched to a stop.

They all breathed an enormous sigh of relief.

'Phew!'

'I'm so glad that's over!'

'Thank fuck for that!'

Harvey noticed that Lola was looking flushed, almost as if she'd just stepped off a roller coaster. She gave them a little smirk and her eyes glistened. 'Well, I don't know about you guys but I quite enjoyed that!'

Harvey looked at her in disbelief. He found her words more frightening than the experience of being mobbed. The four of them had just guzzled a big gulp of danger, a danger he knew too well some people found delicious. And it was quite obvious Lola was one of them. He could only hope the experience hadn't left her craving more.

*

Lola brushed her teeth for the third time that morning but still couldn't shift the taste of stale booze and decay. She seemed to be spending all her time lately either drunk or hung-over. She was so tired she felt like she was trying to drive up a hill with the handbrake on and she looked in the mirror and saw she had eyes like piss-holes in the snow. She padded back into the bedroom and stood facing her assistant.

'Where's that dog?' she asked.

Amina looked puzzled. 'What dog?'

'The one that shat in my mouth.'

Lola gave a little laugh but knew that no amount of making fun of her hangover would be enough to lift her gloom. Which was a real shame, as she was in Madrid, one of her favourite cities in Europe. She sloped across the luxurious, painfully fashionable hotel suite and plonked herself down on a bed so big it could have comfortably slept her whole band. Outside, she could hear a crowd of fans chanting.

'¡Lola, Lola!'

'¡Te quiero Lola!'

'¡Eres maravillosa Lola!'

While she knew she should find this kind of attention hugely flattering, she could only experience it as a thundering din that added to her headache. And was making her feel depressed – because she knew she didn't deserve it. *Oh why am I making such a mess of things?*

Whichever way she looked at it, she really was making a mess of things. She felt desperately exhausted and emptied out by a combination of overwork, overdrinking and overdoing it on the late-night sex. Her voice was suffering and her last few performances had been offensively mediocre. She had no idea what day of the week it was and on TV last night she'd made a joke about being in Italy when she was actually appearing on the most important awards show in Spain. She'd been so embarrassed she'd told the girls she wasn't going out and had guilt-tripped Jake into joining her for a quiet night in. She'd hung the *No molestar* sign on her door so it looked like she was sleeping and crept over to his room, but the two of them had ended up raiding his minibar and then spending so long having sex in his space-age shower that her skin was still shrivelled up like an eighty-year-old scrotum. The worst thing was that, when she'd left Jake first thing this morning, she couldn't find her room anywhere as all the corridors looked exactly the same and she couldn't remember the number. She'd had to creep down to reception in her dressing gown, but as she and the girls always invented funny pseudonyms when she was checking into hotels and she had no recollection of the latest, the staff couldn't work out where she was supposed to be sleeping. In the end, she'd had to ask them to wake up Amina, who'd come down to find her but now obviously knew that she was seeing Jake. And judging from the sympathetic looks she'd been giving her all morning, she really didn't think it was a good idea.

'Would you like an orange juice?' Amina asked, cocking her head as if she were talking to a wounded puppy.

'No thanks.'

'A coffee?'

'Nah, can't face it.'

'How about some breakfast?'

Lola was suddenly struck by an idea for a perfect hangover cure. 'Ooh, you know what I really fancy?'

'Yeah?'

'Some Turkish Delight.'

'*Turkish Delight*? But we're in Spain.'

'I know but they sell it everywhere, don't they? Isn't it, like, international?'

She grabbed hold of her phone and looked up the Spanish translation – *lokum* was what it came up with, which didn't sound particularly Spanish, but what would she know? She was suddenly overwhelmed by a desperate urge to sneak out of the hotel herself and find some. How difficult could it be?

She didn't carry cash when she was away working as everything was bought for her and brought to her, something she hated as it made her feel trapped. *But I'm pretty sure I've got a credit card somewhere . . .*

She convinced Amina she'd gone off the idea and managed to get rid of her by pretending she was going back to bed. She wasn't needed for a good hour, which surely would be enough time to track down some Turkish Delight on the streets of one of Europe's busiest cities. She pulled on a grey tracksuit she'd brought for slumming it around hotel rooms and slipped on a black leather captain's hat, chunky Converse trainers and a pair of wraparound sunglasses that hid most of her face. She had a quick look in the mirror to check she was unrecognizable and then skipped downstairs, boldly sauntering past the crowd of fans.

'Who are you here for?' she asked one casually.

'Lola Grant,' came the comically accented reply. 'We *love* her!'

She smiled and strode ahead, breathing in the air of freedom. She snaked along a street of tall, pastel-coloured buildings and emerged into what she knew from photos was the Plaza Mayor; she immediately recognized the pretty pink walls and shuttered windows, the cobblestoned ground and ornate baroque lanterns. She spotted what looked like a bakery and stepped inside.

'*Hola!*' she managed brightly, almost immediately exhausting her knowledge of Spanish. '*Lokum?*'

'*No, perdona señorita,*' frowned an old woman with dyed black hair and shocking white roots, '*no hay.*'

Lola didn't understand a single syllable but could at least

identify the word 'no'. She walked on, trying another two shops but receiving the same answer. She wished she spoke Spanish – then she could ask someone properly. She felt a stab of guilt that she didn't, considering she was actually half Spanish. Not that her mum had ever told her that but she'd always assumed she must be, especially since she'd been given a Spanish name. *Or should I say saddled with a Spanish name so I'd never be able to forget I was a mistake? She probably got it from that stupid Barry Manilow song – I bet it was the only Spanish name she could think of.* She tried to swallow her bitterness and remembered she was supposed to call her mum to find out how she was getting on in rehab. But she couldn't face it right now.

She strolled on through the streets and soon came to another square, which she recognized as the Puerta del Sol. She looked on the ground for the *kilómetro cero*, which she seemed to remember from a school project represented the centre of Spain. She found it in front of the clock tower and crouched down to get a better look. As she squatted and stared at the map of Spain, she found herself wondering where in the country her dad might live. Her imagination began racing and she revisited her childhood fantasies about what he might be like. Except that now she couldn't help thinking he was probably just as much of a tramp as some of the men she'd dated – like the one she was dating now. *Oh my God, do me and Mum have the same taste in men? Is that why she won't ever talk about my dad?*

She closed her eyes and pictured Jake's face last night when their bodies had almost violently come together and his eyes had bored into her with a passionate fury. But soon the image was replaced by the memory of him slowing down mid-flow to send a quick text, which Lola was pretty sure she'd seen addressed to Sharonne. But she hadn't wanted to ask as she couldn't face the idea of being subjected to yet another lecture about him not looking for a relationship. And she couldn't pretend to herself anymore – there was no longer any question that she'd fallen in love with him.

Oh what am I playing at?

She'd got herself into such a mess she couldn't even talk to her best friend because she couldn't bear him to realize how stupid she'd been. Instead she'd been reduced to sidling over to Belle, Scarlett and Trixie whenever she needed reassurance that Jake was actually a great guy, reassurance that she knew was hollow as they only ever told her exactly what she wanted to hear. She straightened herself up but her body felt like a dead weight and she faltered and had to grab onto a lamp post to steady herself. She felt totally alone and utterly desperate.

But still she couldn't bear the thought of giving up Jake. However low he made her feel, she wasn't sure she could exist without him. It suddenly struck her that her need for Jake was like an addict's need for a fix. She understood why so many pop stars sang about love being like a drug – and from out of nowhere felt a flicker of empathy for her mum. She stood in the Puerta del Sol, at the very centre of Spain, and finally understood just how tough it must be for her mum to fight her addiction. *Because being an addict is hard*, she admitted to herself. *It's really fucking hard.*

She sloped off in the direction of the hotel. Her mission had failed. She'd just have to do without her Turkish Delight.

*

'OK, Spike, speak to you soon,' said Harvey into his mobile as he looked out at the view of Barcelona in the early evening sunshine. A stream of strollers trickled their way down the tree-lined Rambla while the cable car cut across the sky above them. His eyes alighted on the towering monument to Christopher Columbus, the great explorer pointing out to sea in the direction of the new world he was leaving to discover. Harvey thought about their own trip to America in a few months' time and the dazzling rewards it could bring. This was Lola's chance to take her place alongside the biggest names in music. But before then she had a new single to promote and, most importantly, a whole arena tour of Europe to rehearse and then perform – and already he was worried about how she was coping with the frenzied work rate of spectacular success.

Spike's voice broke into his thoughts. 'Yeah, speak to you soon, man.'

'Oh, and Spike?' Harvey added.

'Yeah?'

'I love you.'

'I love you too, blud.'

Harvey looked at his phone and smiled. He was standing in the corridor of the hotel, pressed into the corner and squashed against the window – the spot that he'd worked out had the best reception. He and Spike had only just started saying 'I love you' to each other and it still gave him a little rush of happiness every time he heard it. He only wished Lola could experience the same thing rather than falling for men who always seemed to make her unhappy. Once they were back in the UK, he was going to have another crack at persuading her to go out on a date with Freddy Jones. He knew she fancied him and when he'd first mentioned fixing them up she'd promised she'd think about it, but since then she'd fobbed him off every time he'd brought up the subject. He couldn't help fearing it was because she was seeing Jake. *Which would explain a whole lot more besides . . .*

Just then he heard the sound of the lift doors opening and someone stepping out onto the marble floor and heading in the direction of Lola's room. He rounded the corner to see who it was. It was Jake.

Oh no! So I was right all along . . .

He watched with despair as Jake checked his reflection in a window and then rapped on Lola's door.

'Hey babe,' he called out, 'it's me!'

The door swung open and Lola's grinning face emerged. Over Jake's shoulder her eyes met Harvey's and her smile wilted. 'Oh. Hi, Harvey.'

Jake turned around to face him.

'All right?' Harvey murmured. He looked at Jake, whose eyes drifted down to the floor guiltily. *Stay calm, lad. Stay calm.*

Lola stepped out in her dressing gown and leant on the door frame. 'What are you doing here?' she asked Harvey.

He held up his phone. 'I was just making a quick call. The reception's better out here.'

'Oh right.'

There was a silence and Jake eased his weight from one foot to another.

Lola opened her mouth to speak. 'Jake was just coming over to—'

'It's all right,' Harvey interrupted, 'you don't have to say anything.'

Lola looked at him and hung her head. He hated her feeling this way. He hated her being in this position. And he hated Jake for putting her in it.

'Look, I just remembered,' Jake said coolly, 'I left something in my room. So if you guys don't mind, I'm actually going to shoot.'

'Course you are,' sneered Harvey. 'You come along and cause a load of trouble and then piss off to let other people pick up the pieces!'

Oops! That wasn't particularly calm.

'Harvey!' objected Lola.

'Dude, I don't know what you're talking about,' smirked Jake. 'But I really don't need this shit. I'm going down to find the others.' He walked over to the lift and pressed the call button.

'Jake!' Lola bleated. 'Don't go!'

'No, I'll see you some other time, babe,' he said, stepping through the doors. 'Things are getting way too heavy around here – and it's really not my bag.'

'Harvey!' she hissed once the doors had closed. 'What do you think you're doing?'

'Funnily enough I was going to ask you the same thing.'

'Oh all right, all right. So I've got off with Jake a few times. Why's that such a big problem?'

'You tell me, Lola. You're the one who's finding it a problem – you've been all over the place for the last few weeks.'

She threw up her hands. 'No I haven't. I've just been a bit tired, that's all. In case you haven't noticed, I've been working really hard.'

He looked behind him to check there was no one else in

the corridor. 'I know you have, Lola. But I also know how men like Jake can mess with your head – which really doesn't help things.'

She crossed her arms and gave an exaggerated sigh. 'Honestly, darlin', you're blowing this up into something way bigger than it is. I mean, Jake's blatantly really fit and everything but it's not as if we're going out with each other. I could stop seeing him any time I wanted.'

Harvey gave her a sceptical frown. 'Now you're sounding like an addict promising you can stop using.'

Lola visibly flinched.

'What's the matter?' asked Harvey. 'Are you all right?'

'Yeah, yeah, you just hit a raw nerve, that's all.'

'Oh I'm sorry. But I'm only looking out for you, Lola. And I'm not judging you or anything – I just don't want you to end up getting hurt.'

'I know, darlin'. But I promise I won't. I know exactly where I stand with Jake. And when it stops being fun I'll call it off.'

As she said the words, Harvey heard her conviction waver and he knew she was lying. He'd known it from the look on her face as Jake disappeared into the lift.

'Come on,' she went on, 'what can I do to prove it to you?'

He thought about it for a minute but didn't take long to come up with an answer.

'OK, if you and Jake aren't serious then presumably you're free to date other people?'

She nodded with a smile. 'Blatantly.'

'Well when we're back home, how about I line up that date with Freddy?'

'Fine,' she fired back without hesitation, 'no problem at all.'

'Right. Great.'

'Now is that everything? Because I need to get an early night.'

'Yeah, yeah, I think so. Night then.'

'Night, darlin'. See you in the morning.'

As he watched the door close, Harvey realized she'd gone without giving him a kiss. He swallowed but his throat had gone dry.

He walked back to his room and stopped to look out at Christopher Columbus. Now that he'd persuaded Lola to go on a date with Freddy he really hoped it would go well. He *needed* it to go well. Because if it didn't, he didn't dare think of the consequences.

7

Lola had been holding the can of Twinkle to her lips for so long she was worried her arm was starting to shake. She did her best to keep it still as she leaned seductively on an enormous papier-mâché moon that was hanging from the ceiling of a photography studio on an industrial estate somewhere near New Cross. All around her hundreds of little stars shimmered on a black velvet background. It wasn't particularly subtle but it was the image chosen for the new ad campaign for Twinkle – a campaign that would be fronted by Lola.

'Let's have a little giggle please!' said one of the photographers as the flashbulbs exploded.

'And a dash of mischief!' piped his partner.

Lola obliged, keen to do anything to please the company that would be coming up with the money to make her vision for a spectacular stage show a reality. Not to mention providing her with a priceless platform to launch her career in America.

'And how about a naughty grin?' asked one of the photographers.

'Course, darlin'.' She instantly switched on a grin she was convinced she'd already flashed five or six times during the last hour. 'Whatever you say.'

The stills for the campaign were being shot by Mark and Mark, an American gay couple who were the hottest names in international fashion photography and who Harvey had described as 'performance art'. Lola hadn't understood what he'd meant until this morning, when they'd skipped onto the set looking like twins in matching blue-and-white sailor suits, little cocked caps embroidered with anchors, and blue suede shoes decorated with diamanté studs. Trundling along ahead of them had been a so-ugly-it's-cute French bulldog with its own sailor hat perched on its head. The dog had been introduced as Nancy.

'Oh she's so lovely!' Lola had cooed.

'Urm, he's actually a boy,' one of the Marks had corrected her.

'Oh right,' she'd stuttered, suddenly getting the joke. 'Well in that case, *he's* so lovely!'

Lola spotted Nancy splayed out in the corner, oblivious to the sound of the latest dance remixes of music by Beyoncé, Britney Spears and will.i.am that came blasting out of the speakers around him.

And right now Lola needed the pounding beat to maintain her momentum. This was the third and final day of the Twinkle shoot and so far each day had dragged on for about twelve hours. The first two had been the hardest as they'd started by shooting the TV commercial, which had featured Lola wearing a dark green version of her currently violet halter-neck jumpsuit and catwalking through a similarly starry set towards the camera, where she'd stopped, taken a swig of Twinkle and promised the viewer, 'You too can twinkle like a star.' She hadn't really understood why they'd needed to record so many takes when her contribution had been pretty much the same throughout – in fact almost embarrassingly so, however hard she'd tried to vary it. But she'd done as she was told and was determined to do the same on today's stills shoot, which had a much more relaxed atmosphere and she hoped wouldn't last quite as long.

'And if you could just rest the can on your cheek,' suggested one of the photographers. 'That's it! And then close your eyes as if you're in ecstasy. Awesome!'

Earlier in the week Lola had arrived home from Spain and the next day had started band rehearsals for the *Trouble* tour. But the first session hadn't gone at all well. After Harvey had caught Jake visiting her room in Barcelona, Lola had become convinced her secret was out and everyone around her was gossiping. But then she'd only gone and made things worse when she'd caught Jake chatting to Sharonne, who was maniacally blinking at him like Bambi on speed, and had snapped at the two of them across the rehearsal room, no doubt increasing the tension bouncing around in every direction. This was exactly the kind of atmosphere that was supposed to develop towards the end of a tour – not before it had even started! It had been a relief to know that she'd be stepping away for a few days to film the Twinkle campaign. *Even if my arm is shaking like I've got the worst hangover ever.*

'That's great!' oozed one of the two Marks. 'Now if you don't mind holding your finger up to your lips – almost as if you're surprised by how good it tastes.'

Lola was just about to make a joke about how good it *didn't* taste when she remembered that a handful of Twinkle execs were somewhere on set monitoring the shoot. Harvey had promised to shadow them all day to take some of the heat off her, but even so she couldn't risk joking about what she really thought about Twinkle. She remembered the nickname Harvey had given her, the Mouth from the South, and wondered whether by keeping quiet she was compromising her policy of remaining true to herself or whether she'd simply developed a little maturity. It was a tough call and right now she was too tired to work out the answer.

The truth was, she hadn't had a day off in nearly a month and felt close to collapse. Not that she'd ever complain about working too hard when for years she'd only dreamed about being this successful; she still felt pathetically grateful when a magazine wanted to take her photograph, a journalist wanted to interview her or a TV producer liked her enough to book her on his show. And of course she knew that everyone else on her team was working hard too, but even so the band and backing singers often had time off if she was doing press or a chat show and her Style Council were usually dismissed if she was doing radio or print interviews. Only Amina worked as hard as she did. *Oh and Harvey,* she thought with a little frown.

But then again, Harvey set the working schedule – as Belle, Scarlett and Trixie had reminded her that morning when it had become obvious she was struggling to stay awake. 'You need to stand up for yourself a bit more,' they'd told her, 'and remind Harvey who the star is.' Of course that wasn't the kind of thing she'd ever do, especially not since the two of them had been united in building up her career from the very start. But she couldn't help thinking maybe the girls had a point. *Maybe Harvey should cut me a little slack – I can't work all the time and he should know I need the odd night out to let my hair down.* She spotted him feigning interest as he chatted to two strong-chinned, broad-shouldered Americans from Twinkle's head office. They certainly seemed perfectly happy with the way things were going. She wondered if Harvey had exaggerated their response to the YouTube clip of her falling down drunk in Stockholm. *What if he made the whole thing up just to try and scare me into behaving myself? And what's he doing getting me into the deal anyway if they only want some boring stiff who doesn't drink?*

'You know, Lola's perfect for us,' she heard one of the Americans tell him during a dip in the music. 'She's got that naughty edge but deep down you know she wouldn't step out of line.'

'Absolutely,' agreed his colleague, 'she's a little wild but you know she takes a stand against drugs and is ultimately wholesome.'

Lola bristled as she listened to the men speak as if she wasn't there – and felt her irritation grow as she watched Harvey nod his head in response. *'Wholesome'? Who are they calling 'wholesome'?*

The very mention of the word made her want to suddenly flash her boobs or knock back a whole bottle of vodka and run naked down Oxford Street – or have mad passionate sex with Jake on her roof garden in full view of the neighbours. *Oh wait a minute, we did that the other night . . .* Not that she'd seen Jake much since she'd got back from the promo tour – not since Harvey's little outburst in Barcelona. In fact, she'd seen so little of him she was starting to think he was avoiding her. Thankfully there'd been that one exception, but on that occasion she'd been so eager to please she'd agreed not only to having sex on the roof garden in full view of any prying neighbours but also letting him smoke a joint while they were at it. He'd ended up getting so stoned he'd spent the rest of the night telling her brain-bustingly boring stories about the different types of weed he'd smoked at different music festivals around the world, along with a detailed analysis of the high induced by each. She stifled a yawn at the memory of the conversation. It was a shame it wasn't enough to put her off him.

Oh it wasn't her fault she was in love with Jake. She'd tried everything she could to make herself *not* be in love with him but nothing seemed to work. And now she'd agreed to go for dinner tonight with Freddy, which was pretty stupid because she was only doing it to prove to Harvey that she wasn't in love with Jake, even though she was quite happy to admit to herself that she was. And the worst thing was that she'd actually really fancied Freddy, but now she'd be trying her best to resist him because it would mean going off Jake and she was terrified of losing him. She had no idea how she'd ended up in such a stupid situation. *Why do I always have to fuck everything up?*

'OK, can we be a bit sexy please?' asked one of the Marks. 'Kind of stroke the can a bit?'

As she complied with the instruction she shot a pained smile in the direction of Harvey and the Twinkle execs. *Oh I know the whole Jake thing's a disaster but I don't need anyone else to tell me.* Harvey's expression of concern only made her feel worse. And why should she have to put up with him criticizing her all the time – even if he was doing it for the right reasons? Surely one of the perks of being a star was that you could do what you liked and everyone else had to dance to your tune? *And anyway, what makes him think his life is so sorted? Do I go around criticizing his new boyfriend?*

'OK, that's awesome!' cheeped one of the photographers. 'Let's take a break and start again in ten!'

Lola put down the can of Twinkle and wriggled her right arm until it stopped shaking. She slid down from the fake moon and tried to land gracefully on the floor but stumbled and almost went over on her high heels. She looked up but thankfully no one had noticed. Not even Nancy, who was too busy lapping up a latte Mark and Mark had sent out for and then tipped into a bowl. Lola smiled at the dog as he slopped most of it onto the floor.

She looked over and saw that Harvey was still chatting away to the Americans. *Yeah,* she thought, *it might all be going brilliantly with his new boyfriend at the moment but it won't last long.* And when it did all start going wrong, Lola wouldn't gloat. She wouldn't say 'I told you so'. She'd do just what Harvey had done and express her concern. She'd tell him she only wanted what was best for him and was just looking out for him.

And let's see how he likes it.

*

Spike quickly glanced around the newsroom to check no one was looking and held out his hands in front of him. They were still shaking, even though it was mid-afternoon. He lodged them under his thighs and trained his eyes on his computer screen. *Oh when's this shit going to stop, man?*

He tried to read the same email three times but just couldn't concentrate. He felt gripped by a fear that any minute a huge news story would break and he'd be thrust onto the front line, where everyone would be able to see he was going through one of the worst coke and booze comedowns ever. He slouched so far down into his chair that he almost slid under his desk. He just wanted to disappear and hide away from everyone until the programme went on air – at which time he could slip away and collapse into his bed.

Of course Spike knew that if he were white, straight and posh, everyone in the newsroom would love him being hungover – he could just imagine them all queuing up at his desk to give him a pat on the back. Just the other day Hugh Badcock had got so shit-faced with one of the foreign correspondents at some awards show in Switzerland that they'd ended up missing their flight home. When they'd turned up for work the next morning they'd been greeted by a round of applause. But it was different for Spike; as the odd one out in several ways he had to be twice as good at his job as anyone else in the newsroom if he wanted to prove himself. He certainly couldn't risk anyone seeing the state he was in now – except Freddy.

A glass of something fizzy and fluorescent was plonked down in front of him. 'Come on, champ,' Freddy said, 'get this down you.'

As he raised it to his lips and drained the glass, Spike thought about all the booze he'd downed last night. His flatmate Serenity had texted him during the day to say she'd just heard she'd landed her dream job at her favourite magazine, *Heat*. She'd wanted to go out and celebrate but Spike knew from experience that Serenity's celebrations were always characterized by a complete absence of serenity. To try and limit the damage he'd suggested they go for a meal and they'd met after work in a gay restaurant in Soho called Meat and Two Veg – although neither of them had eaten much meat and certainly hadn't touched any veg. Instead, they'd worked their way through two bottles of champagne before moving on to a gay bar called Rod's, where they'd downed endless shots of vodka with a Brazilian go-go dancer Spike was pretty sure he'd once met on Grindr for a bout of post-club off-his-face sex. Once the dancer had worked them for free drinks and moved on to flirt with someone else, Spike and Serenity had clattered on to a dodgy fetish club called the Butt Hut, where they'd snorted so much coke they'd both been overwhelmed by an uncontrollable urge to have sex. It hadn't been long before Serenity had disappeared into the staff room with one of the bouncers and Spike had ended up going home with a horrendous blonde geezer he didn't even fancy, who he couldn't help thinking looked a bit like Myra Hindley.

Several hours into his crushingly miserable comedown he still hadn't worked out what had come over him. He let out a low moan as he remembered stumbling onto a nightbus outside the Myra Hindley lookalike's flat in Tottenham, then falling asleep and being woken up by the driver at the end of the route in Wandsworth. By the time he'd made it home to Brixton it had been 8 a.m. and he'd had to get ready for work, where he now sat shaking, sniffing and suffering – proper suffering.

Thankfully it was a heavy news day so the entertainment team had been left alone for a spot of forward-planning, which meant Freddy could work himself up about tonight's date with Lola while Spike cradled his comedown. His eyes darted around the room, paranoid that everyone was watching him. But they all seemed to be going about their business hypernormally, which for some weird reason only made him more edgy. A group of middle-aged secretaries dressed in Marks & Spencer's leopard-print were indulging in what they called their regular 'Friday sex talk', giggling girlishly as one of them reminisced about the time she'd drunk one vodka and orange too many, pulled a black man then screamed out loud when confronted by his 'massive willy'. Spike wondered what they'd say if he told them some of the things he'd got up to last night with the Myra Hindley lookalike. He squirmed at the memory. *Oh what was I doing, man?*

'Any better?' asked Freddy softly.

'Not really, blud,' whined Spike. 'I still feel a bit wavey, to be honest. And I just can't get over how stupid I've been.'

'Yeah well, don't beat yourself up about it. We've all been there, you know.'

'No,' Spike corrected him, 'I'm not sure we *have* all been there.'

He watched Freddy nod solemnly as he ran through some of the more shameful details of his night out, ending by shaking his own head in disbelief. He'd no idea how he'd been able to cheat on Harvey so casually. Everything had been going so well between them; they'd had a brilliant time in Rome, wandering through the streets arm in arm and snogging like teenagers in the audience of Lola's concert in the Villa Borghese. Since Harvey had come home they'd spent all their free time together – except last night, when Spike had had a few drinks and suddenly been overwhelmed by a desire to shatter his happiness into tiny pieces. *What if I've gone and fucked up the best relationship I've ever had?*

And the worst thing was it was all so predictable. He was sure Harvey's friends thought it would only be a matter of time until Spike showed his true colours and started behaving badly. And now here he was, doing exactly that. But the weird thing was that he hadn't even wanted to – it was like he'd been somehow driven to it against his will. He wondered whether he was just a bad person, forever destined to ruin everything that was good in his life. The idea of his own badness felt like a poison creeping through his body and turning every last bit of him rotten.

'Oh what am I supposed to do now, man?' he asked Freddy, letting out a long sigh. 'I mean, should I tell Harvey or not?'

'I'm not sure, mate,' came the considered response. 'Obviously telling him would be the *right* thing to do, like. But I don't know him like you do. How do you think he'd react?'

'He'd be proper gutted, man. And I'd always know I'd done that to him.'

'But could you live with yourself *not* telling him?'

Spike crinkled his nose as he thought it over. 'Urm, no – I don't think I could, blud.'

'Well, there's your answer.'

Spike looked at his watch; it was still only four o'clock. He stretched his mouth wide open and slapped his cheeks. He had less than five hours to figure out what to tell Harvey.

*

Lola stepped out of the car and undulated into the restaurant. She was feeling pretty slinky after finishing a shoot everyone said had gone brilliantly. Unfortunately she hadn't had time to nip home to change so had been forced to come out in the violet jumpsuit she'd worn in the studio together with her professionally done hair and make-up. She was slightly worried it was all a bit over-the-top but reminded herself that it didn't matter, seeing as she was only here to shut up Harvey. *I wonder how soon I can get away and if I'll have time to see Jake afterwards . . .*

Inside the restaurant, Freddy was waiting at the table. He'd specifically asked to be seated in a quiet corner so they wouldn't be hassled by other diners – although he'd chosen the restaurant because it was often frequented by celebrities and people working in the creative industries who were less likely to be star-struck. Scran was a fashionable, relaxed venue acclaimed for its contemporary take on unfussy, traditional British food. Freddy looked down the menu to see what was on offer – calves' liver, sausage and mash, corned beef hash . . . He hoped his choice of restaurant would be glamorous enough for Lola. He realized he was scrunching up a napkin in his fists and stopped to straighten it out on his lap. *Calm down, champ, there's nothing to be nervous about, remember?*

A few feet away, Lola was being greeted by a maître d' with a face like a Digestive biscuit and a set of discoloured teeth that seemed to have been arranged in his mouth like crazy paving. 'Hello, Miss Grant. Welcome to Scran.'

'Hiya,' she chirped, 'it's great to be here!'

She followed him through a timber-panelled, cosily lit restaurant full of unpretentious people relaxing on green leather-backed chairs and cushion-covered benches, leaning forward to chat on tables covered by pristine white cloths and decorated with little vases of pink and yellow gerberas. It was so delightfully inviting she found herself suppressing a little squeal. *Well, Freddy certainly scores full marks for his choice of venue.* That is, he would if she were keeping score – which she reminded herself she wasn't. *Because I'm only here to please Harvey.*

She swept round a corner and spotted Freddy furrowing his forehead as he studied the menu. 'Hiya!' she beamed. 'You all right?'

Wow! he thought. *She looks incredible.*

'Yeah, cracking, thanks,' he smiled, standing up. 'Good to see you.'

He was wearing a sea-green polo shirt that perfectly comple-mented his red hair, with the top button undone to reveal a silver chain rolling over the ripples of his upper chest muscles and sleeves that dug into the curves of his bulky biceps. He gave her a little hug and she noticed he was wearing a subtle but strong aftershave that smelled of cedarwood and spices, and as he squeezed her he felt solid and tough. *Hmm,* she thought, *someone's even more handsome than I remembered.*

'You look great,' he murmured, sitting back down as the maître d' pulled out Lola's chair. 'Really gorgeous, like.'

'Oh come off it,' she scoffed, lowering herself into her seat. 'I've come straight from a shoot – I look like a drag queen!'

'No you don't!' he said as the maître d' swept away. 'You look gorgeous, honestly.'

'Well, in that case, thanks darlin'. You're looking pretty good yourself.'

Freddy shrugged sheepishly. He'd actually been heading out in his work suit when Spike had pulled him back and insisted he change into the only casual clothes he had hanging in his locker. His producer had also sprayed him with a few squirts of his own favourite aftershave, something called Terre by Hermès. Freddy hoped Lola liked it – because he really wanted tonight to go well. He'd been thrilled when Harvey had emailed to say Lola was back from Europe and wondered if he'd like to go out for dinner. Finally he had her on her own.

'But a handsome man like you doesn't need telling,' Lola teased. 'And anyway, I've blatantly told you plenty of times already.'

'Yeah, thanks,' he managed, looking down awkwardly. There was a short silence and he reminded himself not to talk too much. *It's not your job to fill all the pauses.*

'Cool restaurant,' Lola said after a few seconds. 'Have you been here before?'

'Yeah, a few times – the food's cracking. But what do you want to drink first? Shall we get a bottle of wine, like?'

'Yeah, go on. I could do with a drink after today.'

He called over a waiter, who was shaven-headed, stubbled and had the kind of uber-masculine look that could have meant he was either extremely straight, or extremely gay and doing his best to butch up. As Freddy chatted to him about the wine options, Lola couldn't help noticing the waiter was shaking with nerves – even more than her arm had been shaking holding up that can of Twinkle all day. *Aha!* she thought. *He must fancy Freddy.*

It looks like this waiter fancies Lola, thought Freddy as he watched him shake more than Spike had done on his coke comedown. And he couldn't blame him; not only did she look amazing but she had an energy about her that in a funny way made him just want to *be* better. He tried to relax and ordered a bottle of Sancerre, which he'd chosen after googling the restaurant's wine list and researching several options. Whatever it tasted like, he couldn't wait till it arrived.

'So how was the shoot?' he asked Lola.

She told him all about her three days posing with a can of Twinkle and he chuckled as she reprised the one line she'd had to deliver what felt like a thousand times. 'You too can Twinkle like a star!'

Oh she's such a laugh, thought Freddy. *I hope she doesn't think I'm boring and uncool.*

I feel so happy and safe with him, thought Lola. *I hope he doesn't think I'm dirty and common.*

The waiter reappeared and served their drinks, spilling a little as he splashed it into the glasses. Lola noticed that not only was he shaking but he also had terrible bitten-down fingernails. *He must have a serious crush on Freddy,* she thought. And she couldn't blame him. How could she have ever let him get away? How could she have allowed herself to be distracted by a blatant tramp like Jake? She watched him fiddle with his silver chain then let it fall onto the contours of a chest she could just imagine tracing with her finger.

Freddy felt embarrassed that the waiter was falling to pieces in front of Lola and tried to distract him by asking about the specials. He took another look at the menu and couldn't help giving a little chortle as he saw cock-a-leekie soup. He was just about to make a knob gag when he stopped himself – he knew Lola was famous for being straight-talking but he didn't want to offend her by being too crude. He needn't have worried.

'This cock-a-leekie soup,' she asked the waiter, raising an eyebrow. 'Does it have real cock in it?'

The two of them burst out laughing and the waiter looked mortified. 'Urm, no, it's urm, it's a chicken-based soup with leeks and barley.'

'Oh I'm sorry,' Lola said, mid-giggle, 'please ignore me. I'll have the scallops and then the roast chicken please.'

The waiter looked at Freddy, who was still trying to control his laughter. 'I'll have the tomato soup followed by the Dover sole,' he managed, wiping his eyes. 'And I'm sorry for laughing too.'

Once the waiter had scurried away the two of them allowed their laughter to come spilling out.

'He blatantly fancies you!' Lola spewed.

'No he doesn't!' Freddy said. 'It's *you* he's into.'

'Leave it to me, darlin'. I'll find out later. And the loser blatantly has to down a glass of wine.'

'You're on!' He smiled and held up his glass. 'Cheers!'

'Cheers!' She took a sip and smiled back at him.

Freddy felt his shoulders drop as he started to relax. He wasn't sure what he'd been nervous about; this was going to be fun. *You never know,* he thought, *I might even manage to impress her.*

Lola stretched out her legs and kicked off her heels under the table; this was going to be fun – much more fun than she'd expected. Although the truth was she hadn't thought about it much beforehand, probably because she'd been too busy being besotted with Jake. Apart from Harvey, the only person she'd told about the date had been Gloria, and that had been because she'd wanted to stem the rumours she was sure were circulating through the band about her affair with Jake, who'd only become twitchy and take it out on her if everyone knew they were sleeping together. She remembered how sweet Gloria had been and how she'd spent ages giving her dating advice, while all Lola had been able to think about was how long it would take for the news to filter through to Jake and whether it might even make him jealous. Not that she was giving the slightest consideration to Jake's feelings right now. *You never know,* she thought, *it might not be too late for Freddy to save me from Jake after all – to turn my head back to where it first started.*

'So come on then,' she said to him, 'what can you tell me about you? You've already interviewed me twice. How about I interview you for a change?'

'All right,' he smiled, 'what do you want to know?'

'Well, you're from Port Talbot, I remember you telling me that. What about your family?'

'OK. I've got one sister who's two years older than me, my mam runs her own hairdressing salon, and my dad's a rugby coach for the national youth team.'

'Oh right, so do you play rugby? Is that why you're built like a brick shithouse?'

He laughed bashfully and tried to cross his legs but then remembered he couldn't as his thighs were too chunky.

Lola couldn't help noticing his thigh muscles bulging against the seams of his trousers and gave a giggle of delight.

'Urm, I don't know about that,' he said, 'but I do play for an amateur team, yeah. I wasn't good enough for much else, I'm afraid – to my dad's great disappointment.'

Lola detected a note of sadness and wanted to make him feel better. 'Yeah, but he must be really proud of you now, being on telly and everything?'

'Mmm, I don't know. I still think he'd be much happier if I were playing rugby for Wales.'

'Well,' she chirped, looking him directly in the eye, 'if you were doing that we wouldn't have met, would we? And we wouldn't be sitting here right now.'

'No, I suppose not.'

'So it's not all bad, is it?'

'No,' he replied, 'it's not all bad.'

She raised her glass and gave him another smile. She imagined how happy the two of them could be together and saw them cuddling in bed on a Sunday morning and laughing over boozy lunches in the pub.

He took a sip of his wine and his eyes sparkled. He imagined sliding his finger under the edge of her neckline and running it down to her cleavage as he massaged her bare shoulders with a flurry of kisses.

'The scallops!' The waiter reappeared and clanked their starters onto the table. 'And the tomato soup.'

'Thanks, mate.'

'Thanks, darlin'.'

As he left they each nodded after him teasingly.

'He's got such a crush on you!'

'No, it's definitely you!'

Lola began eating but was so entranced by Freddy she barely tasted her food.

Freddy was so captivated by Lola he couldn't concentrate on eating and immediately burned the roof of his mouth.

The two of them chatted away about the kinds of things they'd never discuss on camera. And the conversation was much more fun than any interview.

*

An hour later Lola was feeling slightly squiffy and nipped to the loo to check on her make-up. Sure, things had been going brilliantly so far but she didn't want to start letting herself go. Freddy probably met female pop stars like her every day and he was so gorgeous she was sure they all flirted with him. As she reached into her bag for her powder, her phone fell out and she saw she had a new message. It was from Jake.

'Lying in bed thinking of you,' she read. 'What you up to?'

Hmpf! He's never asked me that before – he must have heard I'm on a date. He must be feeling jealous . . .

Sitting at the table, Freddy was feeling the first flush of a few glasses of wine. He wasn't normally very romantic but wondered whether he should hold Lola's hand when she came back. Sure, things had been going brilliantly so far but he didn't want to overstep the mark. He texted his friend Rhodri for advice.

'Hold her hand?' came the instant reply, 'I thought by now she'd be giving you a hand-job ;-)'

He smiled and decided to interpret that as a yes.

Lola smiled as she applied a little powder to her face. She couldn't help feeling a swell of satisfaction at the discovery of Jake's jealousy. *He's the one who keeps banging on about us not being boyfriend and girlfriend. Well let's see how he likes a taste of his own medicine.*

'Sorry, am on a date,' she texted him, suddenly flushed by a surge of adrenaline. She hadn't thought about Jake for the past hour but now that she did she felt gripped by that all-too-familiar craving for him – a craving that only made her miserable but one that she felt powerless to resist. She imagined him lying in bed overwhelmed by jealousy about her date and soon became lost in fantasies about their angry make-up sex. *Don't think about it! Just don't think about it!* Despite herself, she began typing another line. 'Might be free later if you're around?' She checked over the message and hit Send.

Freddy hit Exit, switched off his phone and slipped it into his pocket. As the waiter filled their glasses with the first of a new bottle of wine, Lola reappeared, her charisma so strong it almost entered the room a few seconds before she did. But Freddy could tell from her face something was wrong. She seemed distracted, like she'd just received some bad news.

'Is everything all right?' he asked as she sat down.

'Yeah, course,' she lied. She wondered what Jake would think if he could see her sitting opposite the most eligible news correspondent in the country. She looked at her watch – it was half past ten. There'd still be plenty of time for her to dash across town to Jake's hotel if he replied to her soon. But she hadn't felt her phone vibrate in her bag. She took it out and slipped it under her knee so she'd feel it straight away. She hoped Freddy wouldn't notice.

Freddy noticed Lola check her watch and position her phone under her knee, presumably so she'd feel it vibrate. He wondered what had happened in the loo for her to suddenly lose interest in their date. She leant back in her seat and he felt a distance opening up between them. *So much for holding her hand.*

'So tell me about this producer of yours,' she began with no hint of the flirtation that had danced between them all evening. 'I hope he's not going to be trouble. Because I don't want anyone upsetting my manager.'

'Urm, yeah,' he replied, 'his name's Spike. And he's a really nice guy.' He pictured Spike sweating and shaking at his desk that afternoon and remembered the look of self-disgust on his face as he'd told Freddy what he'd got up to the night before. Freddy didn't want to lie to Lola but it wasn't his place to tell her about Spike's infidelity – and he didn't want to risk that kind of revelation souring the evening. Not that it didn't seem to be souring already. *What on earth's gone wrong?*

'I mean, he's not perfect,' Freddy went on carefully, 'and he's still quite young. But his heart's in the right place – and he definitely *wants* to do the right thing.'

Lola cocked her head in suspicion. *Hmm, that sounds ominous.* 'Well, just as long as he does,' she frowned, 'because you know how I feel about tramps.'

He managed to force a little laugh. 'Yeah, don't worry – I think I can remember.'

Who am I trying to kid? thought Lola. *Banging on about tramps when all I can think about is Jake?* She felt under her knee to check the phone hadn't somehow slipped away. There was still no reply. He was obviously sulking with her because she was out with someone else. He was obviously ignoring her to try and make her feel guilty. Well, it was totally unfair – and she wouldn't stand for it. She began thinking about how she could use tonight's date to make Jake even more jealous. She could always send a quick tweet in the car home saying how much she'd enjoyed a lovely evening with a mystery man. That would get the journos twitching and it wouldn't take long for one of them to work out who her date had been with. *You never know, there might even be a couple of paps waiting outside.* She knocked back half of her glass of wine and felt emboldened.

'Would either of you like dessert or coffee?' asked the waiter, stepping in between them.

Freddy jumped in first. 'Yeah—'

'Actually,' Lola interrupted him. 'If you don't mind, I could do with getting going. I've got an early start tomorrow.'

She watched Freddy's face sag in disappointment. *Oh what am I doing?* she thought. *I'm so stupid, sitting here with a gorgeous guy who's really nice and all I can think about is some total tramp who treats me like shit.*

'No, don't worry about it,' Freddy smiled weakly, 'I could do with getting going too. We'll just have the bill, please,' he said to the waiter.

Oh what am I doing? Freddy thought. *I'm so stupid, sitting here with a gorgeous pop star and thinking she wants to be my girlfriend when she's so obviously out of my league.* He took out his wallet and insisted on paying the bill. It was the least he could do.

'Actually,' Lola said to the waiter, her mischievous look flickering back into life. 'Do you mind if I ask you a personal question?'

'No,' he replied, handing Freddy the card machine. 'Go on.'

Lola looked at her date with a grin. 'If you had to shag one of us two, which one would it be?'

The waiter squirmed and his eyes flickered onto Freddy. 'Urm, that's easy because I'm gay. So it would have to be Freddy. I'm actually a big fan – I always tape the news so I can watch your reports when I get home from work. And I loved that photo shoot you did in your rugby kit.'

'Oh, thanks,' Freddy smiled, remembering the half-naked shoot Spike had convinced him to do for *Attitude* magazine.

Brilliant, he thought sarcastically, *Lola might not fancy me but the gay waiter does.* He handed him back the machine. 'And I'm sorry if we've tormented you, mate.'

'Not at all,' blurted the waiter, obviously overawed to be speaking to his celebrity crush. 'It's been a pleasure, honestly.' He began backing away slowly, not wanting to take his eyes off Freddy until he absolutely had to. Freddy nodded at him and gave a little salute.

Aw, Lola thought, *he really is so lovely and I'm being such a bitch. Maybe I should tell him I just want to be friends?*

All I need now, Freddy thought, *is for Lola to tell me I'm lovely and she just wants to be friends.*

They stood up and faced each other in silence.

Lola looked at Freddy and wished she wasn't in love with Jake. She knew without a doubt that the man standing in front of her could make her happy and she hated Jake for sending the text and messing up their date. She hated Jake and she hated herself for being in love with him.

Freddy looked at Lola and wished he was sexier or more fun and then she'd fancy him. If she'd just give him the chance, he knew he could make her happy. But why would she do that when he was just a big, ungainly, ginger hulk who couldn't even cross his legs properly? He hated himself for not being good enough.

'Well,' Lola said eventually, 'get on with it then.'

'Get on with what?'

'Downing that glass of wine. I was right about the waiter fancying you – so you need to knock it back.'

He rolled his eyes and obliged. *This is just what I need – a disastrous date and a stonking hangover in the morning.* He held up his empty glass with a half-hearted flourish.

'Atta boy!' Lola sparkled. 'And thanks for the meal, darlin'. It was fierce.'

'Don't mention it,' he managed. He was about to suggest they did it again sometime but was frightened she'd say she didn't want to. He held out his arm to guide her to the exit and followed her through the restaurant, trying not to notice as she picked up her phone and checked it for messages.

Lola thrust the phone into her bag. She couldn't believe Jake still hadn't replied to her text. The evening had started so brilliantly and now she just felt miserable. *How dare he ruin things by pissing me around?* Well, she'd show him. If he wanted to start playing games then she could play them too.

By the time they reached the lobby, the maître d' had already signalled to Lola's driver that she was ready to leave. 'Although I'm afraid there are a few photographers outside,' he explained earnestly. 'Perhaps Miss Grant would like to leave by the back door?'

'Oh no!' she trilled, her eyes glistening. 'I'm not bothered about a few pesky paps. Come on, Freddy, let's go!'

She held out her hand and tugged him into the street before he had time to argue. She waited for the paps to spot her and then moved in to give him a kiss on the lips just as they were illuminated by a flurry of flashbulbs.

Take that, Jake!

Freddy was so taken aback he didn't know how to respond – he'd been convinced Lola had been about to blow him out. And anyway, he could hardly launch into a full-on snog in front of a load of photographers. Before he had time to register what was happening she let him go. *Now where did that come from?*

He was still asking himself the question when Lola jumped into her car and it began to sweep away. *So is she interested or not? If she doesn't like me then why's she just gone and kissed me in front of all those paps?*

He shook his head and watched the car drive off into the distance.

Inside, Lola fastened her seat belt and told the driver not to take her home. There'd been a change of plan. She was going to pay Jake a surprise visit.

*

'Well, this is a surprise,' Harvey mouthed, staggering back onto a bench. They were in the square outside his flat as Spike had told him he wanted to talk – and he needed some air. Harvey had instantly known something was wrong but he hadn't expected this. 'What do you mean, you cheated on me?'

Spike sat down next to him and stared straight ahead. 'I went out last night, I got proper wavey and I went home with some blonde geezer.'

Harvey folded his arms across his stomach as if reeling from a punch. 'And do you *like* this guy? Do you want to see him again?'

'No, man! That wasn't the point, I swear.'

'Well then what *was* the point?'

Spike took a deep breath and exhaled slowly. 'I don't know, blud. I really don't know.'

Harvey stood up and began to pace the path in front of them. The news was almost too much to take in. *Spike's cheated on me. He's actually cheated on me.* He could feel every muscle in his body twisting into a tangle of shock, sadness and anger. He made Spike recount every last detail of the sorry story, the tangle of emotions inside him tightening at every turn. As he watched Spike's mouth move, he couldn't believe it was the same mouth that just a few days ago had uttered the words 'I love you'.

A sombre silence fell between them. 'I can't believe it,' Harvey said. 'I just can't believe it.'

Spike stood up and tried to take his hands. Harvey shook him off and turned away.

'I'm sorry, Harvey. I'm so, so sorry.'

'So is this it, then?' he managed eventually. 'Are you and me finished?'

'No! At least I hope not, man. I'm really hoping you'll be able to forgive me.'

Harvey let his arms fall to his side and looked out over the square. It was surprisingly warm for early September, although already most of the flowers were starting to die. On the other side of the lawn a young couple were sitting on a bench, the man's arm wrapped around the woman as she nestled into him. They weren't even speaking to each other, simply sitting there and savouring the experience of being in love. For these last few months Harvey had thought that maybe he too might be able to experience love, that he too might deserve to be in a happy, loving relationship. Clearly he was wrong. And he hated himself for not being good enough. *If only I weren't so old and Northern and boring this would never have happened.*

Spike moved round so he was facing him again. 'What do you think, blud? Do you think you can forgive me?'

Harvey felt so overcome it was like he'd forgotten how to

breathe. 'I'm going to have to think about it, Spike. You're just
going to have to give me some time to think about it.'

But even as he said the words, he could think of nothing
else. And his thoughts were giving way to a familiar feeling of
self-disgust. A feeling that for years had compelled him to try
and destroy himself with drink and casual sex. A feeling which
had grown out of the disgust directed at him during his childhood, when his difference and sensitivity had led him to being
roundly savaged as a freak or queer. A feeling which had left
him unable to love himself or to ever truly believe he was
deserving of love. A feeling he'd tried to fight with three years
of therapy and three years off the booze. But a feeling which
now resurfaced with such intensity he couldn't help thinking it
must be part of him. Part of his identity. Part of his soul.

He knew that once his initial shock had subsided he'd be
able to see that Spike had only gone out to sabotage their
happiness because he was suffering from the same kind of self-
disgust. Already he had no doubt *that* was the point of his
actions last night, whether or not Spike himself could see it.
But even so, how could he ever trust him again? He might not
have *meant* to ruin everything but that didn't change the fact
that he had. Maybe Lola had been right about him. Maybe he
was no better than Jake. And maybe Harvey had only gone and
sought him out because three years of trying to fight his own
self-disgust had failed – and he still wanted to punish himself
for not being good enough. For not being right.

He looked at Spike and realized he was saying something.
'I'm sorry, what was that?'

'Oh nothing,' he frowned. 'Just that I'd probably better
cut.'

'Yeah,' was all Harvey could manage. 'Yeah. I'll speak to you soon.'

Spike gave his arms a little flap as if he wasn't sure how to say goodbye. 'I still, like, love you, you know.'

Harvey flinched. 'Don't, Spike. Please don't say that.'

Spike nodded mournfully and turned to slope away.

As Harvey watched him leave he couldn't believe he'd been so stupid. *All this time I've been trying so hard to make sure Lola doesn't get hurt, I didn't realize I was going to get hurt myself.*

He wanted to call Lola and tell her what had happened. He wanted her to put her arms around him and tell him everything would be all right. But he knew she was on her date with Freddy and he didn't want to spoil it. He really wanted things to work out between Lola and Freddy, then maybe she could avoid Jake dragging her into the mess Spike had just dragged him into. So no, he wouldn't call her.

Besides, she'd been a bit cold with him since he'd caught her and Jake together in Barcelona. The last thing he needed now was to listen to her expressing concern, holding back from gloating or saying 'I told you so' but insisting she'd been suspicious of Spike simply because she'd been looking out for Harvey and just wanted what was best for him.

That kind of advice would only make him feel like a failure. And he felt like enough of one already.

*

Lola felt like such a failure. She stood in the corridor of Jake's hotel banging on his bedroom door but hearing nothing in reply. *Oh what have I done?*

She turned her back to the door and slid down onto the

thick carpet, letting her legs flop out before her. She'd been so convinced Jake had been steaming with jealousy about her date that she'd decided to turn up at his hotel to dazzle him with her post-shoot glamour and milk his anger for everything it was worth. She'd even sat in the back of the car working out her opening line, a casual mention of what a great time she'd had and how she'd laughed so much she was worried she'd split her jumpsuit. She'd planned to coyly feed Jake more and more details about her impossibly romantic evening until she'd wound him up into a raging fury – at which point she'd oh-so-reluctantly allow him to win her back with a bout of earthquake-inducingly passionate sex. It had all seemed so perfect when she'd played it through in her head. But here she was now, ready to put her plan into action – and Jake had disappeared.

'Is everything OK there?' called out a female voice down the hall. Lola quickly glanced up and saw it was coming from a bespectacled busybody who looked just like Dustin Hoffman in *Tootsie*. 'Are you all right, love?'

Lola pretended to itch her forehead, carefully covering her face so she wouldn't be recognized. 'Oh yeah, yeah,' she sing-songed a little too enthusiastically, 'I'm just going to text my boyfriend and see where he is.'

Actually, she imagined saying, *he won't let me call him my boyfriend and he's probably pissed off to shag some other bird.*

'OK then,' the woman replied with a hint of disappointment. 'If you're sure, then I'll leave you to it. Goodnight.'

'Night.'

Lola fished her phone out of her bag and reread Jake's message. 'Lying in bed thinking of you. What you up to?' *Well, what I was up to was trying to make you jealous! Although a fat lot of good it's done me.*

Her mind started racing with panic. All this time she'd been imagining her date with Freddy would be the perfect way to rekindle Jake's fading interest, but now it looked like it had only prompted the opposite effect. She felt humiliated and angry – angry at herself for being so stupid. Jake had never made any secret of the fact he didn't want their relationship to be exclusive, and she'd been so terrified of the idea of him sleeping with someone else she'd carefully avoided the subject of other women for weeks. But now here she was sitting outside the room from where just over an hour ago he'd texted her to say he was lying in bed. If he'd been feeling horny then she knew him well enough to know he wouldn't just go to sleep. *Or even crack one off to hotel porn.*

No, Jake was only ever interested in the real thing. And when he wanted it he usually got it.

So where had he gone to find it?

*

Jake had no idea where he was and he didn't really care. He stretched out on the bed, toked on his joint, and let himself enjoy one of the most accomplished blow jobs he'd ever experienced.

Camden, is that where I am? Or is it Clapham? Or even Croydon? The truth was, he didn't give a rat's ass. He'd find out in the morning when he'd emerge blinking into the daylight, hail a taxi and gaze out of the window at yet another area of London he'd been introduced to by his dick. He pulled back another toke and allowed the weed to fill his lungs. *Man, this is freakin' strong.*

It was so strong it was softening the edges of his consciousness, lifting him away from reality until he felt like he was floating high above the world. Yet at the same time it heightened his sensitivity and enhanced the enjoyment of having his dick sucked to such an extent that after just five minutes he was worried about shooting his load – which wasn't like him at all. And he didn't want this to end for a long time. *Damn, this chick can suck dick. I bet she could suck the chrome off a trailer hitch.*

He leant back and gave a whinny of delight. He gazed at the ceiling, his eyes losing focus until it slowly blurred into a white haze. He was so engulfed by ecstasy he wasn't even sure who was sucking him off anymore. He looked down and saw her jet-black hair bobbing around his midriff, her ebony arms snaking up to gently massage his sides.

'Is that good?' she asked, briefly breaking off and looking to the side to catch her breath.

He didn't answer but directed her head back onto his dick. He pulled deeply on his joint then let it rest in the ashtray next to him. As she resumed sucking, his ass gave a little spasm. *Man, this is so fucking good!*

He heard his phone ping in his shirt pocket to say he'd received a text. He was sure it would be yet another message from Lola and he wasn't going to answer it. Ever since her fag manager had busted his ass in Barcelona things had been way too heavy between them – and there were even times when he was starting to feel pussy-whipped. Sure, when he'd found out Lola was dating some other dude he'd had a brief moment of feeling aggrieved, but that was only because chicks usually put up with him fucking around without doing it themselves. And now he'd had time to reflect he'd come to the conclusion that if Lola wanted to date someone else, that was fine with him. In fact, the news came as something of a relief. But she couldn't expect him to sit in his hotel room playing with his dick while he waited for her to drop by. No, he'd much rather go out and find somebody else to play with it – which was what he'd wound up doing. And boy, was he glad he had.

The woman gently parted his butt cheeks, licked her fingers and then softly began to massage his ass hole, sliding in the tips as he groaned with pleasure. And still she kept sucking – sucking so sweetly he could feel all the muscles quiver on his belly.

'I think I'm going to come,' he shuddered, expecting the woman to pull back so he could shoot his load all over her face. But instead she plunged his dick deeper into her throat, working her thick lips around the base until she brought him to a climax so intense his upper body began to jerk as if he were having a seizure.

'Aaaaaaaaaaaargh!'

He gripped onto her head, coming so far into her he wasn't sure how it was even possible. He felt her greedily glugging him in before softly easing back and releasing him.

'Fuck . . . That was . . . *Fuck!*' He was on such a high he could hardly speak.

The woman giggled and crawled up to kiss him.

And that's when he remembered who she was.

8

'And let's see that one more time!'

Lola swaggered her way across the rehearsal room, her left fist thrust high in the air and her other hand dragging along a line of dancers who slid after her on their knees. She was at Pomegranate Dance Studios in Covent Garden, running through the moves for the tour version of *Miss Chief*, which consisted of lots of air-kicking, aggressive thrusting and ironic crotch-grabbing. Of course the routine had been choreographed to complement the central theme of the song, which was that Lola was a strong woman, fully in command of herself and her team. But, perhaps unsurprisingly, today she was finding projecting that theme something of a struggle.

'And let's see the middle eight formation.'

Lola strode to the front of the room and snapped her way through a sequence of steps while the dancers fanned out in perfect symmetry behind her. She was acutely aware that the choreography only had the desired effect of making her look like she was the leader of the troupe if she actually got the moves right for the dancers to copy. And watching herself in the mirrored wall facing her, she could see only too well that she was messing up the order.

'I'm sorry,' she said, stopping and scrunching up her now sweat-sodden face, 'but can we try that again?'

'Course we can,' cooed the show's director and choreographer Carlson Bent, an unfeasibly muscled gay man with a chest the size of a vending machine and a collection of T-shirts that looked like they were made to fit a ten-year-old girl. Carlson had dazzling white teeth, a smoothly Botoxed forehead, blonde hair immaculately styled into a glossy quiff, and a dimple in his chin that was so perfect Lola doubted he'd been born with it. But she always insisted on working with him because he understood that dance wasn't her strong suit and that she only really did it at all because it was expected of a female performer. And over the last few years he'd learnt to work around her limitations, creating moves that were characterful rather than complicated. Although today she was finding them complicated enough. She scurried to the side of the room and wiped her face on a sweat towel.

'OK,' she breathed, returning to the centre and steeling herself for the next run-through, 'let's give it another go.'

Carlson gave her an encouraging smile. 'You're doing brilliantly, Lola. Now stride forwards to begin . . .'

She concentrated all her energy on following the sequence Carlson had devised for the middle eight of the song. *Shoulders left, pop right, feet together, bend knees, dip down and bounce up again*. It really shouldn't be that difficult but again she messed it up.

'I'm so sorry guys,' she said, turning to face the dancers. 'I've nearly got it, I promise.'

'Don't worry about it!' they chorused back at her, showering her with compliments about her natural rhythm and instinctive ability. But the dancers' flattery only made her even more aware of her own failings. And she was worried that her lack of talent was going to be exposed by their brilliance. Kitty, Jette and Boo were gorgeous girls with boundless energy and a capacity to contort their lithe bodies into positions Lola hadn't even known existed, while Todd, Nate and Junior were a multi-racial trio of street dancers whose athleticism made Lola breathless with admiration and who were collectively so hot Carlson had already decreed they'd be spending the entire show topless. All of which was fine by Lola. She only wished she could be a bit more coordinated.

And the worst thing was, all six dancers had told her they were huge fans of her work and, as they were a few years younger than Lola, seemed to look up to her as some kind of example to follow.

'It's such an honour to work with you!' Nate had said when they'd met.

'You're absolutely my inspiration!' Boo had fawned.

'I want to be just like you!' Jette had joined in.

Whenever they asked Lola for careers advice or tips or guidance, she couldn't help feeling like she'd conned them all into thinking she was someone special. *Why on earth would they want to be like me? I can't even get a few simple steps right . . .*

'OK, let's give it one more go,' coaxed Carlson.

Lola took a deep breath and pressed her fingers against her nose. 'Yep, I'm ready.'

'This is the one!' he piped. 'Now stride forwards . . .'

Shoulders left, pop right, feet together, bend knees, dip down and bounce up again.

'Yes!' she practically squealed. 'Yes, yes, yes!'

Finally!

'OK that's brilliant,' nodded Carlson. 'Now let's keep running it through till it sticks.'

As Lola practised the moves again and again, she couldn't help feeling ground down by the enormity of the task ahead. *Miss Chief* was only one of several numbers in a ninety-minute show, all of which she'd have to commit to memory in just over a month. If it was taking her all day just to learn this one short sequence, how was she ever going to know the whole show by the opening night of the tour?

It was at times like this that she really wished she had a proper boyfriend – someone who'd be able to comfort and support her at the end of a tough day. But unfortunately Jake was becoming more and more distant, not to mention avoidant. Ever since her pathetic attempt to stir up his jealousy by going out with Freddy, he'd virtually ignored her and they'd only spent one night together, when he'd been out drinking with some American friends and had dropped by in the early hours of the morning for what turned out to be upsettingly unsatisfactory sex, at the end of which she'd actually had to fake an orgasm in a desperate attempt to convince him they still had some kind of special sexual connection.

The situation was making her feel increasingly paranoid and anxious. She remembered Jake saying something about his mum being needy and clingy when his dad went away on business when he was little and how it had only repulsed him. Yet here she was all these years later behaving in exactly the same way. And the irony was that if she could just make him love her, she wouldn't *be* as desperate and clingy – and she'd love him so much in return she was convinced she could cure him of all the pain of his childhood, not to mention her own.

Which reminded her, she still had to call her mum. She'd been putting it off for weeks now, mainly out of guilt for being such a bitch the last time they'd spoken, but also out of the fear of finding out her mum had walked out of rehab and started using again. The whole thing was just too horrific to contemplate. Although if she were stronger she knew she'd have the courage to face it. She just needed Jake to love her first. And then everything would fall into place. The more she thought about it, the more it all made sense. *If only I weren't so stupid and ugly and annoying . . .*

'All right, now let's run through the ending.'

If only I weren't such a crap dancer.

Lola sloped into position for a sequence in which she playfully bossed around her dancers, issuing them with orders to do press-ups, planks and stomach crunches while she strutted around inspecting their performance. They lined up on the floor before her while she stepped her way over them and then formed a train to lift her high in the air so she could look down on them, miming an expression of extreme arrogance. Finally, they lined up in a row and she trailed her finger along their fronts, prodding the boys in the chest so that they keeled over and taking the girls aside to bang their heads together. Lola tried her best to get into character but couldn't help feeling like a total fraud. Here she was acting like some strong, authoritative superwoman in absolute control of her world when the truth was she was a needy desperado who couldn't even control her man.

Oh why can't I make him love me?

She thought back to the way she'd felt when she'd written the song, how she'd been so infused with confidence and self-respect and how she'd been so sure that she'd never give in to weakness ever again. Yet here she was less than a year later, falling apart in rehearsal as yet another disastrous relationship unravelled around her. Earlier that day she'd been in such a state about it she'd needed to talk to someone and, as Harvey was obviously out of the question, she'd confided in Gloria. She knew she was supposed to be keeping the whole thing secret but she was sure everyone knew about it by now. And besides, she knew she could trust Gloria. As expected, she'd been brilliant, telling her all about how badly her last boyfriend had treated her and her similar compulsion for bastards. 'I mean I *want* to fall for nice guys,' Lola remembered her saying, 'but somehow I always end up falling for the sleaze-bags.' It had been a comfort to hear Gloria echo her own thoughts. *When will we ever learn?*

'That's great!' crooned Carlson. 'And now if you could move into your final positions.'

In what felt like less than a second the dancers slid onto the floor and arranged their bodies into a mound onto which Lola climbed to end the song by holding her arms up in the air as if she were a heavyweight boxer who'd just won a fight. *Oh who am I trying to kid?*

'That's terrific!' warbled Carlson.

Really? Are you sure?

'OK, now let's try that with music. First positions please everyone.'

Lola scampered off stage to make her big entrance.

'Can somebody hit Play please?' yelled Carlson. '*Miss Chief* – take it away!'

*

The Chief Medical Officer gave Karen a sympathetic smile. Polly Buckingham was a thin-lipped forty-something who looked like she read *The Guardian* and shopped for organic food at farmers' markets and whose pristine appearance was spoiled only by a huge wart that looked like a button mushroom dangling off her left earlobe.

'Well, Miss Grant,' she brayed, 'I think you've made excellent progress. And I agree with your therapist – I think you're ready to go home.'

'Thanks, chief.' Karen breathed in and felt her chest expand with an emotion she initially couldn't identify but thought might be pride – or even dignity.

'So now it's just a matter of paperwork,' said Dr Buckingham, sliding a stash of documents across the desk. 'If you could have a quick read of these and sign here and here.'

Karen's eyes flickered down the page while her peripheral vision took in a photo of the doctor standing with her arms draped around three little girls on a beach that looked like something out of one of those Bounty adverts in the Eighties. Just two months ago this kind of thing would have been enough to make Karen fume with bitterness at an unjust world that had treated her so differently. Now she just smiled. Although she couldn't help wondering what Polly Buckingham would think if she knew all the patients in the Abbey called her Polly Fuckingham.

'And I understand you'll be taking Miss Grant home, Mr Sparks?'

'Yep, that's right,' said Harvey, sitting next to her. 'And I'll keep an eye on her for a few weeks.' He stopped and gave Karen an apologetic grimace. 'Urm, just to check you're all right and stuff.'

Over the last few years Karen had grown fond of Harvey and come to love his gentle brown eyes, shy smile and no-nonsense Northern accent. She put her hand on his and gave it a little stroke. 'It's OK, Harvey, you don't have to explain anything. It'll be good to know someone's there if I'm struggling.'

She wished she'd had a friend like Harvey when she'd been Lola's age, and couldn't help wondering if her life would have turned out differently if she had. *But no, I didn't have anybody. Even Mum and Dad pissed off at the first sign of trouble.* She shook her head and reminded herself to let go of the bitterness.

'And we'll obviously be in touch to arrange your first out-patient appointment,' interjected Dr Buckingham. As she spoke, Karen's eyes were drawn to the wart hanging off her ear. She imagined what would happen if she took out a pair of scissors and simply snipped it off. But before she'd had a chance to picture the scene, the doctor stood up and straightened her pencil skirt. 'And well done, Miss Grant, the work you've done here has been really tough. I know it's only the beginning of the process but I think you can be very proud of yourself.'

Karen wasn't used to being talked to like this by doctors or indeed anyone in a position of authority. She tried to pinpoint what it was that made it so different and could only think it was that she was being treated with respect. She wasn't sure how to respond but Dr Buckingham held out her hand so she shook it.

'Great, well I'll see you again, I suppose,' she managed.

'Yes, I'm sure you will.'

Karen gave her a sincere smile. 'And thanks for everything, Dr Fuckingham.'

Yes! Slipped it in after all!

'Oh, I'm so sorry!' she grovelled as the doctor gasped out loud. 'I've no idea where that came from. Honestly, two months in here and my head's mashed!'

'It's fine, don't worry about it. It's, urm, it's easily done, I suppose.'

'I obviously meant to say thanks for everything, Dr *Buck*ingham.'

'Yes, well, it was my pleasure. And we've enjoyed working with you, Miss Grant.'

Harvey opened the door and swept her away.

'You did that on purpose, didn't you?' he asked as soon as they were in the car. 'Calling her Doctor Fuckingham?'

Karen's eyes sparkled mischievously. 'I might have done, yeah.'

'Well, I've got to hand it to you, it was hilarious. But do you know who you reminded me of when you did it?'

'No, who?'

'Lola. That was exactly the kind of thing Lola would have done. Especially when someone was being nice to her.'

There was a reflective silence as Karen got into the car and clicked in her seat belt. She felt comforted to know that, after all these years of distance, she and Lola might have something in common after all. She gazed out of the window as Harvey started the engine and the car pulled away. The Abbey, which she was pretty sure had never been an abbey but a stately home belonging to a gambling-addicted earl, disappeared behind them. She thought about its nickname, the Abyss, and how low she'd sunk just before she'd admitted herself. And sure, she still looked a mess with her sunken cheeks, ravaged complexion and missing teeth. But inside she felt like she was leaving the clinic a completely different person.

'So how is Lola, anyway?' she asked.

'Yeah, she's great, thanks.'

'Really? She didn't look great when she fell down those stairs in Norway.'

'Sweden.'

'Oh wherever it was. But people don't get off their faces like that when they're happy – I've just spent the last two months having that drilled into me.' She almost stopped mid-sentence as she realized she'd hit on another similarity between mother and daughter. 'Anyway, are you sure she's OK?'

'Yeah, honestly. You know what she's like – she's always been high-spirited.'

Hmpf! People used to say that about me . . .

'And do you think she might come and see me when I'm home?'

Harvey cleared his throat nervously. 'Yeah, I'm sure she will. One day. Once work has settled down a bit.'

'Which basically means not for ages.'

'No! I'll bring it up with her next time I get a chance. I promise.'

Karen arched an eyebrow. 'Hold on a minute. Does Lola even know you've come to take me home today?'

Harvey's hands tightened on the steering wheel. 'Not exactly. She's really busy rehearsing for the tour and everything and I just didn't want to bother her with anything else.'

'Bollocks! You're worried about her, aren't you?'

'No! What makes you say that?'

'Because I might have been a crackhead for the last twenty years but I can still tell when someone's lying. Believe me, I've spent a lot of time around people who do nothing but. And I've told more than a few lies myself – as I'm sure Lola hasn't wasted any time explaining.'

Let go of the bitterness, she reminded herself, repeating the words of her therapist at the Abbey. *Picture it drifting away and floating out into the sky.* At the start of her treatment, exercises like this had seemed far-fetched and just plain daft. But she'd forced herself to get over her scepticism and play along – and had gradually learned to trust that they worked. Now she didn't hesitate to employ the techniques she'd been taught to avoid giving in to the feelings she knew would lead her back to drugs.

There was another silence and Karen looked out of the window. She couldn't believe how far she'd come in just two months. Although at the same time she knew Dr Buckingham was right and a lot of the hard work still lay ahead – forging a new life for herself in the real world. As the Berkshire countryside whizzed by, the September sun strobed through the trees. It was almost as if it were willing her on.

'So come on then,' she said, 'are you going to tell me what's going on?'

'It's no big deal,' Harvey replied, 'but Lola's under a lot of pressure at the moment. I'm sure it's nothing more than that, but I just don't want to add to it.'

'What do you mean, "add to it"? I'm leaving rehab and going home – isn't that good news? Or do you mean you don't want to get her hopes up in case I get out and go straight round to my dealer's?'

'No, it's not that, Karen. Honestly.'

Like hell it isn't. Although she could hardly hold it against him; she'd only known him for five years and he must have come to pick her up from rehab just as many times. *But this time it's different.*

'Anyway, what's going on between you two?' she asked. 'I thought you told each other everything? What do you mean "you're sure it's nothing more than that"?'

'Yeah, we do tell each other everything. But, you know, the new single's out, she's rehearsing for the big tour – there's a lot of stress flying around.'

'You've not fallen out, have you?'

'No, not at all.'

'Is it something to do with that Freddy Jones?'

She spotted his jaw stiffen. *It IS something to do with Freddy Jones.*

Over the last few days the papers had been full of Lola's date with the handsome entertainment correspondent from Channel 3 News. According to one journalist quoting a source close to her, the new couple were so blissfully happy they were already looking to buy a place and move in together. Funnily enough, it was when Karen had first heard the news that she'd known the treatment she'd been having must have been working. Ordinarily she'd have felt a jolt of jealousy as she looked at the photo of Lola kissing Freddy outside some trendy restaurant. It would have reminded her of all the scumbags and scrotes she'd dated over the years – not that she'd ever done much dating, more like shagging when she was off her face or being pimped out to her dealer's mates when she couldn't pay her debts. But on this occasion, she'd felt a stirring of joy at the sight of her daughter's happiness. It was about time she found a nice guy after some of the dickheads who'd made her so unhappy. Mind you, from the tension currently whitening Harvey's knuckles, it didn't look like she was happy at all.

'It's got nothing to do with Freddy Jones,' he stated firmly.

Bollocks! She could tell from his face it had *everything* to do with Freddy Jones. He obviously wasn't as much of a nice guy as the papers were making out. And she might have known – he was a journo after all. And she'd had enough of them offering her cash to dish the dirt on Lola to work out what they were all like. But if Harvey didn't want to tell her the truth she'd just have to play along.

'All right, Harvey, whatever you say.'

She'd give him one thing, though. All this time she'd been thinking Lola was her father's daughter but here was the person who knew her best saying she was just like her mum. For the first time in years she felt a glimmer of hope that she and Lola might be able to salvage something from the wreckage of their relationship. The only problem was, if Lola *was* anything like her mum she'd be in serious danger of destroying herself before they reached that point. And from what

Karen could infer from her conversation with Harvey, it looked like she might already be well on the way.

*

Lola looked at the stack of papers as it thumped down onto the table in front of her. She flicked through a few tabloids and saw they were full of stories about her supposed relationship with Freddy. 'LOLA FINDS SWEETHEART AFTER LIFETIME OF TRAMPS,' read one headline. According to another, the blissfully happy couple were planning a Christmas wedding. *Oh what have I done now?*

She was sitting with Barbara in the lounge area of Musicmaker rehearsal studios, preparing for a big interview with the showbiz editor of the biggest-selling red top in the country. The plan had been to promote the release of *Tramp*, which according to the midweeks was set to enter the singles chart at number one this weekend. But from what Barbara was saying, there'd be another topic of conversation right at the top of the agenda.

'What's going on, doll?' she asked. 'Are you seeing Freddy Jones or not?'

'No, I mean yes. Well, I mean, we did blatantly go on one date, which is when the paps got that picture, obviously. And we had a really nice time and everything but I haven't seen him since. To be honest, darlin', he's fit and I fancy him but I just can't go there right now.'

Barbara nodded, mulling it over. Lola wondered if she'd heard the rumours about her seeing Jake – or if she'd been too caught up in her own long-distance relationship with the German radio producer with the laugh like a hiccup. If she had heard anything, she wasn't letting on. *Good old Barb, always sensitive, never questioning or criticizing. Why can't Harvey be like that?* Ever since her date with Freddy he'd been pestering her about setting up another. No doubt he'd be grinning with glee at all this newspaper coverage.

Barbara folded her arms. 'OK, so what are we going to tell this journo now?'

'Well, I blatantly don't want to string him along but I also don't want to hurt Freddy.' *Not that I haven't hurt him enough already.* Lola thought back to their date and how wonderful it had been until she'd ruined it. Her actions had been selfish and thoughtless and she hadn't been able to shake off her guilt about it since. *Why do I always seem to do the wrong thing?*

'Well, whatever you say,' cautioned Barbara, 'it's got to be good because we don't want to go pissing off Freddy Jones or Channel 3 News. The show's ratings might be on the slide but it's still the most popular news programme on telly – and we need to keep them sweet.'

Oh my God, thought Lola, *how have I got us into this mess on top of everything else?*

'Can't I just tell the truth?' she asked Barbara. 'Can't I just say I really like Freddy but I've just got too much other stuff going on right now – and I'm not in the right place for a relationship?' *Not that that's the whole truth but it isn't exactly a lie . . .*

'Yeah but maybe you should soften the blow a bit. How about warming it up by saying you think Freddy's lovely but you just want to be friends?'

Lola could hear a train clattering along the tracks through the window behind them. 'Yeah, all right. OK. If you think that's best.'

Barbara nodded firmly. 'Great, that's settled. Now let me go and get this journo – he's waiting in reception.'

Lola leant forward and looked again at the stack of papers on the coffee table. Once again she was confronted by the sight of her own image gaily kissing Freddy outside the entrance to Scran. *Oh what was I thinking?* She took the papers and dropped them into the bin.

*

Freddy tried to concentrate as he googled background information on a children's fashion designer he was about to interview who'd been propelled to fame when the Duchess of Cambridge had dressed Prince George in her latest designs to open a sausage roll factory in Skipton. But he was finding it a real struggle. He knew nothing about fashion – let alone children's fashion. *What on earth's a shortall?*

Besides, he had much more pressing personal matters on his mind. If you could call a very public brush-off a personal matter. He picked up the newspaper from his desk and reread its front-page boast of a 'world exclusive' interview in which Lola Grant 'sensationally reveals the truth about her relationship with red-headed reporter Freddy Jones'. He opened the paper at the centre spread but already knew where his eyes would settle – on Lola's description of Freddy as 'lovely' but her admission that she 'just wanted to be friends'. Even though he'd been staring at the words for most of the morning, they still hit him like the bumps and thuds of a particularly aggressive team of opponents on a rugby pitch.

'I'm sorry, love,' said Dolly Dawson with a stomachwrenchingly sympathetic smile. 'Let me know if you want to talk about it.'

'Bad luck, boyo,' boomed Hugh Badcock. 'But look on the bright side – all those housewives will only love you more now you've been dumped!'

He wasn't sure he could take it much longer – and was almost looking forward to interviewing the fashion designer just so he could get out of the newsroom. The worst thing was, all week he'd had to put up with his colleagues winding him up about his 'pop star girlfriend' as the papers had built up their single date into the romance of the year. The last time he'd looked, one had quoted a 'close friend' of Lola's saying she was madly in love with him and the couple were about to start trying for a baby. And now here he was being blown out in an interview with the most popular red top in the country.

As if the date itself hadn't been confusing enough with Lola blowing hot and cold and then launching herself at him in front of all those paps. *What the hell was she up to?* He couldn't call her as he still didn't have her number and he couldn't plug Spike for information seeing as Harvey hadn't spoken to him since he'd told him he'd been unfaithful. Freddy looked at Spike now sullenly tossing a ball from one hand to another as he gazed aimlessly into space, his baseball cap pulled down so far it hid most of his face. Once they'd got through this shoot he'd take him out for a drink and try and cheer him up.

He had no idea how he was going to cheer himself up. What was it with him? Why was it that girls always seemed to blow him out by saying he was lovely and they just wanted to be friends? *Am I too nice, like? Is that what it is?* If it was that, he couldn't understand why so many of the girls he dated wanted to be treated like crap. He knew it was supposed to be something to do with low self-esteem but how could that be true of Lola, who had to be the most popular and successful woman in Britain? Or was it that something was wrong with him? *That's it, that has to be it. I'm just an unsophisticated, unexciting ginger Welsh guy. Why would anyone want to go out with me?*

The only thing was, he'd been convinced when he and Lola had been on their date that the energy between them wasn't just friendly but distinctly flirtatious. That was until she'd disappeared to the loo and come back with a face like thunder. *No, I don't buy all this bullshit about her having too much other stuff going on in her life to commit to a relationship.* That kind of thing was always just an excuse. If she did really like him then surely she'd just ask him to wait a while?

He looked again at the paper and the photo of Lola perched next to the journalist, about to tell all. No, there was more going on than she'd made out in the interview. And what he'd give to find out what it was.

*

'How about this one?' Harvey asked. 'It's cocky and feisty. I love it.'

'Yep, that's fierce,' agreed Lola. 'Put it in the Yes bin, blatantly.'

The two of them were sitting in front of Harvey's laptop in the private kitchen area of Pomegranate Dance Studios, sipping extra-hot skinny lattes and sorting through images of Lola for use in the tour programme and merchandise. The problem was, she'd been so shattered and in such a foul mood on the day of the shoot they were having to reject more than three quarters of the photos.

'What about this one?' asked Harvey, clicking onto a close-up shot of her making a diamond-shaped hole with her fingers and thumbs and winking through it.

'Are you taking the piss?' huffed Lola. 'It looks like I've got a lazy eye. Never mind the No bin – put that in the Trash.'

She took a sip of her coffee. Her relationship with her manager had been tense since they'd got back from Barcelona and that tension had increased when she'd announced in the national press that she just wanted to be friends with Freddy. *Not that it's got anything to do with him,* she thought, gazing in horror at a shot of her looking like she'd only had an hour's sleep. Which, if she remembered rightly, she had; the photo session, her second with Mark and Mark, had taken place the morning after the night Jake had turned up at her flat shit-faced and, once he'd shot his load, rolled over and snored so loudly she hadn't been able to get back to sleep, spending the rest of the night fretting about why she'd faked her first orgasm. 'Nope, get rid of that one,' she frowned.

Harvey clicked it away and it was replaced by a shot of her cuddling the photographers' dog, Nancy. 'Oooh, now that's quite sweet. What do you think about that, Harvey?'

'Hmm, I'm not sure. I think we want to stay focused on you looking strong and in control. You know, so it matches the message of the music.'

Here we go again. He can't resist having a sly dig . . .

She lowered her coffee onto the table and looked him in the eye. 'What's that supposed to mean?'

'Nothing. Just what I said.'

'But you blatantly said it with a snigger.'

'No I didn't.'

'Yes you did. And I know what you're trying to imply, Harvey – that I'm *not* in control and I'm being weak and stupid.'

Harvey minimized the window and snapped his laptop shut. 'Lola, that's not what I meant at all.'

'I don't believe you, Harvey. It's blatantly obvious you still have a problem with me and Jake. And it's about time you got over it. Because for your information, it's all going brilliantly.'

Oh what the hell? It serves him right for being so down on me and Jake from the start. Not that it looked like he believed her.

'Really? Is it really going brilliantly?'

'Yes, actually – it is.'

'But I thought you said you were just having a bit of fun and you could break it off whenever you wanted?'

'Yeah, well, maybe it's got a bit more serious now. Despite you shoving your nose in and doing your best to put him off.'

'Lola, what are you on about?'

'Oh come off it, Harvey. It's blatantly obvious you've not stopped having a go at Jake ever since Barcelona.'

'But that's not true at all – I haven't spoken to Jake once since Barcelona. I wouldn't dream of interfering in your personal life.'

I can't believe you. I have to believe it's you making Jake lose interest. She picked up her coffee and took another swig. 'Yeah, well, if I were you I'd keep a closer eye on your own personal life.'

'And what exactly is that supposed to mean?'

She cast her mind back to Freddy's comments about Spike during their date – and her hunch that something had gone wrong between them. 'Just that if I were you I'd forget about my love life and concentrate on your own.'

'For your information, Lola, my love life's going brilliantly.'

Yeah, course it is. 'Listen, Harvey, I'm only saying this because I'm looking out for you – and I want what's best for you. I just don't want you to get hurt, that's all.' Wasn't that exactly what he'd said to her? She hoped she'd got the words right so they'd make maximum impact.

'Yeah, well, there's nothing for you to worry about,' he trilled. 'And I'm not in any trouble.'

She looked him in the eye and could tell he was lying. What was it Freddy had said? That Spike *wanted* to do the right thing. Which surely implied that he hadn't. 'Listen, darlin', all I'm saying is, just because somebody *wants* to be good doesn't necessarily mean they will be.'

Harvey's jaw fell open in outrage. 'Yeah, well, wanting to be good and trying to be good is a lot better than not even giving a shit about being good – which is what you've got with Jake. And you might think he's going to change but if he doesn't want to then I can tell you now that you're only deluding yourself.'

She could feel her temper spiralling out of control. *How dare he say that?* 'You don't know what you're talking about, Harvey!'

'Oh no, don't I? I suppose you think because you two have great sex that means you've got something special? Well, I've got news for you, Lola – it doesn't. Just because a man wants to shag you doesn't mean he cares about you. It doesn't even mean he particularly likes you. That's something I learnt the hard way. And once the sex starts to dry up with Jake you'll learn it too.'

Lola wanted to throw the rest of her coffee in his face. *How can he know our sex life's starting to dry up?* She couldn't listen to him anymore; suddenly his flat vowels and Northern accent, which she used to love, had become excruciating. 'Listen, Harvey, you're really starting to overstep the mark now. Just you remember who's the boss here.'

Even as she said the words she couldn't believe they were coming out of her mouth. All this time the two of them had called themselves a partnership; it had never occurred to Lola to pull rank. But she just had – and Harvey looked stupefied.

'Well, if that's the way you want to play things,' he mouthed, 'fine. From now on, let's stick to business. At least we'll both know where we stand.'

'Fine,' she growled.

Oh what have I just done?

Harvey opened up his laptop and clicked back onto the photos. 'OK, *boss*, what do you think about this one?' She could see a thick vein throbbing on his forehead; he was clearly still seething.

She took a deep breath and tried to calm herself down. She looked at the picture on the screen and saw herself gazing down the lens with one hand on her hip and a snarl on her face. She wasn't sure what she thought about the pose – or what it said about her. *Punky and rebellious or cold and heartless?*

Come to think of it, she wasn't sure she knew which of the two more accurately reflected the person she was these days.

Was she really still just being feisty or had she turned into a total bitch?

*

A fat gay's a lonely gay, Spike chanted inwardly as he pushed and pulled with a passionate rage. *A fat gay's a lonely gay. A fat gay's a lonely gay.*

It was a mantra that had motivated him to pound his way through a two-hour workout that had already included a five-mile run on the treadmill, a long session lugging heavy free weights, and was now culminating in a stint on the cross-trainer that was feeling as endless as the DFS sale.

A fat gay's a lonely gay. A fat gay's a lonely gay.

Not that Spike was worried about being fat but he was terrified of being lonely – and it was a terror that had increased since he'd gone out and cheated on Harvey. Was he destined to spend the rest of his life sabotaging his happiness every time he fell in love?

He gave a loud grunt and came to a stop, collapsing forwards to lean on the control pad as he caught his breath. He stepped off the machine and his legs almost gave way as they touched the floor. He needed to end this workout now before he did himself an injury. He hobbled over to the stretch area and lay down on a mat to straighten out his muscles.

Guts and Butts was an exclusively gay gym in the centre of Soho and as he looked around the main exercise area, Spike recognized several regulars. Stretching out next to him was a geezer who must have been less than five foot tall but who'd overcompensated by taking so many steroids his chest had expanded to roughly the same dimension. Dead-lifting a barbell was a man whose face was so ugly it reminded Spike of the villain from a Roald Dahl story, though from the neck down he had a body that was so beautiful it could rival that of any superhero. And attempting to catch their eye was Ivor Shufflebottom, a wizened old queen who never seemed to do any exercise but instead sloped around the gym desperately trying to engage people in conversation. As Spike watched him stalk the floor he noticed everyone duck their heads or quickly look away. He wondered whether one day he'd end up like Ivor – so lonely he had to trawl the gym to scrape up every last crumb of human connection.

It had now been a week since he'd told Harvey about his infidelity – a week during which he hadn't heard from the man he loved more than any other. Serenity had tried to drag him out on the town, instructing him that the best way to get over someone was to get under someone. But he hadn't been able to face it and had instead stayed at home rearranging his trainer collection, aimlessly YouTubing pop videos and generally wallowing in self-pity. Things had reached a head last night when Freddy had taken him out for a drink after work and given him a stern pep talk. And that's when he'd decided not to give in but to start fighting back. He wasn't going to be lonely – and he certainly wasn't going to be fat.

He did one last stretch and turned to head downstairs. All day he'd been thinking of the best wording for a text message in which he'd tell Harvey how he felt about him and what had happened. He'd already tried to call several times but was always diverted to voicemail. At least with a text Spike knew he'd read it. He went into the changing room and punched in the code to his locker. He opened up his bag and fished out his phone.

'What up Harvey,' he typed. 'Cant tell you how sorry I am. Please give me another chance. I fucking love you. Spike x'

He reread it and hit Send.

He shut the phone in his locker, undressed and padded over to the showers. As he shuffled along the tiles he became aware of a pair of eyes watching him from behind. He tried to ignore it, switching on the water and feeling it surge down with such force it bounced off his shoulders. He turned to rinse himself on both sides and through the jets of water spotted a generic gay standing just a few feet away drinking a protein shake and looking him up and down suggestively. The man had a shaved head, was wearing tight-fitting Aussie-bum underpants and had the name of some no doubt long-forgotten ex-boyfriend tattooed on his bicep in Sanskrit. He held Spike's gaze as he removed his underwear to reveal an enormous semi-erect schlong.

Man, talk about making it obvious!

Spike couldn't help watching as the geezer strode across the empty changing room, stark naked, his towel casually dangling from the tips of his fingers and trailing along the floor. As he hung it up and stepped under the shower head next to him, Spike could almost feel the desire emanating from his eyes like an electric charge. He knew that several men followed their workout at Guts and Butts with a whole different type of exercise in the showers, sauna or steam room – and the staff not only tolerated it but sometimes even joined in. Spike himself had been known to indulge on several occasions before he'd met Harvey. But he didn't feel in the slightest bit tempted now.

He wasn't actually sure that he and Harvey were still together but he was sure that he wanted to win back his affection. And splashing around in the showers with this geezer would hardly be the right way of going about it.

He watched as the man squeezed liquid soap out of the dispenser and curled his mouth into a lewd grin. He began to work the soap around his dick, sliding his hand up and down the shaft until it was standing fully erect. Sure, the old Spike wouldn't have wasted any time in helping the man soap himself down but the new Spike was different. He wasn't interested in some generic gay making eyes at him in the showers. He was only interested in Harvey. And he was determined to win him back, whatever it took.

He switched off the shower and wrapped himself in his towel. The man's grin wilted and his dick began to deflate. Spike gave him a curt nod and headed back to his locker.

He was looking forward to checking his phone – and seeing if he had a reply.

*

Harvey looked at his phone and reread the text.

'What up Harvey. Cant tell you how sorry I am. Please give me another chance. I fucking love you. Spike x'

It was obviously sincere and he knew Spike well enough to know he'd be really hurt by what had happened between them. But *he* was hurt too – and his argument with Lola had only hurt him even more. His sadness had swelled until it cast a shadow over his soul, while his thoughts endlessly pinballed between the two most important people in his life and what they'd done to him. And right now he was too overwhelmed by all kinds of emotions to work out how he felt about his relationship with Spike – or how he was going to reply to the text.

Besides, now that Lola had reduced their partnership to a purely professional arrangement he couldn't risk neglecting his mounting workload. Which was why, at eight o'clock in the evening, he'd agreed to accompany Carlson Bent on a visit to an old aircraft hangar near Heathrow to check on the progress of the set being built for the show. An eye-wateringly large amount of money was being spent on moving and extending platforms; a twenty-foot long fireman's pole for the dancers to slide down; a travelator that ran the length of a runway thrusting out into the audience; and a podium that would lift Lola high above the stage and then out over the sea of fans for her big encore. Every aspect of the *Trouble* tour was now being upgraded in full expectation of it being extended to include a second leg in the States next year. The more successful Lola's career became, the more pressure this seemed to generate. And even though he was feeling ground down by problems both professional and personal, Harvey was determined not to buckle under the strain.

Carlson led him into the vast space and switched on the lights so the set flickered into vision. It wasn't even half finished but Harvey could already see how it would fit together and felt a little surge of excitement sparkling through the sadness that had swamped his last week. Carlson guided him around, talking him through the progress of each element and updating him on the designer's evolving vision.

After a while, Harvey broke off to stroll to the end of the runway and look out onto the enormous empty space. *In just under a month this view will be completely different,* he told himself. He pictured the opening-night audience screaming at the stage and felt the impact of their energy as they waited to be wowed by the sensational show they'd been promised at the press conference in Paris and in so many interviews since. If he could just draw together all the different creative strands being worked on by all the different artists, designers and musicians, Harvey had no doubt the show really would be sensational. But pulling it off would be a challenge far greater than any other he'd faced in his career so far.

He turned around to speak to Carlson and found himself staring at an empty set. 'Carlson?' he shouted. 'Carlson, where are you?'

Just then he heard the squeak of bare skin on steel and spotted an almost naked Carlson sliding into view down the fireman's pole. He came to a stop at the bottom and sprang onto his feet, revealing that he was covered by nothing but a pair of Aussiebum underpants and a tattoo in what looked like Chinese characters on his bicep – a bicep which, like the rest of his body, Harvey now saw was strikingly well sculpted.

'Here I am,' he drawled, striding down the runway towards him.

Flippin' 'eck! He is seriously fit.

'I thought you and me might put on a little show of our own,' Carlson grinned.

Hold on a minute, said a voice in Harvey's head, *you can't do this – you've got a boyfriend, remember?*

What are you waiting for? asked another. *Spike cheated on you – he can hardly expect you to be faithful!*

Carlson came to a stop right in front of him, so close

Harvey could almost sense his body heat. He felt the desire emanating from Carlson's eyes like an electric charge. His fingers touched Harvey's bare forearm and gently stroked their way down to his hand. As he felt Carlson weave his fingers through his, Harvey's eyes settled on the cute little dimple in his chin.

'So what do you say?' asked Carlson softly. 'Shall we make a start on our opening number?'

Oh go on! Stop fighting it. If you want to have some fun, just do it . . .

Don't do it! You've fought too hard to stop cheating on boyfriends. You're so much better than this!

It suddenly struck Harvey that his response to Carlson's invitation would not only determine the outcome of his relationship with Spike but also the success or failure of his last three years of therapy and abstinence.

Don't throw away everything you worked so hard for . . .

All that hard work and where did it get you? Right back where you started . . .

He had to admit, Carlson did have an incredible body.

Harvey opened his mouth to answer him.

There was only one way he could respond.

*

Lola opened her mouth and stepped up to the mic. She was back at Musicmaker in Bermondsey for a band rehearsal of *Miss Chief*. After a week of tension with both Jake and Harvey she'd had enough of feeling like everything was her fault. She'd had enough of being awash with guilt and self-pity. Now she was ready to fight back.

> *Nothing you can say or do,*
> *Will ever make me bow to you.*
> *The way you act is beyond belief,*
> *Don't forget that I'm Miss Chief.*

As she growled into the mic she tried to reconnect with the strength she'd felt when she'd sacked her last assistant for speaking to the press about her affair with Fox Marshall. It had been great to exercise her power in the eyes of the whole team and remind everyone she was in charge. It was a message she could do with certain people understanding now.

> *I'm smart and strong and I'm the boss,*
> *Losing you would be no loss.*
> *The way you act is beyond belief,*
> *Don't forget that I'm Miss Chief.*

She channelled all her energy into the vocal, feeling elevated by a strength and self-assurance that was returning to race through her once more. Her sense of exhilaration was so intense she was convinced she could feel it reverberating around the room. This was just what she needed – and just what she needed everyone else to witness. She caught sight of Harvey nodding along to the music next to a grinning Mike Henry. She gleamed at him and moved back in to the mic.

> *You think you can walk the walk,*
> *But I can tell you're just all talk.*
> *The way you act is beyond belief,*
> *Don't forget that I'm Miss Chief.*

She hoped everyone in the room could pick up on the

intensity of her emotion. Arranged in their positions around her, Danny, Smudge and Chuck played their instruments with what she was convinced was an increased vigour, while Gloria and Sharonne delivered their vocals as if totally transformed by the meaning behind the lyrics. But it was Jake she most wanted to register her transformation – her argument with Harvey had focused her mind on the problems between the two of them. The more she thought about it, the more she realized she was sick of him treating her like some pathetic weakling he could pick up and toss aside whenever he felt like it. Why should she put up with any more of his shit?

She waited to catch his eye but he didn't give her even the briefest glance. Instead, his gaze was trained firmly in the direction of her backing vocalists. She caught him flash over a cheeky wink, the same wink he'd flashed at her on the day they'd met – and then again on the set of *Lucky Star* when she came face-to-face with Rex Watson. Well, she wasn't going to stand for it. It was blatantly obvious something was going on between him and Sharonne. And she'd put up with it for long enough.

> *You tell lies and you're a cheat,*
> *But I can dance to my own beat.*
> *The way you act is beyond belief,*
> *Don't forget that I'm Miss Chief.*

That was it. As soon as this rehearsal was over she was going to confront Jake and tell him how she felt – that she was in love with him, whether he liked it or not. Why should she have to hide her feelings all the time? It wasn't her fault if he was terrified of real emotion and opening himself up to love. She'd pussyfooted around him for too long. But now she wanted more than a quick shag whenever he was pissed or horny. She wanted to be his girlfriend, to share her life with him, and for him to make a commitment not to sleep with anyone else, especially members of her team. And the more she thought about it, the more she felt sure she deserved it.

> *Don't forget that I'm Miss Chief.*
> *Don't forget that I'm Miss Chief.*

She hoped Jake was paying attention to her lyrics. Because as soon as this rehearsal was over she was going to ram home their message – and a whole lot more besides.

*

Jake rammed his dick into the moist pussy and heard a low groan of pleasure.

Man, that's good!

Fucking had been all he'd been able to think about as he'd gazed across the rehearsal room during endless runs of some bullshit song about Lola being the boss. Like he gave a shit anyway. He held onto the beautifully rounded ass and heard his stomach slapping against it as he slammed himself deep inside the gorgeous black body over and over again. He reached forward to tickle a nipple and couldn't help chuckling to himself as he heard a little cry of delight. *Who's the boss now, Lola?*

Not that Lola could have any idea he was banging her backing vocalist over a stack of old instruments in a storeroom, the first place he'd found that had been free. He'd been so crazy for a fuck he hadn't even washed his cock beforehand. Not that it mattered – this chick was a regular and so horny for him he was sure she didn't care. *And anyway, isn't that what a pussy's for, washing your cock?* Well, this one was sure giving his cock a good wash now.

'Fuck me, Jake! Fuck me, fuck me, fuck me!'

He wished the dumb bitch would keep her voice down. Sure, she was a great fuck but she was also a terrible squealer. And he wanted to keep this one strictly on the down-low.

'Shut the fuck up, babe,' he snarled as he slid deeper and deeper into her.

'But Jake, it's . . . I can't . . . I . . . *Oh!*'

He broke into his sloppy grin. 'Yeah? Are you enjoying that?'

'Fuck, yeah!'

He quickened his stroke and began pounding her so fiercely she had to grab onto a spare drum kit to steady herself. 'Who's the boss, babe? Who's the boss?'

'You are, Jake. You are!'

'You bet I am, babe! And don't you fucking forget it!'

Every muscle in his body began to quiver in anticipation of that sweet rush of ecstasy. *Motherfuck!*

'I'm going to come,' he spluttered, his shoulders already twitching.

'Me too!' she whinnied. 'Me too!'

He burst forth with one final slam, filling her with every-thing he had and stumbling forwards as his legs swayed beneath him. But the dumb-ass bitch was shaking too and had to grab onto a cymbal to stop herself from falling.

It was too late. The two of them collapsed into a heap and the cymbal crashed down onto the floor beside them –

making a noise so loud Jake was sure it was going to give them away.

*

'Jake? Jake? Is that you?'

The door creaked open and Lola stepped in to fill its frame. Her jaw slackened at the sight of them. 'What the fuck's going on here? Gloria, is that you?'

Shit! thought Gloria. *There's no getting out of this now . . .* She looked up and swept her hair out of her face, grimacing as her eyes locked onto Lola's.

'It *is* you!' Lola spluttered.

'Yeah, yeah, it's me,' Gloria mumbled, picking herself up from the floor and feeling around for her clothes. Jake pulled up his trousers and tried to zip away his still erect cock.

'But I thought we were mates,' Lola mouthed, her chin quivering.

'We are but . . .'

'But what, Gloria? Is this how you treat your mates?'

How dare she turn this on me? thought Gloria, so outraged she felt short of breath. But just as she was about to answer back she remembered that, however she felt about Lola, she was still technically her boss. *Don't forget that I'm Miss Chief,* she repeated to herself. She closed her mouth without saying a word.

'Wait a second, Lola,' Jake piped up.

'No, Jake,' Lola jumped in, her voice cracking, 'I won't wait a second – because I've waited long enough already. And while I've been waiting you've been shagging this cheap, tacky, two-faced *bitch*!'

Gloria's face burned with humiliation. *What I'd give to tell Lola what I really think of her . . .*

'You know, it's no surprise your solo career flopped,' Lola went on, 'if this is the way you behave. Fucking your friend's man behind her back!'

'OK, now hold on,' Jake broke in, waving around his hand. 'There's something I need to make quite clear here – Lola, I am *not* your man!'

*

The words hit Lola with such impact she felt her chest judder. To think she'd been looking for Jake to tell him she loved him – and to demand a more serious, committed relationship. And to think she'd confided in Gloria and the two of them had talked about trying to wean themselves off womanizers. She didn't think she'd ever been so humiliated in her life.

'And while we're on the subject,' Jake went on, turning to glare at Gloria. 'I'm not *anybody's* man. That's just not how I roll.'

As Lola listened to him speak she felt like she was sitting on a plane as it landed, being propelled back by a force beyond her control as her ears filled with the sound of the world screeching around her. Her stomach lurched at the smell of sex that still hung heavy in the room.

'But . . . But Jake . . .' she stammered.

'But nothing, Lola,' Jake interrupted, 'I thought I explained I don't want to be tied down. You know, I *did* explain that – several times. Or did you just decide not to hear me?'

Yes I fucking heard you! Lola thought. *But what you said and what you did just didn't match up.* That certainly hadn't been the message she'd received while they were having sex – when she'd looked into his eyes so close to hers their lashes were touching and she felt like she was drowning in love. But what was the point in trying to explain that now? It would only make her feel even more pathetic.

'Lola, I'm so sorry,' Gloria offered, clutching her clothes to her naked body, her face still flushed with that post-sex glow. 'I really didn't plan to do this, it just kind of happened.'

Lola looked at her and could feel the bile rising to the back of her throat. This obviously wasn't the first time she'd had sex with him. *Did she think the same thing as me when she was shagging him?* She remembered what Harvey had said about men being able to have sex without necessarily caring about a woman. And she felt a blast of anger – anger at herself for ignoring so many warning signs and striding head first into trouble.

'Oh give it a rest, Gloria,' she hissed. 'I don't want to hear your bullshit excuses. In fact, I don't want to hear anything you've got to say. And in case you haven't noticed, I don't need to.'

Don't forget that I'm Miss Chief, she reminded herself, trying to salvage the tiniest shreds of her self-esteem. But it was no use. She wanted to fire the pair of them but knew from previous experience you weren't allowed to sack someone just because they'd cheated on you – or had sex with your man. No, there were laws against that kind of thing, laws that could only be bent by paying the employees a shitload of cash. And for that she'd need to speak to Harvey and explain to him exactly what had happened, which was the last thing she wanted to do right now.

One thing was for sure: she couldn't delude herself any longer. Whatever had been going on between her and Jake, it was blatantly over – even if she *was* his boss.

'Lola,' Jake ventured, 'I'm sorry if I've hurt your feelings.'

My feelings? The banality of it was so offensive it lodged like a pain in her chest. *Doesn't he realize I'm in love with him?*

'Oh cut the crap, Jake!' she steamed. 'You don't know anything about feelings – mine or anybody else's. And from now on, as far as you're concerned, I won't be having any feelings. And that goes for both of you!'

She stomped out, slamming the door behind her.

My God what a mess!

This time she really had excelled herself. And she had no idea what she was going to do next.

9

'Come on then, love,' cooed Freddy's mam as the entire family turned to look at him. 'What's going on with you and Lola Grant?'

He'd been wondering how long it would take her to broach a subject she'd been working up to ever since he'd arrived home an hour earlier – and during numerous phone conversations over the past week, all of which he'd manage to cut short by coming out with increasingly outlandish excuses. But now that he was back in Port Talbot, he couldn't fob it off any longer.

'I mean, one minute you're apparently getting married,' she went on, 'the next thing we hear, Lola announces she just wants to be friends.'

Freddy cut into his roast chicken and did his best to look nonchalant. 'Oh it's no big deal really. We just went out on a date and we had a cracking time, like, but I get the impression she's too busy with work to get serious with anyone. She's about to go on a big tour and then she's off to the States for six months – the last thing she needs right now is a boyfriend.'

He omitted to mention the fact that he didn't even have Lola's phone number so had learnt all this from the same newspaper interview they'd read. He popped the chicken into his mouth and did his best to chew it; even though it was moist and smothered in gravy, his throat was dry and his Adam's apple felt like it had swelled to the size of a Granny Smith.

'But I don't understand,' bleated his mam, 'I thought you were moving in together?'

'And trying for a baby,' added his sister Helen in a brief break from shovelling mashed-up food into her one-year-old son's mouth. She'd just returned from maternity leave to work as a beautician in the salon owned by their mam and was struggling to reconcile her previously glamorous image with the reality of being a parent. She brushed away a squashed pea that had somehow attached itself to her left cheekbone.

Freddy swallowed his chicken with a gulp he was sure would be audible down at the steelworks. 'Yeah, well, don't believe everything you read in the papers. Could somebody please pass the gravy?'

'But what about that photo of you getting off with her out-side some restaurant?' asked his brother-in-law Owen, a balding, out-of-shape thirty-year-old who wore shorts in all weathers and had a permanently sweaty top lip. 'You looked more than friends in that – you looked like you were about to get down to business.'

Yeah, thanks mate. Rub it in, why don't you? Freddy couldn't help bristling whenever he was addressed by Owen, probably because his sister's teenage sweetheart had been the golden boy of Freddy's childhood, the star of the Wales youth rugby team coached by his dad and widely predicted to be destined for great things until he'd walked in front of a car aged sixteen and had his career cut short by a permanent leg injury. Since then Owen had piled on weight and developed a serious chip on his shoulder but everyone in Freddy's family adored him; he worked as his dad's assistant and followed him round all day, lapping up his every word. No one seemed to notice when he made sly digs at Freddy or was so jealous of his success he couldn't bear to watch him on TV. Sometimes Freddy thought his parents loved Owen more than they loved him.

'Yeah, well . . .' he struggled, inching back his chair and hearing it shriek across the sparklingly clean tiled floor. 'You can read anything you want into a quick pap shot. Especially when there's a caption next to it *telling* you what to think.'

'But don't they say the camera never lies?' Owen jumped in, looking towards Freddy's dad for some kind of back-up. 'Or did Lola say she just wanted to be friends *after* you'd got down to business?'

Freddy was sure he caught his dad giving Owen the faintest whiff of a snigger. *Don't get wound up,* he told himself, stabbing into an over-boiled carrot. He looked at his brother-in-law and saw a flash of the golden boy who for years at school had been the barometer against which his own failure had been measured. Then he saw his thirty-year-old moobs straining at his shirt and comforted himself with one of his favourite sayings – *Early to ripe, early to rot.* 'Well, I hate to disappoint you, Owen,' he frowned, 'but me and Lola didn't actually get down to business. Like she said, we're just good friends. And I don't know why you're all making such a big fuss about it.'

There was an awkward silence, filled only by the sound of the baby spitting out cabbage all over Helen's top and eventually broken by Freddy's dad clearing his throat, a sure sign he was about to launch into one of his self-aggrandizing anecdotes. 'Did I ever tell you about the time *I* went out with a famous singer?' he began.

'No!' trilled a wide-eyed Owen.

'When was that, Dad?' gleamed Helen as she dabbed at her front with a wet wipe.

For the next half-hour, Freddy's dad dragged out an at-best-mediocre anecdote about the time he'd briefly dated a pub singer called Gladys Glitz he'd met in a working men's club in Swansea in the mid-Seventies. He described her as 'a dead ringer for Olivia Newton-John' and claimed she turned down the chance to work in America because she was so head over heels in love with him. Freddy didn't have the heart to say he knew all about Gladys Glitz because she'd written to him shortly after he'd made his debut on Channel 3 News, begging for his help in relaunching her career and enclosing a CD of Bonnie Tyler covers she murdered with a voice that sounded like a bulldog choking on a cactus and a photo of her with an overly made-up face so puffy she looked like a character from Royston Vasey. Instead he kept quiet, gasping and giggling along with his family as his dad cued their laughter with the occasional pause. For once, Freddy was glad to hear him talk about himself; it gave him a brief respite from talking about Lola.

'So what happened then, Dad?' he asked. 'How did it all end?'

'Well, she started to get really clingy and wanted to see me all the time,' his dad boomed on. 'But I told her, don't try to come between a Welshman and his rugby!'

Freddy sat back and forced himself to laugh at his dad

holding court – the famous 'Big Freddy', tall, broad-shouldered and still with a full head of rust-coloured hair, reliving his glorious youth for his wife, daughter, son-in-law and son. A son who was still known both within the family and around the whole of Port Talbot as 'Little Freddy', even a year after the arrival of 'Baby Freddy'. He couldn't help wondering whether his nephew would still be called Baby Freddy when, like him, he'd reached the decidedly adult age of twenty-eight. He hoped he'd grow up to be the grandson Big Freddy hoped for – and didn't turn out to be as big a disappointment as he was as a son. He popped the final carrot into his mouth and pushed forward his empty plate.

'And that's when I met your mother,' his dad ended with a flourish. 'And I haven't given Gladys a second thought since.'

His family actually gave him a round of applause.

'That's a brilliant story!' fawned Owen, wiping the sweat off his top lip.

'Dad, that's so romantic!' echoed Helen, picking some baby sick out of her hair.

'Oh wouldn't it be nice,' added his mam, 'if one day Little Freddy and Lola could be just as happy as me and your dad?'

Freddy's heart sank. His mam obviously wasn't giving up just yet – and he braced himself for the onslaught continuing all weekend. Of course he knew she was only asking about Lola because she was proud of her son and his famous so-called girlfriend, just like she was proud of his success on TV and would boast about his latest reports to her customers in the salon. Usually her attention came as a welcome relief from his dad's disinterest, but in this instance her pride in him only made his failure to make Lola like him even worse.

'I'm sorry, Mam,' he said, giving her a weak smile. 'But I can't help it if Lola's career's taking off all over the world.'

'No, but it's such a shame. The girls at work will be so disappointed. And the customers have talked about nothing else all week.'

Oh it's not my fault, Freddy wanted to say. *And I'm disappointed too!* But he bit his tongue, unable to shake off the suspicion that it *was* his fault. After all, he could tell himself that girls dumped him for bad boys because of their own low self-esteem, but how did he know he wasn't the one with low self-esteem, always going for girls who were out of his league and would knock him back because he didn't think he deserved love? Well, if that was true then this time he'd surpassed himself, falling for a hugely successful pop star who obviously wouldn't ever consider going out with someone like him. 'Look, I'm really sorry, Mam,' he repeated rather sombrely, 'but you'll just have to tell everybody the truth – even if it is a big let-down.'

'I know, but everyone was so excited about meeting her,' she protested, her diamond danglers rattling from her ears. 'We were going to ask her to one of our girls' nights at the salon.'

Freddy tried not to cringe as he imagined Lola stepping inside MillionHairs and being greeted by his mam with the heavily highlighted Krystle Carrington bouffe she'd refused to change since the Eighties, and her staff made up of either teenage girls who looked like they'd walked straight out of an episode of *My Big Fat Gypsy Wedding* or ageing wannabe cougars with fake tan congealing in the wrinkles of their crêpe paper cleavages. Maybe it wasn't such a bad idea that she'd knocked him back before things had even got going. All right, everyone knew she'd had a tough upbringing, but now that she was the biggest pop star in the country she'd probably only have scoffed at his parents' aspirations of grandeur, their oversized house perched on the hill overlooking the town with its private driveway and portico columns, its wrought-iron gates emblazoned with the names Freddy and Trish, and its over-the-top sweeping staircase leading up to a framed portrait of the entire family shot by a professional photographer in black and white and slightly soft focus. He wondered what she'd make of his dad lording it around Port Talbot in his flash car with its private registration plate FREDDY 8, the number of his shirt when he'd played rugby for Wales. Maybe it was a good thing he wouldn't be finding out.

'But it all seemed so perfect,' his mam bleated, still unable to accept her dream of having a pop star daughter-in-law was over. 'Lola meets Little Freddy just when she's ready to give up bad boys.'

'Or tramps as she calls them,' offered Helen, tugging at Baby Freddy's now filthy bib.

The mere mention of the word made Freddy's chest tighten. He thought back to his interview with Lola on the set of the video for *Tramp*. How she'd explained at great length that she was through with tramps and then had fluttered her eyelashes at him as she'd asked if he knew any nice boys. He could hardly blame his mam for believing she was interested in him – at the time he'd believed it too. But now it looked like he'd fallen for some kind of act and in the process been humiliated in front of his family and his entire home town. He gave out a shaky sigh. He might have known Lola would be trouble; the warning signs were there from the start.

'Anyway, enough about girlfriends,' his dad butted in. 'How are you getting on with your rugby, champ?'

His mam and sister began to clear the plates and Freddy stood up to help them, explaining to the slouching males that he'd just started playing another season for the Welsh Dragons in the London Sunday League. He glossed over the fact that once again he'd been picked for the second team.

'And do you think you'll make the first team this season?' sniped Owen.

'Oh I don't know,' he replied calmly. 'I'm not sure I'm good enough for the firsts.'

Owen's face betrayed a glint of satisfaction while Freddy's dad frowned sympathetically. But for once it didn't bother him. On the contrary, after all the talk about Lola he felt relieved to be discussing a disappointment he knew how to handle.

*

Lola looked at her costume and wasn't disappointed. On the contrary, she was pleasantly surprised. It had been her idea to spend one section of the show dressed as strong female leaders from history. Boudicca, Joan of Arc, Cleopatra – a trio of warrior women who'd together help her project a steely front to the audience and show the world she wasn't to be messed with. And along the way hopefully inspire her female fans to tap into their own inner strength. After months of design meetings and discussions about sketches, her vision was finally starting to take shape.

'Now this is fierce!' she gushed as she gave a twirl dressed in the beginnings of the costume that would transform her into Cleopatra: a jewel-encrusted headdress with a ruby-eyed cobra at its crest; a glittering gold gown which would shimmer as she shimmied under the stage lights; and an ornately embroidered cape with winged sleeves which, when lifted, would transform her into a towering, indomitable presence.

'Now you have to imagine it with a long black wig and all the eye make-up,' quipped the designer. 'Oh, and without any of the safety pins!'

Lucretia Lavelle was a grand but rather haggard heiress-turned-hellraiser who'd first made her name as a fashion designer in the Seventies and since then had become almost as famous for her scandalous affairs and five husbands, including an earl, a high-ranking member of Margaret Thatcher's cabinet and a much younger truck driver from a council estate in Hull. Now single and a senior stateswoman of British fashion with a worldwide reputation, she still had a naughty twinkle in her eye, insisted on dyeing her hair bright purple and would occasionally flash photographers to prove she was wearing no knickers. Before she'd become famous, Lola had watched mesmerized as Lucretia had been interviewed on *Piers Morgan's Life Stories* and had gasped in delight as she'd recounted every detail of her rule-breaking behaviour and rebellious lifestyle. And now one of her all-time idols was designing the costumes for her new show. She felt slightly overcome and more than a little humbled.

'Well, I'm really made up,' she managed, moving over to the mirror to raise her arms and enjoy the full effect of the sleeves. 'And I'm sure Carlson can work these wings into some kind of routine.'

'Now just stand still one minute,' Lucretia asked, lowering herself onto her knees to adjust the hemline of the gown. Lola froze to the spot, unable to quite believe Lucretia Lavelle was kneeling at her feet.

But right now it was just the kind of distraction she needed. For the last few days she'd struggled to try and take her mind off the horror of walking in on Jake having sex with Gloria – and to make up for the fact that she had to face the two of them almost every day at band rehearsals. She wished to God she could have just sacked them; it would have made things so much easier. She just felt so betrayed – and she couldn't get the image of the two of them looking up at her from the floor of the storeroom out of her mind.

Perhaps even worse, over the last few days she'd been surprised to discover she actually missed Jake. Or at least she missed loving him – even if their love had been one-sided. But without it the joy had been sucked out of her world and everything felt different. Even her food tasted different – bland and flavourless. But being struck in the face with evidence of Jake's infidelity had robbed her of all her happy memories of him, contaminating everything they'd done together and souring their entire relationship. Or whatever Jake wanted to call it. Now she woke up in the morning feeling like one of those piñatas children bashed with sticks at parties, tearing them to bits to get to the sweetness inside.

'I'm just going to take this in a bit at the waist,' explained Lucretia, bunching together a handful of fabric. 'I mean, it's not really historically accurate but let's be honest, you do want to look hot.' She gave a loud, throaty cackle and Lola couldn't resist joining in.

Her laughter trailed off as she remembered how she'd felt on stage at Hyde Park and the triumph that had blazed in her eyes as she'd first got together with Jake later that night. All right, the warning signs had been there from the start but she'd been so carried away by such a strong feeling of sexual attraction, she'd somehow thought it would overpower all negativity and conquer Jake's compulsion to sleep around. She wondered how Lucretia would respond if she told her what had happened and asked for her advice. She was certainly a woman of the world who'd lived through her fair share of romantic dramas. Surely she'd understand?

But she fell silent. Right now she wasn't sure she'd be able to trust anyone again. She doubted Lucretia would be capable of shagging her man or selling her story to the press, but then again, she hadn't expected her last assistant to flog her heartache to the highest bidder or to walk in on Gloria on the job with Jake. And she reminded herself that, just like them, Lucretia was working for her and stood to benefit from the professional association – as did everybody who strayed into the very outreach of her orbit. She was racked by a low throb of loneliness and her costume suddenly felt very heavy.

'Can I take this off now?' she asked.

'Absolutely,' said Lucretia, beckoning forward her team of assistants with a click of her fingers. 'We're all done.'

As she watched the designer issue orders, she couldn't help wondering what she was hoping to wring out of her. Was it just the credibility of working with a young, cool pop star or was she looking for something more than that? *Does she want a piece of me too? Does she want to rip into me like a piñata?*

'And might I say you make a divine Cleopatra?' gushed Lucretia. 'The gold really complements your skin tone!'

Does it? Does it really? Lola wasn't sure what to think anymore – what to think about anything. She looked in the mirror as Lucretia's assistants dismantled the costume around her and suddenly had no idea whether she looked absolutely amazing or utterly horrendous.

She wondered who she could ask for an impartial opinion. The only other person in the room was Amina, who as usual was tapping away on her iPad, and she was hardly going to tell her she looked like crap, especially knowing what had happened to her last assistant. Of course there was always Harvey – and from the start of her career he'd made a point of telling her the truth. But she couldn't bear Harvey to know he'd been right about Jake. Oh she wished she had a manager she could talk to about this kind of thing. And why shouldn't she? Surely it was a manager's job to pick up the pieces if their artist made the odd mistake? She resented being made to feel bad about it. And she resented being made to feel like she was being slowly buried under an avalanche of criticism.

Come to think of it, do I really want to expose myself to criticism? Do I really want to hear the truth? She suddenly remembered that she was seeing Belle, Scarlett and Trixie later in the week to shoot the video projections to be shown on the screens during the show. They wouldn't have a go at her about her disastrous fling with Jake or make her feel bad about it – far from it. Of course she knew they were all on the payroll and only ever told her what she wanted to hear. But surely that was the point; she *wanted* to hear it. And she was sick of hearing people make comments she *didn't* want to hear. If she was a star and didn't have to hear them, why would she choose to?

And she *was* a star – a major star. OK, everyone in the team had played a part in her success but ultimately it was Lola the public wanted. It was her name on *Tramp*, which was currently the number one single in practically every country in Europe. It was her voice and her lyrics that had made it the biggest airplay hit of the year in less than a month. And it was her identity as an artist and the experiences that had inspired her music that had kept her album at number one every week since the summer. And all right, it might be glamorous and fun to be the frontwoman of the entire operation but it was also tough and incredibly stressful. *Isn't it about time everyone cut me some slack?*

She watched in the mirror as an assistant removed her elaborate headdress and handed it to Lucretia. She was pretty sure Cleopatra didn't get to become Queen of Egypt by kow-towing to her subjects. And she certainly hadn't gone down in history for listening to her manager tell her she was falling for the wrong kind of man. No, she'd simply steamed on and done exactly as she'd pleased. And now she was remembered as one of the greatest women who'd ever lived.

She turned to Lucretia and gave her a smile. 'OK darlin', who's next? Boudicca or Joan of Arc?'

*

Harvey looked at the National Theatre and saw the poster for a new play about Joan of Arc. He'd offer to take Lola if she hadn't downgraded their relationship to a purely professional one. He hardly thought it would be appropriate now. Since their big row in the kitchen of Pomegranate Dance Studios, all the warmth between them had gradually frozen over – until talking to her had become like skating on a sheet of ice he was terrified of cracking.

'The other day,' he huffed, 'all I said was "All right, Trouble?" and she nearly bit my head off. She told me never to call her that again. But that's what I've *always* called her!'

Spike shook his head incredulously. 'That is proper shit, man.'

The two of them had come back to the Cod Squad on the South Bank, where they'd stopped to eat fish and chips on their very first date not quite three months ago. Although summer had now firmly given way to autumn, the late September sunshine was still warm enough for them to sit outside. The carnival atmosphere of early July had gone and there were far fewer people strolling along and gazing at the river now the first leaves were falling from the trees and the sky had clouded over. But Harvey had wanted to come back here to talk to Spike about their relationship; after nearly two weeks' silence he'd given in to his texts and agreed to meet up to thrash things out. The problem was he also had a confession of his own to make. And now the time had come he found himself doing everything he could *not* to make it.

'You know I'm actually worried something else has happened,' he raced on. 'She's been acting like a total cow with everyone all week and Jake's hardly said a word. He just skulks around the whole time and legs it out the door the second the rehearsal's over.'

'Well, isn't there someone you can ask about it, man?' Spike managed to squeeze in. 'And find out the deets on what's gone on?'

Harvey wrinkled his nose. 'I don't know. The atmosphere in rehearsals is so toxic I'm not sure I'd get a straight answer out of anyone.'

'What about that Carlson? Couldn't you ask him?'

'Oh, there's a waiter!' Harvey almost shrieked. 'Shall we order our food?'

Before Spike had time to argue, Harvey had practically yanked over the waiter and was blurting out his order. Spike followed by asking for the same fish and chips he'd eaten last time and then leant onto the table towards Harvey.

'Is everything all right, blud?' he asked. 'It's just that you've been acting proper shifty and it's making me nervous. And to be honest, I was nervous enough in the first place.'

Come on, lad, Harvey told himself. *You can't put it off any longer.*

'Well, actually,' he began slowly, 'there was something I wanted to talk to you about.'

'Yeah, I know, and I've been doing a lot of thinking about that too. And the—'

'No, Spike,' Harvey interrupted. 'It's not about what you did the other week. *I've* got a confession I need to make this time. And it's about Carlson.'

Spike gave a sad slump. 'Oh yeah? What about Carlson?'

'Well, the other day he tried it on with me.' Harvey could feel the tension lifting his shoulders.

'And?'

Oh go on, Harvey, just tell him!

'And what did you do, man?'

Come on, lad. Spit it out!

Harvey took a deep breath. 'Don't worry, I didn't do anything. But I wanted to. And I had to really fight not to.'

Spike let out a long sigh. 'Is that it, man? I thought you were going to tell me you shagged him or something.'

Harvey thought back to the erection stirring in his trousers as Carlson had run his fingers along his arm and woven their hands together. 'No, Spike, I didn't shag him. But I came really close. And it worried me because I thought I was over all that.'

Spike looked down guiltily. 'Yeah, well, you're a lot more over it than I am – obviously.'

'Yeah but I'm a lot older than you, Spike. And I've spent years trying to figure out why I was always so turned on by that kind of thing, cheating on boyfriends and stuff. And I thought I had it all worked out. I thought that would be enough to make the feelings go away. But it hasn't quite – not yet anyway.'

'Yeah, well, don't be too hard on yourself, man,' Spike offered. 'I was tempted too but I gave in – and at the time I didn't even know why. But as I said, I've been doing a lot of thinking lately. And I'm pretty sure I've started to work it all out, man.'

Harvey nodded. 'Oh yeah, and what have you worked out?'

'Oh, you know, probably that I was trying to punish myself, just like you said you used to. Probably because of the way I was brought up and the kinds of things everyone used to say about people like me. You know, gay people. I suppose part of me, like, still believes them.'

'But Spike,' Harvey spluttered, 'you're the most amazing guy I've ever met. You shouldn't be thinking anything bad about yourself. And I know I was really pissed off when you first told me what you'd done, but I've missed you so much since then.'

'Me too, blud, me too. I've really struggled without you, man.'

As he spoke it was almost as if Harvey could feel his injured feelings knitting back together. This was exactly the kind of thing he'd wanted to hear Spike say. Because he too had stalled without him and shuffled through a life that felt like it had been stripped of all joy. And yeah, he'd been angry when he'd found out Spike had cheated on him and had worried he wouldn't be able to trust him again. But his little encounter with Carlson had relieved some of that anger – by helping him reconnect with the part of him that even now could some-times feel gripped by an urge to destroy his happiness.

'And who knows, man?' Spike went on. 'Some of this dark shit might always be a part of me. And it might take ages for, like, my feelings to catch up with my brain. But I know they will do one day, man. And I'm hoping you'll stick with me to see it happen.'

There was a silence and Harvey remembered the last time the two of them had been sitting here, when *Lost in Love* had blasted out of the sound system and he'd felt utterly uplifted by the possibility of new love. Perhaps it was that sense of hope that he'd missed most over the last few weeks, that he'd struggled to get through the day without. But he knew now that he wanted it back. And if Spike was offering it to him he was ready to seize it.

'All right Spike, I'll stick with you. If you'll stick with me.'

Spike gave him a big, beautiful smile – a smile that on their first date Harvey had thought was like the bright sun breaking through the clouds. Clouds he'd almost forgotten were now filling the sky. 'For sure, blud. You just try and stop me.'

Harvey reached out and took his hand, not wanting to lose a single second of the connection between them. It was as if he could feel the joy and hope rushing back to revive his sapped spirit. When the waiter came to serve their drinks he didn't even look up. And neither did Spike.

'Oh, and Harvey,' Spike added once the waiter had gone, 'if it's not too early to say this again, I love you. I fucking love you.'

'It isn't,' Harvey managed, smiling so widely his mouth could hardly form the words. 'And I fucking love you too.'

*

'Now remember Mummy loves you,' Gloria told Chanelle as she bounced up and down on the bed in her princess pyjamas. 'Mummy loves you lots and lots forever and ever.'

It was something she insisted on telling her daughter every day. Not that anyone had ever told Gloria they loved her – or was ever likely to in the future. *Certainly not now Lola's come along and fucked everything up.*

She rearranged her face into a sweet smile. 'And Mummy loves you a little bit more on your birthday,' she cooed, kissing Chanelle five times around her face. 'Five years old! I can't believe my little baby's turned into such a big girl!'

'I'm a big girl!' Chanelle squeaked, waving around the princess doll she carried everywhere. 'I'm a big girl now!'

'Now come and sit down next to Mummy and I'll sing you a nice song,' Gloria said, a little yawn escaping from her mouth. It wasn't even seven o'clock but for once she'd been happy to be woken up early so she could share in Chanelle's delight at being another year older. Sometimes she looked at her daughter and was frightened by how much she loved her or what she'd be capable of in order to protect her. Theft, violence, even murder – nothing would be too much if Chanelle's happiness were ever threatened. Or if anyone ever threatened to disrupt the happy little world Gloria had created for the two of them. *Anyone like Lola . . .*

As Chanelle snuggled up to the pillow next to her, Gloria put her arm around her and launched into a heartfelt rendition of *Happy Birthday*. Halfway through she couldn't help her voice cracking. *If it weren't for Lola I'd be singing something much better than this. If it weren't for Lola I'd still have a solo career and would be preparing for the opening night of my tour.*

Funnily enough, Gloria had always thought Lola couldn't remember that she'd once had her own solo career. But she obviously could as she hadn't wasted any time bringing it up when she'd burst in on her and Jake having sex like the door-mat wife in some downmarket daytime soap. And what she'd said made Gloria wonder if all this time she'd been sniggering at her failure as her own success grew and grew. 'It's no surprise your solo career flopped,' Lola had practically spat in her face, 'if this is the way you behave.' Gloria didn't think she'd ever been so insulted in her life. And that was saying something!

And she wouldn't care, but Lola had nothing to be angry about in the first place. Jake was more her man than he was Lola's. At least she'd got there first, if that counted for anything. And it wasn't as if she hadn't done the sisterly thing and tried to warn Lola off him, making up some bullshit story about a friend in New York calling him the Pied Piper of trouble. She'd delivered the warning after they'd performed on *Lucky Star* and were celebrating in Club Foot, when Lola had prick-teased Jake but then gone off to chuck her guts up, leaving him practically frothing in frustration. Gloria had spotted her chance and moved in, inviting herself back to his hotel room where they'd spent the rest of the night fucking like rabbits reared on Viagra. It had been the best sex she'd ever had and she resented the fact she'd had to apologize to Lola for it. She reminded herself she hadn't actually done anything wrong. *It's not my fault Lola can't hold her booze – or that she got too shit-faced to nail her target.*

She reached down under the bed and pulled out an enormous present wrapped in bright pink paper and tied with a ribbon. 'Now this is a present from Mummy,' she grinned, handing it over to Chanelle, who immediately began tearing off the paper like a feral beast hunting for food.

'Oh it's a castle for my princess!' she yelped.

'I know, honey,' said Gloria, peeling off the Sellotape to open up the box. 'And there's a handsome prince living inside who can't wait to meet her.'

Chanelle's eyes stood out like gobstoppers as she watched her mum open up the flap of the box and slide out the pink fairytale castle with its pale blue turrets, sweeping staircase and wind-down drawbridge. Waiting inside was a doll of Prince Charming which Gloria began to release by undoing the plastic ties that attached him to the packaging. Chanelle was buzzing in anticipation.

As she gradually worked the doll free, Gloria thought back

to her own feelings about Jake as she'd gradually got to know him. All right, she'd been able to tell he wasn't ever going to be any kind of traditional Prince Charming but then again she was hardly a traditional princess. Of course he'd told her he didn't like to commit to one woman, and she'd heard the rumours about him seeing Lola after the gig in Hyde Park – way before Lola had actually told her about it. And she'd worked out exactly what was going on when Jake had started making excuses and seeing her less and less. But, unlike Lola, Gloria wasn't stupid or desperate. So she'd sat back and bided her time, knowing sooner or later he'd get bored of Lola – which he did, pretty quickly. And then she'd simply upped the ante to reignite his interest in her. On the night Lola had told her she was going on a date with Freddy Jones, Gloria had invited Jake round to her house and treated him to her signature deep-throat blow job, taking full advantage of the fact she'd been born with no gag reflex. And she'd done it on this very bed.

She finally released the doll of Prince Charming and handed him to Chanelle. 'Here you are. Are you going to introduce him to your princess?'

As Chanelle took hold of the doll and laid him down next to his new girlfriend, she began acting out a romantic scene she must have picked up from some Disney film. *I wouldn't get too carried away, honey,* Gloria felt like saying, *because in real life that kind of thing doesn't happen to people like us.* But she fell silent. She couldn't bring herself to destroy the innocence of Chanelle's dreams. Even though she'd just seen another of her own dreams destroyed – the dream of falling in love again, which after Ned she'd all but given up on. That was until she'd met Jake, when she'd allowed herself to think she might still achieve her happy ending. But now he'd broken it all off, saying things were getting too heavy and he didn't want any drama before they went on tour. No, now that dream was dead too – killed once again by Lola.

Unfortunately Gloria had no choice but to grit her teeth and turn up at rehearsals, as usual smiling through the pain. What else could she do? It was Lola who'd ruined her solo career but ironically it was Lola's money that had thrown her a lifeline. It was Lola's money that had paid for Chanelle's princess castle. And more importantly, it was Lola's money that was paying the rent for their home – even if they deserved to live somewhere much nicer than this grotty, dingy shit pit. So Gloria would just have to swallow her humiliation and carry on sucking up to Lola. Because the second she put another foot wrong she had no doubt she'd be out on her ear.

But ever since that demeaning scene in the storeroom, she hadn't been able to stop thinking about somehow getting her revenge. It was almost as if the idea had worked its way inside her soul and wouldn't give her any peace until she'd seen it through. It was about time Lola was made to pay for everything she'd done to her – and Gloria had already worked out exactly how she'd do it. Her debut as a film director had proved a smash hit after their little shoot with the unknown cameraman in Sweden. It was about time she moved into production on the sequel. And this time she'd be stepping behind the camera herself – to make sure the film caused even more of a sensation.

'Chanelle, honey,' she crooned, reaching for her mobile phone, 'why don't I film you playing with your new present? And then me and you can show it to your friends at school?'

'Oh yes please, Mummy! And can we send it to Daddy too?'

'Of course we can, honey,' Gloria breezed, her well-practised smile once again covering up a pang of pain.

Chanelle sat upright and followed Gloria's direction, holding her two dolls up to the camera and winding the castle's drawbridge up and down. As Gloria looked through the viewfinder and followed the action, her imagination began to race ahead to the next time she'd be pressing Record. And whatever action she'd be filming she was sure it wouldn't be the kind of behaviour worthy of a fairytale princess.

No, the way Lola had been bossing everyone around lately, acting like a wasp at a picnic and pissing off her entire entourage, it wouldn't be long before she slipped up and gave Gloria the opportunity to expose her as the self-centred, heartless bitch she really was. And Gloria could hardly wait.

*

Lola imagined her fist slamming into Gloria's face. She stepped forward, threw a punch and gave a little twist at the end. 'How's that?'

'Not bad,' said Tiny. 'But try and keep your elbow in tight. Push it, don't sling it.'

She gave it another go. 'Better?'

'Yeah. Just make sure you exhale from your diaphragm as you punch. So the energy flows out through your fist.'

She gave it one last go, breathing out as loudly as possible. 'Is that it?'

'Good. We're finally getting there.'

Lola jumped up and down on the spot and banged together her thickly padded boxing gloves. She was standing in the ring in Busters, a boxing club in Bethnal Green that dated back to the 1930s and had recently been restored to its art deco glory. The ring formed the centrepiece of a grand hall that had been painted green and beige and was surrounded by raked seating and overlooked on all sides by a gallery. At great cost, the venue had been hired for the day to film one of the videos to be projected onto the screens at the back of the set during the *Trouble* tour. Tiny, Lola's head of security, had been enlisted to teach her some moves as she'd remembered he used to be some kind of boxing champion. Unfortunately, he wasn't proving to be quite such a champion coach. Either that or Lola wasn't much of a student. She wiped a bead of sweat off her forehead with the back of her wrist. *I always thought dancing was hard but this is something else.*

She could hardly complain as she'd been the one who'd insisted on changing the concept for the shoot at the last minute, forcing everyone else to work flat out to make it happen. And she didn't mind admitting to herself that she'd kind of done it on purpose. Part of her had wanted to remind everyone who was in charge and to show them all she was the creative mind behind the tour and not just some kind of puppet. But dressing up as a female boxer had been a great idea and was a perfect fit for the strong woman theme she wanted to run through the show. And it hadn't escaped her attention that it had the added bonus of allowing her to let off some steam. She might not be able to punch Jake or Gloria in real life, but at least she could imagine laying into them as she pounded her fists into Tiny's huge frame.

'OK,' he said, 'now let's try a cross punch.'

She nodded in concentration.

'Take your rear hand, keep your shoulder slightly behind you, rotate all your back-up mass and move your head so it goes over the knee.'

She did her best to imitate him but could feel her hands tensing in frustration, even though Tiny had spent all morning reminding her to keep them relaxed until the point of impact.

'No, it needs to start from your feet and travel up to your fist,' he explained patiently.

She gave it her best effort but was rewarded with a concerned frown.

'Don't cross the body,' sighed Tiny, giving yet another demonstration. 'Go straight out and steal it.'

'But I thought you said it was called a cross punch?'

'Well it is, but you don't actually cross the body.'

'Well, can't you call it something else then? It's blatantly really confusing!'

Carlson stepped in to try and simplify things but only succeeded in making the choreography even more convoluted. To make matters worse, Hettie Spriggs had been hired to direct the video and stood there twiddling the edge of her rockabilly dress as she expressed conflicting ideas about what would work best on camera. Amidst all the chaos, Tiny was insisting on following to the letter Lola's instruction to make her boxing look as authentic as possible. And as no one had benefitted from any time to plan the shoot, everyone seemed to be making it up as they went along. Lola looked at a clock on the wall and saw it was already late morning. They still hadn't shot a single frame.

'You know what,' she snapped, turning on her heel and striding out of the ring, 'I can't be doing with this.' She looked over her shoulder at Tiny, Carlson and Hettie. 'Why don't you lot work out what the fuck's going on and then give me a shout. I'm blatantly going for a break.'

She thundered down the steps and across the auditorium, trailed by Amina and her Style Council, who'd reassembled early that morning for the shoot. She led them all towards her dressing room, which had been set up in the ladies' toilets. She flung open the door and thumped inside.

'I don't know what the hell's going on,' she growled, 'but it's really starting to take the piss.'

'It's outrageous,' agreed Belle.

'Totes scandalous,' echoed Scarlett.

'They need to seriously get their acts together,' spewed Trixie.

Thank God, thought Lola, *finally some people are talking sense!*

She slumped into her chair and let her gloved hands fall to her sides as the girls swept in to touch up her hair and make-up.

'Well, I think you're doing amazingly,' breathed Belle. 'Especially considering all the pressure you're under.'

Yeah, she thought, *I am actually under a lot of pressure*. The tour was opening in ten days' time and it was her name on all the tickets, her name the fans would be screaming and her name the critics would be blackening if the show wasn't a success. Why didn't people realize how hard it was for her? And to top it all, Harvey had pissed off for another big meeting to firm up the second leg of the tour in the States. Not that Lola particularly wanted him around at the moment – far from it. But at least the girls were here.

'Well, all I can say is,' breathed Scarlett, 'it's about time people showed you a bit more understanding.'

'Big time!' added Trixie. 'Especially after all this shit with Jake and that slag Gloria.' Lola had spent the morning filling in the girls on last week's little surprise in the storeroom. They'd all sided with her against Jake and Gloria, despite the fact that just a few weeks ago they'd been going out on the town with Gloria and encouraging Lola to fall for Jake. Of course she hadn't forgotten they were all on the payroll, but she told herself she didn't care. For the moment their advice was exactly what she wanted to hear.

'I actually think you're handling everything really well,' said Trixie. 'Most artists I work with would have cracked up by now. Or started overdoing it on the coke.'

'God,' sighed Lola, 'can you imagine if I suddenly started taking a shitload of coke? That's the *last* thing I need!'

'You say that,' crooned Trixie, 'but a nice little bump might sort you out.'

'Oh come on, darlin', you know I couldn't ever do coke. Can you imagine what the papers would say?'

'Lola, there are loads of people who do coke without the papers ever finding out,' warbled Belle.

'You know, the odd bit of Charlie's not as big a deal as you think,' added Scarlett. 'Everything that's gone on with your mum has probably just turned you against it.'

'And we keep telling you, coke's nowhere near as hard core as crack.'

Lola suddenly remembered she still hadn't called her mum, who according to Harvey was now out of rehab and doing really well. But she just couldn't face it.

'Big time!' burst in Trixie. 'As long as you stay on top of it, coke's perfectly harmless. It's only like having a shot of vodka. And it does make you feel cool as fuck.'

For the first time, Lola could feel her interest sparking. 'Really? Like how? What's it like?'

'Oh it just sharpens you up a bit,' smiled Trixie, 'gives you a little boost. I always think it makes me into the best version of myself.'

It sounded nothing like the state her mum had got in when she'd taken crack. And she had to admit, they were making it sound very tempting. 'But doesn't it turn you into a total bitch?' *Like I need any help on that front at the moment.*

'No!'

'We've had a couple of lines this morning.'

'You don't think *we're* bitches, do you?'

'No. Not at all. It's just . . . Oh, I don't know . . .' She was so strung out she could hardly remember why she had to stay away from drugs in the first place. But she did remember she'd always thought that if she ever started on coke that would be the beginning of the end. *No, I can't, I just can't.*

Presumably Amina agreed with her; Lola noticed that since they'd been talking about drugs she'd started biting her nails and flitting her eyes around nervously.

'Oh thanks, girls,' she said, rallying slightly, 'but at the moment I've just got to get through today. And for some reason that's turning out to be difficult enough as it is.'

'Well, I think you should get back out there and tell them you want to start rolling,' Scarlett said.

'Absolutely,' chipped in Belle. 'You're the artist and the shoot should start when you're ready.'

'Big time!' agreed Trixie. 'I mean, what do they expect you to do? Sit in here fiddling with your fanny?'

'You know what,' Lola steamed, feeling a flush of anger, 'you're all right. And I can't be arsed with this anymore. Come on, it's about time somebody kicked this lot into action.'

She stomped back onto the set with the four girls tottering after her, booting out of the way any kit that had been left in her path.

'Right, let's get on with it!' she boomed to the crew, most of whom seemed to be standing around kicking their heels while Carlson, Hettie and Tiny were still blocking through the action in the ring. She bounded up the steps towards them, banging her gloves together and jumping up and down impatiently.

'Yeah, just give us another five,' cheeped Hettie with that permanent smile Lola was starting to find annoying.

'No actually, Hettie, I'm ready to go now. And I'm sick of sitting around fiddling with my fanny.' She realized she was practically shrieking and most of the crew had dropped what they were doing to stand and gawp at her. But she couldn't care less. And she felt bolstered by the support of Belle, Scarlett and Trixie lined up behind her.

Hettie looked stumped. 'Oh, right, urm, yeah—'

'Look,' Lola interrupted, 'it's about time someone took charge around here. It's perfectly simple if everyone stops trying to overcomplicate things. Carlson, tell me what you want. Tiny, show me how to do it. And Hettie, tell that camera to turn over!'

'Yeah, urm, turn over please.'

Lola looked at Carlson. 'Right, what's happening?'

'Well, we were just saying it would make a great end shot if you came directly at the camera with an uppercut.'

'Right. Yeah. Fine. Let's go.'

Carlson looked at her with a worried grimace. 'Although obviously don't actually hit the camera.'

'Blatantly,' Lola hissed. 'What do you think I am, an idiot?'

'No, sorry Lola, of course not. But if you just stop your fist about an inch from the lens, we'll be able to dip to black.'

'OK,' Lola nodded, banging together a pair of fists that felt fully loaded. 'Tiny, what do I do?'

Tiny stepped up to the camera and briskly walked her through the actions.

'OK, so with this move your hip should go before your punch. Lean back, don't lean forward. Keep your elbow bent and stay in tight. Tuck your chin down to your shoulder then slide the punch off your ribcage and lean back as you throw it. Push your hip forward and release!'

God, why does he have to make it so complicated?'

'So if we just go for a little practice?' he suggested.

'No, fuck that,' she exploded, 'I've got it already. Let's go!'

'Lola, are you sure?'

'Yes! How many times do I have to say it? Hettie, is the camera turning over?'

The cameraman nodded at his director, who forced herself to smile at Lola. 'Yes, we're at speed. So positions please everyone. And standby. And action!'

Lola concentrated all her efforts on remembering the moves Tiny had shown her. But as she stepped up to the camera her heart was racing with so much adrenaline she felt like she was losing control. She looked into the lens and could see the faces of Jake and Gloria looking up at her from the floor of the storeroom. And then, in a flash, it happened, without her even thinking what she was doing. She pulled back her fist, threw it forward with a low grunt and crashed it straight into the lens, not only shattering the glass but knocking the machine off its tripod and onto the floor. It landed with a thud, sending a ripple out through the ring.

Fuck!

She watched in horror as the entire crew rushed forward and began scrambling around to assess the damage.

Fuck, fuck, fuck!

She slowly sank to the floor, her heart still pounding and the taste of shame now burning in her throat.

Oh what the fuck have I done?

Tears sprung to her eyes but her gloves were so big she couldn't even wipe them. She felt them race down her cheeks as her whole body began to convulse. Within seconds she was crying deep, guttural tears. And the worst thing was, everyone in the hall had stopped to stare at her in abject horror.

'Lola?' Carlson whispered, kneeling down beside her. 'Are you all right?'

'No!' she wailed. 'I'm not all right! The tour's starting in ten days and I'm supposed to be excited and everything's supposed to be fierce and I just don't understand why I feel like shit. And now I've gone and fucked it all up and I'm turning into a bitch and everyone hates me. And I hate myself and I just want it to stop!'

As she buried her head in her hands she became aware of a flurry of arms appearing from all sides to stroke and hug her. But it was no use; nothing was any comfort. No amount of

Turkish Delight would make any difference this time. She was overwhelmed by the physicality of her tears and a crippling sadness she hadn't been aware of all day but which seemed to have suddenly erupted within her. She just wanted to melt away and disappear. But she knew there was no way out. And she felt trapped and terrified of what was going to happen.

I've got to pull myself together. I've got to get a grip.

There was only one note of positivity glimmering through her despair.

At least the camera's broken. At least it can't film me in this state.

Because this embarrassing meltdown was bad enough – but having it caught on camera would make things a whole lot worse.

10

As the music blasted out to fill the vast space, Lola held up her arms and felt the dancers lift her high onto the table. She shook to a sound much rockier than her usual style and prepared to launch into the vocal for *Mess It Up*.

> *Worked hard all week,*
> *Doing as I'm told,*
> *Being such a good girl,*
> *Being good as gold.*

'Sorry!' broke in a voice coming out of the speakers. 'Can we stop there for a minute? We just need to reposition that light on Lola.'

Even though she couldn't see what was happening in the darkness before her, Lola recognized the voice of her technical director Vlad, a pigeon-chested thirty-something who always seemed to smell of TCP and had earned the nickname Vlad the Impaler, partly on account of his Romanian parentage but also because of his legendarily large dick – something Lola found extremely unlikely considering his stick-thin frame. Not that she had the remotest inclination to find out, especially at the moment. *The way I feel right now, if I never see another dick again it'll be too soon.*

'Just one more minute, Lola!' came Vlad's nasal voice. '*That's* it! Much better!'

The entire team working on the tour had assembled in a huge aircraft hangar near Heathrow for the first of several production rehearsals. There was just one week to go till opening night and it was time for all the different elements that would make up the show to be brought together. The band, the dancers, the set, the sound and lighting – only the costumes would be added at a later stage. But even so, there were so many problems to fix that the rehearsal was interrupted every other minute. And even though Lola wasn't performing at full pelt it was still very frustrating. She was doing her best to stay calm.

'OK and let's press on,' instructed Carlson's voice over the speakers.

The band began playing and Lola repeated her routine at the start of the song, this time going on to sing the first chorus.

> *I'm heading for a blip,*
> *Mess it up!*
> *Let's sip till we slip,*
> *Mess it up!*
> *Maybe do a strip,*
> *Mess it up, mess it up, mess it up!*

'Sorry, sorry!' interjected Carlson, clearly enjoying feeling like a star with his own mic to speak into. 'Hold it there for a bit, guys. We just need to tweak the dance routine for the new space.'

Lola stepped down from the table as Carlson skipped onto the stage to speak to the dancers. In keeping with the theme of the song, Todd, Nate and Junior were playing barmen, juggling cocktail shakers and performing acrobatic tricks on a chrome bar that had risen through the floor and onto the stage. Kitty, Jette and Boo were dancing around a table as if on a particularly rowdy girls' night out while Lola whipped up their enthusiasm by singing to them from above.

As she leaned on the bar and listened to Carlson's direction, she thought back to her outburst in Busters boxing club and tried not to cringe. Not only had it been hugely embarrassing but it had also been extremely costly; the production had been insured for the breakage of the camera but it had taken hours to find a replacement, pushing the crew fees well into overtime, an additional cost Lola couldn't pretend was down to anything other than her own meltdown. And on top of all that she could tell it had made everyone, not least herself, worried that she might crack up completely as the tension mounted in the final week of rehearsals. Ever since, she'd felt like she was walking a tightrope and could topple off at any second.

'OK,' said Carlson, bouncing off the stage and disappearing into the darkness, 'all done. *Mess It Up* – take it away!'

> *Stuck to the script,*
> *Followed every rule,*
> *Now I wanna scream,*
> *Wanna act like a fool.*

As Lola half sang and half spoke the lyrics, she walked her way through the unstructured, slightly wild choreography Carlson had devised to complement the song's theme of letting go.

And even though she wasn't giving it her all, she could still feel herself being infused with the song's spirit and being turned on by the idea of getting out there and messing it up – an idea that appealed more and more as she drew closer to opening night and felt the pressure she was under ratcheting up another notch. In just one week's time she'd be taking to the stage at the O2 Arena and the whole world would be watching to see if she really was good enough to justify all the fuss – and the huge sales. As she couldn't risk falling ill, she was already taking all kinds of extra-strength vitamin tablets and daily injections of some kind of mineral that was supposed to boost her immune system. She could hardly refuse as there was no way her role could be understudied – she had to make it onto that stage, whatever happened. So why did she just want to go out and get shit-faced?

> *I'm heading for a blip,*
> *Mess it up!*
> *Let's sip till we slip,*
> *Mess it up!*
> *I'm gonna let rip,*
> *Mess it up, mess it up, mess it up!*

Out of the corner of her eye she couldn't help noticing that Jake was staring at Kitty, a gorgeous blonde with bright blue eyes and that killer combination of great boobs and a pencil-thin waist. She caught him flashing her a sloppy grin and felt a wave of revulsion. *How could I have fallen for such a blatant sleazebag? How could I have actually thought I was in love with him?*

Jake must have found Kitty a little too distracting as he

suddenly lost his rhythm and one of his drumsticks came clattering down from his elevated position and onto the set below.

'And just pause it there for a second,' bellowed Mike Henry into his mic. He stepped into the light, stroking his moustache. 'Everything all right, Jake?'

'Yeah, sorry dude, I'm not too sure what happened there.'

I am, thought Lola. *You were thinking with your dick as per usual.* She was about to voice her thought but stopped herself when she heard Gloria tutting loudly from behind; she didn't want to give her any chance of rehabilitating herself by forming some sort of sisterly alliance. Instead she watched in silence as Kitty skipped across the stage, picked up Jake's drumstick and threw it up to him with a flutter of her eyelids. Lola could hardly blame her for falling for his charm – after all, she had. So had Gloria. And as this was her first rehearsal with the band, Kitty probably knew nothing about what had gone on between Jake and either Lola or Gloria. But Lola did think Jake was being more than a little insensitive to both of them. Rather than rubbing salt into her wound, it only reminded her of how stupid she'd been.

'OK, one more time,' called Carlson. 'Take it away!'

> *I'm heading for a blip,*
> *Mess it up!*
> *Let's sip till we slip,*
> *Mess it up!*
> *Wake up in a skip,*
> *Mess it up, mess it up, mess it up!*

God, she wanted to get drunk. So drunk she didn't care *where* she woke up – even if it was in a skip.

Thankfully she'd have the opportunity later tonight. Her record company was throwing a big party to celebrate the success of the single *Tramp*, which was still at number one across Europe after more than a month of release, and *Trouble*, which was now the biggest-selling album for years. Lola intended to throw herself wholeheartedly into the celebrations; for one night only she'd forget all about the show and the pressures of opening night.

This would be her last chance to mess it up for real before the start of the tour. And she didn't intend to waste it.

*

Jake didn't understand what all the fuss was about. All that talk about messing it up. He could think of several things he'd much rather do – and all of them involved that smoking-hot dancer Kitty.

As he pounded out the beat of the song his eyes wandered to watch her stepping through the routine at the other side of the stage. She was wearing some kind of tiny shorts or hot pants with a crop top that showed off her killer bod. What he'd give for a piece of that ass. And it looked like the feeling was mutual. He'd seen it in her eyes when he'd staged his little accident and she'd thrown him back his drumstick with a flutter of her eyelashes.

And all right, it might be a little awkward with both Lola and Gloria there too. But it wasn't his fault if the two of them had grown way too attached to him and caused a major drama. And the truth was, he was kind of relieved he was no longer seeing either of them. Sure, Lola had been a lot of fun and a great lay, but once she'd got serious the fun had quickly disappeared. And yeah, Gloria had given a kick-ass blow job but he was through with having to trail across London to her roachy apartment because she had no babysitter for her dumb-ass daughter. Like he gave a shit.

No, now he was seeing neither of them he felt much freer. And there might have been a pissy vibe in rehearsals for the last couple of weeks but as soon as the band had been joined by the rest of the team the tension had lifted. And there was one person in particular who'd lifted Jake's tension. As he drove the song towards its rousing finale, his eyes fixed on Kitty performing a cartwheel across the stage. He smiled as he realized he'd be seeing her at the party later – and she'd hope-fully be lifting his tension a whole lot more.

And it wasn't as if anyone could object if he started nailing one of the dancers. Surely it was almost expected of a drum-mer? He wouldn't care but he'd been a good boy and kept a low profile ever since that little scene in the storeroom, only banging broads from outside Lola's circle. But that had gone on for long enough now. And the real star of this show was ready to make his comeback.

Mess it up? These guys could mess it up by getting as drunk as they liked. Jake was planning on messing things up in his own way.

*

'OK, so this one's completely different,' Freddy said, 'but I think it'll be cracking.' He was sitting with Spike in Hugh Bad-cock's office, midway through the entertainment team's regular meeting to pitch long-lead stories for the month ahead. Although in this particular meeting, most of his energy had so far been spent on trying to avoid the subject of Lola – and tonight's big party.

'Go on then, boyo,' Hugh said, putting his arms behind his head and leaning back in his chair so Freddy felt like he was talking to his package. 'Let's hear it.'

'Well, as I'm sure you know, for the last few months Rex Watson has been dating celebrity sex therapist Bunny Love.'

Hugh dismissed the story with a wave of his hand. 'Yeah, yeah, old news. Next!'

'No, but get this – they're about to announce they're writing a big sex manual together. And we've been offered an exclusive interview to break the news.'

Hugh leaned forward and began fiddling with his signet ring. 'Hmmm, so they'll talk about their sex life, will they?'

'Apparently so,' offered Spike. 'And according to Bunny it's off the hook, man.'

Hugh shook his head. 'Yeah, well, she always says that. But I want detail. Just what exactly has Rex Watson got under those tight chinos? You've got to take the piss, Freddy.'

Freddy smiled. He knew this story would appeal to Hugh. In his experience one alpha never missed out on the chance to take a swipe at another. And Rex had to be the biggest silverback in the jungle, who'd only climbed to his exalted position by stepping his way over several much smaller and weaker apes – which was why on this occasion Freddy was happy to agree to Hugh's usual demand for a more aggressive approach. 'Oh I'll be sure to get stuck in. And it won't be hard to take the piss; Rex is pretty much setting himself up for it, like.'

'Well, that saves us the bother,' Hugh went on. 'Oh and don't forget, the more noise you can make the better.'

'No problem,' Freddy nodded, doing his best to feign a look of respect.

'Good man. Good man.' Hugh stretched his arms and looked pleased with himself. What he didn't realize was that Freddy had spent the first half of the meeting going through his usual routine to get the stories he wanted to cover commissioned. He'd begun by deliberately pitching a crap story he didn't want to do about fashion photographers Mark and Mark being caught having a threesome with TV producer Cassian Blunt in Spike's gym, precisely so Hugh could flex his muscle by turning it down. And then he'd invented a 'fiercely competitive battle for exclusivity' with the BBC to get the green light for an interview he wanted to do with Blake Striker about his new album, knowing that Hugh would only go for the story if he pretended a rival broadcaster was interested. Although in principle Freddy objected to having to spend so much time pandering to his editor's machismo, over time he'd learnt to work with it as just another part of his job.

If only I can avoid the subject of Lola. This morning a press release had landed in his inbox announcing record-breaking sales for Lola's album and her single, *Tramp*. There was no denying that her success was fast becoming the entertainment news story of the year. Freddy could only hope the information had escaped Hugh.

'And what about your ex-girlfriend, boyo?'

Evidently it hadn't.

'Do you mean Lola Grant?' Freddy asked, managing to look unruffled.

'Yeah. Isn't she having some kind of party tonight? Someone sent me a release bragging about her amazing sales.

Presumably she'll be getting wankered to celebrate. Can you get in there and film it?'

'I'm afraid the record company have hired the venue so it's a private party,' frowned Spike. 'And strictly no press.' So far Hugh had no idea Spike was seeing Lola's manager – and for his sake Freddy hoped it stayed that way.

Hugh dipped his hand into his trousers to work free what must have been an uncomfortably positioned bollock. 'Sorry, chaps, but you know how it is.' He withdrew his hand and rested it on his desk. Freddy made a mental note not to shake it later.

'I mean, we'll double-check,' he said, 'but I really don't think we'll get in.'

'Well, do your best. I'm sure I don't need to remind you our ratings are down yet again. And the channel's really starting to get jumpy. So we've all got to up our game – and be much tougher from now on. Nobody's job's safe.'

There was a tense silence and Freddy pictured himself being made redundant, unable to pay his whopping big mortgage and having to sell his flat. And he could just imagine the re-action of his dad and his brother-in-law when they heard the news. He looked at Spike and widened his eyes. He couldn't let it happen.

'What about the opening night of Lola's tour?' Hugh rattled on. 'Isn't it happening at the O2?'

'For real,' said Spike. 'Next Wednesday.'

'Well, if we can't get into the party can we get into that? And do some kind of backstage report? A big exclusive?'

Freddy tried not to groan. Reporting on Lola's brilliantly successful career really was the last thing he wanted to do right now. But it didn't look like he had much choice – not if he wanted to keep his job.

It looked like Spike had come to the same conclusion. 'Urm, yeah, we can definitely give it a go.'

'Yeah, well, you'll have to do more than that, bro,' Hugh hit back, causing Spike to recoil ever so slightly. 'You'll have to dig around for a juicy news story. Because there's got to be the odd skeleton hiding in Lola's closet and it's about time you two found it – and dragged it out onto our programme.'

Freddy could feel his shoulders twitching. He'd spent the last few weeks trying his best to avoid anything to do with Lola but now he was being forced into it. Well, at least he didn't have to go to tonight's party and pretend to be having a good time while he was secretly sniffing around for scandal. Although Spike would be there – and he'd have to start sniffing.

'All right, boss,' Freddy mouthed rather weakly. 'We're on it.'

'OK then chaps,' said Hugh, standing up to dismiss them. 'I think we understand each other. Now off you go and make some noise.'

He held out his hand, the same hand that just a few minutes earlier he'd thrust down his trousers to reposition his no doubt dirty, sweaty bollocks. Freddy had no choice but to take it.

*

Lola held out her hand and Harvey shook it. If she wanted their relationship to be businesslike then he had no choice but to play by her rules.

'All right, Lola?' he ventured, stepping into her trailer. He daren't call her Trouble after the way she'd reacted last time.

'Hiya,' she replied curtly. He noticed there was no 'darlin'' although, come to think of it, he wasn't sure she'd called him that for weeks.

'Oh hi Barb, *darlin'*,' she trilled, her face brightening up at the sight of Barbara behind him.

'Hello, doll,' Barbara replied, following Harvey inside and kissing Lola warmly on each cheek. 'Good to see you.'

There was an awkward silence as the three of them sat down around a table piled high with presents from fans. A huge bouquet of flowers stood in the centre, blocking the view between Harvey and Lola. Neither of them moved it.

The three of them were meeting for one of their regular sessions to talk through publicity requests for the month ahead. As time was tight Harvey and Barbara were grabbing Lola in her lunch break from the first production rehearsal. Although from the look of things, she was already itching to get back to work.

'Come on then, let's get on with it,' she quipped, checking the time on her watch. 'I've not got long and we really need to kick this show into shape.'

Harvey tried not to bridle at her brisk manner and reminded himself that she was under a lot of pressure. Of course he'd heard about her meltdown on the video shoot the other day, but what could he do about it? She hadn't wanted to discuss it with him – nor had she wanted to discuss her break-up with Jake, which he'd heard about from Amina. She probably assumed that, because Harvey had predicted that particular disaster, he'd be looking forward to a good gloat. But on the contrary, he knew from his own experience how splitting up with someone you'd always known you shouldn't have fallen for could be the toughest kind of break-up because it was sharpened by anger at yourself for being so stupid. And just because his relationship with Lola was now purely professional, that didn't stop him from worrying about her. So before the meeting he'd had a quick chat with Barbara to talk through ways to ease the growing pressure on Lola in the run-up to opening night. And he'd come up with a list of suggestions, which Barbara was now going to present to her as her own ideas. The way Lola felt about him at the moment, Harvey knew she wouldn't accept a single one of his suggestions.

'OK, so first up,' said Barbara, opening her notepad, 'the party tonight. I think we should definitely say no press. If that's still OK with you, Lola?'

'Blatantly. I just want to mess it up, Barb. You know, it's the last chance I'm going to get before the show opens. And I know what I'm like.'

Harvey was sure she was shooting him a stern glare but thankfully the flowers were still standing between them. He couldn't help thinking how ironic it was that in just a few hours' time they'd be celebrating Lola's success in Club Class, the very place where they'd first met. He remembered how a mutual friend had introduced them on the dance floor one night and how he'd instantly liked her, sparkling with delight as she'd told him about her music, promising to send him some songs for him to have a listen. As they'd started working together and become friends, Club Class had quickly developed into their favourite hang-out. He remembered how much fun they'd had in there night after night, revelling in each other's company and laughing uproariously. He could almost feel tears spring to his eyes as he remembered how joyous their friendship had been in those days – and how united they'd been in the hope that one day all their dreams would come true. But now they had and Lola was becoming so hardened and wrapped up in herself he wasn't even sure she'd remember. *Oh I don't know what it is but I just can't make her like me anymore.*

'And what about promo?' Barbara went on. 'Now I think it would be a good idea to stop doing everything for a few weeks, at least until the tour's up and running.'

Lola took a swig from her bottle of water. 'All right, if you think that's best.'

'Definitely,' nodded Barbara. 'I'm sure you've got enough on your plate already. And besides, I fancy a trip to the golf club this weekend.'

Harvey laughed, knowing how much Barbara liked her golf. She was captain of the ladies' team in some kind of publicists versus press league, but often had to sacrifice her game to make way for work commitments – and would be having to do so much more once the tour was underway.

'Knock yourself out, darlin',' Lola smiled. He wondered how long it had been since she'd smiled at him.

'There is one thing though,' Barbara pointed out. 'We've just had a request in from Freddy Jones at Channel 3 News. He wants to do a backstage exclusive on opening night. Now I know the papers blew the whole romance between you two totally out of proportion, but he's obviously still a friend so I thought I'd run that one by you.'

There was a pause and Harvey was sure Lola's eyes flickered onto him. At that moment Barbara realized he couldn't see her properly and moved the flowers out of the way. As soon as he had a clear view of her she looked away uneasily.

'Hmm, yeah, I don't know,' she mumbled.

'It would be a great way to get footage of the first night straight out there,' suggested Barbara. 'Especially if we're going to announce extra dates.'

'Wait a minute,' Lola piped up, 'I don't suppose this has anything to do with the fact Harvey's shagging his producer?'

'No!' he broke in. 'That's got nothing to do with it at all.'

'That is, if you *are* still shagging him?'

Yes, me and Spike are very happy actually, he wanted to blurt out. *And it's not our fault it didn't work out between you and Jake.*

'Lola, it's got nothing to do with that,' he explained calmly. 'But the whole country is convinced you and Freddy were getting married a few weeks ago. So we just have to tread carefully, that's all.'

She looked out of the window with an expression Harvey was pretty sure betrayed a sense of guilt. He decided to gloss over the fact that it was him who'd persuaded her to go on a date with Freddy – and that he'd pestered her afterwards to follow it up with a second date. All right, he'd been convinced the two of them would make a great couple and he'd heard from Spike that Freddy was gutted at being blown out. But nobody could say he hadn't done his bit to get them together. And now he'd just have to step back and let whatever was going to happen between them take its course.

'Look, I don't think we should do an interview or anything,' picked up Barbara. 'But how would you feel if we let him come and do a live broadcast, film a bit of the build-up to the big opening and then maybe the first couple of numbers?'

Lola took a deep breath and glowered at Harvey. 'Hmm, maybe.'

'We could give Channel 3 News exclusivity if they agree to pool their show footage afterwards,' explained Barbara. 'So all the other broadcasters will be able to show it but we don't have to put up with fifty cameras stressing you out.'

It made perfect sense and Harvey didn't see how Lola could refuse.

'Yeah, all right,' she huffed eventually. 'And I actually wouldn't mind seeing Freddy again. He's a nice guy.'

'OK, fantastic,' said Barbara, snapping her pad shut. 'But one last thing. I think it would be a good idea if we're not doing any press to start sending out regular tweets – just to keep the momentum going. And I've noticed you've been a bit quiet on that front lately?'

'Oh yeah,' Lola frowned. 'Sorry.'

Harvey knew how important it was for Lola to maintain her Twitter presence – especially as she now had over two million followers. 'You know, I'm quite happy to send the odd tweet from your account if it makes things easier,' he offered.

'No!' she objected. 'I'll blatantly do them myself. I do write all my songs, you know – I'm sure I can manage the odd tweet.'

'No, of course, I only meant . . .' *Oh what the hell. It doesn't matter anyway.* Nothing he could say right now would reduce Lola's animosity towards him. He watched as she picked up her phone and began tapping at the keypad. To think that just a few months ago she'd been the one convincing him to tweet for her, arguing he could do her just as well as she could. Those days seemed a long time ago now.

She plonked her phone down onto the table and Harvey's pinged to alert him that her tweet had been posted. As he picked it up and typed in his passcode he could feel her scowling at him.

'Still busy in rehearsals,' he read, 'show going to be fierce. Last night of freedom tonight. Am blatantly going to MESS IT UP!'

'How's that, Harvey?' she asked, her eyes blazing with defiance.

'Yeah, great,' he gulped.

He'd already been worried about tonight. Now he was seriously scared.

*

A few hours later Lola was already starting to feel messy. She'd spent the first half of the party being whisked around and introduced to everyone who was working on the tour, from the production manager and tour accountant to an endless parade of roadies, each of them bigger and hairier than the last. Everyone who'd worked on the album had been keen to congratulate her on its success, from producers and co-songwriters to musicians and sound engineers. And all that time she'd been plied with glass after glass of a specially created cocktail, which she was pretty sure someone had said was made of vodka, champagne and elderflower. Whatever it was, it tasted fierce.

She broke away from a deathly dull conversation with a bloke with dandruff and buck teeth she seemed to remember was somebody important at the record company and leant on a pillar to survey the party. The steady stream of cocktails seemed to have lowered everyone's inhibitions below their usual rock-bottom watermark. A beaming Hettie Spriggs had taken to the dance floor to teach Mike, Smudge and Chuck how to dance like rockabillies, letting her out, reeling her back in and twirling her around energetically. Lucretia Lavelle was desperately trying to prove she could still rock out with the best of them, twerking her stringy sixty-something-year-old body around Tiny, backing up onto his groin and occasionally lifting up her skirt to prove it was true she didn't wear any knickers. And Vlad the Impaler was using his hands to mime the dimensions of something Lola could only assume to be his legendarily large dick to gasps of approval from Belle, Scarlett and Trixie. She couldn't help chuckling to herself. *It looks like I wasn't the only one who needed to mess it up tonight.*

Across the dance floor she could just about make out transgender DJ Candy Lunt, who must have been hired to provide the soundtrack to the night. She watched as Candy listened to the next track in her earphones and then mixed into it to a roar of approval from everyone on the dance floor. Lola broke into a mischievous smile as she recognized the first notes of *Mess It Up*.

> *Worked hard all week,*
> *Doing as I'm told,*
> *Being such a good girl,*
> *Being good as gold.*

A rush of adrenaline surged through her and she bounded onto the dance floor, where within seconds she was joined by Kitty, Jette and Boo to recreate the routine they'd been rehearsing all day. They lifted her onto a nearby table and she shimmied and shook her way through the song as everyone at the party cheered her on, their fists pounding the air. She wasn't sure she'd ever danced so well. Why couldn't she dance like this when she was sober?

I'm heading for a blip,
Mess it up!
Let's sip till we slip,
Mess it up!
Maybe do a strip,
Mess it up, mess it up, mess it up!

She looked down and spotted Todd, Nate and Junior improvising around the girls, their bodies jerking and snapping to the infectious beat. And she noticed a defiant-looking Gloria dragging Sharonne onto the dance floor to give it her all, occasionally looking over at Lola to check she was watching. Well, she didn't care if Gloria was a better dancer than she was because *she* was the star of the show – and of tonight's party.

Stuck to the script,
Followed every rule,
Now I wanna scream,
Wanna act like a fool.

The only person Lola realized she hadn't seen all night was Jake, and as she swung her head around to the music she surreptitiously glanced up and down the club to see if she could spot him. Club Class had long been one of the coolest venues in London; created in an old Victorian school, its dance floor stood in what had been the school hall, where the ceilings had been lowered to the level of the steel girders, the walls stripped back to expose the brickwork, and a raised platform which must have been some kind of stage converted into the DJ stand. The staff were dressed all in black, their outfits topped off with mortar boards and the occasional black cane, which they'd run up and down any customers they deemed to be particularly cheeky. And a series of old classrooms leading off the main hall had been reinvented as a VIP room, a chill-out area and a 'detention den', which was where people were supposed to go if they wanted to get naughty. Not that it looked like any of her team needed it. Even Amina had been loosened up by the cocktails and was currently draped across a bare wooden bench straddling Danny, running her fingers through hair that made him look like he'd been electrocuted while he ran his up and under her bra.

> *I'm heading for a blip,*
> *Mess it up!*
> *Let's sip till we slip,*
> *Mess it up!*
> *I'm gonna let rip,*
> *Mess it up, mess it up, mess it up!*

It had been a few years now since Lola had been to Club Class but it was here she'd first met Harvey. She'd lost track of the number of times the two of them had stood at the bar getting shit-faced, nipping into the unisex toilets to huddle in a cubicle and discuss the merits of whichever men they were chasing, only ever splitting up to nip into the detention den for a quick snog – or a little more in Harvey's case. She had a vague recollection of one particular occasion when he'd staggered in there with a tracksuited skinhead who claimed to be a distant relative of David Beckham, only to emerge completely naked an hour later, explaining that the guy had disappeared with all his clothes and his wallet, leaving him to spend the rest of the night hiding his modesty behind one of the barmen's mortar boards. But Lola remembered that he'd carried on drinking and had even gone on to pull some hot Texan who'd been wearing a Stetson he'd swapped for Harvey's mortar board. The two of them had laughed together until they'd been clutching at their stomachs gasping for air. Oh he used to be such fun in those days. *But he's a different person now and he probably wouldn't even remember.*

Everything had changed when he'd given up booze and started taking life so seriously. She spotted him now talking to the buck-toothed record exec, miming fascination at whatever he was spouting on about. In the old days she'd have sneaked up behind him and stepped on his foot or elbowed him in the ribs to try and make him laugh – and he'd have given in too, however important the conversation. She missed the old Harvey. She missed her best mate. She didn't understand how he could have changed into the kind of person who made her feel bad about everything she did, often without even saying anything. *Whatever happened to his promise of being always at and on my side?*

She was suddenly desperate for a drink but all she had to do was look down and a fresh cocktail was immediately thrust into her hand. She downed it in one and threw herself into the routine for the climax of the song.

> *I'm heading for a blip,*
> *Mess it up!*
> *Let's sip till we slip,*
> *Mess it up!*
> *Wake up in a skip,*
> *Mess it up, mess it up, mess it up!*

There was still no sign of Jake but she did spot Harvey's boyfriend Spike standing at the bar chatting to a bleary-eyed Barbara, who was demonstrating her golf swing with one of the barmen's canes but was so unsteady she kept toppling over and hitting him in the face. *Now what's he doing here? Didn't I say no press?* Just because this guy was shagging her manager, she didn't see why that should give him special privileges. And she didn't see why he should think he could swan into her private party and get pissed with her publicist. Well, she wasn't going to stand for it.

She jumped down from the table and onto the dance floor but lost her footing and careered towards Gloria, a head-on collision only averted at the last minute by a quick-thinking Sharonne, who stepped in to break her fall.

'Oh thanks, darlin',' she slurred, standing up and straightening out her top. 'I must have had one too many cocktails.'

She was sure Gloria was smirking at her.

'And what are you looking at?' she barked. 'Or are you trying to pick up some tips on how to be a star?'

Gloria's mouth fell open.

'Well, I wouldn't bother if I were you,' Lola went on. 'You've already had a crack at that – and we all know how it ended.'

Was that too harsh? Oh what the hell! It serves her right for stealing my man. She turned on her heel and stomped away.

Now where's Harvey gone? She stood on her tiptoes to look around but had to lean on the wall as the room started to spin. *There he is . . .*

'Harvey!' she hissed. 'Can I have a word?'

'Yeah, what's the matter? Are you all right?'

'Yeah, course I'm all right. I'm blatantly amazing, actually. But what's the foetus doing here?'

'You what? What foetus?'

'That baby you're going out with.'

'Lola, he's exactly the same age as you, remember? And I didn't think you'd mind so I invited him.'

'Well I do mind, Harvey. I made it quite clear I don't want any journos in tonight then I can relax and mess it up a bit.' *Not that I'm not doing a good enough job of that already.*

'Oh come on, Lola. He might be a journo but he's not working or anything. And he's also my boyfriend.'

All right, all right, rub it in why don't you? It was perfectly obvious just by his presence that he and Harvey had patched up their problems – and she didn't need their happiness ramming down her throat.

'I don't care what he is, Harvey. Journos never stop working, everyone knows that. And everyone knows you can't trust them.'

Oh why don't I just shut the fuck up? She wasn't even sure what she was saying anymore – or why she was saying it. But it just didn't seem fair that Harvey's boyfriend was here when hers had dumped her and now seemed intent on shagging one of her dancers. And of course she knew journos weren't all untrustworthy. She was sure she could trust Freddy. And she'd realized this afternoon when they'd been talking about him that she actually wanted to see him again. She imagined him walking into the club now, picking her up and holding her in his big manly arms. She imagined how lovely it would feel to nestle into his thickly muscled chest and how safe and happy he could make her. Although she was sure he wouldn't want to have anything to do with her since she'd fucked him around so badly. *How have I managed to develop such a knack for doing the wrong thing?* Even when she was in the middle of doing it she couldn't stop herself. *Like right now for example . . .*

She tensed her lips and glowered at Harvey. 'I'm serious, I want him out.'

'But Lola—'

'But nothing. Just get rid of him, Harvey. I can't believe you were so unprofessional as to invite him in the first place.'

He held up his hands in surrender. 'OK, boss, whatever you say.'

She gave a satisfied nod and flounced away, sweeping up a spare cocktail from the bar and knocking it back in one swig. *Oh why can't I stop being so horrible?*

Just then she spotted Jake drooling all over Kitty as a blatant erection strained at his trousers. She suddenly felt like everyone in the club was staring at her and sniggering. *I bet they can't believe how stupid I was to be taken in by him.* She breathed in sharply and tried to shake off a searing sense of shame.

'Are you all right, Lola?' asked a voice behind her. It was Belle, flanked by Scarlett and Trixie. 'Come on,' she said, holding out her arm and putting it around her shoulders, 'don't do this to yourself. Don't let it get to you.'

They huddled around her and straight away she felt bolstered by their support.

'That Kitty's a complete slapper.'

'She's totes a dirty slut.'

'I've never seen such a slag in all my life.'

'No,' Lola corrected them, 'Kitty's done nothing wrong. *Jake's* the slag. *He's* the one who can't keep his dick in his pants. And it makes me feel sick to think I actually went there.'

Trixie squeezed her shoulder in sympathy. 'Well, if you need something to pick you up, we're just nipping to the shithouse for a toot of the old Charlie.'

Lola looked at them and bit her lip. She felt so exhausted and so tired of forcing herself to be strong, she wasn't sure she had it in her to resist anymore.

'You know you're very welcome to join us.'

Well, she *had* said she wanted to mess it up tonight. And even though she'd knocked back countless cocktails, she still wasn't feeling quite messy enough. *Not yet, anyway.*

'Come on,' coaxed Trixie, 'come with us and give it a whirl.'

Oh maybe it's time to try out a new way of messing it up. Maybe my old way's just not working anymore.

No! countered another voice in her head. *Be strong and don't do it. However low you're feeling, this will only make you feel worse.*

'You know, you could always start with a little bump and see if you like it,' cooed Trixie.

Oh come on, one little bump's hardly going to turn you into a full-on cokehead. And coke's completely different to crack, remember?

'All right, all right,' she said eventually, 'let's do it. But just one bump and that's it!'

The three of them sparkled back at her. 'Of course, just one bump, we promise.'

Oh God, what am I letting myself in for?

*

Gloria watched Lola striding out of the toilets flanked by Belle, Scarlett and Trixie and could almost taste the hatred at the back of her throat. She still couldn't believe Lola had humiliated her as she'd staggered around on the dance floor, making fun of her failed solo career in front of Sharonne and in earshot of all the dancers. She wouldn't care but all she'd been doing was having a little fun. It wasn't her fault if she was a much better dancer than Lola – or if knowing that made Lola feel insecure. And the worst thing was, she'd been feeling particularly fragile as she'd just bumped into that horrendous buck-toothed exec who'd dumped her from her record deal. As they'd made awkward small talk, his words had returned to ring in her ears. 'You're not a star,' he'd said, 'not like Lola Grant.'

Well, Lola Grant wasn't acting like much of a star tonight. She'd been shit-faced within minutes, and now that she didn't have her manager to look after her, had spent most of the night crashing around her own party. That was until she'd started disappearing into the bogs with the girls. Gloria wasn't stupid; she'd guessed straight away what was going on. And this little development was the best thing that had happened to her for years. The best thing that had happened to her since she'd lost her record deal. Since Lola had stolen it off her.

She'd stood at the mirror touching up her make-up, propping up her phone next to the sinks so she could film what was happening. But the first few times the girls had gone in there they'd shut the cubicle door after them so she'd only been able to record the telltale sniffing sound. She'd told herself that it didn't matter – she knew she'd get more chances. And sure enough, once Lola had snorted one line of coke she hadn't known when to stop, popping back into the toilets every half an hour for more. Gloria couldn't help scoffing to herself. *Like mother, like daughter* . . .

Before long she'd been pleased to see that the girls were getting sloppy and letting the cubicle door fall open as they snorted a heap of coke off the toilet cistern. They were all so out of it none of them seemed to notice Gloria was always standing there in front of the mirror, endlessly reapplying her lip gloss with her phone at waist height angled towards them. Well, it wasn't her fault if they didn't know how to be discreet. Unfortunately, though, every time she'd wanted to film the action some stupid bitch had appeared and plonked herself in between the camera phone and the cubicle. And now she was starting to get frustrated that she was going to miss out on her chance of revenge.

She followed Lola and the girls across the club and was relieved to see them settle down around a table that was in a quiet corner and under a bright light. *Perfect conditions for filming* . . . She sidled over and nudged herself into a prime position behind a pillar just a few feet away. She pretended to be texting while she zoned out from the music and listened to their conversation.

She cringed as she heard Trixie telling them all a story about the time a condom had fallen out of her snatch three days after she'd slept with some guy. 'Do you think that makes me a slut?' she heard her ask the others.

Oh I can answer that one for you. And the answer's an almighty yes.

'No!' they all chimed. 'Not at all!'

Oh come on, shut up and get the coke out!

She listened for what felt like ages as Belle and Scarlett shared similar stories about discovering days-old condoms inside them. And then their laughter trailed off. 'Well, what do you think, girls?' she heard Trixie ask. 'Shall we have another cheeky line?'

Finally!

She watched as Trixie took a bag of coke out of her handbag, shook a pile out onto the table and then swiftly chopped it up into four lines – in full view of anyone who happened to be watching.

Now they're getting seriously sloppy.

She switched her phone onto camera mode and held it up at the side of the pillar so she could stay hidden behind it. But she kept a close eye on their every move through the viewfinder. She felt a quiver of excitement as she hit Record.

And action!

One after the other she watched the girls lean forward and sniff up the coke through a rolled-up banknote. When it came to Lola, she casually took the note and gave a sharp snort as if she'd been doing it all her life. She reeled back, sniffed and gave a little whoop of satisfaction. As Trixie swept together the remaining grains of coke with the palm of her hand and hoovered the table clean, Gloria hit Stop and held the phone to her chest as she leant back on the pillar.

That's it! I've got it!

She couldn't believe it. This was better than anything she'd ever dreamed of. Her heart began to race as she realized just how big a news story she was holding in her hand. Lola Grant, Britain's biggest pop star and poster girl for the anti-drugs movement, caught on camera on a coke binge.

Gloria clutched her phone and had to stop herself from laughing out loud. Trouble? Lola didn't understand the meaning of the word.

*

Across the room, Harvey was starting to think about how soon he could slip away. The party had been even more of a nightmare than he'd expected. He looked around and was pretty sure he was the only one in the club not off his face and having fun. And he couldn't stop feeling stiff and awkward, knowing he must stand out like a pair of crotchless panties in a convent.

If he were being completely honest, the whole thing had been an ordeal from the beginning. First he'd bumped into a drunk Carlson, who he'd spent the last few weeks avoiding but who now confronted him to accuse him of being a prick-tease. At least he'd now disappeared into the detention den with the photographers Mark and Mark – and Harvey had a pretty good idea from all the time he'd spent in there what they must be up to.

Then Lola had started ranting at him about Spike being at the party and said he had to leave. Harvey had been so angry he'd wanted to leave too but Spike had insisted he stay – although what for he wasn't sure. By now everyone was so out of it they couldn't tell who they were speaking to, never mind who else was in the room. Harvey stepped over Barbara slumped in a corner twirling a cane, muttering something he wasn't even sure was English. He could just about make out the words *Ich will dich ficken*, which he seemed to remember meant something rude in German.

To make matters worse, Harvey had then spotted Jake

drooling all over Kitty just a few feet away from Lola. He'd been so angry he'd marched over and accused him of being insensitive to his artist, at which point Kitty must have realized he'd had a thing with Lola, disentangled herself from him and promptly disappeared onto the dance floor – which had only made Jake furious and hurl a horde of insults at him. 'Interfering fag' was the one that stuck in his mind.

He took a sip of his sparkling water. He'd pretty much had enough and was ready to go home. He'd just check to see Lola was all right first. The last time he'd seen Amina it hadn't looked like she was in a fit state to see her home – or even call for her driver.

He manoeuvred his way across the dance floor and through the crowd until he spotted Lola sitting at a table with her Style Council. As he drew closer he stopped in his tracks. He couldn't believe what he was seeing. Lola and the girls were snorting lines of coke in full view of everyone at the party. He blinked several times as he tried to take it in. *Can this really be happening?*

He looked around to see if anyone else was watching but thankfully they all seemed to be too shit-faced to notice. At least they were this time. He had to make her stop soon.

'Lola?' he called, stepping towards them as Trixie dabbed at the last few bits of coke and rubbed them into her teeth.

'Yeah? What do you want?' Lola looked up and glared at him with pupils that filled most of her eyes. He dreaded to think how much coke must be coursing through her.

'Urm, can I have a quick word?' he managed.

Lola turned to the girls and rolled her eyes. She stood up with a huff and the two of them moved to one side.

'Come on then,' she barked, 'spit it out.'

He spoke in as calm a voice as he could muster. 'What's going on, Lola?'

'What does it look like? I'm just having a little line of Charlie, that's all.'

'But Lola, if this gets out it'll cause a massive shit storm.'

'Oh stop overreacting – everybody does coke. Apparently Ruby Marlow does it all the time.'

'Yeah, but she hasn't been so publicly anti-drugs. And she hasn't just signed a huge record deal in America – not to mention the whole sponsorship set-up with Twinkle, which will be gone in a shot if they get wind of this.'

'Yeah, well, they won't, will they? There's only us here – and I said no press, remember?'

'But that's not going to stop people talking, Lola. And you know as well as I do how easily gossip gets out.'

She folded her arms and ground her teeth. 'Oh cut the crap, Harvey. I can tell what's going on here – you're just trying to keep me under control like you always do.'

'That's not true, Lola.'

'It is, and I can tell you now it's not going to work. A bit of coke's not that big a deal – it's in a completely different league to crack.'

'Is it? Is it really?'

'Yes, Harvey, it is. And to be honest I need a bit of something to get me over the last few weeks. For your information I caught Jake on the job with Gloria and that's why it all ended. And I'm sure you're really happy about that but I've blatantly found it quite hard.'

She broke off and her chin gave a little tremble. Even

though she was stoked by all the cocaine, Harvey told himself to remember she was still the same person underneath her anger.

'Lola,' he ventured. 'I'm not happy about that at all. In fact, I'm really sorry to hear it.'

'Bollocks!' she snarled, beads of sweat breaking out on her forehead. 'I can hear you saying "I told you so" without you even opening your mouth.'

Harvey gave a sigh and massaged his temples. Nothing he could say would make any difference. 'Lola,' he tried, 'you've got to understand that just because I tell you the odd harsh truth that doesn't mean I'm not on your side anymore. It's my job. I'm your manager. And I *was* your mate. But if you don't allow people who are close to you to give you honest criticism then you're going to turn into a monster. I've seen it happen before when an artist's career takes off – it's the oldest cliché in the book.'

She gave a loud sniff and the left side of her face began twitching wildly. 'You know what, Harvey, I can't believe you're actually calling me a cliché.'

'I wasn't calling you a cliché, Lola. I was talking about some of the things you've been doing. Like taking coke, for a start. Now *that's* a cliché.'

'Yeah, well, if it is I don't want to hear it. You're right, Harvey, you *were* my mate – in the past tense. And you *were* my manager. As of this moment you're not anymore.'

Did I just hear her right? Harvey felt like he'd been winded. *Did she actually just say what I think she said?*

'But Lola—'

'Oh give it a rest, Harvey. I can't do this anymore. You can hand everything over to Amina first thing in the morning. She'll deal with all the day-to-day stuff. As for everything else, I can look after myself.'

He could almost feel the sense of victory vibrating off her. But as she ranted at him her words began to distort, overpowered by the thud of the loud music and the pounding of the blood rushing to his head.

Is this it? Is she ending everything in the same place where it all started?

'Lola, are you really sure about this? Are you sure it's not just the coke talking?'

'Yes, I'm sure, Harvey! And that's exactly the kind of thing I don't want to hear anymore. Just because I've snorted a few lines of coke doesn't mean I've turned into some madwoman who can't think straight.'

Well you could have fooled me.

'As it happens I've been thinking about this for a while. And I'm sorry but I've made my decision. I don't want to discuss it.'

'Right. OK. I'll get going then.'

'Blatantly. I'm off to mess it up. And I haven't finished yet.'

No, there's clearly a whole lot more to come.

But as of tonight he wouldn't be around to clear it up.

11

Gloria hit Play and rewatched the footage on her phone. Perfectly lit and in sharp focus, Belle, Scarlett and Trixie burst into view cramming as much coke as they could up their noses. And then came Gloria's favourite bit. Lola leant forward and casually snorted an entire line in one stroke – with all the insouciance of a practised addict. It was better than Gloria remembered. Even if she had now watched it close to fifty times.

She put her phone down on the kitchen table and took a sip of her rather bitter-tasting instant coffee. It was early in the morning and she was waiting for Chanelle to wake up so she could drop her off at school before making her way over to rehearsal. Although there was no rush to get there. She had no doubt everyone else involved with the tour would be nursing killer hangovers this morning – including Lola. But not Gloria. She'd left the party shortly after her little shoot with much more important things on her mind than Lola's stupid mantra about 'messing it up'. And for once she'd bolted out of bed this morning way before her daughter, excited to revisit last night's stroke of luck. It was about time she had some good luck after all the shit she'd been through.

She'd hardly slept all night as a plan had formulated in her mind. For maximum impact she wasn't going to release the footage to the press till the opening night of Lola's tour. And she couldn't risk contacting too many journalists in case one of them got in touch with Lola's dyke publicist. So she'd decided to offer the footage exclusively to Freddy Jones at Channel 3 News – Britain's highest-rated news programme. Of course, contacting Freddy was a high-risk strategy seeing as Lola had been on a date with him and it had been splashed all over the papers. But Lola had told her what had happened, and the way Gloria saw it, Freddy couldn't be happy about being prick-teased in public then dumped in a national newspaper. No, she had a hunch that like her he'd be hungry for revenge. Although perhaps not quite as hungry as she was.

She took another sip of her coffee and stood up to pace the room. She wondered how much money she should ask for. How much would it cost to put down a deposit on a house? *Nothing too fancy, just somewhere nice and cosy for me and Chanelle – in a nicer area than this shithole.* She looked out of the window at the scrap of scrubland that was supposed to be a park but saw much more use as a dog toilet. A muscled white boy in a tight vest and chunky silver jewellery trotted past with an unleashed pit bull terrier which stopped to squat next to a drunken wino crashed out on a bench. She looked away in disgust. *Never mind, we won't be here much longer.*

Then again, if she sold the footage of Lola would that make her guilty of blackmail? Or extortion? What did any of those charges actually mean? She had no idea and didn't dare ask anyone as she didn't want her story to leak out before the big night. Oh maybe it would be safer not to ask for any money.

She couldn't risk breaking the law and then losing custody of Chanelle. Maybe it would be better to go for maximum destruction and then sell her story afterwards – especially if she portrayed herself as the wronged woman who'd exposed Lola's hypocrisy to the world. Surely that would fetch a good price? *You never know, I might even get a record deal out of it.*

But there was only one problem: how did she get hold of Freddy? She didn't have any numbers for him and couldn't risk making contact on Twitter. It was way too public and she'd have to ask him to follow her before she could send him a direct message. No, she'd have to set up an anonymous email account and then send a confidential message to the Channel 3 newsdesk and mark it for Freddy's attention. She'd tell him to give her his phone number if he was interested in a major scandal involving Lola Grant. That was the way to do it. And if she didn't give anything away in the first email, no one could trace it back to her. She sat down and picked up her phone, running a quick internet search on Channel 3 News.

Her finger hovered over the Contact icon but a thought entered her head and stopped her from clicking. *Wait a minute, can I really trust Freddy? What if he doesn't realize Lola was two-timing him and he's still under her spell?* She did seem to have a way of duping people, although Gloria had no idea why they all fell for it. But what if Freddy took Lola's side, got hold of the footage and decided not to run with it – or, even worse, somehow turned it against Gloria? Sure, it wasn't very likely when this was the kind of scoop that made a journalist's career. But she couldn't take any chances. No, what she needed was some kind of back-up plan, a way of releasing the footage to the world at the same time as Channel 3 News. A way of holding some kind of public premiere for her film that would coincide with Lola's opening night.

Aha! That's it!

She was suddenly hit by an amazing idea. An idea so amazing it made her jump up and knock over her coffee. An idea that would allow her to stay in complete control of the news story – and use it to inflict as much damage as possible on Lola. She gasped out loud at her own brilliance.

She wouldn't send that email just yet. Before she did, there was something she needed to investigate.

*

Lola yawned as she stared at her coffee machine and it drifted out of focus. She tried to concentrate. Where was she supposed to put the water? And how many spoons of coffee was she supposed to add for one cup? *Oh why do they always have to make things so complicated?* She'd bought the machine when she'd first moved into the flat but hadn't ever felt brave enough to use it. She didn't really know why she was trying now. She stood no chance.

After just a few hours' sleep she'd woken up that morning with one of her worst hangovers ever – coupled with what she could only assume was a shocking coke comedown. For the last hour or so she'd flitted around her flat picking things up and putting them down again, starting jobs only to abandon them after a few seconds, and doing everything she could to fight the bone-numbing, breath-quickening, bladder-loosening fear of her whole life coming crashing down around her. But there was no escaping it – however much she told herself that extreme anxiety must be a side effect of a cocaine binge. She wanted to scream out loud but wasn't sure her own head could cope with the torture. And she couldn't even make herself a cup of coffee.

She leaned back against the worktop and let out a long sigh. Everywhere she looked her possessions still sat packed away in boxes. She wished she'd listened to Harvey when he'd wanted to rent her a temporary apartment while this one was done up rather than waiting for the builders to start work when she went on tour. She remembered him saying she'd need some kind of sanctuary when things got tough, which he predicted they were bound to. And she could see now that he'd been right.

Oh why did I fire him? What the hell was I thinking? Actually she knew exactly what she'd been thinking. And again Harvey had been right when he'd said it was the coke doing the thinking for her. He was always right. She only wished she'd realized that before she'd sacked him. Or maybe she had. Maybe that was one of the reasons *why* she sacked him.

Come to think of it, she wasn't even sure she *could* sack him. It wasn't as if she'd ever been in this position before. Mind you, she didn't remember them ever signing any kind of formal contract. And you heard about artists firing their managers all the time. Anyway, it was too late to start worrying about it now. She'd been such a bitch she was sure that even if she asked him back he'd only refuse – and with good reason. But what happened now if something awful blew up? If something went wrong with the tour before it opened? She'd made a big deal about being able to look after herself, but now that she was on her own she didn't mind admitting she'd been talking complete crap. And she was utterly petrified. She tried to tell herself again that it was only a side effect of the coke. But it didn't make any difference.

She turned back to the coffee machine and managed to insert what she could only hope would be the right amount of coffee and water. But if she wanted a latte did she add the milk now or once the coffee had brewed? She grabbed a carton of semi-skimmed from inside the fridge but could barely think straight and put it down on the worktop. She leant forward onto the edge, let her head flop down and closed her eyes. She couldn't believe she was actually on a coke comedown. How different was this to the kind of comedown she'd witnessed her mum going through day after day, year after year? She felt another stab of fear.

As she stood bent over the worktop she wondered how her mum had felt the first time she'd taken crack. Or had she started on normal coke and graduated to crack once she was hooked? *Like mother, like daughter,* tormented a voice in her head. *Like mother, like daughter.*

She lifted up her head and had another look at the coffee machine. *Oh forget the milk, I'll just have it black.* But which button was she supposed to press? There were loads of them flashing in her face, each of them a different colour. It was all too much. The slightest thing made her feel like her whole life was hurtling out of control.

How could I have been so stupid? And what if somebody saw me? Now that her fear had found something to latch onto, it rocketed out of control, crushing her in its grip until she felt like she was going to explode. She tried to calm down and regulate her breathing. *Come on, Lola, nobody saw you. Now pull yourself together and snap out of it!*

She gave up on the coffee machine and switched it off at the mains. One thing was for sure – there was no way she could go to rehearsals feeling like this. Not that they'd accomplish anything seeing as everyone had been shit-faced at the party. No, she didn't think anyone would complain if she rang in sick and gave them all the morning off. And besides, there was something much more important she needed to do. Something she realized she'd been putting off for months now. And something she couldn't avoid any longer.

She reached for her favourite sunglasses and wrapped them around her face. She remembered how she'd given them to Freddy at her album launch and he'd returned them when she was on the set of *Lucky Star*. She wondered what he'd think if he knew what she'd got up to last night. Then again, he'd probably stopped caring about her ages ago, right after she blew him out in a national newspaper. *Nice work, Lola, that was another smart move.*

Anyway, she'd have to think about Freddy another time. Right now it was time she visited her mum. She could pick up a coffee on the way.

*

Karen opened the door and was met by the sight of a huge black umbrella filling the frame. As it turned around she was stunned to find that standing underneath was Lola.

'Hiya, Mum.'

She was wearing an old black tracksuit and trainers with a pair of huge wraparound sunglasses despite the fact it was throwing it down. The rain bounced off the windscreen of a dark car that sat purring on the other side of the street.

'Lola! What are you doing here?'

'Oh thanks, Mum. I thought you'd be pleased to see me.'

'I am, no I am. Sorry, it's just a surprise, that's all.'

'No, well, I guess it was a spur-of-the-moment thing. Anyway, aren't you going to invite me in? It's blatantly pissing it down.'

'Yeah, yeah, course. Come in.'

Karen stood to the side and Lola slid past her and into the flat. She wished she'd known her daughter would be coming. She was wearing old jeans and a faded T-shirt, hadn't touched her hair since she'd got out of bed and wasn't due at the dentist's to sort out her teeth until next week. But she wondered whether that was the point – whether Lola had wanted to turn up unannounced to see how she was getting on with her life. If it was, she told herself that it didn't matter. *The important thing is she's here.* She took Lola's umbrella and shook it outside then closed the door.

'Well, this is very nice,' Lola said, looking around the living room.

'Oh I know!' she burst out. 'I'm so happy here, Lola. I mean, I still need to add the odd personal touch and stuff but I already feel really settled. Harvey helped me with it all – he said I'd need a sanctuary when I got out of rehab. And he was spot-on.'

Lola was still wearing her sunglasses but Karen was sure she detected a slight flinch at the mention of Harvey's name. It was obvious they still hadn't patched up their differences, whatever they were. She'd have to find out what had gone on at some point soon. Although she wouldn't push it just yet – it had been months since she'd seen Lola and the atmosphere between them was still a bit edgy. She reminded herself to tread carefully.

'Let me show you around,' she suggested brightly.

'OK, great.'

She gave Lola a little tour of the flat, proudly showing off her double bed with its headboard padded and pleated in faux leather, a gigantic plasma screen TV which took up almost an entire wall of the lounge, and a cream leatherette sofa with a handle which when pulled made it recline. 'Get a load of this,' she beamed as she demonstrated how it worked. 'Isn't it fab?'

'Yeah, Mum,' Lola smiled, her sunglasses still clamped to her face. 'It's fierce.'

Around the time Lola had bought her flat in Shoreditch she'd also invested in this one-bedroom place in Dulwich, not too far away from Karen's home in Tooting but far enough away to distract her from temptation. Of course it had been bought in Lola's name, presumably so that Karen couldn't do anything stupid like sell it to buy drugs, but the understanding was that she could stay here rent-free. And she could see now that it had been a shrewd strategy. Knowing she had a new home to go to when she came out of rehab had made her feel a fresh start might just be possible – and had played no small part in the fact that after three months she was still clean. It was the longest time she'd stayed off drugs in more than twenty years.

'You know I've been clean since early July now,' she shouted from the kitchen as she boiled the kettle. 'I'm even starting thinking about training to be a drugs counsellor. My therapist at the Abbey thinks I'd be really good.'

'That's great news, Mum,' Lola called back. 'Congratulations!'

Is it my imagination or is she being a bit warmer with me today? She certainly didn't seem to be as prickly as she'd been the last time they'd spoken on the phone before that big anti-drugs gig in Hyde Park. But she couldn't help thinking there was something wrong. Something she couldn't quite put her finger on. If she'd bothered to be much of a mother before now she might have developed some kind of intuition. Although there was no point regretting that now. It was much more important to concentrate on rebuilding her life – and rewriting some of her mistakes. She walked back into the lounge with two steaming mugs of tea.

'Here you go, get this down you.'

'Thanks, Mum.'

Karen watched as Lola's sunglasses steamed up and she reluctantly removed them, revealing eyes rimmed with black circles, sallow skin and a haggard-looking face. On top of that, she couldn't stop sniffing, kept having to wipe the sweat off her forehead and her left cheek gave way to the occasional twitch. So Karen had been right, there was something wrong. In fact, if she wasn't mistaken her daughter was going through some kind of comedown. And she might not be much of a mother but that she *did* know about.

'Lola,' she said softly, 'are you all right?'

'Yeah! Why do you say that?'

'You just look a bit worn out, that's all.'

'Yeah, sorry, I am a bit. It's been totally full-on rehearsing for the tour.'

She obviously wasn't ready to tell the truth and Karen didn't want to push it. 'Well, you have to make sure you look after yourself. I know the times I made the biggest mess of things were when I was feeling vulnerable.'

Lola laughed weakly and nodded. Karen noticed her eyes alight on a picture of the two of them standing on the mantel-piece. It was the first time she'd ever put up anything like a family photo in her home. It had been taken on a holiday to Brighton when Lola was about eight years old during one of Karen's brief periods off drugs. They'd stayed somewhere her mum and dad had taken her when she was little and had spent a whole week paddling in the sea, singing along to Lola's favourite Spice Girls songs and racing excitedly around the pier. Karen remembered the two of them riding the roller coaster over and over again and asking a passer-by to take a photo of them when they were flushed with adrenaline; it had captured them screaming with joy as the sea breeze blew their hair high in the air and the sun lit up their faces. Of course as soon as they'd got home Karen had gone all out to sabotage their happiness with her biggest drug binge ever. She looked at Lola now and wondered how much of it all she could remem-ber. Her features had settled into an expression of what looked to her like sorrow. Karen's chest tightened as she realized just how much she'd put her through. *If only I could make it right. If only it's not too late.*

'Is it that Freddy Jones again?' she ventured. 'Is it some-thing to do with him?'

'No. What are you on about?'

'Oh I don't know. I just got the impression he'd been treat-ing you badly. And maybe you were finding it a bit hard.'

'God, Mum, not at all. All that stuff I said in the paper about wanting us to be friends, that was actually true. Trust me, if I was going out with Freddy I wouldn't be in all this trouble now.'

'Oh, so you *are* in trouble?'

She shook her head and firmly set down her tea. She obviously didn't want to talk about it. 'No, sorry, I didn't mean that. I've just been overdoing it a bit, that's all. I think I need to take it easy – at least till the tour's up and running.' She crossed her legs and folded her arms. 'Anyway, I'm bored of talking about me. How about you? What did you mean about making a mess of things when you were feeling vulnerable?'

Now it was Karen's turn to be evasive. 'Oh, you know, just the shit that happens in life.'

'No, I don't know, Mum. You've never told me about the shit that happened in your life.'

No and I'm not going to either. For your sake.

But Lola wasn't giving up. 'I mean why do you think you did make such a mess of things? Did some guy piss you around? Did my dad get you up the duff and then dump you?'

At the mention of Lola's dad, Karen's mind flashed back to that holiday in Spain and the look on the stranger's face as he'd chatted her up in the club, putting his arm around her and buying her drink after drink as he made jokes in his heavily accented English. Where had he said he was from? He wasn't Spanish, that much she could remember. She seemed to think he was from somewhere in Eastern Europe, not that it mattered. All that mattered was what he'd done to her, slipping some kind of powder into her drink and then luring her away to a derelict warehouse where two other men had been waiting. She gave a little whimper as her mind flickered and flashed with memories of the three of them beating and raping her, hitting her round the head so hard she hadn't been able to see properly for days afterwards. Just thinking about it stopped her breath and she clutched onto the side of the sofa for support.

'Mum, is everything OK?'

'Yeah, yeah, I'm totally fine. I just think my body's still getting used to things, to be honest. You know, after everything I put it through it's probably still expecting me to pump it full of crack any minute.' She did her best to laugh at her own lame joke.

Can we please move on now?

There was no way she could tell Lola what she'd really been thinking – or the true story behind her conception. She'd decided long ago to let her think her dad was some charming and handsome Spaniard who'd seduced her on some kind of whirlwind holiday romance. She hadn't even told her own mum and dad the truth about what had happened, convinced at the time that they wouldn't believe her. She'd only gone out that night after having a massive row with them about wearing a skirt they said was too short and made her look indecent – like she was 'asking for it'. As if to prove a point she'd hitched it up another inch and then stormed off into some sleazy bar with the express intention of flirting with every man in there. And she had – which was why she knew the police wouldn't believe her if she'd told them a man had got her hammered, spiked her drink and then calmly led her away to destroy her life.

So instead she'd come up with some bullshit story about falling over drunk and waking up bruised on the beach the next morning with no idea how she'd got there, when the truth was she'd been shaken awake by a middle-aged Spanish woman as she lay battered and bleeding at the side of the road. A middle-aged Spanish woman who for a while she'd been convinced must have been an angel, giving her a hot bath, dressing her wounds and then taking her to a doctor she knew for a morning-after pill. A middle-aged Spanish woman who'd saved her life and whose name had been Lola, a name she'd given to the baby daughter who'd arrived nine months later. The daughter she'd tried to protect for the last twenty-five years from the full horror of everything that had happened to her in Spain.

Even now she was just as determined to protect Lola from knowledge she told herself could only corrode her soul. *How could she ever live with the truth?* Karen herself had struggled with it all her life and look where it had got her. Well she wasn't going to let that happen to Lola. She'd failed in every other area of motherhood. In this one at least she was determined not to – even if it did mean Lola would go on imagining she'd done something to be ashamed of. No, however much Lola persisted she'd just have to go on avoiding her questions.

'So you're still not going to tell me?' Lola frowned. 'You still don't think I deserve to know?'

'Oh Lola,' she sighed, 'sometimes things just aren't as simple as that. As you go through life I'm sure you'll find out that everyone has their own story – and a lot of people have their own struggles. You don't always need to know exactly what's gone on in their lives to understand them. And just because people do bad things it doesn't mean they're bad people.'

Her words seemed to make a real impression on Lola. She

turned to look at her and Karen was suddenly confronted by an image of herself when she'd been young and vulnerable – before she'd erected the hard front that had made her so difficult to love. As difficult to love as for so long she'd found Lola. But as she looked at her now she felt herself drawn in by a vulnerability she herself could just about remember feeling. And at that moment Karen knew for sure that she *could* love her. In fact, she knew that she *did* love her – and always had done.

'Lola, I'm sorry I've been such a shit mum,' she said slowly and clearly. 'I'm sorry I haven't been a mum at all really. But if it's not too late I'd like to start trying.'

Lola nodded seriously. 'OK, I'd like that too.'

'Great. Well let's not rush things. You've obviously got a lot on your plate at the moment.'

'Yeah but I'm up for it if you are. Just let me get the first night of this tour out of the way and then we'll have a go.'

They smiled at each other and came together for a hug, the first hug Karen could remember them having since Lola had been a little girl, probably since the time they'd gone on holiday to Brighton. And it wasn't the tightest hug in the world but at least it was something they could build on. She'd just have to wait less than a week until the tour had opened.

'Oh, actually, Lola,' she remembered, 'speaking of the tour, I've got you a little present.'

'Oh, right. Thanks, Mum.'

She disappeared into the kitchen and came back with a box covered in some old Spice Girls wrapping paper she'd managed to hunt down on eBay. Lola looked at it and laughed.

Karen hoped she remembered how happy they'd been as they'd sung her favourite music together.

'Now don't open it yet,' she said. 'It's for the first night of the tour. To wish you good luck.'

'Thanks, Mum. And are you going to come? It's at the O2.'

'Come? I wouldn't miss it for the world.'

*

Lola bounced onto the back seat of the car. 'Take me to rehearsals please!' she called to the driver.

She clicked her seat belt and leaned back, clutching her mum's present to her chest. Even though the rain was continuing to pelt down she could feel her mood lifting and her fear beginning to dissipate. *Oh my God, that was completely amazing.*

It would have been amazing enough to find out her mum was finally clean and making a new life for herself. But she'd even seemed serious about improving their relationship. For the first time since she was about eight Lola actually felt that her mum loved her. And as they'd hugged each other goodbye she'd been struck by the realization that she too could learn to love her mum.

Now that she thought about it, she wasn't sure she'd ever stopped loving her, even if her mum's actions had sometimes made her difficult to love. But she'd actually apologized for being a crap mum. It was a lot to take in. But it was all good. And it made her feel so much more positive about her own future to know that her mum would finally be a part of it.

As she listened to the sound of the car's windscreen wipers battling against the rain, she told herself that last night's coke binge had only been a minor blip. OK, so she'd been stupid to give into temptation after holding out for so long. But it wasn't the end of the world and she certainly wasn't going to go any-where near coke again. She was even going to lay off the booze – at least until the tour was up and running. If her mum was taking steps to sort out her life after twenty-five years, then she could hardly fall straight into the abyss she'd just vacated.

No, as of this moment she was going to snap out of her self-pity and enjoy the brilliant life she'd fought so hard to create. So what if she'd let herself down and snorted a load of coke? It didn't matter if it was definitely a one-off. So what if she'd fallen for yet another tramp and only ended up having her heart broken? If the heartache finally taught her a lesson then it wouldn't have been a wholly bad thing. And so what if she'd fucked up and fired her manager when she was totally off her face? She was sure once they'd had a bit of time apart she'd be able to go back to him and ask if they could start again. *Surely if I apologize for being a total bitch he'll forgive me and agree to come back?*

She took a deep breath and could feel her chest expanding. The more she thought about it, the more she realized she had nothing to feel frightened or depressed about. Nothing else mattered because for the first time in nearly two decades her mum had looked at her like she loved her. She'd even given her a present! She lifted it to her ear and gave it a little shake. She was dying to open it but she'd promised her mum she'd wait till the first night of the tour. Instead, she'd just have to concentrate on rehearsals and start thinking about today's schedule. She put the box down next to her and reminded herself that right now, the important thing was for her to focus everything she had on the tour and making the opening night as brilliant as it could be. Especially now that her mum would be there.

*

As Freddy undid his tie he felt all the happiness leak out of him. Just a few hours ago Spike had told him that Lola had been having some kind of relationship with the womanizing drummer in her band. He'd let the news slip when he'd been talking Freddy through the events of last night's party at Club Class – and it had hit him with as much impact as a twenty-stone prop slamming into him on the rugby pitch.

But at the same time it had suddenly explained so much. Lola hadn't been interested in him at all. All the time she'd been stringing him along, either to distract herself from this womanizing drummer or to try and make the bloke jealous. He wondered whether that was why she'd grabbed hold of him after their date and kissed him in front of all those paps. Had she even spoken to this drummer on the phone when she'd gone to the loo? *Could that explain why she came back to the table in a completely different mood?*

He was so angry he let loose a low growl. He was sitting in the rather tatty changing rooms of his rugby club, trying not to choke on the smell of cheap deodorant as he got ready for the team's regular Thursday night training session. Everyone else had already gone out onto the pitch but he'd arrived a bit late. He normally struggled to make it at all but today he'd finished work earlier than usual as he wasn't in the programme. He and Spike had been taken off roster for a day of forward-planning when it had been confirmed they'd been granted permission to film their exclusive report on the opening night of Lola's tour. Although right now Freddy couldn't think of anything he wanted to do less. Especially since Hugh was still so keen on them searching for a skeleton in Lola's closet – and dragging it out and onto the programme.

Even though he was late for training, Freddy took off his clothes slowly, lost in the jumble of thoughts whirling around his head. Could he work up this story about Lola seeing her drummer and expose her as a fake for singing to the world that she was through with tramps? But how could he even prove this guy *was* a tramp? And hadn't Spike said they'd already split up? Freddy could hardly go on the national news and announce that Lola had just had a fling with another bad boy; if it had now ended she could still hold her head up high and claim she'd turned her back on tramps. No, he needed something much harder than that. And he had just five days to find it.

As he pulled off his trousers he was hit by the first stirrings of an idea. Apparently Lola's affair with this drummer was the reason she'd had a massive row with Harvey at the party – a row that had been so bad it had culminated in her sacking him. Spike had also said Lola had gone ballistic when she'd seen him and had thrown him out of the party, which surely implied she had something to hide. Freddy remembered him saying she was completely shit-faced and had almost fallen flat on her face on the dance floor, although that was hardly headline news when half the world had already seen her tumble arse over tit down a flight of stairs in Stockholm. But when he added together all the different factors – the affair with the drummer, the arguments with Harvey and Spike, and getting herself so shit-faced she couldn't stand up – it did sound like her life was hurtling out of control. And he knew that a major star going into meltdown was just the kind of story Hugh loved, even if it was just the kind of story he hated. But there was no point worrying about that now – however he felt about it, he had to go ahead and file some kind of story. And at the moment this was the best he could come up with.

And anyway, why shouldn't he tell the world Lola was cracking up after the way she'd treated him? She hadn't shown the slightest interest in his feelings when she'd openly flirted with him on their date, on stage at the gig in Hyde Park and on camera in front of millions of viewers. No, the more he thought about it, the more he felt used and duped; Lola had simply toyed with him and then tossed him aside as soon as he'd served his purpose. And as usual, he'd simply rolled over and taken it – Mr Nice Guy, always aiming to please and never wanting to upset anyone. Well, he'd had enough – and for once he *wasn't* going to roll over and take it.

He stopped and looked at himself in the mirror. He was now wearing his full strip, including the skintight top he was sure was too small for him and always made him feel self-conscious. Freddy looked at his muscles bulging out like some kind of cartoon superhero and scoffed at his own reflection. *Me, a superhero? That's a joke.* He didn't think he'd ever felt like less of a hero. He thought about what he was about to do to Lola. Was he the kind of journalist who dug around for scandal and then went all-out to hurt people? Evidently he was, whether he liked it or not.

He sat down to put on his boots and reminded himself that it was no use feeling guilty if he didn't have any choice. And anyway, everything Lola did was so successful at the moment, one news report about her going off the rails would hardly end her career – it wasn't as if she was doing drugs or anything. But it would save his career, and that's what he had to remember. The only problem was, could he actually make his story stand up? Sure, he had lots of gossip to work with, but there was nothing concrete. What he really needed was some kind of evidence, preferably something visual that would work well on TV. And then he could go big – big enough to satisfy his editor. But where would he find it?

He took a deep breath and jumped to his feet. His whole body felt tense and he jiggled up and down to try and release some of the stiffness. It was no use. To work off this level of tension he needed something much stronger. He didn't think he'd ever been so up for a game of rugby. He ran out onto the field, ready for battle.

*

As Harvey powered through the water, he hoped the tension would start to leave his body. But with every stroke and every breath it clung onto him, gnawing away at his insides and driving him on. He didn't think he'd ever swum with such energy or vigour.

Ten lengths. Twenty. Thirty. Nothing made any difference.

He wondered whether he'd ever be able to stamp out his scorching anger at the injustice of what Lola had done. Or his deep sadness at her destruction of their friendship, the best friendship either of them had ever had. Or his humiliation at the thought of how everyone else must be reacting to the news of his sacking. Carlson was probably having a good old laugh about it. And he didn't dare imagine how smug it must have made Jake. He squeezed his eyes shut and tried not to think about it.

Forty lengths. Fifty. Sixty. Still he felt no better.

But the funny thing was, even though he was devastated at the way Lola had treated him, that didn't stop him from panicking that somebody else might have seen her snorting coke and would go blabbing to the press. Should he call Barbara and warn her about it? No, it wasn't his problem anymore. Lola had made it quite clear how she felt. She wanted him to hand everything over to Amina, which he'd done first thing that morning, even though Amina had been paralysed by what looked like a hideous hangover and he wasn't sure how much of his information she was actually taking in. But he'd done as he was told and his only option now was to step back with love. Even if Lola did sometimes make herself difficult to love.

Seventy lengths. Eighty. Ninety.

Right, that's it. If a hundred lengths weren't going to make him feel better, keeping going to two hundred certainly wouldn't do it.

He hauled himself out of the pool and splashed his way over to the changing rooms. The minute he entered he almost choked on the sickly scent of expensive aftershaves sprayed one on top of another by the gym's affluent clientele. As he opened his mahogany-panelled locker and began to towel himself down, he heard the famous theme tune to Channel 3 News coming from the big plasma TV fixed high up on one of the walls. He lowered himself onto a bench and watched Amanda Adams appear on screen and read the headlines. The latest unemployment figures, flash floods in Yorkshire and Lola Grant—

Just as Amanda started talking about Lola, some fat Greek bloke who always insisted on styling his hair whilst stark naked switched on the hairdryer. *Oh no! But I can't hear the TV!*

Harvey felt a little spasm of panic and jumped to his feet. *What if someone's blabbed and Lola's coke binge is about to be plastered all over the news?*

He wrapped his towel around him and rushed closer to the TV, where he could actually hear what was being said. He stood fixed to the spot and endured a long report about a minor altercation between Lavinia Trout and some gobby fish-wife on a market in Grimsby and then an interview about unemployment with some businesswoman with librarian boobs straining to get out of a dress way too tight for her middle-aged spread. Surely if Lola had been busted for taking coke it would have easily trumped this round-up and made the top story? So why on earth had they mentioned her name in the headlines?

After what seemed like forever, the presenter announced that Channel 3 News had secured exclusive access to the first night of Lola's tour. Harvey let out a sigh of relief. *Is that it? A trail for next Wednesday's programme?*

As she explained that Freddy Jones would be the only journalist allowed backstage, he returned to his locker and began patting his hair dry. Oh maybe there was no need to worry about Lola's coke binge making the news. Because of libel laws, no journalist could run the story without cast-iron evidence. And as far as Harvey knew there wasn't any.

For the first time since last night he was starting to feel a little less tense. He padded over to the mirror and stopped to inspect his reflection. He looked tired and a bit frazzled but at least he was still standing – and would live to fight another day. After all, he'd fought his way through much worse than this and had always survived. He forced out a little smile and broke away to start slipping on his clothes.

As he pulled on his trousers he remembered that Spike was going to meet him outside the gym to come back to his place for a late dinner. And he was determined to enjoy himself. It was no longer his responsibility to worry about Lola. Besides, it didn't look like there was anything to worry about.

*

Over near Heathrow, rehearsals for the *Trouble* tour were being wound down for the evening.

'Well done everyone!' called out Carlson. 'If we can do as well as that for the next five days we've got nothing to worry about.'

Oh save your breath, thought Gloria. *Some of us aren't worried in the first place. In fact, some of us couldn't give less of a shit if we tried.*

No, Gloria had a whole different show to prepare for – one that would be much more deserving of the title *Trouble* than Lola's tacky tour. But before she could begin rehearsals she needed to hold one key production meeting. And now looked like the perfect time.

As the band and dancers grabbed their coats and bags and bolted out of the door, Gloria sidled over to the tech desk and perched on the edge.

'Hi Vlad,' she purred, 'how's it going?'

'Fine thanks,' he answered without moving his eyes from his computer screen.

He didn't seem remotely interested in her presence. She subtly inched up her skirt to flash him a bit of leg. 'I'm not sure we've actually met before. Well, not properly anyway. I'm Gloria. One of the BVs?'

She held out her hand and her eyes sparkled at him.

'Oh yeah, Gloria. Good to meet you.'

As he shook her hand she spotted a glimmer of interest in his eyes.

That's more like it . . .

'Night, guys!' called a voice behind her. She looked around and saw Lola leaving with Amina trailing after her.

'Night!' yelled Vlad.

'Night!' Gloria shouted, trying her best not to scowl. Lola had been a silly cow in rehearsals all afternoon, bursting with enthusiasm and forcing them all to go over the same bits of the show time and time again to make sure everything was perfect. And she'd been annoyingly chirpy for someone who'd spent all night snorting coke. It wasn't right – nobody on a comedown should be that cheerful. *Well by the time I've finished with her, cheerful's the last thing she'll be.*

But first she needed Vlad to take the bait. And she was dismayed to see he'd turned back to his screen and was tapping away on the keyboard. She casually unzipped her top to reveal a bit more cleavage. *It's about time I got my money's worth out of these girls*, she thought, leaning forward so he'd get a decent eyeful.

'You know, I'm so impressed by your contribution to the

show,' she gushed with such conviction she almost fooled herself. 'I was just saying to Sharonne how amazing your video projections are looking.'

Vlad broke away from his computer and smiled at her. 'Yeah, turned out well, didn't they?'

Yeah, and they'll be turning out a whole lot better once I've got my hands on them.

'Funnily enough,' she went on, 'it's the screens I wanted to talk to you about.'

'Oh yeah. What do you want to know?'

'Well, I wondered if I could ask you a little favour. My brother's studying IT at uni and he's absolutely brilliant. But would you mind if he came and sat in with you some time? I've already told him about some of the stuff you're doing and it's exactly what he wants to do when he graduates.'

'Urm, yeah, maybe, urm, leave it with me and I'll have a think. I mean, we're obviously really up against it at the moment.'

'Oh I know, Vlad. And I've no idea how you manage with all the pressure you're under. But if you could squeeze him in for just one day I'd be ever so grateful.'

'See you tomorrow, guys!' called out Carlson as he sloped out of the door.

'Yeah, see you!' Gloria called after him.

Finally they were on their own.

'So how exactly do the screens work anyway?' she asked, fingering the zip around her cleavage suggestively.

'Well, it's all digital, obviously,' Vlad explained, struggling not to stare at her boobs. 'So we feed in the finished films on a memory stick, cue them up and just click on one little icon when it's time for them to play. It's that simple.'

'My God, even *I* understand that,' Gloria fawned. 'And I'm hopeless with technology!' She gave a flirtatious giggle to make her ineptitude sound more convincing. 'So is that just a normal memory stick then?'

'Yeah, just your regular thirty-two-gig pen drive from any old computer shop.' He ejected it from the hard drive and held it up to show her.

Hmm, that looks promising. She knew it wouldn't be too difficult for her to copy the master sequence, edit in her own little piece of movie magic and substitute the new version on Vlad's hard drive just before opening night. And then all those lucky fans at the O2 would be getting two shows for the price of one – and she'd be getting maximum value out of her debut as a film-maker. She shivered with excitement as she pictured Lola prancing around the stage screeching along to one of her awful songs while the footage of her snorting coke was projected onto the screens behind her. Oh yeah, that would be so much better than just sending the clip directly to Channel 3 News. Especially as Gloria had just heard Freddy Jones and his crew had already been granted permission to film the show on opening night – and their programme started broadcasting at nine o'clock, just half an hour after Lola was due on stage. They'd be ideally placed to capture the fans' outrage as their idol was humiliated. It was all falling together perfectly.

But Gloria knew her plan would only work if she had access to the tech desk so she could copy the file and smuggle it out of the building. Which was where her little brother Clinton would come in. She just needed Vlad to let Clinton shadow him for a day. But he didn't seem that keen. *Oh what's his problem? All he does all day is sit around on his bony arse pressing a few buttons. Why should he care if someone watches him?*

She told herself not to get irritated. She'd just have to try a bit harder to win him round. It wasn't as if she'd had any difficulty on that front in the past. In fact, she prided herself on having ways of getting around any man. And one way in particular she was confident would work even on a man nick-named the Impaler.

But God he was ugly. She'd seen better legs on an oil rig and when he smiled his face reminded her of a diseased ferret straining out a dump. On top of all that, he looked distinctly like the kind of man who didn't clean his bits properly and had never heard of manscaping. She tried not to think about it. *Think about Chanelle. Think about the money. And think about Lola's face as she finally gets what she deserves.*

'Oh Vlad,' she breathed, running the tip of her tongue along her top lip, 'I hope you don't mind me saying this but I've always been so turned on by talent.'

'Really?' He switched off his computer and stepped towards her. *Now* she had him.

She slid across the desk so the insides of her knees were touching the outsides of his thighs. 'Absolutely. And I've been wanting to come and chat to you for ages.'

'Are you serious?'

'Yeah. But you're always surrounded by hangers-on. This is the first time I've had you all to myself. And I've been waiting for so long . . .'

He inched closer and Gloria was overwhelmed by the smell of TCP. 'Yeah, well, I'm glad you did.'

'Oh, Vlad, you've no idea how good it feels to hear you say that.'

She tried not to retch as she leaned in to kiss him. Within seconds he was ramming his tongue down her throat and pressing his growing erection against her groin. She immediately understood how he'd earned his nickname. His dick was the size of a small bulldog and, by the looks of things, just as lively.

Come on, Gloria. You've got to go through with this now . . .

This was it – her chance to resurrect her career, turn her entire life around and punish Lola in the process.

She took hold of Vlad's belt and undid the buckle.

12

Freddy leaned onto the railing and squeezed it with both hands. He and Spike were standing in the lift on their way up to the Channel 3 News boardroom. They'd been summoned to a top-secret emergency meeting and all Freddy had been told was that it had to take place outside the newsroom. It sounded ominous.

'Man, do you think we're in for a bollocking?' asked Spike, a look of terror on his face.

'I don't know,' Freddy gulped. 'I'm worried it could be much worse than that. I'm worried we could be about to get sacked.'

Last Friday the two of them had recorded their exclusive interview with Rex Watson and celebrity sexpert Bunny Love but it had turned into a disaster. Freddy had started the shoot ready to rip Rex to pieces by taking the piss out of his plan to write a sex manual, but every time he'd tried, Rex had smiled serenely and said he didn't care if he was making a fool of himself – he'd fallen madly in love with Bunny and realized that some things in life were more important than his career. He'd also said that his first experience of love had made him realize some of the mistakes he'd made in the past, and

Freddy's instincts had told him this was a major scoop so he'd spent the rest of the interview quizzing Rex about his plans to turn his back on his nasty past. But when he'd returned to the newsroom and shown the finished interview to his editor, Hugh had gone apeshit, accusing Freddy of producing a puff piece, letting Rex walk all over him and giving one of the country's most hated figures a platform to rehabilitate his image. So much for Freddy's instincts. In the end, his package had been hacked down to less than two minutes and dumped right at the end of the programme. But it looked like that wasn't the end of it. It looked like the incident might be about to cost him his job.

The lift doors pinged open and Freddy and Spike gave each other a solemn nod.

'Here we go, champ,' Freddy said, patting his producer on the back.

Spike opened his mouth to reply but nothing came out.

As they strode forwards and into the boardroom, Freddy could feel his legs beginning to wobble beneath him. *Come on, mate. Hold it together!*

Waiting to greet them were an obviously fired-up Hugh Badcock, who was manically twiddling his signet ring, and his deputy editor Janine Jury, who as usual was chewing gum and swigging Diet Coke.

'Freddy, Spike,' Hugh beamed at them. 'Come and sit down.'

Uh-oh. This doesn't look good.

Freddy shut the door and he and Spike took their seats at the other end of the board table. Hugh introduced them to a grim-faced lawyer who looked like something out of a Ken

Loach film and who Freddy couldn't help noticing was wearing a fluorescent orange vest underneath his white shirt. But what was a lawyer doing there?

This really *doesn't look good.*

Freddy told himself he should probably get in there first with some kind of apology for the Rex Watson debacle. At least that way he might save some face – and earn some goodwill.

'Look,' he began, laying his hands down on the table, 'can I just start by saying I'm sorry about the whole Rex Watson thing? I know what I delivered wasn't what you were looking for and I'll just have to try harder in the future.'

Hugh looked surprised. 'Oh, great. Well, it's good to hear that, Freddy. But we didn't ask you here to talk about Rex Watson.'

'Oh. Right.'

'We asked you here to talk about Lola Grant.'

'*Lola*? What about Lola?'

Hugh looked at the other two and then launched into his story. 'Well, while you were out filming with Rex, a confidential email marked for your attention arrived on the newsdesk.'

'Oh, right. I haven't seen it, sorry.'

'No,' explained Hugh, 'as you were out it was passed onto me.'

'OK. And what did it say?'

Hugh slid his laptop across the table and Freddy grabbed it from the centre.

'Have a read,' Hugh said, 'but it's basically from someone in Lola's entourage who says they want to remain anonymous. Now whoever this person is, they say they have exclusive footage of Lola snorting coke that they're going to play onto the screens on the opening night of her tour.'

There was a long silence.

'Fuck,' was all Freddy could say.

'What the fuck?' echoed Spike.

'Exactly!' smiled Hugh and Janine in perfect unison. 'Isn't it fucking brilliant?'

Freddy didn't answer. 'And who else has seen this email?'

'Just that blonde bird on the newsdesk, whatever her name is,' brayed Janine. 'But I've already had a word with her and she'll keep schtum.'

'And obviously we don't want anyone else to find out about it,' added Hugh. 'Of course, once the footage has been played to thousands of fans in the O2 there'll be no keeping it secret anymore. And am I right in thinking as part of the deal we have to pool our show footage after we've broadcast it?'

'For real,' croaked Spike, his dark knuckles turning white as his hands gripped onto the sides of his chair.

'But that doesn't matter too much,' reasoned Hugh. 'What matters is that we'll be the first to break the story – we'll be the only ones allowed in the O2 and the only ones broadcasting live.'

Fuck, thought Freddy. *How the fuck has this happened?*

'Yes, that's what we negotiated,' he confirmed gravely.

Fuck. Fuck. Fuck.

'So as far as anyone else is concerned it'll be our scoop,' Hugh grinned, his face more animated than Freddy had ever seen it. 'And I'm sure you don't need me to tell you it'll make shitloads of noise.'

Freddy tried to swallow but his throat was too dry. All right, he'd been angry with Lola when he'd found out she'd been seeing her drummer – and his anger had helped him decide to go through with Hugh's request to come up with some kind of grubby story. But this was something else. This would destroy her career – and ruin her life.

'And is it definitely coke?' he ventured somewhat lamely. 'I mean, in the video?'

'Well, that's where our legal expert comes in,' chomped Janine.

'It's difficult to say without seeing the footage,' began the lawyer. 'To be on the safe side you might have to say it shows her "snorting a white powder *believed to be* cocaine". And say that if it is, stressing that "if", it'll prove her to be a hypocrite.'

'OK,' Freddy nodded, making a mental note.

'But our viewers aren't stupid,' Janine butted in, her eyes gleaming with aggression. 'They'll see for themselves that Lola's a cokehead.'

'If she *is* a cokehead,' Freddy pointed out.

'I think we can trust this source,' countered Hugh. 'They seem to know what they're talking about and they're offering us a broadcast exclusive if we can guarantee them a slot – in writing.'

'And can we?' asked Freddy, a small part of him still hoping for some way out.

'*Can we?*' Hugh spluttered. 'We can do more than that – we can guarantee the top story. Fuck it, we can guarantee the whole programme if we need to!'

Freddy did his best to look excited. 'OK, great, I suppose I'd better crack on with it then.'

'Good man. We're taking both of you off-roster for the rest

of the day so you can start preparing. And if I were you I'd get onto this source ASAP. He or she wants an answer by close of play or they say they'll go to another broadcaster.'

Freddy gave a sharp sniff. 'OK boss. I get it. And I'll get onto them right away.'

He stood up to leave and Spike followed, his chair scraping along the floor with a high-pitched screech.

'Good man,' repeated Hugh. 'But this time, don't let me down.'

'Oh don't worry,' Freddy nodded. 'I won't.'

*

'La la la la la la la la laaah.'

Lola was determined her voice wouldn't let her down.

'La la la la la la la la laaah.'

As she moved up a key she remembered to keep her mouth wide open and to sing from her diaphragm.

'La la la la la la la la laaah.'

She stopped and smiled. Even though she was aware of her limitations as a singer, she could tell her voice was sounding better than ever. And the discovery came as a relief because she really wanted her vocals to be up to the standard of every other aspect of the show, which was starting to take shape as something very special. In rehearsals they were now running through the set list in full costume; the other day Lola had tweeted a selfie of her dressed as Cleopatra and the response from the fans had been insane. And earlier that day she'd spent a long time rehearsing and perfecting her big entrance at the start of the show, which involved her shooting up from underneath the stage and onto a raised platform at the back before stepping her way down the stairs to join the dancers. Once she'd nailed the sequence she'd felt a rush of excitement and couldn't wait to do it for real for the fifteen thousand fans – not to mention the TV cameras – on opening night. But before she did, she just needed to spend a bit of time working on her voice.

'That's sounding delicious, Lola,' reassured her teacher from her seat at the piano. Bella Figurini was a former opera singer with the look and temperament of a Mediterranean mamma but the speaking voice of an Essex dinner lady. The truth was that she'd been brought up by Italian parents in a flat above Papa Razzi, the restaurant they ran on the high street in Chelmsford. Now in her early sixties, Bella's own singing voice had started to deteriorate so she'd diversified into teaching and gave lessons in the music room of her home in Primrose Hill, which was filled with posters and photos commemorating her glory days, as well as fifteen cats that only ever seemed to lie around sleeping but somehow still managed to cover Lola and her clothes in a thick coating of their moulted hair. Not that Lola particularly minded – it was a small price to pay for a session with the best vocal coach in the business. Even if she was also the biggest gossip Lola had ever met.

'Oh you'll never guess what I heard the other day,' Bella whispered, her eyes rounding and the big blue veins standing out on her bust. 'Ace Bounder's only been shagging Lucretia Lavelle. I mean, can you believe it? She must be older than me!'

Lola responded with the requisite gasp of amazement. She decided not to mention the fact that Lucretia was doing the costumes for her show in case Bella plugged her for more information. And she made a mental note never to tell her vocal coach anything about her own personal life. *Unless I want it broadcast to the whole music business, that is.*

'And what's next?' she asked, eager to move on.

'Let's try some broken chords,' chirped Bella, her fingers returning to the keys. 'Repeat after me. Aaa, eee, iii, ooo, uuu.'

'Aaa, eee, iii, ooo, uuu.'

'That's great. Let's try it one more time but remember to take a breath after the second chord.'

'Aaa, eee, iii, ooo, uuu.'

'And try it again with less tension in the lips.'

'Aaa, eee, iii, ooo, uuu.'

That's it! thought Lola. *It's blatantly sounding fierce.*

'Oh, get a load of this,' Bella spouted, leaning towards her over the keyboard. 'Someone told me the other day Shereen Spicer's shagging one of her backing dancers. Can you believe it? And not only that – apparently she's a total cokehead.'

Again Lola gasped but tried not to get drawn in.

'Have *you* ever seen her doing coke?' pressed Bella.

'Oh no, I hardly know her – I've only met her once.'

It didn't take much to imagine how Bella would respond if Lola told her she'd been shagging her drummer, caught him dipping his dick in her backing vocalist and then went out on a coke bender to get over it. The news would be all around London in the time it took Lola to complete a set of scales.

'Urm, do you mind if we do a bit of work on resonance?' she asked, keen to divert the attention back to her voice.

'Not at all,' smiled Bella, clearly disappointed Lola wasn't taking her on. 'So let's go aaa, eee, iii, ooo, uuu. Crescendo first, a little vibrato, sustain and then fade out.'

'Aaa, eee, iii, ooo, uuu.'

'And again.'

'Aaa, eee, iii, ooo, uuu.'

'Delicious. Absolutely delicious!'

Lola performed a little jig on the spot.

'So what's the gossip from *your* tour?' wheedled Bella. 'Is there anyone you've got your eye on?'

'Oh no,' she trilled, comforting herself that technically she wasn't lying. 'Not at the moment anyway. I've not got the time to start messing around with men. Honestly darlin', I'm just really focused on the show.'

And she *wasn't* lying. In fact she'd been so focused on rehearsals lately she'd hardly thought about Jake and hadn't even noticed Gloria. It was as if she'd developed tunnel vision and nothing mattered to her other than having an amazing show to reveal to her fans on opening night. And immersing herself in work was actually making her feel much better about herself and some of the mistakes she'd made recently. Not only that but it was making her more determined to turn her back on the bitch she'd somehow slipped into becoming over the past few weeks. She was even thinking of a way of apologizing to Harvey while she was on stage on opening night. Of course she didn't want to embarrass him, especially when news of him being sacked still hadn't leaked out to the press. But she was sure she could come up with some way of publicly admitting she'd been wrong and asking him to come back without causing offence.

'OK, now let's do some work on pitch control,' Bella broke in. 'So let's start with some lip trills, with your fingers either side of your lips. Brrrr. And then take a quick breath and open up for eeee.'

'Brrrr. Eeee.'

'Not bad, but imagine the sound's in the front section of your mouth. So you're spinning it around and letting it resonate. And again.'

'Brrrr. Eeee.'

Lola felt great. In fact, she'd never felt better. Once again, her music was coming to the rescue. And once again it was going to save the day.

'That's delicious,' gushed Bella. 'And one last time.'

'Brrrr. Eeee.'

As she channelled all her energy into making her voice resonate, Lola felt another tremor of excitement. With everything going so well she was sure her opening night was going to be fierce. In fact, if she carried on through the next few days as focused as she felt now, how could anything possibly go wrong?

*

'Mmm, that's delicious,' sighed Sharonne as she sipped her glass of champagne and smacked her lips. 'Just what I needed.'

Jake looked at her and smiled. The two of them were lying naked in the Jacuzzi in his hotel suite, the bubbles dancing around her nipples – nipples he just wanted to lean over and nibble the hell out of. But he told himself to take things slowly. He couldn't risk anything going wrong this time.

'Cheers, babe,' he winked, bringing his glass closer to hers.

'Cheers,' she said, her eyes meeting his with a naughty twinkle – a twinkle he was pretty sure told him he was going to get what he wanted.

And it was about time. Ever since he'd been caught boning Gloria and Lola had caused such a big fuss, Sharonne had been avoiding him as if he were a leper. It hadn't bothered him at first, especially not when he'd met that hot-as-hell dancer Kitty. But then that interfering fag Harvey had stepped in to pour cold water all over that one and ever since he'd felt like everyone on the tour was turning against him. Of course, he couldn't give less of a fuck about Lola and Gloria. But now Kitty had poisoned the other female dancers against him and the three of them were making him feel about as welcome in rehearsals as a pork chop in a synagogue. Well, he'd had enough and now he was ready to fight back. And he couldn't think of any better place to start than right here in his hotel Jacuzzi with Sharonne. He took a sip of champagne and felt the bubbles froth in his nostrils. *So many bubbles,* he thought. *And hopefully we'll be creating a few more soon . . .*

After just half a glass of champagne he was starting to feel seriously horny. He slid his way through the water and put his glass down on the side next to her. He leaned in to kiss her temple and felt her eyelashes flickering shut against his chin. He began softly nibbling his way down her cheek and towards the edge of her mouth. And then he stopped. She gave a little whimper and put down her glass.

Looks like good old Jakey boy's back in business.

He seized the moment and moved in to kiss her lips, gently parting them to slip in his tongue, as under the water the bubbles bounced around his now rock-solid cock.

He had to admit, Sharonne had it all going on and she was one of the best-looking chicks he'd ever screwed. He'd first wanted to bang her back in Berlin, but on that occasion Lola had managed to distract him with a well-timed hand-job. Not that it had distracted him for long. No, he'd just waited a few days till they were in Stockholm and Lola had gone out with Gloria and the other girls, winding up so drunk she'd fallen downstairs outside some club. In all the fuss afterwards she hadn't thought to ask what he'd been up to – or worked out that he'd spent the night boning Sharonne in the hotel sauna. Well, the Swedes *were* famous for their love of saunas. He'd only wanted to find out if they'd get his balls swinging too . . .

And boy, had Sharonne got his balls swinging that night. So much, in fact, that he'd gone back for more several times afterwards – in Amsterdam, Rome, Madrid, Barcelona and then back in London. And yeah, Lola might have had her suspicions that something was going on, snapping at the two of them whenever they so much as said hello to each other, but thankfully she had no proof and he'd managed to convince her she was just being paranoid. He dreaded to think what would have happened if she'd found out he'd been banging *both* her backing singers. She'd whipped up enough drama about him screwing one of them.

'Hold on a minute,' Sharonne panted, pulling back. 'I really don't want to get my hair wet.'

Is she fucking serious? We're in a fucking hot tub!

'OK babe,' he managed, mustering up a mischievous smile, 'I promise not to push you under.'

He moved back in to kiss her but could tell there was still something holding her back. 'What is it? Is everything all right?'

She pulled back again and this time cupped his head in her hands. 'Actually, I really shouldn't be doing this. I've got a boyfriend now – and he's very possessive.'

Is that all? Like I give a shit about some dumb-ass boyfriend.

'Well, I won't tell him if you won't,' Jake breathed into her ear as he ran his fingers down her arm.

'Yeah but there's something—'

He put his mouth to her lips. 'Sssh. Don't worry about it, babe.'

Your boyfriend, your problem.

'No but he's—'

'Oh knock it off, babe. Tonight's about me and you. And you know how good we are together. Don't you remember the first time we hooked up in Stockholm?'

She giggled and he could feel her body start to give way. Her mouth gradually opened and she returned his kisses with a new passion. He spotted his chance and moved his hand down under the water to stroke the insides of her thighs until she began to part her legs.

'Oh Jake, I . . . I . . .'

'Yeah?' he teased, sliding his body into the gap between her legs and tickling her tongue with his. 'Yeah?'

But she didn't reply. As he felt the last remnants of resistance leave her body he spotted his chance, nudged the tip of his dick onto her pussy and eased himself into her. *Man, that feels good.*

He listened to the jolt of pleasure catch in her throat and knew the last thing she was thinking about was her boyfriend.

Whoever the fuck he is, he sure ain't her boyfriend now.

*

The following morning, Freddy arrived at the aircraft hangar where Lola and her team were holding the last day of rehearsals. He was due to meet Barbara Bullock to run through the logistical details of their shoot and had been told by security he needed to walk down a long corridor bordering the main rehearsal space to find her. As he opened the door and stepped inside, all he could think was he hoped he wouldn't bump into Lola. He reassured himself that was hardly likely with her being in the middle of a dress rehearsal.

'Freddy!'

A familiar south London accent stopped him in his tracks. *No, it can't be.*

'Freddy, is that you?'

Lola froze to the spot. She'd had no idea Freddy was going to be visiting rehearsals today and couldn't believe she'd just bumped into him.

He turned around and the two of them stood staring at each other from opposite ends of the corridor.

Oh no, he thought, *how am I supposed to face her knowing the trick I'm going to pull tomorrow?*

Oh no, she thought, *how am I supposed to face him knowing how much I've messed him around?*

'It *is* you!' she called out, hoping she looked pleased to see him.

'Yep, it's me all right,' Freddy replied, hoping she couldn't read the dread on his face.

As she walked over to him, he saw she was dressed in some kind of suit of armour.

'Hiya.'

'All right?'

There was an awkward moment when neither of them was sure whether to hug or kiss each other. They ended up doing neither.

'Sorry,' Lola said, gesturing to her armour. 'It kind of gets in the way a bit.'

'Oh, that's fine,' Freddy said. 'Don't worry about it.'

Well, she's obviously looking for an excuse not to kiss me, he thought.

Well, he's blatantly relieved he doesn't have to touch me, she thought.

'What is it, anyway?' he asked.

Lola flashed him a weak smile. 'I'm supposed to be Joan of Arc. Can't you tell?'

'Oh, right, yeah.'

There was a silence.

'So what brings you here then?' she asked.

Freddy didn't want her to think he was hanging around like some lovesick loser on the off chance he'd bump into her. 'Oh, work, you know. I'm here to see Barbara to plan tomorrow. My producer's gone to the O2 to do a tech recce. We're going to be filming backstage, like.'

'Oh, yeah, of course.' Lola tried not to look too disappointed; part of her hoped he might have arranged to come here hoping he'd bump into her.

'So are you doing your dress rehearsal then?' he asked.

'Yeah, we're running through the show twice. I'm just nipping back to my dressing room to make a quick call while they fix a problem with the sound.' *Well, I don't want to put him off by telling him I'm going to the bogs for a piss.* Not that it would matter in the slightest; he'd obviously gone right off her already.

'And, urm, how's it going?' he asked.

'Yeah, it's, urm, it's great thanks.'

There was another pause. Freddy tucked his hands under

his armpits. Lola began fiddling with the collar on her costume. In the distance a pair of half-naked dancers clattered across the corridor on roller skates, the sound of their wheels on the tiled floor echoing in the silence behind them.

This is awful, thought Lola, thinking back to the way she'd knocked him back in a press interview. *I messed him around so badly he blatantly can't stand the sight of me.* She felt so guilty she just wanted the conversation to be over.

This is excruciating, thought Freddy, thinking forward to what he was about to do to her tomorrow. *She won't be able to stand the sight of me once I've done my report.* He hoped she couldn't sense his guilt and just wanted the conversation to be over.

'So how've you been?' he asked, finally breaking the silence.

'Oh, you know, up and down. But work's been keeping me busy.'

Yeah, he thought, *she obviously hasn't found the slightest moment to think about me.*

'Me too,' he found himself saying. 'It's been non-stop lately.'

Oh, she thought, *he doesn't seem remotely bothered about me.*

'Yeah, well, don't let me keep you,' Lola said, the words tumbling out of her mouth before she realized she didn't actually want to say them.

'No, I, urm, I'd better be going.' Better be going? He was actually early.

At that moment, more than anything else, Lola wanted to say sorry, to apologize to Freddy for messing him around. But his tone was curt and businesslike so she didn't think he'd appreciate it. Instead she kept quiet.

At that moment, more than anything else, Freddy wished

there was some way he could apologize to Lola for what he was about to do. But her tone was stand-offish and anyway, he could hardly blow his story the day before it broke.

'Well, yeah, urm, good luck,' he mouthed.

'Yeah, thanks. Maybe I'll look out for you backstage.'

They stood facing each other and did their best to smile.

As he looked into her eyes, Freddy remembered her impish expression when they'd first met and she'd told him he was much more handsome than he looked on the telly. There *had* been something between them, he hadn't imagined it. And even though it had all soured since then, he found himself realizing he didn't want to say goodbye. But there was no point; the situation was impossible.

As she looked him in the eye, Lola remembered his bashful expression on the set of the *Tramp* video when he'd called her fit and then quickly corrected himself to say she was pretty. There *had* been something between them and she'd been stupid to let it slip away. And even though it had all gone wrong since then, part of her realized she didn't want to say goodbye to him now. But she'd blown it – and it was impossible.

'Bye, Freddy.'

'See you, Lola.'

Their eyes lingered on each other and neither of them moved away.

Lola felt like she was lying in the bath, sinking down into the water as the world became distorted and unreal around her. *Go on, darlin', don't let him slip away a second time!*

Freddy felt like he'd just pulled the plug out of the bath and the water was seeping out and draining away around him. *Go on, champ, give her a chance and tell her how you feel!*

But something stopped them both.

They turned away and sloped off in opposite directions.

*

Later that evening, Gloria sipped hot honey and lemon as she recovered from a day of dress rehearsals. She'd just put Chanelle to bed and was sitting at the kitchen table next to her brother. Clinton was the baby of the family and had grown up slightly in awe of his big sister, despite their mother constantly putting her down. And even though Gloria's solo career had flopped, she knew he still thought of her as a star, especially now that he hung around with a crowd of computer geeks who didn't know the first thing about the music business – and were shocked at the very idea of taking drugs. As she could tell he was as he sat in front of his laptop watching the footage of Lola snorting coke.

'Shit!' he gasped. 'This is unreal. People just aren't going to believe it!'

Oh they will, thought Gloria. *I'll make sure they will.*

'Yeah, well, this is why you've really got to keep it secret,' she explained. 'I can't risk this getting out before opening night.'

He nodded seriously. She knew she could trust him. She could trust Clinton with her life.

And so far he hadn't let her down. He'd spent the day in rehearsals shadowing Vlad on the tech desk. And while he'd genuinely loved finding out about how it all worked, he hadn't forgotten to copy the files from Vlad's computer as well as working out a simple way for Gloria to substitute the new file once they'd created it. Which was exactly what they were about to do now.

'So where do you want me to cut in the new footage?' he asked as he clicked into a film-editing programme.

'During the opening number,' she replied. The set list for the show had already been locked down and Gloria had decided to premiere her little movie during Lola's biggest ever hit, *Tramp*. 'I think we should let her get going a bit first though,' she added. 'How about cutting it in about two thirds of the way through the song?'

'All right,' he nodded, 'coming right up.'

As she watched him cut, paste and click, once again Gloria's imagination jumped ahead to opening night. She told herself that Lola's public disgrace would make up for everything she'd put her through – including the indignity of having to suck off Vlad. She shivered at the memory. Going down on him the other day had been stomach-turningly gross. For a start, she'd been right about him never having heard of manscaping and had ended up with a forest of his pubes stuck between her teeth. And she'd discovered to her horror that the smell of TCP wasn't limited to his breath but covered his whole body. But at least her strategy had worked; Vlad had come to her begging for more every day since, complaining most girls couldn't handle sucking his dick because it was much too big. Well, Gloria wasn't most girls.

As Clinton dragged the cursor to the start of the new sequence and prepared to play it through, she quickly checked her emails on her phone. There was one she wanted to reread. It was from Freddy Jones at Channel 3 News.

'We're on board,' she scanned. 'And if your footage is genuine, we can confirm it will be broadcast on our programme on the opening night of Lola's tour.'

Oh my footage is genuine all right. Unlike Lola Grant – who's about to be exposed as a lying fake.

'But we're only filming the first two songs,' she read on, 'so please make sure your footage is played at the start of the show.'

Don't worry, Freddy, it's all being taken care of. Although something told her that once the audience had seen her little film, *Tramp* wouldn't just be the opening number – it would also be the grand finale. And Lola wouldn't be invited back for an encore.

She exited the email and put her phone down on the table. So her hunch had been right and she wasn't the only person who wanted revenge on Lola. Well, in just two days time she'd be getting just what she wanted. And so would Freddy Jones.

*

'Oh my God, it's Freddy Jones! Freddy, I'm *such* a big fan!'

Spike watched as a fat woman with bridesmaid hair, glittery lip gloss and legs that were somehow the same width all the way down began quivering with excitement.

'You're so much nicer than all the other news reporters!' she gushed as Freddy cowered in embarrassment. 'And so *lovely!*'

'Oh thanks,' he mumbled. 'Thanks a lot.'

'Would you mind if I took a quick photo?' the woman asked, her face and neck blushing. 'The other mums at school will be so jealous!'

Spike noticed Freddy's mouth twist into a little grimace. He knew how much he hated being the housewife's favourite. But he was way too polite to show it. 'No, not at all,' he managed.

'I'll take it,' Spike offered, standing up. The woman handed him her phone and slipped in next to Freddy. 'That's it, man!' Spike said as she flashed her brightest smile. 'That's beast.'

'Oh thanks!' she fawned, taking back the phone to inspect the picture. 'I can't believe I've actually just had my photo taken with Freddy Jones!'

'Well, it was good to meet you, like,' Freddy said, obviously eager to move her on.

'You too!' she beamed, her rolls of flab wobbling as she squealed with glee. 'And I'm really sorry about you splitting up with Lola Grant.'

'Oh yeah, urm, yeah, we were only ever just friends really. Anyway, have a good night.'

'So will you be interviewing her again?' The woman obviously couldn't take a hint.

'Urm, yeah, urm, I don't know, maybe. Actually, I won't be interviewing her but I will be live at the first night of her tour tomorrow.'

After which we won't be allowed anywhere near her again, thought Spike.

'Well, in that case I'll be watching!' the woman squeaked, leaning forwards and planting a little peck on Freddy's cheek. 'And thanks for the photo!' she called out as she trotted back to her table.

'Well,' Freddy sighed, 'Lola Grant might have dumped me like a ton of bricks but at least I've still got my fan club at the school gates. Come on, champ, get the drinks in.'

Spike attracted the attention of the barman and ordered a pint of lager for Freddy and a vodka and Coke for himself. They were in a pub called the Cock and Bull, which was just around the corner from the newsroom and a favourite hang-out for journalists. Freddy had said he needed a bit of Dutch courage if he was going to get through the next day – and Spike had needed a dose too for what he was about to say to him.

When the drinks arrived they began throwing them down. Freddy whistled as the alcohol hit home. 'Mate, this story's going to be really tough – the toughest yet.'

'You're telling me, blud.' Spike fished out his phone to reread the latest email that had arrived a few hours ago. 'Lola Grant is a cokehead slag,' he recited, 'and it's about time everyone knew it!'

Man, somebody sounds vexed. And whoever it is, it doesn't sound like they'll be backing out either.

'And you've still no idea who could have sent it?' Freddy asked.

Spike shook his head. 'Nah, blud. I mean, it's obviously someone she's crossed who wants some kind of revenge. But why would anyone hate Lola?'

There was an awkward silence. Spike couldn't believe he'd ended up in this situation. He'd already been dreading having to report on Lola's tour and announce to the world that she was having some kind of meltdown. But now it turned out he was going to have to produce a news report revealing she was a cokehead and in the process destroy her career. Not to mention his relationship with Harvey.

And he had no doubt that if they went ahead with the story it *would* destroy his relationship with Harvey. Because he might not be Lola's manager anymore, but that didn't mean he didn't still care for her. And there was no way he'd forgive Spike for doing this to her – or for scuppering any chance he might have of being reinstated as her friend and manager. He'd already given Spike another chance when he'd cheated on him over the summer. And OK, they'd grown stronger as a couple since then, but Spike knew there was only so much betrayal one person could take.

So over the course of the day he'd come to a decision. He couldn't live without Harvey. It was only since he'd met him that he'd understood what it meant to be happy – and why people talked about finding another person who made them feel whole. It was like Harvey had opened some kind of door and invited Spike into a whole new world, a world he hadn't even known had existed but at the same time had always longed for. Well, he wasn't going to go and slam the door shut in Harvey's face now. No, he didn't want to produce the news story and he was determined to find a way to wriggle out of it. The only problem was, he couldn't do it alone. He couldn't succeed unless he had Freddy on his side. He took a deep breath and began to speak.

'Freddy, I really don't think we should do this.'

'You what? What are you on about? We haven't got any choice, Spike. At least not if we want to keep our jobs.'

Spike had to admit he was right; Hugh Badcock had made it quite clear they were looking for excuses to fire people. And once word got around that Spike was the kind of journalist who backed out of a tough job, no other broadcaster would take him on either. His career would be over and he'd have no alternative but to move back in with his parents. He felt a twinge of fear as he thought back to their reaction when he'd told them he was gay.

'No son of mine is a filthy queer,' his dad had spat in his face. But how was he supposed to *stop* being gay just to please his dad? And how could he ever be happy suppressing his sexuality now that he'd known what it meant to rejoice and take pride in himself – in every aspect of himself?

It was too horrendous to contemplate. If he went ahead with the story he'd lose Harvey – but if he didn't he'd lose his career and have to move back in with his parents. Then again, he could always get a job in a bar or a shop, the kind of job that would pay him just enough to stay in the flat with Serenity. Or maybe Harvey might even ask him to move in with him? Surely he could make it work somehow. Yes, he had to stick to his guns. He *had* to persuade Freddy not to go ahead with the story.

'But aren't there some things in life that are more important than careers?' he attempted. 'Isn't that what Rex Watson said the other day?'

Freddy snorted. 'Yeah and look how that ended up. We both got a massive bollocking.'

'But that doesn't mean we were wrong, man. Just because Hugh Badcock thinks we were.'

Freddy arched an eyebrow. 'Look, mate, I appreciate this is going to be really difficult for you and it's going to cause problems with Harvey. But there's less at stake for me. Lola knocked me back, remember?'

'Yeah but she's single again now,' Spike protested, knowing even as he said the words that they sounded lame.

Freddy laughed. 'Yeah, well, she didn't show the slightest sign of being interested in me when I bumped into her this afternoon.'

'Oh come on, blud, she was in the middle of a dress

rehearsal. And, you know, she probably felt guilty about messing you around.'

'More like she thinks I've served my purpose now. And she doesn't need to use me to make her drummer-boy jealous anymore.'

'I'm sure that's not true at all, man. I've seen the way she looks at you and I don't think you should give up on her yet. Come on, blud, what if there's still something to fight for?'

Freddy raked his fingers through his hair. 'But Spike, do we even know the real Lola anymore? What if she's just been putting on a front the whole time? I mean, you read the email – she's a cokehead. So if she's lied to the world about taking drugs, how do we know she hasn't lied about everything else?'

Spike let out a long sigh. It wasn't looking good. But he wasn't giving up just yet. And he knew Freddy well enough to know that deep down he wouldn't want to go through with the story either – however much Lola might have hurt him.

'The thing is, man,' he attempted, 'I've learnt a lot of things over the last few months. And one thing I know now is that sometimes people do bad things without being bad people. I mean, everyone has their own story and their own struggles. I should know, I've taken all kinds of drugs and made all kinds of mistakes in my life. And there must have been, like, plenty of people who've looked at me and thought I was a liar, or a druggie, or just a shitload of trouble. All of which was true, man. But they wouldn't have known what was going on in my head or what was making me act like such a dick. Harvey didn't know either – not really. But for some reason he believed I was a better person than that and he took a chance on me. And it's only because he believed in me that I was able to, like, *become* a better person and give all that shit up. So, you know, maybe Lola's the same, man. Maybe she just needs, like, someone to believe in her.'

Whoa, that was quite a speech! Where the hell did that come from?

Freddy rubbed at his forehead with his hands. 'Yeah but Spike, Lola's got millions of fans who believe in her. Why should *I* make any difference? And anyway, I tried being the nice guy with her and that didn't get me anywhere. Maybe she'll respond better to me being nasty.'

Spike roofed his eyes. 'Freddy, what are you talking about, man? Did you actually just say that? Come on, you heard that woman just then – that's not why people love you. And yeah, I know they might not all be the kind of women you'd like to go out with. But they still think you're great. So don't go trying to change what makes you special, man.'

Freddy hung his head and didn't reply.

Is this it? Have I won him round? Have I actually done it?

'I'm sorry, mate,' Freddy said eventually. 'But I've got to go ahead and do this. I completely understand if you want to bail out. But I can't.'

Spike felt like he was going to slide off his stool. 'You can't?' he almost cried out. 'Or you won't?'

'All right, I won't. But you know, maybe I've got my reasons too. Maybe I've got my own story and my own struggles. And I'm a good person most of the time so maybe for once I'll just have to go off and do a bad thing. And hope you're right – hope it doesn't make me a bad person.'

There was a heavy silence. Spike felt hollowed out and wanted to howl into the air in desperation. The only option he could think of was to call in sick tomorrow. But Hugh would know he was only faking illness to get out of the story – particularly if it ever got out that he was seeing Harvey. And besides, pulling a sickie wouldn't be fair on Freddy; the two of them were a team. As his producer, Spike was his wingman. He knew that if his correspondent had made a decision, he had to stick with him.

'Oh it won't make you a bad person,' he managed, nudging Freddy on the shoulder. 'Of course it won't. And if you really have decided to go ahead, I'll be right by your side.'

Freddy nodded. 'Thanks, mate. Let's just get it out of the way now, shall we? We can try and pick up the pieces afterwards.'

'Genuine,' Spike croaked. 'But I might need another drink first, man.'

Freddy thrust his hand into his pocket and called over the barman.

As he did so, Spike looked over to the fat woman who'd recognized Freddy when they'd arrived. He gave her a wave and she returned it with a bright smile.

He couldn't help wondering if she and the rest of Freddy's fans would love him quite so much tomorrow night.

13

Lola bolted out of bed and bounced into the kitchen. It was the morning of her opening night and she couldn't wait to get to the O2 and reveal her amazing show to the world.

She looked at the coffee machine but decided not to bother; caffeine was the last thing she needed right now. In fact, she was on such a natural high she felt like she could fly out of the window and down the river to Greenwich. If anything she needed something to calm her down rather than crank her up. She looked in the cupboard for some chamomile teabags and switched on the kettle.

This is it. This is the culmination of everything I've worked for. And everyone would be there to witness it. Not just fifteen thousand fans, the TV cameras and entertainment journalists but all the important people in the music business, including the execs from her British, European and American record companies, not to mention the marketing men from Twinkle – and, of course, her mum. But she felt confident. The way she felt at the moment she knew she'd be able to thunder through the show. She could already hear the fans cheering so loudly they were drowning out the sound of the kettle boiling.

She poured the hot water onto the teabag and told herself

that she really needed to try and relax. She couldn't stay in this excitable state all day; by tonight she'd be burnt out. No, she'd just have to drink as much chamomile tea as she could, even if she did think it smelled like her wee after eating a truck load of asparagus. She fished the bag out of the mug and thought about Harvey. She only kept chamomile tea in the flat for when he came round. Not that he'd been round lately but all that would change after tonight. She'd composed a little song she was going to sing to him in between the first and second numbers, when Channel 3 News were still filming; that way he'd definitely see it, even if he was only watching at home.

She sipped at her tea and tried not to wince at the taste. The more she thought about it, the more she realized tonight was the night she'd be turning around her entire life. She was even going to make sure she bumped into Freddy backstage and invited him out for a drink. She'd been stupid not to apologize and tell him how she really felt when she'd seen him yesterday. But tonight she'd have one more chance and was determined to make the most of it. Because all right, she might have fucked things up between them, but she wasn't going to dwell on her mistakes anymore. From now on, Lola was all about the future. And if she got it right this time, Freddy might just be a part of that future.

No, there was no doubt about it: tonight was going to be the best night of her life – both professionally and personally. And most importantly, she felt ready. She didn't think she'd ever felt more ready in her life.

*

In the Channel 3 newsroom, Freddy sat at his desk packing his bag. Next to him, Spike was unplugging his phone and shutting down his computer. It was mid-afternoon and time for them to set off for the O2.

He'd just presented a brief outline of his plans for tonight's programme to the afternoon meeting, obviously omitting to mention his story's headline but telling the team he was going to break a major scandal involving Lola Grant, one that Hugh Badcock had interrupted him to boast would 'destroy her career'. As he'd watched his colleagues' faces light up at the prospect, Freddy had felt sickened right through to his soul. What was he doing?

He'd spent most of last night tossing and turning in bed, going over and over in his head everything Spike had said to him in the Cock and Bull. And, even though he'd chickened out from telling Lola how he felt when he'd bumped into her at the dress rehearsal, he couldn't help wondering whether Spike had been right and there really was still something worth fighting for. *What if Lola does still like me and I'm about to ruin my chances by laying into her live on TV?*

His thoughts were interrupted by the sight of Hugh Badcock striding out of the toilets and across the newsroom as he did up his fly. 'All right, boyo?' he boomed. 'Good luck!'

'Thanks,' Freddy managed. 'Thanks a lot.'

'Oh, and when you get back, let's me and you arrange to go out for a drink one night. Have a little chat about your future. Because, you know, this is the kind of story that can make a journalist's career. And it's something we should definitely build on.'

'Great,' Freddy swallowed. 'That'd be cracking.'

'But first of all let's see how much noise you can make with this one. Don't forget, the harder you can make Lola fall, the juicier the story is for us.'

Freddy tried to avoid looking at Spike. 'Thanks, boss.' He made a show of glancing at his watch. 'Urm, we'd better get going.'

'OK,' Hugh said, backing away and shouting across the newsroom, 'but remember, I don't just want this story to be noisy – I want it to make my ears bleed!'

'Yeah, yeah, I'm on it.' Freddy tried not to sigh out loud. Shouldn't he be all fired up about this?

Once Hugh had disappeared into his office, Freddy scooped up his bag and headed for the door with Spike at his side. But as he walked towards the lift, he could feel his heart starting to pound. Something was rising up within him – something he couldn't name but which had been repulsed and sparked into life by Hugh's words.

I don't want Lola's downfall to be the making of my career. And this isn't the kind of story I want to build on in the future.

No, however much he tried to convince himself, now that it came down to it, Freddy knew he couldn't go ahead with tonight's report. But how could he possibly get out of it if the story was going to break anyway?

Unless I try and stop the story breaking in the first place. Unless I can somehow stop the footage being played in the O2 and convince Hugh the whole thing was some kind of hoax.

But could he do that? Could he really pull it off? He'd certainly be up for trying. But if he did, he'd have to act fast.

He followed Spike into the lift and as the doors shut he turned to face him.

'Right then, champ. We're not doing this.'

'What? Are you for real, man?'

Freddy folded his arms purposefully. 'Yes. We can't do it, Spike. It's not right. I'm not going to attack Lola – and I'm not going to let anyone else attack her either.'

'But I thought you said we had no choice?'

'Well, we have no choice if we wimp out and just let the story happen. But we do have a choice if we man up and *stop* it from happening.'

Spike's face illuminated at the first glimpse of a new hope.

The lift came to a stop and the doors pinged open onto the ground floor.

'But you know,' Freddy went on as they walked through the security barriers, 'we've not got much time so we need to get on with it. And I really need Harvey's number.'

They stepped into the street and saw that it was raining. They ran to shelter under the canopy of the crew garage where they were scheduled to meet their cameraman Big Phil. Freddy looked around to check no one could hear them as Spike scooped his phone out of his bag and his fingers flew over the keys.

'Here you go, blud.'

Freddy took hold of the phone and breathed in deeply. He knew that once he'd told Harvey what was about to happen he'd have no option but to see things through. And he'd have to do everything he could to stop the story breaking. He really hoped he was up to it.

He hit Call.

*

Lola picked her way between the piles of flight cases filling the vast scene dock of the O2 and walked out onto the empty stage. She'd purposefully arrived early for the soundcheck so she could have a bit of time to herself first. She was determined to savour every second of a day she wanted to keep alive in her memory for the rest of her life.

And now she was here everything suddenly seemed much more real. Of course she'd been living and breathing the show for the last few months. But holed up in rehearsal venues it had been easy to kid herself she was creating an explosion of artistic expression purely for her own benefit – not something she'd actually be performing to real people and real cameras in the real world. But there was no kidding herself anymore. Waiting for her in the car park of the O2 had been the seven tour buses and sixteen trucks that would be transporting the entire team and equipment from London to all the major cities in the UK and Europe – not to mention the planned second leg in the US. She felt a twist of tension tightening in her stomach.

Please let me get through tonight.

Please let me be as good as I can.

I promise I'll never be a bitch again.

She slowly crept down the runway that extended from the stage and walked all the way to the edge. She stopped and gazed out at the empty auditorium. Everywhere she looked, endless rows of blue seats stretched as tall as skyscrapers, and as she peered up at the top they began to swim out of focus and make her feel dizzy. Even though the arena was huge, she felt almost claustrophobic, as if the towers of seats were about to topple forwards and tumble onto her. She imagined looking out at the same view when the auditorium was filled with fifteen thousand fans, each of them holding up their camera phones ready to film the show and be the first to upload it onto YouTube.

Thinking about her fans reminded Lola to tweet them a quick message. She reached for her phone and took a selfie standing at the foot of the runway with the empty auditorium behind her. She attached it to a new tweet. 'Shit the bed! This place is blatantly massive. Looking forward to causing some trouble for you all later x'

She hit Send and closed down Twitter. From now on she'd have to ignore her phone and concentrate on psyching herself up for the show.

'All right, Lola?' bellowed a voice from the back of the stage. It was Mike Henry, dressed in a brand new tour T-shirt featuring the slogan *Here Comes Trouble* on the front and the dates of all the shows Lola would be performing on the back. Her knees buckled slightly as she saw them stretching out before her. Manchester, Munich, Marseilles . . .

'Hiya, darlin',' she called back, 'how you doing?'

'I'm great thanks. But the question is, how are *you* doing?'

'Oh, you know, a bit nervous. But I'm still up for it. I'm blatantly bang up for it.'

'Atta girl!'

Mike turned around to greet the band as one by one the musicians stepped onto the stage and began staring out at the auditorium.

'Fuck me, that's big!' said Danny.

'Fucking hell!' echoed Smudge. 'Are we really going to do this?'

'Too fucking right we are!' piped Lola, striding over to them and forcing herself to be jolly. She couldn't believe it had been less than four months since she'd met these guys. Already they'd been through so much together they were starting to feel like family – albeit a very dysfunctional one. And now she was about to share with them the most important night of her life. 'Come on guys, this is going to be fierce!'

'Fierce?' gulped Chuck. 'Or fear*some*?'

'*Fierce*!' she said, straining out a laugh. 'Now will everyone stop trying to make me nervous?'

She went around hugging them all, soaking up everyone's words of encouragement. When she came to Gloria she stopped and there was an awkward moment as the two of them stood facing each other just a few feet apart.

'Good luck,' Gloria quipped casually.

'Thanks,' Lola managed to grin back at her. 'Have a good show.'

'Oh I will,' smiled Gloria. 'I'm really looking forward to it.'

Oh well, thought Lola, *at least everyone's up for it.*

Even Jake seemed enthusiastic. 'Good luck, Lola!' he called out from behind his drum kit. 'I'm sure you'll rock the roof off this joint.'

Yeah and I'm sure you've started shagging some other bird. She could tell from the look on his face he was getting his end away. Not that she cared anymore. She only felt sorry for who-ever the new girl was.

'Thanks!' she called back at him. 'And I'm sure you'll shag the shit out of it.'

He smiled at her with the sloppy grin that just a few weeks ago had driven her wild. Now she felt so little she could even crack jokes with him. She couldn't believe how quickly she'd moved on. And tonight she was planning on moving on even further . . .

But first of all she had a show to perform. And right now she had a soundcheck to get through. She turned back to take another look at the empty auditorium. The next time she'd be standing on this stage it would be looking very different.

*

Harvey sat in his dressing gown stroking Pickle and staring at the phone. He couldn't believe what he'd just heard.

Freddy Jones had called to warn him that tonight someone would be going all out to destroy Lola's career – and her life. And from what he'd explained, Harvey couldn't think of a better way for them to do it. Well, he might not be her manager anymore – or her friend for that matter – but he couldn't stand by and let this happen.

He jumped out of his seat and grabbed his phone. Freddy had said he was going to set off for the O2, so Harvey had promised to back him up by making a few calls. He decided against calling Lola; she already had enough to worry about with tonight's show and he knew that finding out about this could be just the thing to push her over the edge. And besides, she probably wouldn't answer anyway; the last time they'd spoken she'd made it quite clear she wanted nothing more to do with him.

He thought about calling Amina but reasoned she'd be with Lola, who might overhear the conversation. So he decided that instead he'd go straight to the person responsible for the screens during the show, the person best placed to remove the threat posed by the anonymous source. He dialled the number of the show's technical director, Vlad. But there was no answer.

Is he busy? Or is he just ignoring me because I've been sacked? He was sure he'd feel humiliated if he weren't so frightened for Lola. He dialled the number again but still there was no answer. He left a voicemail asking Vlad to call him urgently.

Next he tried Barbara. Surely she was still speaking to him? But again there was no answer. It obviously hadn't taken long for word to get around that he was out of a job. Again he left a voicemail.

In desperation he began searching for the number for Carlson. The two men hadn't exchanged a word since Carlson had accused Harvey of being a prick-tease in Club Class. Well, there was no point dwelling on that now. He'd just have to swallow his pride and give him a call. He dialled the number and held his breath. Again there was no answer.

'I'm a bit *tied up* at the moment,' came Carlson's camp voice, 'but leave me a message and I'll give you a tinkle as soon as I can.'

Harvey let out a low groan. He left another voicemail and began to pace the room. Pickle jumped down from the sofa to trail along beside him.

What on earth am I supposed to do now?

He stopped to look up at the ceiling and rubbed at the stubble on his chin. He hadn't bothered showering or getting dressed for days and had hardly left the flat since his bust-up with Lola. He'd just wanted to hide away from the world and fester in a pit of self-pity. But now he'd have to pull himself together and snap out of it. Because there was nothing else for it: if he was going to try and save Lola from public disgrace he'd have to get out there and spring into action. But first he had to make himself look human again. And as soon as he did he was going to dash across town to the O2. He only hoped that when he got there someone would let him in.

*

Vlad, Tiny, Carlson . . . One after the other they called into Lola's dressing room to wish her good luck.

'You'll totally nail it!' they all seemed to agree. 'You'll blow everyone away!'

'Oh thanks,' she mumbled, feeling less confident by the minute.

'Now I'm going to be watching from out front,' explained Carlson, 'so I get a real sense of what it's like for the fans.'

'All right, darlin'. Sounds like a good plan.'

'But I'll come straight round afterwards to see you,' he promised. 'And I'm sure you'll have a great show.'

'Yeah, thanks, darlin'. See you later.'

She closed the door softly and turned back to her dressing room. Well, she called it her dressing room but it was actually a suite of rooms; there was a changing room fitted with white wardrobes and mirrors bordered by built-in spotlights; a bedroom with a king-size bed and a huge pile of plump pillows; a separate lounge area with three plush, bum-swallowing sofas; a little kitchen crammed full of pre- and post-show treats; and a bathroom stocked with the latest range of luxury beauty products by Laura Mercier. All of the rooms were filled with the fragrance of several vases of fresh flowers sent by friends, which competed for space alongside all kinds of peculiar presents from fans. It was absolutely amazing but she couldn't help thinking she didn't deserve it – and panicking that everyone was expecting her performance to be just as amazing. She felt herself gradually being consumed by an upsurge of that recurring conviction of not being good enough, which no amount of success seemed able to smother. In fact, it only seemed to make it worse. *Oh why can't it just finally go away and never come back?*

The truth was, she'd have been much happier in a dressing room a bit less ostentatious. She remembered some of the dumps where she'd got ready to go on stage just a few years ago when she'd been trying to kick-start her career by performing up to three PAs a night in any old club that would take her. She had a particularly vivid memory of applying her make-up in the ladies' loos of a gay club called Dirty Den – ladies' loos which had been full of gentlemen having sex in the cubicles and had stunk of a sickly mix of poppers, vomit and the latest aftershave by Dolce & Gabbana. Of course, in those days there hadn't been any good-luck presents from fans, and the only friend or colleague who'd travelled around with her had been Harvey. Now, on the other hand, she'd stupidly sacked Harvey and was instead accompanied by her ever-present assistant Amina as well as her three-woman Style Council, not forgetting Lucretia Lavelle, who'd called in to inspect the costume she'd designed for the opening number. Lola gave her a little twirl.

'That's sublime!' Lucretia beamed. 'Absolutely sublime!'

For her big entrance Lola was wearing a variation on her outfit from the *Tramp* video; Lucretia had recreated the persona of a futuristic feminist crusader but dressed her in a shorter hot-pant catsuit in metallic silver and rimmed with real diamonds. The costume was complemented by high-heeled thigh-high boots similar to the ones Lola had worn in the video, but the hairpiece had been deemed too fiddly to remove in between numbers so had been replaced by a silver space-age helmet which had an inbuilt microphone, didn't obscure too much of her face and could be whipped off in between numbers to reveal her signature jet-black spiky hair. The look was about to be completed by a liberal application of silver glitter eyeshadow and lip gloss at the hands of Scarlett. Lola smiled at her reflection and slid into the make-up chair.

'You look totes amazing,' frothed Scarlett. 'Let's hope the audience is full of hot men.'

'Ooh, speaking of hot men,' chirped Lucretia, 'you'll never guess who my date is tonight.'

'Now let's see,' mused Lola, feigning ignorance. 'Ace Bounder?'

'Yes! How did you know that?'

'Oh, let's just say gossip spreads fast around this industry.' As she said the words she felt thankful no one in her entourage had blabbed about her fling with Jake – not to mention her coke binge when they'd split up.

'Anyway,' Lucretia went on as she headed for the door, 'I'd better dash. I don't want to be late for my date!'

Lola knew that Lucretia had a pair of seats in the box that had been reserved for her friends, execs from her record companies and everyone who'd worked with her on the album and singles. Not forgetting a shoal of celebs like Ruby Marlow, Blake Striker and Shereen Spicer – and now, apparently, Ace Bounder. She kind of wished they weren't all coming on the opening night. She picked up her state-of-the-art stun gun and fired a laser beam at her reflection. 'Fuck me, girls, I'm really starting to brick it.'

The three of them gasped in surprise.

'But you've nothing to be nervous about!'

'You'll be totes wicked!'

'You're going to fuck the shit out of it!'

Lola took a ragged breath. 'Thanks. I blatantly hope you're right.'

'Well, you know if you're really nervous you could always have a little bump of coke,' Trixie offered.

Lola shook her head firmly. 'Oh no. No thanks.'

'But it'd give you that extra kick. And I thought you really enjoyed it the other night?'

'Yeah it was a good laugh and everything, but I really don't want to get into it when I'm working. And to be honest, I'm not sure it's for me anyway – I mean, the way I feel at the moment, I don't even want to get pissed anymore. I just want to get out there and sing. Sing, sing, sing!'

She watched the girls peer at her like she'd said something stupid.

'Well, if you change your mind,' Trixie mouthed slowly, 'I always carry a few wraps in my bag. So if you need a boost just say the word.'

'All right, darlin',' Lola said, anxious to move the conversation on. Then she remembered something else that might give her a boost. 'Oh, Amina!' she shouted through to the lounge.

'Yeah?' replied her assistant, popping her head around the door.

'What happened to that present from my mum?'

'Oh yeah, just a minute.' She disappeared and then came back holding the box covered in Spice Girls wrapping paper Lola's mum had given to her.

'Thanks, darlin'.' She tore off the paper to reveal a big box of Turkish Delight, which she could see from the label had been bought from the same bakery in Tooting that she and her mum used to visit after picking up her mum's dole from the jobcentre next door. Every fortnight they'd bought themselves exactly the same box and had sat on the bench outside chomping their way through the sugary sweets – and for just a few minutes Lola's little head had filled with fantasies of her mum telling her she wasn't going on to her dealer's but had decided to give up drugs and be a normal mum after all. A normal mum who loved her daughter.

The memory brought tears to Lola's eyes. *Oh come on, darlin', don't get upset now. You need to stay focused! You need to get back in the zone!*

'Are you all right, Lola?' asked Amina.

'Yeah, yeah,' she said, knuckling the tears out of her eyes. 'Sorry, I don't want to ruin my make-up. But do you mind if I just have a quiet minute?'

The girls stepped back and busied themselves as Lola looked at her reflection in the mirror and tried to regain her composure. She opened up the box and popped one of the sweets into her mouth, biting into it and feeling the gorgeous goo slither and slide around her tongue. It tasted exactly as she remembered – and so much better than all the other brands of Turkish Delight she'd bought or other people had given her since. It reminded her of how far she'd come since she'd been that scared and lonely little girl sitting on the bench with her mum outside the bakery in Tooting. It reminded her of the last time she'd seen her mum and how she'd felt truly loved by her for the first time in years. And it reminded her of how happy she was that her mum had finally conquered her addiction and was gradually rebuilding her life. Just that morning she'd texted Lola to wish her good luck and say how much she was looking forward to seeing the show. Well, Lola now felt inspired to give her a show she'd enjoy – and deliver the performance of her life.

She slowly closed the box and put it to one side. She'd save the rest for later; it would be her little treat to herself to celebrate the success of the show. She looked again at the label on the front of the box and smiled. It was the best present ever – and a much better pick-me-up than any coke. In fact, it had given her just the boost she needed to dispel her self-doubt and see her through to her big entrance. Because she *could* do it. She *was* good enough. How could she not be when her mum believed in her? How could she not be when her mum *loved* her?

She looked at a clock on the wall. It was six thirty. There were just two hours to go until she burst onto the stage.

*

Freddy looked at the famous O2 Arena lit up against the night sky. With its distinctive yellow spikes poking through its white domed roof he couldn't help thinking it looked like some weird kind of spaceship, which for some unfathomable reason had touched down next to the Thames. And tonight it looked even weirder than usual as its canvas roof was being thrashed by sheets of heavy rain that ran down it in torrents and flowed into the drains. It was an eerie, ominous sight. He shuddered at the realization of what he was about to do. *Oh please let me be able to pull it off . . .*

He listened to the sound of his breathing as the Channel 3 News van beamed its way through the security barriers and onto the forecourt. Everywhere he looked there were posters of Lola, animated advertisements announcing the opening of the tour and groups of fans who'd arrived early and were hiding under umbrellas singing her songs. *If only they knew the danger she's in . . .*

Behind the steering wheel Big Phil spotted the Channel 3 News satellite truck and swung the van round to park up next to it. Freddy remained in the passenger seat and watched him jump out and race through the rain to chat to the engineers. He already knew they'd chosen to broadcast from a position in the scene dock that was near enough to the stage to look like it was in the centre of the action but far enough away for his own microphone not to be drowned out by the sound of the music. Although he had no idea what he'd be saying into it. If everything went according to plan, his original script would be redundant. But he'd have to worry about that later. First he had to act against the instincts of any good journalist and take decisive action to kill his own story.

'OK blud,' said Spike, leaning towards him from the back seat, 'what's the plan?'

For the entire journey Freddy had been pretending to rehearse his lines in his head whilst the truth was he'd been mulling over this very question. 'Right mate, me and you need to split up. I need you to go with Phil and shoot actuality of the fans arriving, the dancers warming up backstage and all the stuff we agreed with Barbara.'

'OK, man. But what's the point if we're going to kill the story?'

'Well, that's just it – we don't know if we *can* yet. But while I'm trying I need you to make it look like we're doing what we're supposed to. We've no idea who this anonymous source is so we can't risk anyone getting suspicious. Not even Barbara.'

'Genuine. But what will you do, man?'

He pressed his lips together firmly. 'Well, I looked online and the technical director's someone called Vlad. I'm going to get in there and find him and show him the email about the screens. Hopefully that will get him to switch the footage. That is, if Harvey hasn't spoken to him already.'

Just then his phone pinged and he scrolled through to read a text from Harvey. It said that he was really sorry but he hadn't been able to get hold of anyone so was rushing across town to join Freddy at the O2. Unfortunately though he was stuck in traffic and wouldn't be there for at least an hour. *Shit.*

'OK, so Harvey *hasn't* got hold of the techie guy. But let's not panic – I'll just have to do it on my own.'

'But how are you going to do that if you can't tell anyone what's going on?'

'I don't know,' Freddy frowned, rooting around in his bag for his backstage pass and hooking it around his neck. 'That's the part of the plan I haven't got to yet.'

'Well, good luck, man. If anyone can do it, you can.'

'Thanks, mate. I only hope you're right.'

*

Inside the O2, Gloria could hear the sound of the rain lashing against the roof. It sounded like something out of a disaster film. Well, she couldn't think of anything more appropriate. She'd cast Lola as the victim in the biggest disaster movie imaginable, and if she could just pull off this final step in her plan, tonight it would be having its world premiere.

She texted Vlad to ask him to come to her dressing room and then sneaked across the arena to his technical booth. But when she looked through the small window in the door she saw another two engineers hanging around talking about football. She listened for what felt like ages while they compared the form of their favourite teams, using the pronoun 'we' as if they themselves had made some sort of contribution to their success. *For fuck's sake, can't you talk about this outside?*

Just as she was beginning to despair, the two men decided to go for a fag break. *Thank fuck for that!*

She stepped to one side and once the men had rounded the corner slipped into the booth and shut the door. Her heart was thumping; after that little hold-up she knew she didn't have much time to switch the footage on Vlad's computer and cue up her own carefully re-edited version. She inserted her memory stick and looked at the instructions Clinton had scribbled on a piece of paper, deleting, dragging and clicking until she read on the screen the words he'd told her to look out for.

'Edit complete. Would you like to render your changes?'

Too fucking right I would.

She hit the Render button and was told she'd have to wait thirty seconds until her changes had registered. As she stared at the screen she began picking at a hangnail on her thumb. *Oh come on! Hurry the fuck up!*

The computer erupted in a loud sound she didn't recognize but Clinton had told her that would mean her substitution was complete. She felt a surge of joy and wanted to whoop out loud. But she stopped herself and remembered to exit the screen so Vlad wouldn't be able to tell anyone had tampered with his work.

'Gloria?' came a voice from behind her. 'What do you think you're doing?'

Fuck!

Her heart hammered in her chest as she turned and saw Vlad. 'Oh hi, honey,' she managed to smile, 'I was just killing time while I waited for you.'

He creased his forehead. 'But I thought you asked me to go to your dressing room?'

'Well, yeah, I did, but I got bored waiting so I thought I'd surprise you here.'

He didn't look convinced. 'But I went round there as soon as I got your message.'

Fuck! This ugly fucker's not going to fuck this up now!

There was only one thing for it; she knew what she had to do. She stood up and moved towards him. 'Oh I know, Vlad, but I always get so horny before a show.'

'Really?'

She ran her finger along his belt. 'Yeah and right now I'm so horny for *you*.'

She gently tugged him over to the chair and pushed him down onto it. Just one more blow job and that would be it – she'd never have to degrade herself again.

'Jesus,' Vlad whispered, his mouth flickering into a grin as he hit her with a blast of TCP, 'you're so fucking sexy.'

She smiled and lowered herself onto her knees before him. As he closed his eyes she quickly reached behind him and clicked out of the editing programme. The computer reverted to Vlad's screensaver and she knew that her work was done.

Well, almost . . .

*

It was nearly seven o'clock and Harvey was only just arriving at the O2. He'd had a disastrous journey across the city and at one point had been stuck behind a dustcart for the best part of an hour while a team of bored-looking binmen sauntered along collecting rubbish from both sides of a narrow street he'd only driven down to try and save time. He looked at his watch. There were just ninety minutes to go until Lola made her entrance.

He'd forgotten his umbrella but there wasn't time to worry about that now. He held his coat over his head and raced through the pissing rain, across the car park and over to the artists' entrance. He thundered to a halt in front of a hard-faced security guard standing in the doorway chomping on an enormous bag of crisps.

'All right, lad,' he panted, trying his best to sound nonchalant. 'I'm Harvey Sparks. Sorry, I've forgotten my pass.'

The security guard shook his head. 'Sorry, buddy. No pass, no entry.'

'But I'm Lola's manager.' *Well, at least I was until last week.* 'And I really need to get in and speak to her.'

The man plunged his hand into the bag of crisps and

jammed a fistful into his mouth. 'Sorry, bud,' he spluttered, spraying Harvey's cheek with potato, 'but I can't let anyone in unless they have a pass. Not unless I get the OK from my boss.'

'Tiny?' Harvey's face brightened; he'd hired Tiny himself and the pair of them had known each other for years. 'Yeah, great, speak to Tiny.'

'If you don't mind waiting outside for a minute,' the man said, guiding Harvey back into the rain and shutting the door in his face. 'I'll try and get hold of him now.'

Through the glass door he watched the man slowly put down his crisps, make a big show of licking his fingers and then turn his back to him and start speaking into his walkie-talkie. *Oh come on! Get a move on!*

After a few minutes the man opened the door with a smirk of satisfaction. 'I'm sorry but your request's been denied.'

Harvey felt like he'd been slapped in the face. 'But . . . But . . .'

'If you really want to get in you're just going to have to call the artist. I'm afraid she's the only one who can override Tiny.'

Oh for fuck's sake!

He didn't bother to reply and stepped back under his coat and out into the rain. He desperately wanted to avoid calling Lola but what choice did he have? He'd repeatedly tried to phone Vlad, Barbara and Carlson but he didn't want to call anyone in Lola's wider entourage as he had no idea who this anonymous source was.

With a heavy thud he realized what he had to do. He took out his phone and cleared his throat.

He dialled Lola's number and listened to it ring as he felt his trouser legs soaking up rain.

It clicked to voicemail.

Shit!

He decided not to leave a message but instead to text her.

'Lola, you're in danger,' he typed, realizing he must sound like a character in some over-the-top disaster film. 'Call me urgently. And whatever you do, don't start the show until you've spoken to me. Sorry, I wouldn't be doing this unless I had to. Harvey.'

All right, it might sound a bit dramatic, but there wasn't time to refine the wording. He added a kiss and hit Send.

Oh please read it, Lola. Please, please, please read it! His thoughts were interrupted by a cluster of camp male fans waving around pink umbrellas and belting out the chorus to *Mess It Up*. As he watched them skip towards the public entrance he remembered that at the very least he still had a seat reserved for the show; before he'd been fired he'd arranged to watch it from the front row next to Lola's mum Karen. And he might have forgotten to bring his umbrella but at least he'd remembered his ticket.

He just needed to get into the O2, even if it was through the front entrance. He darted through the rain and joined the flood of fans.

*

'Scrumpity scrumpity scrump.'

In her dressing room Lola was midway through her vocal warm-up.

'Scrumpity scrumpity scrump.'

She listened to the recording Bella Figurini had made on her iPod and repeated her lines out loud.

'Scrumpity scrumpity scrump.'

She heard her phone ping with a text message and pressed the Pause button on the iPod. All afternoon her phone had been pinging and ringing but she'd ignored it; it was only people wanting to wish her good luck and if they needed to speak to her urgently they could always call Amina. Right now she needed to zone out from the world and focus on the show.

'Do you want me to get that?' asked Amina.

'No thanks. But could you do me a favour and shove it on silent?'

She watched Amina pick up the phone and kill its sound.

Just as she was leaning towards her iPod to press Play she caught sight of Trixie firing her laser gun into the mirror.

'This is cool as fuck! Make sure you fire a few shots at Jake!'

'Oh I can't be arsed thinking about him anymore,' Lola shrugged. 'And I'm pretty sure he's got a new bird anyway. Here, you guys don't know who it is, do you? I feel like I should speak to the poor cow – and warn her about what he's like.'

Belle, Scarlett and Trixie looked away guiltily and began fussing with clothes hangers and hair straighteners.

Lola shifted onto the edge of her seat. 'Hang on a minute. Is it one of you three?'

'No!' squeaked Belle. 'I haven't shagged him for ages. Not since you pulled him after the Hyde Park gig.'

'Me neither,' squealed Scarlett. 'And I only shagged him once – the night we shot the *Tramp* video.'

'I only shagged him once too,' stammered Trixie. 'After the party in Club Class. But you did say you'd moved on . . .'

Oh my God, thought Lola. *All three of them have shagged him. They've all blatantly shagged him!*

She looked at her assistant and raised an eyebrow. 'Amina, don't tell me you've been there too?'

'Sorry, no, I don't really get what everyone sees in him.'

'Well, don't apologize,' Lola piped. 'You should be proud of yourself – it looks like you're the only woman on the tour who *hasn't* shagged him.'

She glanced at the three girls shuffling around nervously and burst out laughing. The whole thing was suddenly hilarious.

'So you're not mad at us?' ventured a contrite-looking Trixie.

'God no,' Lola snorted. 'I think it's piss funny. That man is blatantly such a tramp!'

'Big time!' agreed Trixie. 'But he *is* a wicked fuck.' She looked at Belle and Scarlett and the three of them gave in to a gale of giggles.

Lola pulled a face. She couldn't for the life of her think how she'd ever found Jake attractive. Or how she'd knocked back Freddy so she could carry on chasing him. Well, that was the last time she was going to make that mistake. *Which reminds me, what's happened to Freddy? Aren't I supposed to be bumping into him somewhere?*

She looked at the clock. There was less than an hour till she'd be making her entrance on stage. If she didn't bump into Freddy soon it wasn't going to happen. 'Actually, girls, do you mind if we move over to the wings now?'

'What, already?' asked Amina.

'Yeah, I'm kind of getting itchy feet here.'

Amina began to gather her things and Lola jumped out of her chair and onto her feet. It was time for her to tell Freddy what she should have told him yesterday. And this time she wasn't going to back out.

*

Just a few metres away, Freddy crept along the brightly lit breeze-blocked corridor trying not to draw too much attention to himself. He wove his way through an endless carousel of dancers, musicians and roadies, all the time wondering if one of them could be the anonymous source trying to destroy Lola. *If I could just find this Vlad . . .*

He spotted a security guard and strode over looking as confident as he could. 'All right, mate? Where can I get hold of the technical director?'

'What, Vlad?' Freddy couldn't help noticing the man had a picture of a topless woman with her arms behind her head tattooed onto his bicep.

'Yeah, that's him.'

The man sucked at a row of stumpy teeth that gave him a mouth like a Toblerone. 'You need to get through to the techie area and for that you'll need Access All Areas.'

Freddy read the pass around his neck. 'Backstage – media.' *Shit!*

'So will this not do?' he tried.

'Afraid not, pal.'

'But what if I just need to ask him a quick question about our shoot? Honestly, it'll only take a minute, like.'

The man looked at him and frowned. 'Yeah, well you'll just have to hang around here and hope you catch him.'

But I don't even know what he looks like!

'OK, never mind,' he managed to sing-song. 'I'll go and ask someone else. Thanks anyway.'

Thanks for nothing!

Freddy drew in a long breath. The worst thing was, he was probably standing just a few metres away from this Vlad. And he wouldn't care, but there didn't seem any logic about the areas that had been designated accessible or inaccessible for someone with his pass. He couldn't get through to the technical director, but right in front of him was a sign pointing to Lola's dressing room. He looked at it and mopped a hand through his hair.

The last thing he wanted to do was follow the sign. Harvey had made him promise not to contact Lola herself in case he freaked her out before the show. But what else was he supposed to do? Anything had to be better than what was waiting for her once she went on stage.

He followed the signs around a corner, along a corridor lined with a rail of costumes and all the way to a door labelled with the word 'Artist'. Thankfully there weren't any security guards standing in front of it. Maybe this would be easier than he thought.

He strode up and steeled himself to come face-to-face with Lola. He reached out and gave a loud knock. There was no answer.

She wasn't there.

But if she isn't in her dressing room where the hell is she?

*

Spike stood in a corridor biting his nails while Big Phil crouched on the floor shooting a pair of half-naked dancers as they stretched their limbs on a handrail.

'Everything all right, doll?' Barbara asked. 'Are you getting what you need?'

Fuck knows, man, he wanted to reply. *That depends on Freddy . . .*

'Yeah, this is, like, cool thanks,' he managed to mumble.

'Well, hopefully Lola will be out of her dressing room shortly. So you might get some footage of her having a chat with the band.'

'Cool, that'd be sick.' He did his best to smile at her but the truth was he was terrified of coming face-to-face with Lola. He'd only ever met her once or twice and the last time they'd been in the same room she'd thrown him out of it. She probably wouldn't be too happy to see him hanging around the O2 now – minutes before she went on stage for the first night of her tour.

'Oh look,' Barbara chirped, 'here she is already.'

Spike's stomach sank as he watched Lola round the corner. She spotted him and strode over in a hot-pant catsuit and high-heeled thigh-high boots. He had to admit, she looked amazing. But she was wearing so much stage make-up that under the harsh strip lighting she looked more than a little severe. *Man, please don't let her be vexed with me!*

'Hiya, Spike,' she sparkled, 'how's it going?'

'Yeah, urm, what up, Lola?'

'Listen, I'm sorry I was a total bitch last week.' She reached out and put her hand on his arm. 'I've just had a lot of shit going on lately but I think I've got it all sorted now. And once the tour's up and running it'd be nice if me and you could spend some time together. Something tells me we've got a lot in common.'

Spike couldn't believe it. *Am I hearing her right?*

'Urm, yeah, urm, yeah. That'd be, like, beast. But . . . But . . .'

'But what about Harvey?'

His face contorted in awkwardness. 'Yeah, man. Sorry but, you know, I love him. I proper love him.'

'Yeah, well, don't worry because I love him too. And I know I need to make things up to him – which is why I've got him a little surprise tonight.'

'For real?'

'Blatantly. But don't say anything. I don't want anything to spoil it.'

'OK, I promise.'

'Anyway, where's Freddy? I can't find him anywhere.'

Shit! Spike had never been any good at lying – and there was no way he was going to be able to start now.

'He's urm, he's—'

'Lola!' an old rocker with a handlebar moustache shouted through from the scene dock.

Lola turned to wave at him. 'All right Mike, I'm coming!'

Phew!

'Listen,' she said, turning back to Spike, 'I've got to go. But will you tell Freddy I'm looking for him?'

'For sure.'

She leaned forward and kissed him. 'And I'll see you soon, yeah?'

'Yeah,' he croaked. 'See you soon.'

He watched her skip into the distance and shook his head in disbelief. Lola Grant had actually just apologized to him, said she wanted to be friends and then promised she was going to make things up with Harvey. *Man, that was off the hook!*

'Oh, and good luck with the show!' he shouted out after her.

'Thanks, darlin'!' she called back.

For a few seconds Spike couldn't do anything other than stand there smiling to himself. But then he felt a shiver of fear as he remembered what was going to happen when Lola hit the stage.

He really hoped Freddy was managing to do what he needed to. Because until now Spike had been determined to divert the impending disaster to protect himself, but now he found himself also wanting to protect Lola.

*

Jake watched from the scene dock as Lola marched down the corridor towards him. She was flanked by Tiny on one hand and Amina on the other and behind her trailed Belle, Scarlett and Trixie. *And I've screwed all three of them,* he couldn't help thinking.

'Hiya!' Lola boomed brightly.

The band and dancers turned to face her. 'Hi, Lola!'

She flashed everyone a huge smile and held out her arms. 'Come on, gather round and let's have a chinwag.'

As everyone moved to form a circle, Jake spotted the camera-man from Channel 3 News zoom into Lola and press Record. He was with some black dude he could only assume must be the fag producer going out with Harvey, as well as Lola's publicist, Barbara Bull-dyke or whatever she was called. Not that he gave a shit; right now all he cared about was Sharonne.

Jake glanced over at her standing between Smudge and Chuck, all three of them clearly stoked and ready for the show. In fact, Jake felt like the only one who wasn't remotely fired up about it. The truth was he couldn't wait to get the show out of the way and then he could pay Sharonne a visit in her dressing room. That was way more his kind of show.

'Well, I just want to wish you all good luck,' began Lola, closing her eyes and squeezing the hands of Mike and Danny on either side of her. 'We've all worked really hard on this show and given it everything we've got. So, you know, we deserve it to be fucking fierce!'

Her words were met with hollers of approval. Jake rolled his eyes and couldn't resist looking at his watch. In the distance he could hear the sound of the audience filing into the arena and taking their seats.

'Anyway,' Lola went on, 'I know I haven't always been the easiest person to work with.'

You can say that again!

'But I just want you all to know how much I appreciate everything you've done – even when I was being a total bitch.'

As everyone heaved out a laugh, Jake looked across at Sharonne and managed to catch her attention. He shot her a quick wink but she widened her eyes in warning and put her finger to her lips.

What the hell's eating her? Don't tell me she's about to start getting heavy too . . .

He noticed her shoot a nervous look at Tiny, who was standing with his lips clenched and his arms folded, glaring at her. He realized that Tiny must have seen the way she'd responded to his wink – and he didn't look happy.

Motherfuck! Don't tell me he's *her boyfriend?* Most boyfriends he could handle – but most boyfriends weren't Tiny.

'So, you know, thanks for putting up with me,' Lola chatted on, 'and I hope from now on things are going to get much easier. Because tonight's blatantly where the fun starts. Now let's get out there and slay the shit out of this show!'

Jake winced as everyone roared into his eardrums, hugging each other and slapping out high fives. He wished they'd all quit going on about the dumb-ass show. He had something much more important on his mind.

As the huddle gradually dispersed, he blinked in horror as Tiny stomped over to Sharonne and took her to one side. He watched him growing more and more animated while Sharonne did her best to placate him, all the time feeling the goosebumps race up his arm. There was no avoiding it – Tiny obviously suspected something was going on between them. *Well, I hope Sharonne keeps her goddam mouth shut.*

Not that he was going to stick around to find out. No, there was no way he was going to risk getting on the wrong side of a former boxing champion who now earned his living lugging around his super-size chest to protect Lola.

He grabbed his drumsticks and disappeared onto the stage. He'd just have to wait there until the show started.

*

On the other side of the stage, Karen Grant shuffled into the auditorium and felt her breath catch in her throat. *My God, this place is massive!*

Already it was almost full of people crawling like insects up the stairs and along the aisles. As tracks from Lola's latest album blasted out of a wall of speakers that looked as big as Karen's flat, excitement zipped through the air like an electric charge.

Karen spun around and looked at the stage. Most of it was hidden behind a silver sequinned curtain, but there was a runway that thrust out into the audience and she was pretty sure she could spot several screens at the back, presumably onto which the films Lola had already recorded would be projected. Karen gulped as she suddenly realized just how much work must have gone into the tour – and how much energy everyone must also be channelling into this, the opening night. She hoped Lola wasn't too nervous and was feeling confident enough to storm her way through her performance. She closed her eyes as she tried to transmit a message through to her. *Come on, girl, you can do it!*

She opened her eyes and looked at her ticket. She read her number and counted down the rows as they led her to a seat directly in front of the runway. She couldn't believe it: she must have been given the best view in the whole arena. She'd originally been offered a seat in some box where Harvey had told her VIP guests would be served with complimentary drinks. But it had all sounded very daunting and besides, she was trying to keep away from temptation so had opted instead for a seat in the auditorium next to Harvey – well away from any bar. Except that this had been arranged before Lola had come to visit her last week, and since then Harvey had been in touch to say he was no longer her manager and he wouldn't be watching the show after all. Karen still had no idea what had gone on between them but she knew it must be serious and she hoped it wasn't weighing too heavily on Lola.

Thankfully the last contact she'd received from her had been entirely positive; a text message had arrived about an hour and a half ago in which Lola had thanked Karen for the Turkish Delight and invited her back to her dressing room after the show. She held the phone to her chest as she felt the invitation warming her up from within. She slid into her seat and waited for the show to begin.

*

Lola slid into the tent that had been set up in the wings for her quick costume changes, disappointed that she hadn't bumped into Freddy. But before she had a chance to work out how else she was going to find him, a sound engineer began fussing with her microphone and battery pack while Belle doused her with yet another blast of hairspray, Scarlett touched up her already immaculate make-up and Trixie fiddled with imaginary imperfections in her costume. Outside she could hear her album playing as the fans chanted her name.

'Lola! Lola! Lola!'

'Lola?'

She looked up as a head popped through the door. 'Oh hi, Vlad, how's it going?'

'Great, thanks. We're ready when you are.'

She was hit by another rush of adrenaline. She filled her lungs and let out a long breath. Freddy would have to wait.

'Yep,' she replied eventually. 'Is it time then?'

'More or less. Once you give me the word, I'll cut the DJ set, dim the lights and start playing the Twinkle adverts and the album promo. And then there's the long intro from the band. But it's all on a sequence, basically, so once it starts we can't stop. And you'll only have fifteen minutes till you're on.'

She smacked her cheeks with her hands then jumped up and down on the spot. She was buzzing with so much nervous energy she felt like she could blast through the roof like a rocket. 'All right, let's go!'

Vlad smiled and slipped away, followed by the sound engineer.

Lola sat down at her dressing table and the girls carried on bustling around her. Fifteen minutes wasn't long but it felt like an eternity. What was she supposed to think about for fifteen whole minutes?

I know! I'll have a look at my phone and check my texts. Reading everyone's good luck messages was bound to put her in the right frame of mind before the show.

'Amina? Have you got my phone, darlin'?'

Amina passed it to her and she began scrolling down the long list, absorbing everyone's good wishes one after the other. Then her eyes alighted on a message from Harvey.

'Lola, you're in danger,' she read. 'Call me urgently. And whatever you do, don't start the show until you've spoken to me. Sorry, I wouldn't be doing this unless I had to. Harvey x'

She felt like a switch had been flicked and the floor had disappeared beneath her.

Don't start the show? I just have!

Within seconds her heart was thumping so furiously she was worried the sound was going to start registering on her mic. Her stomach swayed and she thought she was about to throw up.

What's Harvey on about? Is he trying to get back at me for sacking him or am I really in danger?

There was only one thing for it. She dialled his number and waited for him to answer. But her call wouldn't go through.

Fuck!

She tried again but again it failed. She told herself it must be because she was sitting right next to fifteen thousand people all using their phones – all waiting for her to make her entrance.

'Lola! Lola! Lola!' she heard them chant.

Fuck!

There were only fifteen minutes until she'd be propelled up and onto the stage.

But Harvey says I'm in danger.

What kind of danger?

And what the fuck am I supposed to do about it?

She wiped away the beads of sweat breaking out on her forehead. All of a sudden she felt like she was being roasted in some kind of furnace. She picked up a tour programme and began fanning herself. *Here Comes Trouble*, it read, almost as if to taunt her.

She wondered if she could just pretend she needed the toilet and run away – as far away from the danger as possible. But she looked at her reflection and remembered she was wearing a hot-pant catsuit and two inches of stage make-up. And could she ever really escape anyway? She tried to swallow but her Adam's apple swelled to the size of a brick in her throat.

'Is everything all right?' asked Amina.

'I don't know,' mumbled Lola as if in a trance. 'I'm not sure.'

The four girls froze and stood staring at her in the mirror. Lola's eyes settled on Trixie.

'Trixie, darlin'? Have you still got that coke?'

14

From his position in the wings of the O2, Freddy heard the DJ set end and some sort of advert for Twinkle begin playing on the screens. He looked at his watch; it was quarter past eight. If everything was running to time he had just fifteen minutes to save Lola from being robbed of her dignity – and publicly disgraced. He really had to get a move on.

But he still couldn't find her. He dashed through the wings, almost forgetting he was trying not to draw attention to himself. In his mounting panic he nearly tripped over a dancer free-running between the floor and the walls and narrowly avoided colliding with a pair of roadies wheeling along a ten-foot-tall slide in the shape of a high-heeled shoe. He spotted a staircase leading up to the back of the stage and a little tent set up at the bottom. There was a laminate pinned to one of its walls. He drew closer to read it and spotted the word he'd been looking for – 'Artist'.

Thank fuck for that!

The only problem was, this time there was a bodyguard the size of a garden shed standing by the entrance. *How am I supposed to get past him?* He remembered the text that had just come through from Spike telling him Lola wanted to see him.

He searched for it on his phone and opened it up on the screen.

'Lola looking for you blud,' he read. 'And proper excited about show. Hope you can save it!'

Even in his panic, he couldn't help feeling a flicker of excitement at the news Lola was looking for him. But what did it mean? He'd have to find out – just as soon as he'd managed to divert disaster.

He strode up to the security guard. This time he wouldn't let himself be talked down. 'All right, mate? Mind if I have a quick word with Lola?'

The man had an AAA pass pinned onto his chest and Freddy read his name – Tiny. Presumably it was meant to be ironic. He might have laughed if he weren't so stressed.

'Sorry, fella,' Tiny replied, his face expressionless. 'Not possible. The show starts soon.'

'Yeah but apparently she's looking for me. Here, have a read of this.'

He handed Tiny the phone and watched as he quickly scanned the text message.

'Yeah but that doesn't prove anything,' he glowered at him. 'Anyone could have sent that.'

Don't let him fob you off, mate!

'But she's just told my producer she wants to see me. And I need to speak to her about something really important.'

Tiny let out a loud huff, his nostrils bulging so wide Freddy could see right up his nose. 'Listen, fella, I'm having a really shitty day and right now I don't need any more grief. I'm tell-ing you – Lola's busy.'

Freddy looked him in the eye and held his nerve.

'And I'm telling *you* I need to speak to her!'

*

Lola was sure she could hear Freddy's voice coming from the other side of the canvas. She was leaning over a line of coke chopped out on her dressing table, trying not to notice Amina's look of disappointment. She could hardly blame her; she too was disappointed – disappointed in herself. But she was also desperate – more desperate than she'd ever imagined she could be. Trixie handed her a rolled-up note and she lifted it to her nose.

'But you don't understand,' came the voice from outside. 'I have to speak to her – it's really urgent!'

Lola froze rigid.

Just a minute, it IS Freddy's voice! And he seems to know what's going on . . .

She dropped the rolled-up note onto the table and rushed over to the entrance.

'Freddy!' she burst out, flinging open the canvas curtain. 'What the hell's going on?'

'All right, Lola?' he said with a nervous smile.

Their eyes met and she immediately felt safer.

'Come in,' she squealed, grabbing his hand and almost yanking him after her. She came to a stop in the centre of the room and folded her arms. 'Come on then, what's going on?'

Freddy took a deep breath and she saw his thickly muscled chest strain at the buttons of his shirt.

'Look, I'm going to tell you this quickly because we need to move fast.' There was something about the musicality of his

Welsh accent that Lola found instantly calming. 'Someone close to you has got footage of you snorting coke and they've tampered with tonight's show and it's going to be played on the screens during the opening number.'

'Fuck!'

Not even Freddy's accent could make her feel calm about that. It was worse than she thought. She spotted the line of coke on her dressing table and felt a shudder of shame. Had she really been about to snort it? She inched across the room and positioned herself in front of it so Freddy wouldn't see.

'But everything's started now,' she yowled. 'And Vlad said once it's started it can't stop.'

'Well, I really need to speak to Vlad. I've been trying for ages but nobody will let me anywhere near him.'

At the entrance to the tent, Tiny was standing open-mouthed. Lola had no idea what had got into him but ever since the pre-show huddle he'd been all over the place.

'Tiny,' she barked, 'get on that walkie-talkie and radio through to Vlad. Tell him he needs to switch the footage straight away.'

Tiny snapped out of his daze and picked up his walkie-talkie. 'Security to technical. Do you read me?'

Lola reached for her bottle of water and took a swig. The way he was talking was like something out of a bad cop film. She looked at Freddy and he gave her a reassuring smile.

'Roger,' came a voice from the walkie-talkie. 'What's the problem?'

'You need to change the footage,' Tiny said somewhat cryptically.

*Oh what's the matter with him? How's Vlad supposed to under-
stand that?*

'What?' It sounded like Vlad couldn't even hear him. From
his position in the middle of the arena he must be almost
deafened by the sound of the fans chanting.

This is all I need!

Lola thought her legs were going to give way and she clung
onto the table for support. Belle, Scarlett and Trixie stood
gawping at her in shock. Amina's brown skin was in the
process of turning white.

'You need to change the footage!' Tiny repeated louder.

'What footage?' Vlad replied.

'On the screens!'

'What?'

'On the *screens*!'

'But why? It's all cued up and ready to go.'

Oh for fuck's sake!

Lola snatched the walkie-talkie off him. 'Vlad, this is Lola,'
she shouted in as clear a voice as she could. 'I don't know if
you can hear me but Freddy Jones is coming to see you. I need
you to listen to him and do as he says. Just do as he says. Do
you get that?'

'Roger,' came the reply.

She wasn't sure how she was supposed to respond and
thrust the walkie-talkie back at Tiny.

'Tiny, take Freddy round to see Vlad now. And Trixie, give
him your pass.'

Freddy took the AAA pass and reached out and squeezed
Lola's shoulder. 'Don't worry, I'll fix it.'

She looked in his eyes and felt like she was going to faint.

She trusted him. She trusted him completely. But Vlad's technical booth was practically at the other side of the arena – and at the top of three flights of steep stairs. How the hell was he going to get there in time?

*

As she ran her tongue over her teeth and sauntered past the tent labelled 'Artist', Gloria pictured Lola pacing around inside, working herself up into a frenzy about the show but remaining completely oblivious to the disaster that awaited her once she stepped foot on stage. God, it felt good – it felt really good. So good in fact it almost wiped out of her mind the memory of having to get down on her knees and blow Vlad a few hours ago.

Although if she were completely honest, Gloria wouldn't have cared if she'd had to suck a mile of cock to get the outcome she wanted from tonight's show. She was so excited she almost skipped over to her position in the wings to stand by and wait for her entrance. She could hardly believe that after everything she'd been through, after everything Lola had put her through, it was finally time for payback. She looked at her watch. *Just ten minutes to go . . .*

She was distracted from her thoughts by the sound of raised voices coming from Lola's tent. *Hmpf! The silly bitch is obviously having some kind of tantrum before she goes on.* She was probably worried that the world was about to realize she had no talent. Well, some people – some people like Gloria – had cottoned on to that one years ago. And she could hardly be expected to feel any sympathy for her now. *Not when she stepped in and snatched away my career – not to mention my man*. And come to think of it, from what Gloria remembered, Lola hadn't felt any sympathy for her on either occasion. Well, she'd enjoy watching her regret that later.

And boy, would she regret it. Gloria looked at the tent and wondered how nervous Lola would be if she had any inkling of what was actually coming to her. The idea was so intoxicating she could hardly bear to imagine it.

*

Inside the tent Lola held out her arm and swept the line of coke into the bin.

'Do me a favour, girls,' she said sternly. 'Never offer me any coke ever again.'

Belle, Scarlett and Trixie were speechless.

'I'm serious,' Lola went on, pacing the floor. 'You know, I might be about to lose everything because of that shit.'

There was a tense silence filled only by the sound of the fans on the other side of the stage continuing to chant her name.

'Lola! Lola! Lola!'

It was so loud it almost drowned out the sound of the album promo Lola could just about hear playing on the screens.

Shit, that means there's only ten minutes to go . . .

'Lola! Lola! Lola!'

I hope to God they're still chanting like that at the end of the show.

'Anyway,' she spewed, reaching for her bottle of water, 'I don't want to talk about that now.'

No, there'd be plenty of time for that kind of thing later. Plenty of time to regret taking coke – and to work out who it was that had filmed her and was now trying to use the footage to destroy her. But right now she needed to figure out what the hell she was going to do with the show. Surely she couldn't go on stage knowing what might be waiting for her?

God, I wish Harvey was here!

'Amina,' she croaked, 'what the fuck am I supposed to do? Should I just cancel the show?'

Amina stepped towards her and put down her iPad. She looked at her thoughtfully – with an almost maternal concern Lola hadn't seen in her before. For some reason it made her want to cry.

'Oh, tell me what you think, darlin',' she almost blubbed in her face, 'what you honestly think. Please don't do what everyone else does – please don't tell me what you think I *want* to hear.'

Her eyes flitted across to Belle, Scarlett and Trixie and they all looked down to avoid her.

Amina stiffened her mouth. 'Lola,' she said firmly, 'I think you need to be really brave and just get out there. If you don't, people are going to wonder what's happened – especially when Channel 3 News are supposed to be broadcasting clips of the show while you're still on stage. It'll be a big story if you cancel at the last minute, and whoever it is who filmed that footage might still have it – or might still blab. Some people might see pulling out of the show as an admission of guilt.'

'Fuck,' Lola gasped, 'I hadn't thought about that.'

'Well, don't think about it. Let's just worry about tonight for now.'

'OK. But do you think Freddy can switch the footage? Do you think he can even get over to Vlad in time?'

'I think if anybody can, he can. He's a good man, Lola, one of the best. I can tell – I can always spot them.'

'Yeah, well, I wish I could say the same. And then maybe I wouldn't be up to my neck in this shitstream.'

Amina rolled her eyes affectionately. At that moment Lola realized just how badly she'd underestimated her – and vowed to make a better effort to appreciate her in future. She took hold of her hand and squeezed it.

'Now why don't we keep trying Harvey?' Amina suggested.

At the mention of his name Lola felt a rumble of reassurance. She decided to give his phone one last try.

*

Harvey was in the disabled toilets holding his wet trousers under the hand drier when he heard his phone ring. It was Lola.

Thank fuck for that!

'Lola!' he practically barked into the phone, stepping away from the loud burring. 'Lola, I've been trying to get hold of you for ages!'

'I know, darlin', and I know everything that's going on – Freddy's just filled me in.'

Harvey was surprised how good it felt to hear her voice; it was as if all the bad feeling between them had instantly evaporated. The machine snapped off.

'He's trying to sort things now,' Lola went on. 'But I really need you here too, darlin'.'

'All right, I'm on my way. But you'll have to send someone to let me in – everyone knows I'm not working for you anymore and they've already struck me off the list.'

He heard Lola clearing her throat. 'All right, I'll send Amina down now. And I'm sorry, Harvey.'

'Sorry? For what?'

'Oh, for everything. For not listening to you when you were right. Because you're always right, Harvey. It's just sometimes hard for me to take it.'

Even though he was standing in a disabled toilet damp and half naked, as he listened to her words Harvey could feel himself welling up with emotion.

'Don't worry about that now, Lola. We can talk about that later.'

'Yeah, all right. Just as long as you let me give you a little surprise first.'

Harvey could feel his chin wobbling. 'I think I can handle that. Just as long as you don't give it to me when you're on stage.'

'All right, darlin',' Lola swallowed, the emotion clearly getting to her too. 'But only if you'll agree to come back as my manager. *And* my best mate.'

'Agree? You just try and stop me.'

*

As Freddy and Tiny dodged their way through the few fans still lingering in the front-of-house areas, Freddy felt grateful nobody was trying to stop them. The odd security guard called out to ask what they were doing but Tiny replied and Freddy barely even registered what he said. All he could think about was getting through to Vlad and switching the footage before Lola stepped foot on stage.

He banged into a pear-shaped man cramming a last-minute hotdog into his mouth.

'Sorry!' he shouted back at him.

The man did a double-take as he recognized Freddy from the TV and dropped his hotdog on the floor.

'Really sorry, mate!' Freddy called back over his shoulder.

As he carried on running he could feel a sweat patch beginning to form on his shirt – something he ordinarily had to watch out for before a live broadcast. He loosened his tie to try and cool down but the truth was he didn't care. Right now all he cared about was Lola. And the way she'd looked at him in that changing tent had made him think she still cared about him too. Spike had been right, there *was* still something there between them – and whatever it was, it was spurring Freddy on with a new spurt of energy.

*

Lola allowed herself to be led through the wings by a smiling stagehand. She looked at the name on his laminate – Vaughan.

'It rhymes with porn,' he joked, following her gaze. She'd have laughed if she didn't think she was about to wet herself with fear. This guy obviously had no idea what was going on behind the scenes – or in her head.

'Just try not to be too nervous,' he offered brightly. 'You're going to be great.'

Am I? She could feel her entire body gripped by such an acute state of panic that she seriously doubted it. She wasn't even able to walk without trembling. She had no idea how she was going to dance – let alone sing.

'Thanks, Vaughan,' she creaked. 'I'll do my best.'

He left her standing in a small chamber under the stage and closed the door to seal her in. From now on she was on her own, completely on her own. At least until the platform she was standing on shot up and propelled her onto the stage – and into view of the thousands of fans who were still chanting her name.

'Lola! Lola! Lola!'

More than anything in the world she wished they'd be quiet. Didn't they have any idea how little she deserved their adulation? Didn't they realize how badly she was about to let them down? She concentrated on regulating her breathing and could feel her inhalations falling into rhythm with their chants.

'Lola! Lola! Lola!'

She heard the album promo come to an end and the band's intro to *Tramp* kick in. There was a roar of excitement from the audience that made the wooden walls rattle around her. She knew from rehearsals that very soon the dancers would be joining the band on the stage. And then it would be time for her entrance.

There were just five minutes to go. Five minutes until her entire future would be decided.

Come on, Freddy. Don't let me down!

*

Spike followed Barbara through the arena and slid into position next to Big Phil on a podium about a third of the way back from the stage. He'd just been in the satellite truck editing the backstage footage that would be laid under Freddy's live broadcast. Although he knew the footage Phil was about to shoot of the performance would be much more important.

447

That is unless Freddy manages to kill the story . . .

The truth was Spike had no way of knowing how Freddy was getting on as for some reason he hadn't replied to his texts. The first he'd get wind of it now would probably be when he watched Lola perform in front of the screens.

He felt his shoulders seize up as six dancers sizzled their way onto the stage to the sound of the band's rousing intro. Lola couldn't be far behind. And, judging from the thunderous roar coming from the fans, they couldn't wait to see her.

He only hoped they weren't about to witness her execution live on stage.

*

Freddy burst into the technical booth without pausing for breath. He'd just flown up three flights of stairs and was hissing out air like a deflating balloon. Three men looked up at him, their faces illuminated by a row of computers.

'Which one of you's Vlad?' he panted.

A weasel-faced man who for some reason smelled of TCP stood up to shake his hand. 'I'm Vlad – and you'd better tell me what's going on.'

'There's no time to explain properly,' Freddy replied, 'but somebody's hacked into your computer and edited footage of Lola doing something she shouldn't into the video for the first song.'

'Fuck!' Vlad dropped into his seat and quickly opened up the timeline on his computer. Freddy swept into position behind him and watched as he dragged the cursor along the edit. 'There it is!' he said, pointing at a chunk of pink appearing on an otherwise green oblong. 'That's got to be it!'

'Well, can you cut it out?'

Vlad looked at a timer in the corner of the screen.

'That video sequence doesn't kick in till Lola hits the stage,' he explained, 'which is in less than one minute's time.'

Freddy gulped.

'It'll be tight,' Vlad went on, 'and I'll need the changes to render, which will take about thirty seconds.'

Freddy looked at the timer. *55 seconds.*

The three techies stared at him in expectation.

'Let's do it!' he boomed.

Vlad's fingers instantly began zipping over the keyboard and Freddy leaned forward to watch.

Oh come on! Please hurry up!

'That's it,' Vlad commented with a blast of TCP, 'we've made the cut. Now for the substitution.'

Freddy looked at the timer. *43 seconds.*

He felt as if his stomach were being run through an old mangle. He was so overwhelmed with fear he could almost taste it at the back of his throat.

'Done!' Vlad gasped. 'Just let me hit Render.'

33 seconds.

Hadn't Vlad said this would take about 30 seconds? He hoped to God there was enough time.

'Changes rendering,' read the computer.

Oh come on! Why's it taking so long?

To try and distract himself he glanced up and out of the window, over the heads of the fans and down onto the stage. The dancers were beginning to move into formation around the bottom of the staircase, presumably to welcome Lola when she made her entrance at the top.

15 seconds.

He wondered what must be going through Lola's mind right now. And how on earth she could be feeling in the right state of mind to perform.

5 seconds.

If the render didn't finish now, he'd have failed – failed to protect Lola and failed to save any future the two of them might have had together.

Oh please God let it work!

The computer gave off a loud ping.

'Render complete,' he read.

Thank FUCK for that!

'That's it,' Vlad announced. 'We did it!'

Freddy held onto the wall and exhaled with a loud moan. Through the window he saw Lola shoot up into the air and land on her feet on the stage. It was as if someone had set off a small bomb in the arena; it erupted into more noise than he'd ever imagined his eardrums could take.

He'd done it. He'd actually done it.

Now it was all down to Lola. But she looked terrified. She was so stiff with fear she could hardly move down the stairs. And when she opened her mouth to sing, her voice sounded throaty and hoarse.

'You know what,' Vlad broke in, 'I think I know who did this.'

'Really?' asked Freddy. 'Who was it?'

'Lola's backing singer, Gloria. I caught her in here earlier and asked what she was doing but she talked her way out of it.'

Freddy didn't know why, but he was pretty sure Vlad blushed.

'Anyway, she left this,' he went on, ejecting a memory stick from his computer and handing it over.

Freddy took hold of it and turned back to look at the stage. 'Thanks, mate. I'll take care of this.'

But first he needed to take care of Lola. His face twisted into a grimace as he watched her stumble off the bottom step and almost fall flat on her face. Thankfully the fans didn't seem to notice; they carried on roaring so loudly they were making the glass in the window vibrate. But Lola was obviously struggling. And she needed his help. There was nothing else for it; he'd have to rush back to the wings and somehow give her the signal that she could stop worrying and relax into her performance.

'Tiny!' he shouted over to her bodyguard standing at the door. 'Are you ready for round two?'

*

Lola did her best to strut her way across the stage but felt so stiff she was in serious danger of tripping over her own legs. A jet of steam burst into the air beside her and despite the fact she'd rehearsed her reaction to it several times she almost shrieked into her microphone with fright.

Shit, I really need to get it together!

She realized her helmet was skew-whiff and readjusted it so the mic was back in front of her mouth. As she floundered along the travelator, she reminded herself that *Tramp* was supposed to be an anthem to female empowerment and did her best to infuse the lyrics with the appropriate emotion. But right now empowered and strong couldn't be any further from the way she was feeling. All she could think about were the images playing on the screens behind her. She glanced over her shoulder for another look and recognized the footage Hettie had shot of her dressed as a boxer. *So far so good!*

But there was no way she could perform the whole song in this stressed-out state. As she staggered off the travelator and into the second verse, she mixed up her moves and leapt off a rising podium straight into an explosion of strobe lighting. In her confusion she dropped her gun and had to quickly bend down to scoop it up before one of the dancers kicked it into the audience. By the time she opened her mouth to sing the next line her voice had gone up an entire octave. *Fuck me, this is a disaster!*

The worst thing was, she knew that if Freddy had managed to switch the footage he'd have done it by now; because of the way the sequencing worked any changes had to be made before the song started. So there was a chance she was panicking needlessly. But when was this footage of her snorting coke supposed to come in? After the first verse? During the second? She had absolutely no way of knowing. And the suspense was shattering her self-belief – and ruining her performance.

Thankfully the audience didn't seem to notice. However much she slaughtered the song they just carried on cheering. She stumbled into the second chorus and fired her gun at one of the dancers. As she swivelled around to shoot another, she caught sight of a flash of red hair standing in the wings. It was Freddy.

Oh my God!

He gave her the thumbs up and nodded brightly.

Oh my God, oh my God, oh my God!

He'd done it. He'd actually done it.

The news was enough for her to feel a huge surge of energy and confidence – much more than she'd have received from any coke.

And she knew just what to do with it. It was all going straight into her performance.

*

As he took his place next to Freddy in the wings, Harvey stroked his AAA laminate. He'd enjoyed showing it to the crisp-munching security guard who'd refused to let him into the artists' entrance as he'd returned to storm through the doors with a smile. And he'd enjoyed feeling it bounce around his neck as he'd dashed along the corridors, making sure Lola's roadies and stage crew could see he was back in business and back in Lola's life. But as her newly reinstated manager he couldn't forget he had a job to do; he needed to make sure the crisis had been averted.

'All right, lad?' he said to Freddy. 'How'd you get on?'

'Job done,' Freddy smiled without taking his eyes off Lola. 'I've just given her the nod now.'

'Brilliant news! Well done!'

The two of them looked out at Lola as she scorched her way across the stage. Harvey listened to her voice soar out over the fans and watched in wonder as she powered her way through a dance routine he knew she usually found tough. There was no doubt about it: she was on fire – and the crowd was going wild.

'So who's this Gloria then?' broke in Freddy.

Harvey tore his eyes off Lola and pointed out the backing

vocalists swaying to the beat at the side of the stage. 'Gloria's the one on the left. But why do you ask that?'

'Well, according to Vlad she's the one who switched the footage.'

'Fuck. Are you serious?'

'Yeah. He caught her with this just before the show.'

Freddy handed him the memory stick and Harvey slipped it into his pocket. He'd make sure he destroyed it as soon as he was home. And hopefully that would be the end of the whole sorry saga. *Except what if there's another copy of the footage? Gloria must have shot it on her phone . . .*

'Listen, lad,' he said, 'I need to nip off and tie up some loose ends.'

'So I take it you've been given your job back?' Freddy smiled. 'Congratulations.'

'Yeah, thanks. But don't congratulate me just yet. There's something really important I need to do first.'

*

As Lola thundered her way through to the middle eight, Gloria looked behind her and checked the screens. Surely her footage should have been played by now? She'd told Clinton to edit it in about two thirds of the way through the song. But they were already past that point and all she could see was that stupid film of Lola prancing around pretending to be a boxer. *What the fuck's going on?*

She continued swaying to the beat as she tried to piece together what could have happened. She'd been meticulously careful about following Clinton's instructions when she'd been substituting the footage. And the computer had made the sound he'd told her to listen out for which said her substitution was complete. So what the hell had gone wrong?

As she watched Lola thump her way through a dance routine even she had to admit was impressive, she started to wonder if maybe she'd been rumbled. But she couldn't work out how on earth that might have been possible . . .

I listened out for the sound from the computer.

I remembered to shut down the screen.

I picked up the memory stick . . .

She froze to the spot.

Shit! I didn't pick up the memory stick!

How could I have been so stupid?

She felt the tips of her fingers tingle with tension. She'd fallen at the final hurdle. And the worst thing was, it hadn't even been her fault. If Vlad hadn't been in such a hurry to shove his fat dick in her mouth, she might have been able to concentrate on what she was doing.

But that had to be it; when she'd left he must have spotted the memory stick and realized she'd been up to something. That would explain why Lola had been in such a fluster before the show – and why she'd acted all weird when she first came on stage. It would explain why Freddy Jones had suddenly appeared in the wings and given her a thumbs-up to signal that everything was OK. It would even explain why Harvey had made a surprise reappearance and pointed Gloria out to him.

Well, they were obviously all in on it together. And once again Gloria was the loser.

Once again the whole world had turned against her.

Once again she'd tried to shine, only to see her efforts stamped on by people who wouldn't give her a chance.

Oh it's all so unfair!

Sharonne hissed in her ear and snapped her back to reality. 'Gloria, what are you doing?' Gloria saw her frown and remembered to keep moving to the beat.

There was nothing else she could do now. She'd just have to get through the show and then face whatever was coming to her. Although she had a pretty good idea what it would be. And the very thought of it made her feel sick with dread.

Lola might not have had any reason to sack her before. But she certainly did now.

*

Harvey burst through the door of Gloria's dressing room and immediately began scouring every surface for her mobile phone. He felt his way along her dressing table, looked under endless G-strings, wrestled his way through a tangle of tights and singed his fingers on a pair of hair straighteners.

Shit!

He sucked on his fingers and pulled open Gloria's top drawer. But all he could find were jars of cocoa butter and beauty products, as well as a silver contraption which could have been an eyelash curler or might just as easily have been a piece of torture equipment. He yanked open another drawer with such force he managed to pull off the front and was almost buried under an avalanche of tampons. But still there was no sign of her phone.

He remembered that he had Gloria's number programmed into his own phone and quickly fished it out of his back pocket. As he pressed the Call button he stepped back to listen. After an agonizing pause the ringer began to sound from an armchair in the corner.

Phew!

He raced over and picked up Gloria's phone. He was relieved to find that she hadn't set a passcode.

Bad move, Gloria!

He went straight into her photo album and began flicking through the videos. He trawled through countless clips of her little girl, including one particularly cute one that showed her playing with a fairytale castle on her birthday. He paused for a second as he realized how hard it must be for Gloria to bring up her daughter on her own. He might even have felt a stab of sympathy for her if she hadn't gone all out to destroy Lola. But the fact remained that she had. And he had to find the video and delete it.

His eyes alighted on the next clip along, a darker film that looked like it had been shot in a nightclub. He pressed Play and tried not to groan out loud as Lola and her Style Council burst onto the screen snorting line after line of coke. He felt a prickle of regret as he remembered that shortly afterwards Lola had sacked him. Even though she'd now apologized, it was still very painful. Well, he'd just have to turn back time to a few moments before that incident and wipe it from the record.

He hit the Delete button and watched as the video disappeared from the screen. If Gloria tried to tell anyone she'd seen Lola snorting coke now she'd have no evidence to back up her claim – and nor would she be able to prove Harvey had broken into her room and deleted the footage from her phone. He picked up a tour T-shirt and wiped his fingerprints off the handset just in case. No, there was no way anyone would believe her now. They'd be much more likely to assume she was an embittered backing vocalist jealous of Lola's success. Which, of course, she was.

From now on Lola was safe. And everyone close to her could breathe easily.

What was it Freddy had said?

Job done.

He couldn't have put it better himself.

*

On stage, Lola was blasting her way through to the end of the song. As she belted out the lyrics she invested them with so much emotion she finally felt she might actually deserve some of the adulation emanating from the audience. And she might have written the song nearly a year ago, when she'd been dumped by Fox Marshall, but it was only since the last few months and the break-up of her relationship with Jake that she finally felt fully committed to its message.

She looked at Jake now, banging away on his drums, his shirt split to the waist to show off his torso but with no sign of his signature sloppy grin or the arrogance that usually illuminated his penetrating green eyes. She wondered what had happened to knock him off his perch but she couldn't bring herself to care. She pictured him in twenty years' time when his looks had faded and his sex drive had dimmed and everyone would realize there was nothing else to him. She knew for sure he'd end up a sad and lonely loser living a life empty of love.

She sensed the dancers moving into position behind her, stepping towards the front of the stage and preparing to bring the song to its stirring climax. As she stormed through her final lines, she realized with a rush of energy that her feelings towards Jake weren't entirely negative; looking at him now she did feel a flutter of gratitude. Because he was the man who'd finally convinced her she was through with tramps. Her head might have warned her off them for a long time beforehand, but it had taken her experience with Jake for her emotions to finally catch up. And now she knew beyond all doubt that she didn't feel the slightest tickle of attraction towards him – or any other tramp for that matter.

She was, on the other hand, gripped by a powerful attraction to Freddy – and it was helping drive her through the song. She could feel his eyes watching her from the wings and more than anything she wanted to turn around and look back at him. She couldn't get over what he'd just done for her. His actions had been nothing short of heroic but the weird thing was, his heroism didn't make Lola feel that familiar sensation of being unworthy. On the contrary, it made her feel good about herself. And as she dropped down into the crouching pose that ended her routine, she knew it was a feeling she was finally ready to embrace.

*

Freddy tore himself away from his view of Lola and crept through the wings towards the position in the scene dock where they'd agreed they'd be broadcasting live. It was almost pitch-black so he had to shine his phone onto his watch to find out the time. There were twenty minutes to go till the programme began at nine o'clock, and just a few minutes after that he'd be on air. He didn't have the slightest idea what he'd be saying; his own success in saving Lola from public disgrace had left him with nothing to report on. Well, he'd just have to call Hugh and tell him straight – and then face whatever his boss wanted to throw at him. Although he had a pretty good idea what it would be.

He picked up his phone and dialled the number of the studio gallery. It was a shitty thing to do to land his colleagues with no top story just a few minutes before they went on air. But there was no point feeling guilty about it. He knew he'd done the right thing.

'Hello,' Hugh answered.

Freddy tried his best to sound upbeat. 'All right, boss?'

'Yeah, how's it going, boyo? Has it all kicked off over there?'

'I'm afraid not. It turns out there was no footage of Lola snorting coke after all – the whole thing was a hoax set up by some jealous backing singer.'

Well, it's only half a lie. And much simpler than telling Hugh the whole truth.

'Oh no. You're not serious?'

'Unfortunately I am.'

Or should I say 'fortunately'?

'Well, what the fuck am I supposed to do now?' Hugh spat. 'I mean, I can move you down the running order but I'll still have a five-minute hole to fill.'

'I know, mate. I'm really sorry. But I can easily give you five minutes on the first night of the show. It's been amazing so far and we got some cracking footage backstage.'

Hugh let loose an exaggerated sigh. 'Is that seriously what you're offering me — Lola's first show? That's not news, Freddy!'

Yes it is, it's just not bad news.

'Isn't it?' he managed with a hint of defiance. 'Why can't we run a good-news story for once?'

'Because that's not how you make noise, boyo. And you promised to make my ears bleed!'

'Yeah, I know, I'm sorry about that.'

Actually, I'm not sorry at all.

'Yeah, well, sorry's not good enough. This story was handed to you on a plate – and you still managed to fuck it up.'

Well, I wouldn't put it like that exactly. Although he kept quiet, realizing it was better for Hugh to think he'd fucked it up rather than deliberately killing the story himself.

'Anyway, I need a story, Freddy. I can't just broadcast a black hole. You're on at half past nine – and if you can't deliver you can consider yourself unemployed.'

Freddy nodded gravely. 'All right, boss. Leave it with me.'

He ended the call and stood staring at his phone.

Just when he'd solved one problem, he collided head-first into another.

What the hell was he going to do now?

15

Sitting in the audience of the O2, Karen Grant was transfixed by the sight of her daughter. She was only on the second number but already Lola had got over her wobbly start and was flying through the show. Who'd have thought it? After everything Karen had done wrong as a mother, she'd somehow managed to bring up a superstar.

But wasn't that the kind of thing they'd talked about in group therapy at the Abbey? Hadn't she learnt that a bad upbringing can sometimes be what inspires a person to try harder and prove themselves – to show the world they're worthy of love? Of course it didn't excuse Karen's catalogue of mistakes as a mother – and nothing could ever make up for the horrors she herself had been put through when Lola had been conceived. But she couldn't help wondering whether in a funny way this was how their lives had always been meant to unravel. *I mean, if the past hadn't happened in the way it had, I probably wouldn't be sitting here watching Lola on stage now. And I wouldn't be feeling so proud.*

'All right, Karen?' boomed a familiar Northern voice behind her.

'Oh hi, Harvey!' she shouted out to him as he slipped in next to her. 'You made it after all!'

Harvey leaned in to speak into her ear. 'Yeah, and it looks like I'll be sticking around for a long time yet.'

'Oh that's fantastic news,' she chirped, knowing that whatever had happened between Lola and Harvey, from now on she wouldn't have to worry about her daughter. 'Honestly, that's absolutely fantastic. And isn't she amazing?'

'She is that,' Harvey smiled, turning back to look at the stage. 'Our girl's done good – really good.'

Karen followed his gaze and watched Lola leap off a table and into the arms of three unfeasibly muscular male dancers. 'You know what,' she glistened, tears forming in her eyes, 'I think this could be the happiest day of my life.'

She breathed in as deeply as she could, feeling herself fill up with the crowd's energy and positivity. After this she knew she couldn't ever go back to her old lifestyle of abuse and self-destruction. It felt like the final step in her recovery – a recovery which had begun when she'd seen Lola ask her to give up drugs live on Channel 3 News.

So yeah, she was right, this *was* the happiest day of her life.

And she couldn't imagine how it could possibly get any better.

*

On stage Lola powered through to the end of *Mess It Up*, strutting down the runway as Kitty, Jette and Boo criss-crossed around her, performing all manner of cartwheels and capoeira. She wasn't sure where her energy was coming from but she didn't think she'd ever performed so well in her life.

The dancers grouped around her at the end of the runway and together they struck the pose that ended the song. They were hit by applause so loud Lola could feel it vibrating on her tongue as she opened her mouth to catch her breath. *Fuck me, this is beyond fucking fierce!*

The audience were making so much noise someone took the decision to turn the house lights onto them, which of course only made them roar even louder. In the front row, standing just a few feet away from her, Lola spotted her mum, flushed with joy and waving her arms in the air wildly. As their eyes met she felt an upsurge of happiness.

'Thanks, guys!' she shouted over the applause, addressing the crowd for the first time. 'You lot are the best audience ever!'

She tried not to recoil from the impact as they roared their response.

'But there's one very special person in the audience to-night,' she went on, 'and that's my mum. So please give her a big cheer everyone!'

She looked at her mum beaming up at her and suddenly felt overwhelmed by the urge to give her a hug.

'Would you guys like to meet her?' Lola offered, giving a little wince in expectation of their ear-splittingly loud reply. 'Would you guys like to meet my mum?'

As the noise levels hit new heights, Lola signalled to a pair of security guards to lead her mum up and onto the stage.

'You know what,' she explained over the crowd's roars, 'I've sometimes been really down on my mum. I seem to remember slagging her off once when I was shit-faced on Channel 3 News. But I think it's about time I apologized because my mum hasn't always been the best mum in the world, but I haven't always been the best daughter either. And, you know, I've made some mistakes in my life too.'

And that's putting it mildly!

'We love you, Lola!' someone called out from the left of the runway.

'Thanks,' she smiled, 'but I was just thinking when I performed that song that it's fun to joke about messing it up and everything, but getting completely obliterated isn't really something to boast about. And when I look back I'm not sure my reasons for messing it up have always been that great.'

Her eyes settled on Harvey and she flashed him a knowing look, just as the security guards guided her mum into position next to her.

'But I guess I'm my mother's daughter after all,' she grinned, taking her mum's hand. 'And I'm really proud to stand here in front of you all and say that. Because my mum's a top bird and right now she's the one who deserves your applause – you know she hasn't been anywhere near drugs for three months. Three months!'

Lola held up her mum's hand and the crowd erupted in approval.

'And I know for sure she's never going to mess it up again – and neither am I, for that matter. So tonight's for you, Mum. And I love you very much.'

There it was. She'd said it. She'd actually just said it. Something she never thought she'd be able to bring herself to say. And not only that but she'd done it in front of fifteen thousand witnesses, not to mention the camera from Channel

3 News. And the funny thing was, it had actually been quite easy. And it had all felt so right.

'I love you too, Lola,' her mum replied, her bottom lip trembling. Lola moved her mic closer to her mouth so everyone could hear her. 'I love you too, Lola,' she repeated, looking shocked as her words reverberated around the arena.

The two women moved together and hugged each other tightly – much more tightly than Lola could remember ever having hugged anyone before. And as she clung onto her mum while the audience's cheers rang out in her ears, she realized that from now on, the two of them would never grow apart again. It didn't matter that her mum wouldn't tell her anything about her dad – or what had happened to her on that holiday in Spain. The truth was, Lola wasn't even that interested in finding her dad anymore. Because for the first time in her life she had a mum. And that was more than enough for her.

*

Standing in the wings, Freddy breathed a sigh of relief.

It looks like Lola's just given me a story.

Not only had she just reconciled with her mum live on stage but she'd even referenced the first interview she'd given to Channel 3 News – and he'd learned from experience that Hugh loved broadcasting anything that bigged up his own show. It stoked his ego, which Freddy knew was just as significant as any news agenda.

He looked out towards the podium where Spike and Big Phil were standing. Their agreement had been to film only the first two numbers of the show so he wasn't sure whether they'd have cut as soon as *Mess It Up* ended. But he spotted

Phil looking through the viewfinder of his camera and the tell-tale little red light shining out from the front that signalled he was still recording.

Cracking! I might just have held on to my job after all!

*

Harvey followed Lola into her changing tent and stood watching from the doorway as she dried her face with a towel. She'd just performed the fifth song of the night and had come to the end of the first act of the show. A video she'd recorded to accompany an album track was now playing on the screens as the dancers performed an elaborate routine to entertain the audience while she quickly changed.

She stood in the centre of the room with her arms in the air as a sound engineer swiftly removed her battery pack and Belle, Scarlett and Trixie swept in to dismantle her first look and construct the second. It was time for her to appear in front of the audience as Cleopatra. Harvey could only imagine how they were going to respond.

Lola looked up and their eyes met. It was the first time they'd been anywhere near each other since their bust-up in Club Class. He flashed her a huge grin. 'All right, Trouble?'

'Harvey!' she squeaked. 'I'd be all over you if I weren't dripping with sweat.'

He smiled bashfully and scratched his cheek. He wanted to move in and kiss her but the girls were buzzing around her and he knew she had to stand still while they did their thing. She shrugged at him and he understood. Amina thrust a bottle of water into her hand and she took a long swig.

'So how am I doing? Am I getting away with it?'

Harvey laughed. 'Well, I've only seen bits so far but I think you're just about getting away with it, yeah.'

She drained her bottle of water and threw it at him in mock outrage. 'Come on, darlin'! You can do better than that!'

He chuckled at her. It was as if the past few weeks had never happened. 'You're fucking amazing, Lola. Better than you've ever been. Better than anyone I've ever seen.'

'Thanks, darlin',' she chirped as Trixie stripped her down to her underwear. 'That's more like it.'

'Now please try to keep completely still,' said Belle, attaching a long black wig to Lola's head. When she stepped back Trixie immediately swooped in to fasten on Cleopatra's headdress and then Scarlett began painting her eyebrows. Through it all, Harvey couldn't help noticing that Lola looked only at him. She shot him a crafty wink. At that moment he understood that, however close she might have grown to the girls over the last couple of months, now she'd repaired her friendship with him they wouldn't get a look-in. It really would be just like it always had been.

'Anyway,' she went on, 'now that I've got you all to myself, I think it's about time you heard my latest song.'

Harvey looked at the girls and felt a little self-conscious. Lola glanced at the backs of their heads, stuck her tongue out and pulled a little face. She and Harvey burst into a fit of giggles. As she began to sing a cappella, it was like they were the only two people in the room.

> *We met when we were really drunk,*
> *We both loved music and the odd hunk.*
> *You're from up north and I'm from down south,*

> *But we both knew how to give it some mouth.*
> *From the start you always made me grin,*
> *I love you like a brother – you're my twin.*

Harvey could feel a wave of happiness flooding through him and stretching his grin all the way across his face.

> *Now you've grown up and matured,*
> *But through it all our friendship endured.*
> *I'm sorry I've been such a stupid bitch,*
> *You put up with me being a total witch.*
> *But missing you cut my heart with a knife,*
> *Flippin' 'eck Harvey, come back into my life!*

As she beamed up at him, Harvey gave her a round of applause. 'I'm back, Lola – and next time you won't get rid of me that easily!'

'Oh don't worry,' she quipped as the girls stepped back to inspect their work, 'there won't *be* a next time!'

Lola stood up and turned to face herself in the mirror and Harvey gave a loud whistle. Her costume was complete – and she looked incredible. But he knew that her quick change had been timed to the second and he'd already spotted a stagehand waiting in the doorway to escort her back onto the stage. He recognized the first few notes of *Miss Chief* and knew that it was time for her to leave. As she swept out of the tent she beckoned him to follow. The two of them followed the stagehand's torchlight and glided through the wings.

'So who's this anonymous source?' she whispered as soon as they were out of earshot of the girls. 'Are you going to find out who did the dirty on me?'

'Don't worry,' he soothed, 'Freddy found out already.'

'Oh yeah? And who was it?'

'Gloria.'

'*Gloria!* Fuck me, what a bitch!'

'Yeah, well, I don't think anyone will argue with you there.'

She shook her head. 'Well at least it makes sense. And I suppose she thinks she had good reason – I did blatantly lay into her when I caught her on the job with Jake. But even so, I didn't think she'd be capable of this.'

'No, and we can talk about it later. But I don't think it would be a good idea to keep her on the tour.'

Lola took a deep breath as the stagehand manoeuvred her into her position on a crane. 'No,' she agreed, straightening up and taking hold of a mic held out to her by a sound engineer, 'and to be honest I don't want her anywhere near me again. But can we give her some money or something? Hasn't she got a little girl to look after?'

'She has,' confirmed Harvey, 'and if we pay her off we can get her to sign a confidentiality clause.'

He stepped back as the crane clicked into action and began raising Lola away and towards the stage.

'Don't worry, I'll take care of it. You just concentrate on the show!'

*

From his position in the scene dock, Freddy could hear Lola tearing her way through the show. She'd already been on stage for nearly an hour so he reckoned she must be about halfway through by now. He readjusted his earpiece and listened to the voices of Hugh Badcock and Janine Jury yelling orders at

Amanda Adams from the studio gallery while she was in the middle of a heavyweight political interview with the Home Secretary Lavinia Trout.

'Ask her about her hippie dresses and Pixie boots!' Hugh bellowed at her. 'Ask her why she wears such shit clothes!'

He looked at Spike, who was also connected to talkback, and roofed his eyes. He could just imagine Hugh and Janine Jury salivating at the sight of Lavinia like a pair of Staffies eyeing up a Scottie. *Well*, he thought sarcastically, *they're going to love my report. It doesn't slag anyone off and is entirely positive.*

'Two minutes to air, Freddy!' came the voice of the programme assistant in his ear.

His mouth tightened. *God I hope I can get away with this . . .*

As he gave a little jig on the spot, he found himself thinking back to the first time he'd met Lola, when he'd interviewed her live at her album launch at the beginning of the summer. He remembered waiting to go on air just like he was now and Lola chatting to him as he listened to the PA count him down in his earpiece.

'One minute to air!'

He smiled as he remembered Lola asking him where exactly he was from in Wales and how she'd told him he was much more handsome in real life than he was on the telly. Now here he was four months later reporting on the first night of her tour after having stepped in to save the show from sabotage and scandal. Back then he'd never have imagined that he'd be in this position now – let alone that he'd be looking forward to seeing Lola after the show to ask her out on a date. One he was now convinced would end much more happily than their first.

'Thirty seconds to air!'

'Good luck, blud!' chipped in Spike.

Freddy smiled at him and told himself he needed to refocus on the present and concentrate on what he was going to say on air. But all he could think about was the way Lola had looked at him when they'd spoken in her changing tent before the show. More than anything else he wanted her to look at him in the same way again.

'Ten seconds!'

Through his earpiece he could hear Amanda linking into his broadcast from the O2. He remembered how nervous he'd been as she'd introduced his first interview with Lola. He didn't feel nervous anymore.

'Cue Freddy!'

'Yes, Amanda, I'm here at the O2 as Lola Grant is performing on stage just a few feet behind me. And so far it's been an extraordinary evening . . .'

For the next few minutes he talked the viewers through the build-up to the show backstage, the crowd's reaction to Lola's first couple of numbers and then her surprise reunion with her mum after *Mess It Up*. At appropriate moments he knew his voice would be underlaid with the footage Big Phil had shot and Spike had edited and sent back to the studio, although they'd agreed to cut out all evidence of Lola's shaky start on stage. And at no moment did he give the slightest hint of any of the backstage drama that had been the real story of the night.

'Fifteen seconds to VT!' boomed the PA in his ear. He needed to wind things up. Thankfully, Hugh had been silent for his whole broadcast. He hoped this was a good sign.

'So it's been a great night here at the O2,' he fizzed, 'and the *Trouble* tour has cemented Lola Grant's status as the hottest star in Britain. But I'm sure many of the fans in the audience will be going home not just thinking about the show but also about the showstopping reunion between mother and daughter. Amanda.'

He held his smile to camera as he knew he might still be in shot for a few seconds.

Well, I did it. And I'm pretty sure I got away with it too!

'And you can relax, Freddy,' came the voice of the PA. 'Thanks, sweetheart.'

'My pleasure,' he replied.

'Man, that was the bomb,' chirped Spike. 'Nice work, blud.'

'Thanks, champ. All we need now is the word from Hugh. And then we can start to enjoy ourselves!'

Freddy screwed up his face as he waited for his editor to holler into his earpiece. Not that he really cared what Hugh thought – but he did want to hold on to his job, at least for the time being. At least until he could find another job that wouldn't put him under so much pressure to cause trouble.

'All right, boyo, you're in the clear,' bawled Hugh's voice into his ear.

Freddy stepped to one side where it was a bit quieter. 'OK so you're happy?'

'Well, I wouldn't say that exactly. But you didn't disgrace yourself, put it that way. And I'm sure a few of your housewives enjoyed hearing about that soppy little mother-daughter reunion.'

Freddy felt a surge of anger. Hugh might be his boss but how dare he speak to him like that?

'You know what, mate,' he began, 'why don't me and you sit down tomorrow and have a little look at our viewing figures? Because I think lots of our viewers would like to hear the odd good-news story – even if some of them *are* housewives.'

There was a pause during which Freddy could hear the sound of the VT playing in the studio mixed with the sound of Lola performing on stage and the odd gasp from some of his colleagues in the gallery.

'Listen, Freddy,' Hugh roared, 'when you've worked in news for as long as I have, then you might be qualified to tell me what the viewers want.'

'Oh that's interesting because I was under the impression that since you've been editing the programme our ratings have gone down.'

The sound of Hugh's indignation beamed up over London, bounced off a satellite in the sky and came hurtling back down into Freddy's earpiece.

'Well, I can't help it if I've been saddled with some leek-munching sheep-shagger who thinks the idea of a big news story is the first night of a pop star's tour. It isn't news if it doesn't bruise. You just remember that, boyo.'

'Oh I will,' he replied calmly. 'But you remember one thing for me, Hugh. I don't like people taking the piss out of my country – and I don't like being called "boyo". It's patronizing to Welsh people and believe it or not, I'm proud of being Welsh. So you can stop it right now or I'll have you for discrimination.'

The gasps from his colleagues in the gallery were so loud they almost drowned out the sound of Lola on stage. But

Freddy was glad everyone could hear their conversation – and he knew it would protect him. There'd be plenty of people who'd witnessed Hugh's anti-Welsh insult so it would make it much tougher for him to get rid of him. *And anyway, it's about time someone stood up to him.*

'Oh and while we're on the subject,' he added, 'it's also patronizing to black people to call them "bro".' He glanced at Spike and saw his face gleaming with delight. 'And you wouldn't want anyone to think you're racist, would you, Hugh? Not on top of everything else?'

For once Hugh was unsure how to reply. Freddy could just imagine him struggling to contain his anger, seething in humiliation like a dick-swinging silverback who'd just been challenged in front of his entire troop of gorillas. Well, he didn't care. And he knew it might make things difficult at work from now on, but he also knew that if Hugh was staying on as editor he wouldn't be sticking around for long anyway.

He couldn't help smiling as he heard Hugh stammering into his earpiece. 'I don't know what you're talking about, Freddy. I love Welsh people – and I love black people too.'

'Listen, Hugh, let's not even go there. I'll see you in the office tomorrow and we can talk about stories that are coming up. I'm not interested in anything else. And to be perfectly honest, right now I'd like to watch Lola perform the rest of her show.'

'Yeah, well, I've actually got a programme to edit,' Hugh blasted into his ear. 'So I need to go too. See you tomorrow, boyo.'

There was an awkward pause and Freddy could hear his colleagues chuntering amongst themselves.

'Sorry,' Hugh came back at him. 'What I meant was, I'll see you tomorrow, *Freddy*.'

Freddy could feel a smile smooth his face. It was only a small triumph. But it was a triumph all the same.

As he pulled out his earpiece he realized Hugh hadn't ended the conversation in his usual way by calling him a 'good man'. He couldn't help thinking it was ironic. *Because I am a good man. And tonight I think I've proved it. Proved it to Lola – and proved it to myself.*

He couldn't care less about proving it to Hugh.

*

Gloria rushed off the stage and ran through the corridor into her dressing room. By the time she burst in she was out of breath and had to lean onto the back of the door to fill her lungs. *Now where's my fucking phone?*

She knew she needed to change her costume for the next number and only had four minutes while a video Lola had recorded was playing on the screens. But before she could even think about that she had to look at her phone to reassure herself she still had a copy of the footage of Lola snorting coke. If she did, there might still be a chance she could salvage something from the whole sorry saga.

Gloria spotted the handset resting on the armchair exactly where she'd left it. She darted over and began tapping into it to access her videos, scrolling through until she came to the clip of Chanelle opening her birthday present. But after that there was nothing.

Shit! Someone must have deleted it while I was on stage!

She threw the handset across the room and watched it

shatter into pieces. There was no denying it; she'd lost the fight and, even worse, she'd lost it to Lola. *I hate that fucking bitch! I absolutely fucking HATE her!*

And not only that but when her video had been deleted all her hopes of clawing her way back to her rightful position in the music industry had been deleted along with it. What was she supposed to do now?

She stared at the phone on the floor and felt hollowed out by a mixture of grief and fear. There was no question now that she was going to be sacked. The most she could hope for would be some kind of dignified exit. At least Lola wouldn't want the world to know the real reason why she'd been fired. Maybe she could come up with a bullshit line about artistic differences and get herself some kind of pay-off to keep quiet? It would be quite a climbdown from her original plan but she didn't see what else she could hope for. Not that it would stop her mum from crowing. And what was she going to tell Chanelle? She'd fucked up so badly even Clinton was bound to be disappointed. *Oh it's so fucking unfair!*

She ripped off her costume and began to throw on the next. If she was going to try and scramble out of this disaster with any kind of consolation prize, she knew she'd have to get back out there and finish the show. After which she could hide away from the world and work out how she was going to go about picking up the pieces and rebuilding her life.

Just then there was a knock at the door.

She froze. 'Who is it?'

'It's Harvey. Can I have a quick word?'

She took a deep breath and dusted herself down. It was time for her to face the consequences of her actions.

'Yes,' she croaked, closing her eyes to compose herself, 'come in!'

*

On stage, Jake clung onto his drumsticks and scraped them back through his hair. He was desperate to take a piss and the video interlude that was currently playing was supposed to be his opportunity. But glaring at him from the wings was Tiny, his eyes flaming with menace as he pounded his fist into his palm.

What the hell am I supposed to do now?

It was all such a disaster – and he couldn't pretend it was anyone's dumb-ass fault but his own. He wouldn't care but Sharonne had even tried to warn him about her boyfriend and he'd just shrugged off her concerns and screwed her anyway. *Man, how could I have been so stupid?*

It suddenly occurred to him that maybe he could blame Sharonne and say she'd seduced him against his will. But there was no way that would work – not when he'd spent months boasting to Tiny about having banged everyone else in Lola's entourage. No, there was no way out of it. As soon as he stepped foot off the stage, Tiny was going to tear a chunk out of his ass. And the very thought of it was making him sweat like a lesbian at a make-up counter. What if Tiny fucked up his face and left him with scars? What if he broke one of his arms and he couldn't play his drums? *Man oh man, I've really excelled myself this time!*

It was enough to make his dick stay limp for the rest of his life. How was he supposed to be turned on by the idea of sex in the future when the last time he'd got laid he'd wound up in this mess? He wouldn't ever be able to relax or enjoy screwing anyone again.

He looked at Tiny and managed to send him a weak smile. But it was no use. Tiny glowered back at him and continued to pound his fist into his palm. *Man, this sucks. This really sucks!*

And the worst thing was, he was still desperate to take a leak. It was going to be a long show. And not only that but it was going to be followed by an after-show party that for once he *wasn't* looking forward to.

*

Harvey wove his way through the wings and took up position next to Tiny. He was excited to see the next instalment in Lola's game-changing performance but he was also aware he still had a few issues to iron out with certain members of her team – and specifically those who'd frozen him out as soon as he'd been fired.

'Oh hi, Harvey,' Tiny greeted him. 'Did you call me earlier?'

'Yeah, yeah, I did actually. And one of your lads tried you on the walkie-talkie too.'

'Sorry, fella. I had a bit of bad news and I've not been able to think straight since. I just found out Sharonne's been cheating on me with that dickhead Jake.'

Harvey shook his head in disbelief. He had to hand it to Jake – he certainly had some gall. But at least that explained why Tiny had been ignoring him and meant he hadn't been freezing him out after all. 'Oh I'm sorry, lad,' he offered. 'That man's got a lot to answer for – to a lot of people.'

'You can say that again. But I think it's about time someone taught him a lesson.'

Harvey couldn't argue with that. In fact he'd been hoping to teach Jake a lesson himself since he'd openly insulted him in Club Class. Well, it looked like Tiny was going to step in and save him the bother – and do the job much more forcefully than he ever could.

He felt his phone vibrate and he lifted it out of his pocket to see he'd received a text message. He opened it up and saw it was from Carlson.

'Sorry,' he read, 'only just got your voicemail. Have been bonkers busy with show. Is everything OK?'

'Great thanks,' Harvey typed. 'Am actually watching from wings. Me and Lola made up and I'm back as her manager.'

He hit Send and wondered what Carlson would make of the news. The response arrived almost instantly. 'Welcome back! Always good to work with another sister ;-)'

He looked at his phone and smiled. That was probably the closest he was going to get to an apology from Carlson. But it would do.

As for Barbara, she'd already returned his calls and apologized it had taken her so long, explaining she'd had her hands full looking after Channel 3 News as well as her German girlfriend, who'd flown in for the opening night. Which meant the only person he still had to speak to was Vlad. But he figured he could let that one go; Vlad would have had more than enough on his plate today. And besides, he was probably embarrassed about letting Gloria get away with switching the footage without even noticing.

But thinking about Gloria did remind him that tomorrow he'd have to find a new backing singer. He already had someone in mind and after tonight's triumph he knew that every vocalist in town would be falling over themselves to land the gig. Although it would be tough to step into Gloria's shoes at the last minute and the new girl would have to spend all day tomorrow rehearsing with Mike Henry. He looked at his watch; he had more than half an hour to spare until the show ended so he could quickly make a few calls.

Oh and there was something else he wanted to do. Something that was even more important than replacing Gloria. But for that he'd have to find Spike. And now that he'd finished his live broadcast he knew just where he'd be.

*

Lola pounced off the stage and into the wings, her whole body blazing with the thrill of knowing she was searing through the show. And it had all gone so quickly. Well, it had done once Freddy had told her she had nothing to worry about. She wondered where he was now. She wanted to thank him for everything he'd done and invite him back to her dressing room after the show for a little celebration. *And hopefully a little more than a celebration . . .*

She was met by the stagehand Vaughan who guided her back towards her changing tent. Just as she rounded the corner she spotted Freddy leaning on a pillar watching the action on stage, his tie now removed and his sleeves rolled up to reveal the tight cords of muscle on his forearms. She couldn't believe she'd described him as lovely when she'd first met him. Well, he was lovely, but he was also wonderfully, gloriously sexy. She felt herself being drawn towards his gentle smile as the stage lights shimmered across his relaxed, happy face. She thought about sneaking up behind him, looping her arms around his knee-knockingly gorgeous chest and nibbling softly on his earlobe. But she told herself not to get over-excited. She had to quickly change into her final costume and didn't have time for that kind of thing now. Although there'd be plenty of time later . . .

'Freddy!' she shouted out to him. 'Freddy, over here!'

Well, she thought, *I might not be able to snog him but that doesn't mean I can't talk to him.*

Freddy swivelled around and came face-to-face with Lola.

Wow! he thought. *She seems to get more gorgeous every time I see her.*

'Quick!' she shouted. 'Come over here and help me get changed!'

As he bounded over she felt a smile sweeping across her face. In fact she was so pleased to see him it was almost as if it was charging through her whole body.

'Cracking show tonight, Lola,' he almost sang in his beautiful Welsh accent.

'Thanks, darlin'.' She took hold of his hand and linked her fingers through his. As their skin touched she felt a tremble of desire. She imagined their bodies coming together in a hot, sweaty tangle, her legs clamped around his sturdy frame as her mouth locked onto his and she gorged herself on every last drop of him. *So much for not getting overexcited . . .*

Freddy took hold of her hand and felt his skin shiver as his body came into contact with hers. He imagined lowering her softly onto his bed and sliding himself into her, drawing her head towards his so their mouths could lock together and he could look deep into her eyes to drink in every last drop of her. *Come on, mate, don't start getting overexcited . . .*

He felt a little tug on his hand. 'Follow me,' Lola said, pulling him along to her changing tent. 'Oh and this is Vaughan,' she added, pointing to the stagehand, 'Vaughan as in porn.'

She squeezed Freddy's hand and he tried not to chuckle.

'All right, Vaughan? Pleased to meet you.'

The three of them rushed into the tent and straight away a group of girls handed Lola a towel and a bottle of water and began pulling apart her outfit. Within seconds she was down to her underwear.

'Sorry,' Freddy said, averting his eyes. 'I don't want you to feel indecent, like.'

Well, actually I do, he corrected himself, *but we'll save that for later . . .*

Indecent? she thought. *Give me a few hours and I'll show you indecent . . .*

'Oh don't worry about it,' Lola cooed. 'I just wanted to grab you for a minute to say thanks for everything you did for me tonight. And I hope you've not got yourself in too much trouble with your bosses.'

Freddy tried not to stare at her half-naked body but the tent was so small and so full of mirrors he couldn't avoid it. 'Oh it's all right, Lola, it's nothing I can't handle.'

'But how can I possibly thank you?'

He cleared his throat. 'Actually, there is one thing . . .' *Come on, champ. Now's your chance to finally convert that try.*

'Oh yeah? And what's that?'

'I wondered if you fancied going out on another date with me and seeing if we can start again, like.'

His eyes flitted around the room nervously. He really wished they were on their own.

Her eyes lit up with joy. She was glad they weren't on their own or else by now she'd be ripping her clothes off and forgetting all about going back on stage.

'I'd love to, Freddy,' she managed as she heard a little gasp escape Belle, Scarlett and Trixie. Her eyes met Amina's in the mirror and she gave her a knowing smile. 'But I think I owe you an apology first. And I've got lots of explaining to do.'

'Lola, you really don't need to explain anything, honestly.'

'No,' she said, swigging on her water, 'I *do* need to explain myself. Because I want you to know that I might have done some bad things in life but I'm pretty sure I'm not a bad person. I've just never had much self-control, that's all. And I've never been very good at finding my Off switch.'

'Yeah, well, maybe I can help you there,' Freddy smirked. 'Maybe I can help you find it.'

Belle, Scarlett and Trixie now squealed out loud.

Amina let loose an elated sigh.

'Yeah but Freddy,' Lola teased. 'I'm not sure if you switched me on I'd ever want you to switch me off.'

Freddy's eyes flared. 'Oh I think we can work with that.'

The two of them stopped still and stood staring at each other.

My God, she thought, *what if I'm actually falling in love with him?*

Wow! he thought. *I think I might actually be falling in love with her.*

'Lola! Lola! Lola!'

On the other side of the stage, fifteen thousand fans were chanting for her to come back and perform the encore. But inside the little changing tent Lola and Freddy couldn't even hear them.

'That's it,' one of the girls eventually broke in, stepping back to inspect Lola's final look. 'I think you're ready now.'

She turned to the mirror to check herself out. She was dressed in dark matador trousers, a fitted red top and a cute Spanish-style hat similar to the one she'd worn when she'd performed earlier that summer on *Lucky Star*.

'You look beautiful,' Freddy nodded. 'Really beautiful.'

Lola was just about to tut or scoff when she stopped herself. If Freddy thought she was beautiful, then maybe she was after all.

'Thanks, darlin',' she crackled. 'Just one more song to go.'

'Great. I can't wait to see it.'

'But there is one other thing I need to tell you. And this is really important.'

Oh no, he thought, *is this when it's all going to come crashing down?*

Look at his cute face, she thought, *all nervous and worried when I'm blatantly only winding him up.*

'Go on than,' he rasped. 'What is it?'

'You can only take me out on one condition.'

'Oh yeah and what's that?'

'You take me somewhere they serve cock-a-leekie soup.'

The two of them exploded into giggles as everyone else looked on, puzzled. Freddy was doubled over clutching his stomach when Lola's assistant stepped forward and told her it was time to leave.

'Good luck,' Freddy almost choked through his laughter.

'Thanks, darlin',' she hooted back at him. 'And will you

come to my dressing room for a little party afterwards? There's someone I want you to meet.'

'Oh yeah?' Now it was his turn to be puzzled. 'And who's that?'

'My mum.'

Oh I know I'm going a bit fast, she told herself, *but it's taken me ages to get to this point. And I can't be arsed holding back now!*

She's moving a bit fast, Freddy smiled to himself, *but I can hardly complain when it's taken so long to get here. And at least it means I don't have to hold back!*

Lola began backing away reluctantly. 'I've got to go, darlin'. But I'll blatantly see you later.' She gazed into his eyes until she disappeared through the doorway.

As she ran towards the stage and into the fans' cheers, she could feel her heart thumping in her chest. But it was no longer thumping with the thrill of knowing she was ripping up the show. Now it was thumping with the thrill of knowing she was falling in love with Freddy.

She raced up the back staircase, ready to make her final entrance. There was only one song left to perform. And the way Lola was feeling, there was only one song it could possibly be.

*

Spike was sitting in a box high up in the arena surrounded by record company execs quaffing cocktails with brash American businessmen, shy-looking songwriters and a smattering of celebrities. He spotted former opera singer Bella Figurini gossiping away with Shereen Spicer and Ruby Marlow, both of whose manic nose-twitching offered some explanation for their regular trips to the ladies' room. Squatting down on the floor just in front of them, gay photographers Mark and Mark were giving their crystal-collared dog a bowl of champagne, which it lapped up before erupting into a loud burp. And squashed onto the seat next to Spike, Lucretia Lavelle was perched on Ace Bounder's lap, jangling her jewellery and giggling out loud as Ace's hand disappeared up her skirt – where Spike could only presume she was wearing no knickers. He tried not to stare and shuffled a few rows back onto an empty seat in a quiet corner. He was much happier hiding back here anyway. It had already been quite a day and right now he just wanted to sit back and chill.

He looked down at the dark stage and waited for Lola to reappear to perform her encore. The audience were loudly chanting her name, desperate for one final blast of a show everyone now knew would be going down in pop history as the moment Lola Grant took her place alongside the greatest megastars in music. But much as Spike was looking forward to seeing her back on stage, he was even more excited about seeing Harvey.

Just after the live broadcast Harvey had arranged to meet him here in the box. But that was over half an hour ago now and there was still no sign of him. Spike pulled down his baseball cap and tried to merge into the shadows as he watched footballer Slam Carter doing his best to chat up a disinterested Candy Lunt. Seeing as Slam had recently made a series of homophobic remarks in press interviews, Spike assumed he didn't realize Candy was transgender. But Candy was clearly aware of his reputation; she scowled and turned her back on him to talk to a woman Spike recognized as the director of the

Tramp video, who looked like she'd turned up to a fancy-dress party as Amy Winehouse.

'All right, lad?'

Spike's spirit lifted as Harvey slid in next to him and kissed him on the lips. *Fuck, I love this man. I really fucking love him.*

'Sorry I'm late,' Harvey said. 'I had a few jobs to do.'

'Oh don't worry about it. Is everything OK, blud?'

'Yeah, yeah. How about you?' He took off Spike's baseball cap and gently traced his finger over the indentations it had left on his forehead.

'Yeah, I'm cool thanks, man,' he said, closing his eyes and savouring the sensation of Harvey smoothing his skin. 'And the show's sick!'

Harvey smiled and kissed his forehead. 'Listen, Spike, there's something I want to—'

He was interrupted by an explosion of noise coming from the audience. The two of them jumped to their feet and watched the stage blast back into life as the sound of a Spanish guitar announced Lola's reappearance dressed as a female matador. She skipped down the stairs and sprang straight into her final song.

> *Like a vision,*
> *He waltzed into my world . . .*

As he listened to Lola's vocals, Spike could feel the song giving him a little glow – just like the summer sunshine.

'Do you remember this was playing on the night we met?' Harvey said into his ear.

'Yeah, man – and on our first date.'

Harvey put his arm around Spike's shoulders and drew him towards him.

'Well, in that case it's quite appropriate it's playing now.'

'Why? What do you mean?'

Harvey dropped down onto one knee. 'There's something I want to ask you, Spike.' He took out a little box from his pocket.

Man, is this really happening?

Even though they were in a room full of people overlooking a packed arena, Spike suddenly felt as if the two of them were being privately serenaded by Lola.

> *That hot summer's night,*
> *It felt oh so right,*
> *And I was lost, lost,*
> *Lost in love.*

Harvey raised his eyebrows. 'Will you marry me, Spike?'

Spike could feel the smile on his face charging through his entire body. He took hold of the box and opened it up to reveal a beautiful gold ring.

'Of course I'll fucking marry you, man,' he beamed, knowing his gold tooth would be twinkling away at Harvey. 'I couldn't think of anything that would make me happier.'

As Harvey drew himself up and their mouths locked together, Spike felt himself filling up with all the positive energy emanating from the audience. This was the best feeling ever. Because not only did he love Harvey but Harvey made him love himself too. And he knew that with Harvey by his side, for the rest of his life he'd be a better man – and so much happier than he'd ever imagined he could be before he'd met Harvey and they'd first listened to *Lost in Love*.

So yeah, his fiancé was right, Lola's choice of song was appropriate – proper appropriate.

*

Lola snapped and kicked her way across the stage, giving the song everything she had and eager to end the night on the highest note possible.

> *The blaze of the sun,*
> *The beat of the drum,*
> *And I was lost, lost,*
> *Lost in love.*

As she belted out the lyrics she found she was pouring into them a deeper emotion than she'd ever felt before. And she knew that if she strayed even slightly away from this emotion, all she had to do was glance into the wings and catch sight of Freddy. Because she hadn't realized it when she'd written the song but *Lost in Love* was about him. She understood now that Freddy should have been her summer romance – and as soon as she was off this stage she was going to start making up for lost time.

> *My head turned,*
> *My heart burned,*
> *And I was lost, lost,*
> *Lost in love.*

Standing in the audience to the left of the runway, Lola spotted Barbara smooching with her girlfriend; the two of them held up their clasped hands and gave her a cheer. As she twirled around she caught sight of Amina standing in the wings, her eyes directed not at Lola but at her boyfriend Danny. Now was it Lola's imagination or was that a ring twinkling on her finger? She'd been so caught up in today's drama she hadn't noticed it before, but she'd be sure to ask about it after the show. And if Amina *had* just got engaged, Lola would have to make her after-show party a double celebration. Actually, make that a triple celebration: Harvey had told her he was going to propose to Spike during the encore and she knew from what Spike had said to her earlier that he'd accept. She imagined the two of them now looking down on her from the box, swaying to the music in each other's arms.

> *I was lost, lost,*
> *Lost in love.*

It seemed the song's sentiment was catching; everyone around her was lost in love. She wondered if that could be because she herself was feeling the first stirrings of love. Now that she was, she couldn't help wondering how she'd ever got away with singing the song before – or how on earth she'd managed to write it. Because she thought she'd been in love before – with a series of tramps that started with Nicky, moved on to Fox and ended with Jake – but she was beginning to realize it was only with Freddy that she was finally going to understand the true meaning of love.

As she strode to the end of the runway and repeated the chorus of the song, she closed her eyes and pictured Freddy.

I was lost, lost,
Lost in love.

And then the dancers stopped and the music dipped. This was the point of the show at which Lola had time to say her thank-yous. And tonight she knew there were some thank-yous that were particularly well deserved.

'Thanks a lot, guys!' she shouted out over the crowd. 'You've blatantly been the best audience ever!'

She smiled as their adulation hit her like the heat when you step off a plane. She paused for a moment to catch her breath.

'While I'm at it, I'd also like to say thanks to my band, my dancers and everyone else who worked on the show. Because it's been a real team effort and everyone I've worked with has been fierce. Fiercer than fierce!'

Well, almost everyone – but that doesn't matter now.

'But the biggest thank-you of all goes to someone you probably all know – and his name's Freddy Jones.'

She turned to look at him standing in the wings and when their eyes met her stomach gave a little spasm.

'And I don't know if you remember when I said in an interview that me and Freddy were just good friends, but that was blatantly a load of crap. Because as I'm sure you all know you can't want to shag your friend!'

The entire audience burst into laughter and Lola couldn't resist shooting Freddy a mischievous look. From the way he grinned back at her she knew she wouldn't have to wait long for her wish to come true.

'Sorry, there I go again with my big gob. But Freddy's been a real hero tonight – and saved me from getting into all kinds of trouble. Although I've realized now that in our own different ways we're all trouble. Because we're all human and we've all lived through shit that makes us do stupid things. But it's only once we've got over the shit that we can stop causing trouble and fall in love. And, you know what, I think I'm going to like being in love.'

A low rumble of approval rose to a roar.

'Is there anyone else who likes being in love?'

The roar grew and Lola grinned.

'Is there anyone else who likes being lost in love?'

The crowd hollered in affirmation.

'I can't hear you!' Lola joked, cupping her hand to her ear. 'Is there anyone else who likes being lost in love?'

She could feel herself glowing as the crowd managed to make even more noise.

And then the music kicked in for its final blast.

> *I was lost, lost,*
> *Lost in love.*

And with one last burst of energy, Lola slammed her way through the final steps of her routine. Then the lights snapped off and all of a sudden the show was over.

That was it. She'd done it. And she'd ended up doing a whole lot more besides.

Under cover of darkness she rushed off the stage and into Freddy's arms. Into a life filled with happiness – and one free of trouble.

If you enjoyed *Nothing But Trouble*,

you'll love *Shot Through the Heart*

The Silver Screen has never shone so bright . . .

Mia Sinclair is the First Lady of Love, a beautiful film goddess known across the globe for her romantic roles. But in real life she has more trouble finding love than she does in the movies. And she knows just who to blame – the paparazzi.

Leo Henderson is a British photographer working in LA, loving the lifestyle and shooting the stars – especially when they don't want to be photographed.

When Mia meets Leo, the sparks fly. But could dating a paparazzo be the biggest mistake of her life? And how will she cope when Leo becomes jealous of her friendship with co-star Billy Spencer, the hottest actor in town, but a man hiding a secret he's worried could destroy his career?

Out Now
Turn the page to read an extract

1

'Well it sure is good to meet you, Miss Sinclair.'

'You too, Dan.'

'You know, I can't believe I'm actually on a date with the First Lady of Love.'

Mia tried not to wince – that nickname was starting to become a curse.

'Don't be silly,' she said, flashing him what she hoped was her best movie star smile. 'And please, call me Mia.'

Oh I hope tonight goes well, she thought. *I'm not sure I can cope with another disappointment . . .*

Mia's date was taking place in Sky High, an exclusive lounge club perched above the outdoor pool of the Mirage Hotel with some of the best views of Los Angeles. Sitting opposite her was Dan Morrison, a solidly handsome thirty-something dressed in an understated navy suit. Dan was sipping a glass of Merlot while Mia was working her way through a rather bitter pomegranate juice.

'So I hear you're new to LA,' she purred. 'Why did you decide to move here?'

'Oh things in Seattle were getting way too stressful,' Dan explained. 'I was a doctor in an Emergency Room but wanted a more relaxed lifestyle. Now I've re-trained as a carpenter I'm much happier.'

'A carpenter?' Mia breezed. 'Oh how creative and . . . manly.'

Did I actually just say that? she thought. *That was way too corny!*

Dan fiddled with his tie and looked down bashfully.

Mia had been fixed up with Dan by her trainer Cole, a black guy with pecs so big you could shelter from the rain under them. Not that it ever rained in Los Angeles. In fact, in the eight years that Mia had lived here she could count on one hand the number of days when there hadn't been a bright blue sky over the city. Which was one of the things that she loved so much about the place, having grown up in Cleveland, Ohio – a dreary city where the sky always seemed to be grey. She'd dreamt for years of escaping to LA and when she eventually arrived here, it had turned out to be everything she'd wanted it to be. Since then, she'd worked hard to create what she sometimes thought of as a fairytale life for herself; she had a great career, wonderful friends and a fabulous home high in the Hollywood Hills. In fact, the only thing that she didn't have right now was a man to share it all with. And according to Cole, Dan could be just the man to fix that.

'I guess I just love making things,' he explained rather earnestly. 'And I know it might sound dorky but I love the feel of wood. I just think it's a beautiful material.'

'Wow,' breathed Mia. She couldn't think of anything else to say. 'Wow.' She stared wistfully at the indentation at the bottom of his neck.

According to Cole, Dan Morrison was kind, dependable

and very much one of the good guys. In fact, Cole always called him Nice Man Dan and from what Mia had seen so far, he wasn't wrong.

Being fixed up with potential boyfriends could be difficult for Mia because invariably she knew very little about them and they knew so much about her. This unsettling one-way intimacy gave her date a massively unfair advantage. For a start, if he liked going to the movies, chances were he'd already seen her naked in one of her many love scenes. And if he read the papers or had access to the internet, it was more than likely that he knew some very private things about her already – the kind of things that were quite revealing and which you wouldn't normally give away on a first date. Details about her unhappy childhood in Cleveland for example, her youthful dreams of becoming a film star, and her mother's death just as her movie career was taking off. A quick Google search would also reveal the media's nickname for her – the First Lady of Love, a title she'd earned after appearing in a string of hit chick flicks. Dan was obviously well researched on this front and she hoped he wouldn't mention it again. The irony was that Mia wasn't sure she'd ever been in love – despite countless attempts, many of them soul-destroying. In fact, she was starting to wonder if she even believed in love anymore – and to worry that she was becoming cynical and jaded. But that was the kind of thing she kept private. There was no way Dan could have learned *that* from the internet.

'So tell me about your relationship history,' she asked. 'How come a great guy like you's still single?'

'Oh well, I recently broke up with someone so am only just back on the market, I guess.' Dan explained that his last girlfriend, Angelique, was a nurse in a plastic surgeon's who'd left him for one of her clients, a famous porn actor who'd gone to the clinic for a penis enlargement. 'What a douche-bag,' he moaned. 'I could never cheat on a woman – I've too much respect for them. In fact, I don't think I've ever been unfaithful in all my life.'

Hmm, that's another tick, thought Mia. *He's doing pretty well here.*

Whenever Mia went on a first date there was a checklist she always worked through, imagining cheesy sound effects from a TV quiz show when contestants got the answers right or wrong. Is he punctual? Bleep bleep – correct answer. Does he have his own career? Bleep bleep – full marks. Has he ever cheated on a girlfriend? Bleep bleep – three out of three.

It wasn't that Mia was being cold or ruthless in her search for a man, just that she was trying to look after herself. She'd seen her mother lose her security, dignity and, for a long time, her happiness after her father had walked out on the family when Mia was still very young. Her mom had had to take on extra shifts at the hospital where she slaved away as a nurse and worked herself into the ground over the next ten years, just to survive and bring up her daughter. Ever since then she'd warned Mia not to make the same mistake with men as she had. 'Don't fall for a bad boy,' she'd lectured, time and time again. 'Find yourself a nice, dependable good guy – someone who isn't trouble.' Over the years, Mia had vowed never to fall into the same trap as her mom. There was too much at stake; she'd seen first hand how much could be lost through falling in love with the wrong kind of guy.

'You know,' Dan went on, 'maybe I'm not the most exciting

of guys but I never thought Angelique would cheat on me like that. Maybe that's my problem though – maybe I'm just too nice.'

Bleep bleep! For Mia, a man could never be too nice. She didn't understand why so many women fell for bad boys, those sexy scoundrels who had trouble written all over them. She was different. She wanted her very own good guy – and perhaps she'd just found him.

*

'So Leo, let me get this straight. Are you saying you're breaking up with me?'

Across town, Leo Henderson was in Dirty Dick's, an English-themed pub popular with LA's expat crowd, just metres away from the seafront in Venice Beach. Dirty Dick's was one of his favourite drinking haunts as it was really close to his house, served more than twenty different real ales, and had the atmosphere of a British pub, which reminded him of home. And with its candlelit recesses at the back, it was a surprisingly good setting for a quiet, intimate date. In fact, Leo had used it for that very purpose on several occasions. Tonight though he was here with a completely different purpose. Tonight, he was here to have a difficult conversation with his girlfriend Eden. And by the end of the conversation, she'd hopefully be his *ex*-girlfriend.

'Yeah, I'm sorry Eden but I've thought about this a lot and things just aren't working for me at the moment.'

'But I don't understand,' she said. 'Is it something I've done?'

The problem was that it *was* something she'd done. But he

didn't want to upset her by saying that. He paused for a moment to choose his words carefully.

'No, no, it's nothing you've done. I just think our lives are moving in different directions, that's all.'

Is that a cliché? he wondered. He hoped not but he was really struggling to get through this. And anyway, it was true.

When he'd first met Eden six months ago her name had been Barbara and she'd been a Pilates instructor teaching stay-at-home mums and former film stars in a local old folks' home. He couldn't deny that he'd been attracted to her stunning good looks and incredible body but more importantly for Leo, she'd been a Buddhist with a bit of a hippie outlook on life. As a paparazzo, he had more than enough madness in his professional life and liked nothing more than a laid-back, calm personal life. Eden had seemed like the perfect fit.

But ever since she'd signed a deal to appear on a daytime TV show as a fitness expert, things had changed. It was as if her first taste of fame had somehow corrupted her. She'd adopted her stage name, given up Buddhism almost overnight and started talking endlessly about her 'profile' with a manic glint in her eye. When she released her first Pilates DVD she treated herself to a boob job and went out for a 'relaunch', which basically consisted of going to a film premiere in a low-cut top, perspex hooker heels and a mini skirt that looked like a pelmet. When she saw the photos in the press she became almost crazed in her desire for more. She kept pestering Leo to snap her coming out of restaurants with a few semi-famous friends – and he started to wonder if that was the only reason she was going out with him in the first place. As she got more and more angry with him for refusing, it began to dawn on him that the two of them couldn't last much longer.

'I'm so sorry, Eden.' He gave her a smile that he hoped wasn't too sympathetic or patronizing.

'Well all I can say is, you sure know how to pick your moments. You do realize I'm on *The Wendy Williams Show* tomorrow?'

He took a swig of his beer. 'Well I guess that's kind of it to be honest, Eden. Boob jobs and TV shows – it's not really what I signed up for.'

She suddenly perked up, as if hit by a good idea. 'Actually, I could always tell Wendy about being dumped – open my heart on air and turn on the tears. She loves a good sob story.'

Leo was beginning to struggle not to sound impatient. 'Eden, will you just listen to me for a minute? It's this obsession with chasing fame that's my whole problem.'

'Well maybe it wouldn't *be* such a problem if you'd actually bother to pap me now and again.'

'But we've already been through all that – you know I don't like to mix work with pleasure. It's way too complicated.'

'It's not complicated at all, Leo. In fact, it's quite simple. My career's moving to another level and you just don't want to deal with it.'

'But Eden, it's not that I don't want to deal with it. It's that I don't want to give up my job – not when I love it so much. And I just don't see how a pap can possibly date a target.'

How many times have we had this conversation? The fact that they were having it yet again only strengthened his resolve that he was doing the right thing.

And it wasn't as if he had many rules in life. In fact, he only had one, and that was never to let his relationships get mixed up with his work. A paparazzo dating someone famous could never work. For a start, both sides wouldn't know when they were being used. And the way Leo saw it, whatever trust there was between them could only ever break down.

'Oh, Leo,' Eden pouted, 'but we've always been so good together . . .'

She swivelled on her seat and crossed her legs – legs that had always driven Leo wild. As he looked at them stretching out beside him he was reminded of just how gorgeous she was and couldn't help thinking back to the great sex they'd had. Eden was right: they *were* good together. So was he really doing the right thing by ending it?

She leaned forward and began nibbling on her finger flirtatiously. 'Oh it just seems such a shame to throw it all away. I mean, we both know there's a real chemistry between us. And chemistry like that doesn't come around every day . . .'

Leo was starting to feel a bit hot and undid another button on his shirt. He had to admit, most men would kill to have a girlfriend as good-looking as Eden. As he breathed down his neck to cool himself down he thought about how tough it would be never to sleep with her again. *Oh maybe just one last time*, he thought. *That couldn't hurt, could it?*

Just then he sensed a buzzing sound from his jeans pocket and realized he'd received a text message on his phone. 'Look, I'm sorry Eden but I really need to get this.'

As he keyed in his security code he felt relieved to have been rescued from a moment of weakness. The last thing he needed right now was to end up back in bed with her – it would only make things even more difficult. Eden must have realized that her last-ditch attempt to save the relationship had failed as she gave a loud huff and swung her legs back under the table.

On the screen of his phone Leo read a text from his photographic agency, Shooting Stars. 'Mia Sinclair on date in Sky High – arrived 9 p.m.'

Straight away he wanted to take the job as pictures of the First Lady of Love with a new man always sold for good money. But he couldn't leave Eden before they'd properly talked things through. He wondered how much longer it would take.

Because this assignation with Mia Sinclair was his kind of date. Totally uncomplicated – and purely professional.

*

As Nice Man Dan told her about his charity work helping to build a village in a remote part of Africa, Mia Sinclair leant back on the heavily cushioned sofa and relaxed into a date that she was enjoying more and more. She often chose Sky High as the venue for first dates as she loved its tasteful gold and green furniture and the pulsing Brazilian music they played. Most of all though, she loved the fact that the bar was private and heavily guarded from the paparazzi.

Because Mia hated the paparazzi. Without doubt they were her biggest enemy. Ever since she'd had her first hit movie and suddenly become public property, they'd ruined every attempt she'd made at starting a new relationship. In the last month alone there'd been three casualties of their unrelenting pursuit of pictures. First there was Seth, a shy but sexy writer who spent all his time indoors hunched over a computer and consequently looked a bit like a mole. But he was sweet and sensitive and Mia liked him a lot. After their first date she'd kissed him goodbye in front of the restaurant and the two of them had been almost blinded by the camera flashes as the paps had pounced, each of them desperate for an exclusive. As someone terrified of any attention at all, Seth had completely freaked out and ended it with her later that night.

It was all very upsetting but she'd picked herself up again and soon felt strong enough to start dating a guy called Hart, a real head-turner of a model who she knew would be used to having his photo taken. He did indeed seem to love being in the spotlight. But when she'd found out that he'd tipped off the paps about their third date so that he could be photographed basking in *her* spotlight, she'd forced herself to dump him without a second thought. The truth was, though, that she'd been devastated and had gone on to spend the entire weekend stuffing herself on takeaway pizza as she YouTubed over and over again his two-minute guest appearance on *America's Next Top Model*.

And finally there was Buck, a tough-talking baseball player with a soft centre who'd said he wanted to take things slowly after recently coming out of a painful break-up. Just when she'd started to think she might be falling for him, photos of them stepping out together had been splashed across trashy tabloids and gossip websites, one of which quoted a so-called friend to come up with the headline 'Marriage within a month for the First Lady of Love' – not the easiest read for someone wary of getting serious. Unsurprisingly, Buck had ditched her like a shot. Again, she'd been devastated but this time she'd had to deal with the public humiliation as well.

She sighed slowly like a deflating tyre. The way Mia saw things, the paparazzi really did have a lot to answer for.

'You know I've seen all your movies,' Dan said, interrupting her thoughts. 'You're very talented. And if you don't mind me saying so, from what I've seen on screen you sure do seem like a lovely lady.'

Now it was Mia's turn to be bashful. 'Oh that's very kind of you,' she said. 'But I have to let you know that in real life I'm nothing like the characters I've played.'

Mia felt that she had to make this point on first dates as she was starting to worry that men were confusing her with the kind of needy, clingy characters she played on screen. Not that there was anything wrong with that kind of person but she'd played so many of them that she sometimes thought men would assume she was a total desperado and run a mile.

Her first hit had been a movie called *Harassment*, in which she played a naïve young secretary whose boss suggests they fake a case of sexual harassment, sue their employer and split the proceeds. Only their plan falls apart when they fall in love, the harassment suit collapses and they're left with nothing but each other – although by this stage they're so in love that they realize that's all they need to be happy. Then there was *Lapping it Up*, in which she played a lapdancer with a heart of gold who gives up her dream of becoming a prima ballerina to elope with a customer who tells her he's a billionaire businessman but is actually a gangster on the run from both the police and the Mob. Obviously, he's heart-breakingly handsome, so she forgives his deception and falls for him anyway, joining him as he flees across the border to a new life in South America. And her last big hit was *The Princess and the Pauper*, in which she played a plucky British royal who renounces her title and claim to the throne to marry a dashing American divorcee who whisks her away from the glamour of her family's palace to live happily ever after on a pig farm in rural Tennessee.

Mia sipped her drink and thought back over her film roles. They might be weak and needy but none of them seemed to have any problem finding somebody to love them. Why was it so difficult for her? Sure, she had more to contend with – a public persona as the First Lady of Love and a squadron of hairy, sweaty paps trailing her everywhere. But however much she reminded herself of this it didn't stop her from feeling increasingly lonely, an emotion she'd never had to portray on screen. What she wanted now more than anything else was to be on a solid team of two, to know that she always had someone on her side, whatever happened. And she really hoped Dan would be that guy.

'So how about you?' he said. 'How come you're still single?'

Mia breathed in confidently. This is what she was good at – this was where the acting came in.

'Oh, you know, I'm so busy with my career at the moment that I just don't get the time to sit around pining for a man. Although, then again, if one should happen to come along . . .' She allowed herself to trail off with a giggle.

Was that all right? she wondered. *I hope I'm not coming across as too cold.*

Dan asked about her next film and Mia explained that she was about to finish making a movie with Billy Spencer, who everyone was calling the hottest actor in town. It was a period piece called *War of Words* and she was hoping it would be a big departure for her. True to form, she played a romantic novelist volunteering as a nurse on the frontline in the Second World War who has an explosive and passionate affair with a radical war poet. But the difference this time was that there was no happy ending and her soldier lover dies on the battle-field, leaving her character desolate and heartbroken. Mia had never starred in a weepie before so there was a whole different emotional journey for her to get her teeth into. And because the film didn't have a formulaic happy ending, it was being taken much more seriously – it wasn't even finished yet and there was already talk of film festivals and awards.

'I just heard we have to do a few reshoots for the ending,' Mia explained. 'But we're all excited about it – and I'm hoping it means I get to play more serious roles from now on.'

'Well I think we should drink to that.' Dan held out his glass and she brought hers to meet it with a cheery chink.

'To new beginnings!' Mia smiled.

'New beginnings!'

They sipped their drinks and held each other's gaze.

All I need now, Mia thought, *is someone to walk me down the red carpet.*

*

'Well I don't need you,' Eden spat. 'My DVD was the fourth biggest seller in Walmart last week!'

Leo sat there and took the flak. As he was breaking up with her he thought it was only right to let her express her anger – even if it was all directed at him.

'Exactly,' he offered, 'I'm sure you'll find someone much better than me. Someone who's famous too and then you can go out and be photographed together.'

'You know, when I think of all the men I turned down because I was dating you,' she ranted. 'You do realize I was hit on by Hart Blakemore last week? I mean, he's only the most famous male model in the world! His last girlfriend was *Mia Sinclair*!'

At the mention of Mia's name, Leo wondered how her date was going in the Mirage. He really hoped he could make it across town in time to catch her exit.

'You know, I always knew you'd be trouble,' Eden rattled on. 'My girlfriends warned me you were a bad boy. And man were they right.'

Leo wondered what time it was and if he could have a quick look at his watch without her noticing.

'And don't think I don't realize that all your bullshit about hating fame is just a cover. I can see right through you, Leo. You just don't want to admit that you're a dog – a dirty dog who can't commit.'

Leo was happy to sit there and take it like a man but this kind of comment really hurt him. He tried not to show it.

'You'll probably have another girlfriend by next week – if you haven't got one already!'

He stared at his beer and tried not to let her get to him. It was proving difficult.

Leo was aware that lately he'd built up a reputation as something of a bad boy, purely because he'd had so many girlfriends. His friend Ronnie joked about him being irresistible, having to fend off female admirers wherever he went. He had no idea why they all seemed to fall for him. Was it the British accent? Was it the motorbike? Was it that wonky grin they all seemed to talk about?

Whatever it was, the problem was that he had a knack of attracting girls who wanted to be famous – and who wanted his help to get there. Before he knew it he'd racked up a string of failed relationships, Eden being just the latest example. But the truth was, he'd only ever wanted one special girl – just one who *didn't* want to be famous.

Leo's phone vibrated again and he apologized and fished it out of his pocket.

'The problem with you paps,' Eden snarled, 'is you've got no feelings. You're just a bunch of cold-hearted sleazeballs!'

He tried to block her out and read the message. Apparently Mia Sinclair had just asked for her check and looked to be winding up her date. He really needed to get going soon or he wouldn't make it to the Mirage in time. If Eden didn't hate him enough already, she was going to hate him a whole lot more when he walked out on her, leaving her with a wad of cash to pay the bill.

'Well screw you, ass-wipe. *Screw you!'*

He took a deep breath and prepared to tell her that he was leaving. Across town he had an urgent assignation with Mia Sinclair, the First Lady of Love.

*

A nicotine-blonde waitress with a face like a King Charles spaniel brought over the check and plonked it down on the table between Mia and Dan. 'Have a great night!'

They finished the last of their drinks and Mia felt a glow of satisfaction that the evening had gone so well. Dan really did seem to be everything she was looking for in a man. But she couldn't allow herself to feel totally satisfied yet – it remained to be seen how he'd cope with the paparazzi, who were no doubt waiting outside the hotel that very moment. She gulped at the idea of subjecting him to the final – and without doubt the biggest and most difficult – test of the evening.

*

Leo was on his bike zipping down the Santa Monica Freeway, winding his way in and out of the traffic to get to the Mirage as fast as he could.

He was trying to relieve his guilt about dumping Eden by telling himself that there was no way things could have ever worked out between them. And she was wrong about him having no feelings; the problem was that he couldn't photograph anyone he did have feelings for. In fact, when he went to work it was almost like he had to switch *off* his feelings and adopt a different persona. And if he stopped being able to do this, he wouldn't be able to carry on doing the job he loved.

When he eventually made it to the hotel and parked up outside, he spotted a cluster of faces he recognized; the pack of paps in LA might have been big but most of them knew each other well from working the circuit. At the back of the pack Leo spied a bald head and a pair of little sticky-out ears and recognized his best mate Ronnie. He worked his way over to talk to him.

'Evening, partner.'

'Hey buddy, how'd it go with Eden?'

'Oh you know – it went. But at least it's out of the way now.'

'That's the spirit. And you still made it here in time to collect your pay check.'

'Looks like it. She's not come out yet then?'

'Not yet. But she's due any second – one of the valet boys has just gone to get her car.'

Leo followed Ronnie's eyes to the small group of people standing by the main entrance – two sniffy-looking doormen who were clearly gay but trying to butch it up, a pair of rich kids kissing like it was a whole new experience, and a fat man smoking a cigarette with the concentration of an addict about to catch a transatlantic flight. Mia Sinclair was nowhere to be seen. *Phew! Looks like I made it in plenty of time.*

Leo was just about to turn away when he spotted the faces of the doormen light up. And he knew just what that meant; they'd caught sight of Mia Sinclair.

When she emerged, it was hard not to stop and stare at her. She had baby blonde hair, a fresh complexion and piercing blue eyes. Tonight she looked incredible in a figure-hugging pastel blue dress with matching high-heeled sandals and a striking diamond necklace. And in case there was any doubt that the show was about to begin, she was glowing with an almost visible aura which Leo had come to recognize as good old-fashioned star quality.

Her date must have gone well as she was smiling brightly on the arm of a rather handsome man who was focused on her so intently that he almost tripped down the first step. Whoever he was, his presence next to Mia meant the paps had their story.

'Ker-ching!' beamed Ronnie.

In a matter of seconds, Leo and the rest of the pack jumped into Mia's path and snapped away, all the time shouting her name so she'd look into their lenses. As the couple pressed forward and fought their way down the steps, using their hands to shield them from the brightness of the exploding flashbulbs, Leo darted around them to get the best shot, sometimes holding up his camera as high as he could and angling it downwards without looking through the viewfinder – a trick known to paps as the 'Hail Mary'.

To the casual observer, this sudden eruption of noise, movement and relentlessly blinding flashes must have looked frightening and almost violently intense. The balding fat man dropped his cigarette and watched from the entrance open-mouthed. But for Leo – and Mia too – this was simply the reality of everyday life.

'Mia!'

'Over here, Mia!'

'To me, Mia!'

'No, to me, Mia!'

'Who's the dude, Mia?'

'Who's your new man, Mia?'

'Oh come *on*, Mia!'

Within seconds, Mia and her date had reached the bottom of the steps and slid into their waiting car. Leo spotted the man take the driving seat and thrust a bunch of notes into the hand of the valet. For a few seconds he sat there frozen, clutching the wheel with a horrified expression on his face. Then he hit the accelerator and the pack of paps scrambled out of the way and rushed to their cars and bikes. Whoever this guy was, if they got a shot of him kissing Mia goodnight, or better still going into her place, then it really would be payday.

*

'Phew!' gasped Dan. 'That was intense.' He whistled and shook his head.

'Welcome to my world,' chirped Mia, desperate to defuse the tension. 'Don't worry, you kind of get used to it after a while.'

Dan raised his eyebrows and punched the steering wheel. He didn't look like he wanted to get used to it.

Oh no! she thought. *Here we go again . . .*

Mia gazed out of the window and saw the bright lights of Sunset Boulevard whizzing by. Film posters glared down at her from all angles, often so big that they covered the sides of entire buildings. Right ahead was one for the DVD release of her last film *The Princess and the Pauper*. It featured a huge image of her wearing a tiara and gazing into the eyes of her leading man with a regal yet familiarly love-struck expression. Under the picture was the tag line 'Can love truly conquer all?' Right now she sure hoped it could.

They turned off Sunset and onto Laurel Canyon Boulevard.

'Wait a second,' said Dan, looking in the mirror, 'are they following us?'

She twisted her neck and saw four or five paps on motorbikes hot on their tail. 'I'm afraid so,' she soothed, patting his knee. 'Don't worry – it's perfectly normal.'

'Normal? This is what you call *normal*?'

Mia shrugged and sank back into her seat. She didn't like to tell him that as well as the motorbikes, they were also being followed by the cars behind and in front of them as well as four or five others she recognized trailing further back. In her head she heard a loud nee-noo sound effect from the TV quiz show she'd been imagining earlier. If coping with the paps was Dan's final test of the evening, it looked like he was about to fail miserably.

One of the motorbike riders inched alongside their car and edged just in front of them to get a clear view. Mia spotted a sticker of the British flag attached to the back of the bike. The pap held out his camera and turned it round at them, flashing away on the off-chance he'd get a decent shot.

Dan held out his hand as if to bat him away. 'Jeez, this is insane!'

'I'm sorry, Dan. It isn't always like this, I promise. They just haven't seen you with me before so they're chasing a story.'

'But I don't do drama, Mia. I'm just a regular guy.'

'Yeah, well there are ways to deal with it, you know. I have a car with blacked-out windows, which I drive if I don't want the paps to see anything. And there's always security . . .'

'Security? Blacked-out windows? I make furniture for a living, Mia. This really isn't my thing.'

Uh-oh. It sounded like Dan would definitely be joining Seth, Hart and Buck on the casualty list. Mia bit her lip to stop a tremble becoming anything else. For just a moment this evening she'd dared to imagine a future for her and Dan. She'd dared to imagine that she might finally have found love. With Nice Man Dan, who unfortunately wasn't quite nice enough to put up with the reality of dating Mia Sinclair.

*

Leo and the other paps raced down Mulholland Drive, heading off Mia's car to arrive at her place before she did. They'd worked this route several times before so knew exactly where they were going. After a few minutes they turned off Mulholland and down a much quieter side street, stopping when they recognized the entrance to Mia's house.

One after the other they parked their cars, threw down their bikes and quickly assumed their positions, cameras at the ready to start snapping away. At times like this, paps like Leo not only had to put to one side all emotion and sensitivity; they had to stop viewing the stars they were following as human beings and see them simply as targets. He knew that to many people this might seem cruel but if he was going to be any good at his job there was only one thing he could focus on – and that was the picture. And right now Leo was wondering what would happen with tonight's big picture.

He was surprised when the car eventually appeared but pulled up outside the property and didn't go through the gates. He assumed that the date hadn't gone well after all and the man wasn't being invited to spend the night. *Never mind*, he thought. *If we're lucky we might still get a kiss.*

*

'Well thanks for a lovely evening. Are you sure you don't want to come in for a nightcap?'

'Gee, I'd love to Mia but I've got an early start tomorrow.' For a fraction of a second his eyes flickered towards the paps snapping their conversation through the windscreen.

'Oh, OK,' she swallowed. 'I understand.'

Mia was crestfallen but didn't want to show it. She could

feel her chin start to wobble but did her best to smile through it. By now she was *really* glad she was an actress.

She wanted to kiss Dan goodbye but knew that the paps would go crazy if she did and she'd be answering marriage rumours for the next few weeks. Before she had time to think about it, Dan moved in to kiss her and she puckered up, ready to meet his lips. He went for her cheek but the flashbulbs exploded anyway. *Oh great*, thought Mia. *Tomorrow it'll be all over the papers: 'The First Lady of Love – dumped again!'*

'Well, goodnight then, Dan.'

'Yeah. See you around, I guess.'

But as he said it, she knew he didn't mean it.

She clutched the door handle and, before pulling it, stopped for a moment to compose herself. *Whatever you do, don't let the paps see you're upset.*

She took a deep breath and opened the door.

*

As Mia stepped out of the car, Leo was at the front of the pack, snapping relentlessly as she walked over to the security gates and began tapping in her code. The look on her face was steely and no-nonsense; she was obviously determined to give nothing away.

Leo stood watching as the gates to the house slowly opened and Mia disappeared behind them. The rest of the paps looked at each other and shrugged. The show was over.

But not for Leo.

Like most stars, Mia lived in a heavily gated property sur-rounded by bushes and trees and Leo knew from previous experience where to find a good peephole. As the other paps began looking back over their pictures, Leo slipped away and started scaling a huge tree with his bare hands, his camera dangling from around his neck. He straddled a thick branch with his legs and inched along until he came to a spot where, if he held his camera at the end of his outstretched arm, he could just about shoot through the leaves.

Leo would do almost anything to nail an exclusive shot. And right now he might just nail a dynamite one of the First Lady of Love at the end of another disappointing date.

*

As Mia walked up her driveway she could hear the pack of paps on the other side of the gates, chatting amongst themselves as they compared the shots they'd taken.

'Mmm, not bad.'

'That's a good one!'

'That's freakin' awesome!'

She stopped for a moment and sighed. The night had ended in disaster and she just wanted to go inside and forget about it. *Those damn paps! Why do they always have to ruin everything?*

Following her every move from several feet above, Leo was just about to start snapping when Mia sloped off and disappeared into her front porch. *Oh no! Why can't she stand still and look towards the camera?*

Sheltered from his lens under the roof of her porch, Mia's whole face began to tremble. She remembered her strict rule of not letting down her guard until she was safely behind the walls of her home. She took out her keys and prepared to enter her sanctuary.

Leo frowned and switched off his camera.

*

Mia opened her door and entered the empty house, slamming the door shut and slumping back against it. *Thank God*, she thought. *Safe at last.*

She loved her home but at times like this it felt like a prison, barricaded away from the rest of the world. And she found it exhausting to have to live her life as if she were permanently under siege.

She tried to snap out of it by reminding herself of how lucky she was. It wasn't so long ago that she'd been stuck with her mom in a tiny apartment in Cleveland struggling to make ends meet and dreaming about one day leading the privileged life of a movie star. But it was no use; however strong those memories were, they couldn't stop her from feeling overcome by a devastating feeling of loneliness.

And yeah, she didn't want to turn into one of those needy, desperate characters she played on screen. But as she stood staring into her empty house, all she could think was that there was a big, gaping emptiness in her life too. And however brave a front she put on for the world, she knew that only love could fill it. The problem was, she was beginning to lose hope that she'd ever find it.

She sank to the floor and buried her head in her hands. Within seconds she could feel the tears trickling down her face.

Outside she could just about make out the sound of the last pap's motorbike as it revved its engine and sped away into the night.